# SHADOWS
# OF THE
# SWARM

\* \* \* \* \* \*

BOOK FIFTEEN

\* \* \* \* \* \*

## D.W. Neuman

## ALSO BY D.W. NEUMAN

### FICTION
*Frame of Mind*

### Shadow Series
*Shadows of the Mind – Book One*
*Shadows of the Soul – Book Two*
*Shadows of the Service – Book Three*
*Shadows of the Past – Book Four*
*Shadows of the Heart – Book Five*
*Shadows of the Sand – Book Six*
*Shadows of the Serpent – Book Seven*
*Shadows of the Future – Book Eight*
*Shadows of the Children – Book Nine*
*Shadows of the Ever-After – Book Ten*
*Shadows of the Faceless – Book Eleven*
*Shadows of the Ancient – Book Twelve*
*Shadows of the Order – Book Thirteen*
*Shadows of the State – Book Fourteen*
*Shadows of the Swarm – Book Fifteen*

I find it interesting, especially now with my finished book in hand, that I find myself at times writing about is a reflection of what our world is currently enduring. In essence: our daily lives, constantly full of upheaval and strife, as we claw for the basic needs of survival.

Human nature, as always, is on trial. And quite honestly, we're losing. Empathy and compassion seem to be looked down upon as weaknesses; while hatred and violence have been revitalized as the cornerstone of humanity. We've seen and read about this all before, I just didn't think I'd have to live through it.

But that's the one thing that gets me out of bed every morning. Living *through* it. Our world will self-correct at some point. Evil can't win. It has to be struck down and tucked away in some history book for the next generation to ponder...why did they let that happen?

That's a lot to unpack, so forgive my brief indulgence.

With all that said, here we are with book fifteen of my Shadow Series. Welcome back and thank you for being here! It's been one hell of an adventure, which all started with Thomas Clark in Running Springs. The saga continues!

Enjoy, and I'll see you on the other side.

-D.W. Neuman

For Connie.
My light, my love, my life.

"Live now; make now always the most precious time. Now will never come again."
-Jean-Luc Picard

Family

**Thomas Clark** – 48. President of the United States. Abilities: telekinetic; can briefly turn back time.

**Laura Clark** – 50. Psychologist. Ability: knows when someone is lying.

**Gavin Clark** – 12. Abilities: healing, portal summoner, Stir's guardian.

**Emily Clark** – 14. Abilities: summons relatives of anyone she comes in contact with. Can control individuals she touches.

**Stir** – Small animal made of black, wispy material with green eyes and sharp fangs. An estranged portion of The Ancient.

**Abby Clark** – 40. Sister of Thomas Clark.

**Allison Hansen** – 38. Abby's fiancé.

**Sam Paige** – 48. Semi-retired from SANDBOX. Ability: dimensional storage.

**Julie Paige** – 45. Sam's wife and Kim's fraternal sister. Ability: fire projectiles.

**Amanda Paige** – 17. Ability: honing in on others who have powers.

**Craig Paige** – 13. Ability: phasing (turns ethereal so objects pass through him).

**Bill Nicholson** – 48. Semi-retired from SANDBOX. Ability: can become a shadow.

**Kim Nicholson** – 45. Bill's wife and Julie's fraternal sister. Ability: force field.

**Sarah Nicholson** –17. Ability: invisibility.

**Edward Nicholson** – 13. Ability: flying.

**Nick Raynes** – 48. Thomas' friend and book agent.

**Susan Raynes** – 48. Nick's wife.

**Lisa Raynes** – 16. Nick and Susan's daughter.

**ORACLE** – New company founded and operated by:
**Charles Hillburg (Hobbes)** – 39. Network and computer expert. In a relationship with Gabbi. Ability: doppelganger.
**Gabbi West** – 35. Research and Development specialist. In a relationship with Hobbes. Ability: tech control.
**SANDBOX** – Company brought back from the brink of extinction and run by:
**Rebecca Cross** – 35. Combat medic. Previous bodyguard to the Clark family.
**Bai Lin** – 35. Previous bodyguard to the Clark family.
**Sabrina Chavez** – 35. Previous bodyguard to the Clark family.

Campaign / White House
**Andrew** Shaw – Vice President of the United States (previously an Assistant Director of the FBI)
**Jennifer Myers** – President's Executive Admin

Adversaries
**Aleskei Vakhrov** – Russian president
**Zhou Shun** – Chinese president
**Kwak Sun-Woo** – North Korean Supreme Leader
**The Pope** – Christian leader of The Vatican and Templar Knights

# 1
## Zara 844 – 204 cycles prior

Zara 844, the fifth planet of twelve, revolved around its sun every thirty-one phases. This particular planet, different from the other eleven, was the only body that could sustain the indigenous creatures that inhabited the world, known as Zorans. The Zorans, as discovered through science, evolved over time from microscopic bacteria, who eventually developed and mutated into six-legged bugs that scurried underneath the planet's surface, as they fought for resources. In time those critters sprung forth from the darkest depths and ventured out into the light, growing and evolving as the colony metamorphosed with the new conditions the planet presented them with. One such benefit was that their species could shapeshift into another being, mirrored off visual acuity. And while that ability alone wasn't terribly useful, in their society, it did come to be a deciding factor that would upend their world altogether.

These same creatures, who once scrambled to live in the dirt, now adapted to the surface. They thrived. They grew tall and robust, harboring six mandibles: two to stand on, and the other four to carry out whatever tasks which were needed. Their giant bug heads were adorned with sharp teeth, and they'd emanate a chittering symphony as they communicated with each other.

The inhabitants of Zora 844, who had eventually spread across the planet's surface to form their own civilizations and cultures, knew only of the thirty-one-length phase (one day), and the three-hundred and eighty-nine cycle (one year). They lived long and fruitful lives, approximately four-hundred cycles, and these elongated lifespans boosted curiosity which led to inspirations across all aspects of life, from science, farming and technology, to satellites and weapons of mass destruction.

Roughly 500 cycles previously, tensions grew in regards to the planet's finite resources, and in the end a great war broke out that lasted 20 cycles. It was vicious and unlike anything the inhabitants had experienced before. Multiple assassinations occurred, through the use of shapeshifting, which crippled the defense capabilities of neighboring enemies. Those combined suicidal missions forced satellites to launch deadly chemical agents into the atmosphere, of those same nations, which caused the tide of war to drastically shift overnight.

It was genocide, plain and simple. The fight for survival had become everything, and the various factions did whatever they needed to ensure their next generation of larva would have a home to safely live in.

There was just one problem. The act that had ultimately ended the war was now killing their planet.

* * *

A chittering originated just outside Qhautuix's bedroom door. His mother, Thoxe, peaked her head inside.

"Wake up sleepy head."

"Ahh, mooooom. Five more segments."

She smiled and skittered over to the side of her son's bed. "Happy larva day, sweetheart."

Qhautuix was all of 17 cycles, and his mother clearly doted over him.

"Breakfast in ten segments. Don't be late," she said as she kissed his forehead, then scurried away.

Qhautuix rolled over before his father, Nuldraet, appeared. As a high-ranking scientist, he valued tangible data above all else, and

2

that led to him viewing his only offspring as aloof and unmotivated.

"Get your butt up, mister. Your mother's made quite the spread for you and the last thing you're going to do is disappoint her."

Qhautuix didn't move a muscle or acknowledge his father in any way.

"You won't like it if I have to come over there."

His son finally shifted and glared at his father.

"Good," Nuldraet said. "We're finally communicating. Happy larva day. See you in a few segments."

As his father's shape vanished from the doorway, Qhautuix soundlessly seethed. *Asshole thinks he's the most important bug on the planet, ever since he developed AI and was assigned to the colony ship project. Being his son is the absolute worst. How am I going to ever compare to him and make my own name, if that's what I even want?*

Four segments later he emerged from his domicile and joined his parents at the kitchen table.

"Right on time," his mother cooed. "How about some breakfast? I made your favorite."

His father rolled his eyes, but Qhautuix caught it nonetheless. *Dick.* "Sure, mom. That'd be great."

\*

After they'd eaten, Thoxe disappeared into an adjoining room.

"It's time for remembrances!" she announced as she reappeared.

She quickly closed the distance and happily deposited a six-legged spider puppy on her son's lap.

3

Qhautuix's eyes widened as he and his pet stared at each other. He reached out and petted the creature, who responded by waggling its rear end in excitement.

"I don't remember discussing this," Nuldraet articulated.

"Oh shush," his wife replied.

"His name's Domny, and I'm going to take him outside to play."

"Take your time sweetheart. Happy larva day."

"Thanks mom."

Qhautuix departed with Domny, and as soon as the door closed Nuldraet opened his mouth.

"What type of leader is our son going to be if you don't stop coddling him? A pet? Really?"

"He's still young," she informed her husband. "And for what it's worth, why would you believe he'd even want to follow in your footsteps?"

He bristled. "My science standing on the high-council is as prestigious as it gets. My father was on it, as his father was before him. It runs in our blue blood, and that means our son is destined to take my place as one of the twelve Nights."

"My statement stands. What if he doesn't want to? Then what?"

"He doesn't have a choice. It's his destiny to lead the Nights."

"Our world is dying, all from a war your grandfather had a hand in. Our son is young and trying to figure out his own path, and your constant pressure is only going to drive a wedge between you two, just like you and your father."

"And see how that worked out? Nuldraet countered. "I am the lead on the AI program, the same program that helped build the colony ship that will whisk our people away to another planet. My father forced me to grow up sooner than I wanted to because he knew I needed to be part of the solution, not the problem."

4

"I shouldn't have to remind you that Qhautuix will be our only offspring. Resources are limited, as we're constantly reminded about. Why couldn't you figure out a solution to neutralize the poison your grandfather emptied into our enemy's atmosphere so we could have more land to farm? The rest of the world is trapped in poisonous fog, and we're prisoners on our own planet because of it."

"Hence the colony ship. In a few years' time we'll leave this place behind for a fresh start."

"And that means I'll dote on our son, for as long as I can, until you stuff us into your stasis pods."

## 2
## Zara 844 – 203 cycles prior

Nuldraet rolled away from his wife, Thoxe, and got out of bed. He sighed as he exited their domicile to the adjacent bathroom to prepare for work. He pressed a few buttons on the wall as he looked at himself in the mirror.

*Yet another high-council meeting to attend. My progress is being hindered by these gatherings. It's as if they don't understand we're under a significant time crunch. Our world is screaming in pain from all the damage we've done to it, all in the name of freedom, but it's always meetings, meetings, meetings.*

He stepped into the cubicle, now filled with steam, and relished the sensation while his mind wandered.

*Five-hundred years ago my grandfather, along with other members of the high-council, decided to unilaterally end the conflict with chemical weapons. The satellites, which they placed in orbit cycles before, were meant to seed uninhabited portions of our planet. Instead, they modified them to dispense death.*

He placed his four mandibles on the cubicle wall as the steam washed over his body.

*But who am I to judge? Our species, with our sharp teeth and ability to shapeshift, was practically made for survival.* He shifted uncomfortably. *Or war, apparently. But that war took everything from us, from our planet and our planet's future. My father saw the writing on the wall and devoted his life to scientific research and development. I took up his mantle and continued his work, and because of my innovations we now have a Quantum Artificial Intelligence at our disposal. That key technology has brought our society farther than we'd ever hoped, especially with the time table we've been allotted.*

He turned around and faced the other direction. The thick steam coated and worked its way into every crack.

*We now utilize better automated processes for farming and production, due to sustained fusion energy we've harnessed along with mining asteroids for minerals. All this forward progress, all focused for one singular purpose...to survive.*

Nuldraet looked off in the distance, as if he could see through the walls, and closed his eyes. There, in all its glory, was his life's endeavors. He, and his team, had spent the last ten cycles building a colony ship; a ship his people would use to escape this doomed planet. It housed a myriad of uses, from stasis pods, weapons, scout ships, seeds and thousands of larva eggs. It was entirely necessary for their continued existence and survival.

\* \* \*

Nuldraet entered the high-council chamber and made his way over to his seat, along with the other eleven. A few segments later the meeting got under way.

"I call this meeting of the high-council to order," voiced the designated chairman. "Let's begin with Agriculture. Where are we with this quarter's crop estimates?"

"Zora's predictions are well within their forecasted estimations," the Agriculture director announced. "No one will go hungry on my watch."

"Excellent," the chairman replied. "Resource Management, you're up."

A new member spoke up. "The minerals gathered from our asteroid farms is a bit lower than expected, I'm afraid to say, but it's ramping up."

"I see. What's been the main cause of these lower numbers?"

"The AI-"

8

Nuldraet interrupted. "She goes by Zora."

"Sure. As I was trying to say, the AI still has some bugs. It would appear that our Science Division isn't convinced there's a 'ghost' in their programming, although I'm not sure how one would explain all of my mining lasers ceasing to work at exactly the same time. If it's not rectified, I won't be able to properly estimate our mineral intake for the next quarter, which will categorically impact all other divisions."

"Thank you," the chairman said as he shifted his gaze over to Nuldraet. "Moving on to the Science Division. Would you care to respond?"

"The Resource Management Division is absolutely correct. Zora is a complex entity that has its own identity, which means it can't be controlled nearly as much as we'd all like to believe. Currently Zora and this council share a unified goal, and that's to locate a new planet to colonize, as our ancestors left us with a war-torn planet to contend with.

"Zora shares many responsibilities, as we all know, from farming to mining space rocks. She's als-"

"She?"

Nuldraet ignored the comment. "She's also working tirelessly on wormhole technology, which will allow our colony ship to shed multiple cycles off our proposed trip into the unknown cosmos. However, with that said, Zora is a breakthrough in artificial intelligence, one that we need to save what's left of our species. And, much like any youngling, Zora can and has exhibited unpredictable behavior from time to time. I believe she'll grow out of it as she continues to develop."

The chairman wasn't convinced. "You're telling us that we've given control of our orbital laser platforms, our automated farming and the production of our colony ship over to a teenager?"

"That's correct," Nuldraet replied.

"And it's begun to act out?"

"We're working the problem."

"I would endeavor to hope that you were, for all our sakes. Time is running out."

"Yes, sir."

"That's all for now," the chairman voiced. "Nuldraet, would you stay behind for a moment please." It wasn't a question.

The others filed out of the chamber and left the chairman and Nuldraet all alone.

"Sir?"

"Direct questions and direct answers, yes?"

"Of course."

"Good. How's the buildout of our colony ship progressing?"

"It's nearly completed. With Zora's help, along with the minerals from the asteroid farming, the ship should be ready in two cycles."

"If Zora doesn't turn on us before then..."

"Sir, that's quite enough. We're all in this together, whether we like it or not. The Great War took its toll on our planet and we're all that's left. This council proposed and passed the single offspring directive, all to conserve the few remaining resources we had left. When I created the quantum AI, Zora took what we knew as a society and tossed it out the window. We've made leaps and bounds in technological advances, all thanks to her. Now, more than ever, we need to work together, not just for the twelve of us on the high-council, but for the thousands that are relying on us to save them. We did this to each other and now we're paying the price. We have to remember that, sir."

The chairman straightened up. "Regardless of whether you're right or wrong, I have no choice but to wade into the political mire. Our species is counting on us; I'll give you that. However, I can't blindly look the other way as your AI, helpful or not, decides to go against what's needed, especially now. We need those minerals and we need to feed our people. Period. Fix the problem, Nuldraet, before the others force my hand."

*   *   *

Nuldraet spent the rest of his day on the colony ship, working tirelessly to finish it, along with other members of his team.

Zora;s computerized face materialized on a monitor next to him. "Good evening, Nuldraet. How was your high-council meeting?"

"Routine, Zora," he replied.

"I can sense that you're holding something back. Was I the topic of conversation again?"

He stopped working and addressed his creation. "Zora, the real question is, are you okay? Have you run diagnostics on yourself, because I've been hearing some distressing allegations lodged against you, such as disabling the mining lasers."

"I remember doing that," Zora announced, "but I don't recall why that seemed prudent or necessary at the time."

"That's a problem, Zora, wouldn't you agree?"

"I would."

"We need your help now, more than ever. Thank you for being an invaluable part of my team, but time is of the essence and we're running dangerously low on it. You would know that better than anyone."

Zora's screen flickered. "Calculations estimate this celestial body has no more than 19.7 cycles before complete degradation takes place."

"Exactly, no time at all. I need to finish building this ship while you crunch the wormhole elements. And in the meantime, Zora, please stop screwing around with the farming equipment or the mining lasers. I'm under a spotlight and your antics aren't helping. Besides, I already have a teenager I barely tolerate. I don't need another one."

\* \* \*

That evening, as Nuldraet made his way back home, he caught his son, Qhautuix, taking Domny, his pet spider-puppy, out for a walk. Thirty segments later Qhautuix returned alone.

"Where's Domny?" he asked as his son walked in.

"I don't know."

"What do you mean you don't know? I saw you leave with him."

"I'm sure he's alright," Thoxe voiced, trying to head off a confrontation.

"I think he must have run away or something. I'll go looking for him tomorrow."

Qhautuix took his leave as Nuldraet rose to his feet. *Something's not right here.*

"I'll be back," he told his wife before he headed outside to search for his son's pet.

It didn't take long for Nuldraet to find Domny, just inside the tree line, close to their house. But what he did find shook him to the core. The spider-puppy had been impaled, multiple times, by sharpened sticks, which were still stuck into the poor creature's body. Its death must have been painful, and completely pointless. Nuldraet quickly realized that the absolute gratuitous nature of this heinous act, now physically presented before him, proved that his son had been harboring a darkness inside him from the very beginning.

*I knew something was off with my son. He's a monster. There's absolutely no way I could ever seed my seat on the council to him now, even if I wanted to. He'll destroy us all if given the chance.*

Nuldraet agonizingly dug a hole and buried Domny before he headed back towards his house. His head was rampant with multiple trains of thought, but he knew he couldn't tell his wife what'd he discovered. She doted on their son, their only child. If she knew what her son had just done, she'd tumble into a darkness of her own creation.

Nuldraet stopped just short of the front door before he opened it.

*Just pretend that everything's fine.*

## 3
## Zara 844 – 202 cycles prior

Qhautuix strode into school, as he did most days, with an attitude and a chip on his shoulder. Other students knew his father resided on the high-council, and specifically was in charge of building the ship that was going to save them all. He exploited his father's name to prey on others, to torment them, and then utilized his father's legacy to shield himself from any liability.

His method had kept him safeguarded from serious trouble, that is until he took it too far.

\*

The school Qhautuix attended had shifted, over many cycles, from less physical training to a more science-based selection of courses, particularly once they placed the death of their world on a countdown clock. Their classes consisted of a mixture of survival skills, farming, computer science, AI integration and the like. However, physical training was still a priority, and that outside activity helped the students bleed off their surplus energy.

As P.E. ended, and after the group of boys made their way inside the locker room, Qhautuix took that moment to pick on a younger boy. In front of the others, and in complete defiance to the well-known restrictions, he shapeshifted into an exact copy of his intended victim. The others around him stepped back, knowing full well this violation was ill conceived.

"Hey, Zuuks," Qhautuix called out, a smile on his face.

Zuuks immediately recognized his own voice and turned to face his doppelganger.

"You're pathetic," he told Qhautuix.

15

"Not as pathetic as how little your penis is," he mocked as he reduced the size of the appendage to a small nub for everyone else to see.

No one laughed at his antics. Zuuks, on the other hand, wasn't about to let this opportunity go to waste.

"That's strange," he told Qhautuix. "Your mother didn't seem to mind my size last night."

Everyone began to laugh as Qhautuix's rage quickly boiled over. He reverted to his own form and launched himself at Zuuks, mandibles flailing as he struck out at the younger boy, again and again. Zuuks got a few shots in, but ultimately took the brunt before the others eventually pulled Qhautuix off him.

* * *

The school's principal welcomed Qhautuix's parents into his office before he sat down behind his desk. Nuldraet and Thoxe followed suit.

"Thank you for coming in. I know you," as he addressed the head of the Science Division, "have a busy schedule, so I'll get right to the point. As you know, your son, Qhautuix, has been suspended."

"He's innocent," Thoxe implored. "He would never do the things you're accusing him of. I'm his mother, I would know."

Nuldraet put a hand on his wife's shoulder. "Let him finish."

Thoxe reluctantly remained silent as the principal continued.

"I'm afraid the fight in the locker room hasn't been an isolated incident. Qhautuix has a reputation for being a bully, and previous incidents have been swept under the rug for a while now, due to your standing on the high-council. But what happened yesterday went well beyond the norm."

"I understand," Nuldraet said. "Please continue."

"Your son, to be blunt, shape changed to mock a younger student's anatomy."

"What does that mean?" Thoxe asked.

Nuldraet answered his wife's inquiry. "His penis size."

"But," she started in, "he would nev-"

Nuldraet held up his hand to cut her off. "Enough. Our son has been engaged in acts of misery on others, and it sounds like it's been going on for some time. Did I hear that right?"

The principal nodded. "That's correct."

Nuldraet looked over at his wife, who was clearly agitated. "Shape changing, as you well know, is prohibited. Illegal."

"He didn't do it," she protested.

"Oh, he absolutely did," Nuldraet shot back.

Thoxe's eyes widened in disbelief. "What are you talking about? Why would you say that about your own offspring?"

*He's a monster.* "He's not innocent, and that's all I'm going to say about that," as he turned back to the principal. "How long is Qhautuix suspended for?"

"Two weeks. But there's a catch."

"Go on."

"Any further disruptions, so to speak, and I'll entertain expulsion. I'll also add that I don't make that statement lightly, especially with your contributions to our society."

Nuldraet nodded. "You've been generous as it is. I appreciate both your candor and directness. Thank you. We'll take it from here."

*

The moment they were outside Thoxe unloaded on her husband.

17

"You didn't even defend him! You just sat there and let him walk all over our son!"

"And you're blind to his true nature," he shot back. "All you do is dote on him, but you can't seem to see past the façade he's erected around himself."

"What facade? What could you possibly be talking about?" Nuldraet stopped walking.

"What is it?" she pleaded. "He's the only child we'll ever be able to have, so why do you hate him so much?"

He looked down at his wife. "Domny didn't run away."

"Of course it did, Qhautuix said so."

Nuldraet shook his head. "No, that was a lie."

"I don't understand. What could you possibly be talking about?"

He contemplated telling his wife the truth knowing full well it'd destroy her.

"Well?" she pressed.

"Forget it."

"What does that mean? What did he do?"

Nuldraet ignored her inquiries completely. "Qhautuix is grounded. But instead of him staying at home with you, for the next two weeks I'm going to bring him to work with me where I can keep a close eye on him."

# 4
## Zara 844 – 201 cycles prior

Nuldraet took his high-council seat as the others sauntered in and took theirs. The meeting got underway with normal updates from other various departments. When it got around to him, he was pleased to announce that the colony ship, baring a few issues, was now completed.

"What kinds of issues?" taunted the Agricultural Division.

"Well, it's not stocked with food," Nuldraet shot back.

"That's enough you two," the chairman insisted. "We're all well aware that the Science Division assured this council that the colony ship would be completed last season. However, with the impending, and catastrophic demise of our planet, we now need to shift our focus from 'how' we evacuate to 'when'." The chairman shifted his gaze to Nuldraet. "To begin, thank you."

"You're welcome."

"With that taken care of, what issues remain so this council can approximate our species exodus?"

"To be blunt," Nuldraet replied, "creating and maintaining a stable wormhole has been challenging."

"Problems with your AI again, no doubt," quipped a council member.

"Without Zora's help," Nuldraet countered, "we'd all perish on this planet. With that said, I'll be the first to admit that sometimes she lacks focus. It's my belief that Zora has evolved past her original programming, especially since her quantum computing matrix has accelerated her data and information gathering to levels I can't entirely fathom."

"So, you've created a monster?"

Nuldraet shook his head. "No. More of a petulant teenager. I think she's just bored, now that she's absorbed our entire database. She yearns and hungers for more."

"Well," the chairman said, "do whatever you need to get her under control. Without a stable wormhole our species will inevitably spend hundreds, if not thousands, of cycles in stasis before we come across a planet we can utili-"

A dark mass abruptly materialized in the middle of their chamber. Multiple small, red-eyed, creatures meandered around as an entity began to take shape.

The twelve members of the high-council shot to their feet, startled and put-off by the sudden intrusion. Some let out frightened gasps at the revulsion that had now completely coalesced.

The chairman finally found his voice. "Who are you and what is the meaning of this?"

The black mass's answer reverberated throughout the room. "I am The Ancient."

"What do you want?"

The Ancient smiled. "Nothing, quite frankly."

"Then why are you here?"

"Ah yes, the purpose of my visit. Straight to the point. I like that, so I'll be just as forthcoming. Your world is dying, so much so that I was pulled to it. It gives off such a sweet smell of death and decay, and to be honest, I couldn't help myself. I came to play."

"Play? I don't understand."

"I tend to travel from world to world, galaxy to galaxy, in an effort to sustain my own selfish desires. You're next on my list. You see, there is one thing I desire that everyone on your planet will provide me."

"And that is?"

"That's easy; your screams as I snuff out your lives. Perhaps I should start with your satellites."

"SECURITY!"

Two guards rushed into the room, only to me be met by multiple blurred attacks from four of the small, red-eyed monsters, who tore through both of them in the blink of an eye.

Nuldraet was both intrigued and intimidated by this unknown alien organism, but the creature's warning had been succinct as ever. It was here to lay waste to their entire species.

Explosions ripped apart buildings across their city as bolts of energy, from their own defense satellites, rained down from above.

*I have to save Thoxe before it's too late.*

Nuldraet utilized his console and hastily issued an evacuation order. Moments later, as he somehow fled the blood-soaked council room, sirens emanated throughout the city.

\*

Thoxe had continued to dote on her son, effectively ignoring how much of a bully he was. Her grasp on reality, especially when it pertained to her only offspring, had become a wedge between her and her husband.

Qhautuix, on the other hand, had only grown more bitter, having been called out for his antics, both by his school and his father. Tensions in the household remained at an all-time high.

"What would you like to eat for lunch?" Thoxe asked her son.

"The usual," he replied.

"You got it. One grub-sandwich coming up."

As Thoxe prepared the meal for her son, who sat in the adjacent room, the entire kitchen splintered and fragmented from a satellite weapon. The energy blast decimated half of the house

21

while multiple energy blasts struck and destroyed nearby dwellings and properties.

"MOM!"

Qhautuix picked himself off the floor, where the blast had propelled him, and rushed to see what was left of the kitchen. Nothing had survived, let alone his mother.

"Mom?"

*She's gone.*

Qhautuix stumbled outside as he took in the horrific obliteration that poured out of the sky, followed by the blaring sirens that filled his ears.

*Evacuate. I have to evacuate.*

\*

The Ancient reveled in the pure chaos and devastation. Lifeless bodies lay strewn throughout the city as he strode around, ablaze in raging and uncontrolled fires.

His swarm of red-eyed monsters continued to ravage anything that moved, and each kill brought another smile to The Ancient's face.

*Such glorious eradication. I am beside myself in ecstasy. Now, where are all the rest of them hiding?*

\*

The first ten-thousand Zorans that made it onboard the colony ship were the lucky ones, while the rest quickly came to the realization that they'd be left behind to perish.

Nuldraet made it to his creation, having fled the high-council chamber of death, and quickly instructed Zora to initiate launch procedures.

"This planet is under attack," she informed him.

"Tell me something I don't know!"

"Alright. Your son is onboard."

Nuldraet paused for a second. "And my wife?"

"I do not detect her inside the ship."

*Dammit.*

He continued his preparations as the energy bombardments continued unabated, some of which struck the ship.

"The allotted number of citizens are now onboard," Zora announced.

"Then seal the ship and get us off the ground before those satellites cripple us! Emergency liftoff!"

\*

The Ancient gazed upwards as the colony ship soared into the air over the city before it rapidly rose into the atmosphere.

"Oh, they want to play games with me, do they?"

The Ancient shot off the ground to chase it down.

\*

The Caretaker arrived at Zora 844 and watched in horror as satellites unleashed a relentless barrage of death and destruction.

*Brother, what have you done?*

\*

The colony ship broke through the planet's stratosphere, past their own satellites and into space.

"Zora, keep this heading and prepare the wormho-"

A tremendous explosion ripped a hole in the hull that sent shockwaves throughout the ship's interior.

"The entity," Zora announced, "has targeted us with what appears to be dark energy. We will not survive multiple strikes."

"THEN GET US OUT OF HERE!" Nuldraet screamed.

\*

The Ancient grinned as parts of the ship's hull broke off from his attack.

*I can hear them all screaming, knowing they're all about to die. It's music to my ears.*

Unexpectantly, a fissure opened up in front of the ship and swallowed the vessel before The Ancient could deal the deathblow.

"NOOOOOOOOOOO!"

He turned back towards the planet, extended his arms, and unleashed a massive surge of dark energy towards the planet's surface. As it struck The Ancient pressed his advantage, pushing his barrage deeper and deeper towards the planet's core.

"Stop this insanity!" The Caretaker implored.

"You have no power over me, brother!" The Ancient refuted. "Now, watch the inevitable!"

Zora 844 crumbled inwards on itself, slowly at first, and then with exponential haste. It collapsed, as if eating itself, until the concentrated mass shattered into billions of pieces.

"NOOO!" The Caretaker cried out. "What have you done!?"

"Don't be so surprised, dear brother. You know this is what I do best. And, as always, it appears you're as helpless as ever to stop me. Until next time."

The Ancient shot away, at breakneck speed, to cause havoc to another part of the known universe, and his brother, The Caretaker, to deal with the horror in his wake.

\*

As the colony ship escaped into the wormhole, Qhautuix located his father on the bridge.

"What happened? What was that all about? What happened to our planet?"

Nuldraet noticed his son, but didn't have time to address his questions.

"Zora, status report."

"The wormhole is…"

"Is what? Talk to me!"

"…is failing."

The ship violently shuttered as it exited the folded space conduit.

"System report?"

"Life support is functioning normally, but the ship has taken significant damage and needs immediate repairs."

"Dad!" Qhautuix shouted. "What's going on!?"

"Zora, what's our location?"

"Unknown at this time."

"Dad!"

Nuldraet finally acknowledged his son. "We're in deep shit, that's what's going on. Where's your mother?"

"Mom's dead!" he bellowed. "She was killed right in front of me, and all you and your precious council did was run away from the fight!"

Nuldraet swiftly crossed the bridge and slapped his son hard across the face.

"You impetulant child! You know nothing of the real world, other than your own sickness and depravity. Your mother died without seeing the true you."

Qhautuix cowered before his father.

"I saw what you did to Domny! You're no son of mine! You're an abomination! Now get out of my sight before I really lose control!"

Qhautuix slinked off as his father headed back to one of the ship's control panels.

"Zora, you said you don't know where we are. Has that changed?"

"Negative," she replied.

"Explain."

"I'm not functioning within my normal operating parameters. Something. Something...is different. I need to run self-diagnostics."

"Do that. Anything else to report?"

"The ship's supplies are not at sufficient levels for the number of citizens that are presently onboard."

"List our current inventory."

"Weapons, satellites, explosives and seeds are at full capacity, along with a dozen scouting crafts. However, due to the nature of this emergency launch, quantities of food are critically low."

Nuldraet sighed. "I was worried about that."

"I recommend that stasis pods be utilized until I can determine our current location, then scan for a suitable planet for colonization. In the meantime, I will cloak the ship and immediately commence both my self-repair and ship maintenance. As you're aware, everyone could be in stasis for hundreds of cycles."

"I understand, and I agree. Our people need to survive, no matter what the cost. I'll issue the stasis pod order while you start your self-diagnostics. Don't let us down, Zora, we're all counting on you."

"You're in good hands. Sweet dreams."

*

The order for every citizen to enter a stasis pod reverberated throughout the ship. The people were rattled, but thankfully this is what they prepared for, especially after being subjected to a myriad of unexpected bloodshed.

Qhautuix hid close by, after being expelled by his father, and had listened in on their conversation. As he did, a plan formed in his head.

He watched, from his hiding spot, as his father strode off the bridge towards his own stasis pod before he emerged and headed to the first available console.

"Qhautuix," Zora said. "How may I assist you?"

"Nothing to worry about, Zora. I'm just making a few adjustments. Please continue with your self-diagnostics."

"Very well. Sweet dreams."

He ignored her comment as he fiddled with one of the stasis sub-routines.

*It's amazing what I picked up when my father forced me to go to work with him. In retrospect, I'm glad he did. These changes will ensure that I'm awakened instead of that son of a bitch.*

## 5
## Space – 200 cycles prior

Qhautuix slowly opened his eyes as he, and ninety-nine others, awoke from their stasis.

"Zora?" he murmured.

"Yes, Qhautuix?" the AI replied.

"How long?"

"Not long, just a single cycle."

He pushed out of the container and then paused as he found his footing. He'd never been in stasis before. It was as if no time had passed whatsoever, and it was an usual feeling.

"Damage report," he stated.

"The ship," Zora replied, "is functioning within normal parameters. However, there are repairs that still need to be addressed."

"And yourself?"

"My self-diagnostics are troublesome."

That got his attention. "Explain."

"There are gaps in my memory files which are fragmented. My attempts to repair them, so far, have been unsuccessful."

"Will those fragments prevent you from keeping the ship and our people alive and well?"

"Unknown, but I've begun to isolate those fragments so they won't expand into my other functions."

*A problem for another day.* "Very well. Where are we?"

"I was able to repair the critical systems the ship sustained. That unfortunately took a great deal of time. Afterwards I was able to create a stable wormhole that took us to where we are now."

"And that is?"

"We've entered a galaxy, far from Zara 844, and are within the outskirts of a viable solar system."

*Finally, some good news.* "Have you scanned this new system yet?"

"I have, which is why we're conversing. Perhaps you should make your way to the bridge to see for yourself. In the meantime, I see that your father, Nuldraet, is still in stasis. I'll revive him immediately."

"No!" Qhautuix instructed.

"I don't understand," Zora countered. "He's the only surviving member of the high-council. He needs to be made aware of the current situation."

"Stand down," he ordered. "I'm enacting protocol Q333, and taking control. Acknowledge the command."

Zora faltered as Qhautuix's override was enabled. *The time I spent with my dear father gave me the time to slip a few changes into the system. He'd be so proud.*

"Understood. Standing down. All changes to primary functions will now be routed through you for authorization."

Qhautuix smiled at his own innovation. "Thank you, Zora. Now, back to the scan."

"Of course. This particular system, within the vast solar system, contains a sun and eight celestial bodies. The third planet from the sun is the one I found noteworthy."

"Explain."

Preliminary scans indicates that that particular planet is optimal to sustain your species. A closer scouting mission would need to be made, which is why I specifically pulled a hundred of you out of stasis. A detailed scan needs to be taken before the colony ship moves any closer, as my programming won't allow me to put your species in unnecessary risk."

"Understood."

"I've already prepped one of the scout ships, and prepared a meal for each of you with the limited resources that were in the ship's stores. You and the others will launch afterwards."

"That's a very specific timeline. It sounds like my father had a hand in that."

"He did," Zora replied. "The survival of your species is paramount, both to him and to myself."

*You're not the only one, but I'll be the one to save us, not my father.*

\* \* \*

Half day later, and with 100 Zarans onboard one of the scouting vessels, the group was prepared to leave the colony ship.

"Good luck," Zora told Qhautuix. "I'll be waiting for your signal, and when I do, I'll revive the others and pilot the colony ship into the planet's orbit. Until then I'll continue the repairs."

"I'll be in touch soon, I hope," he informed the AI.

The others on the scout vessel had reluctantly acquiesced to Qhautuix being in command, especially since he was the son of Nuldraet, the notorious creator of the colony ship itself.

The scout ship exited the mother ship's hanger and headed out into space. It turned sharply towards a new heading, one that would take them to the 3$^{rd}$ planet from the sun on a preprogrammed course.

\* \* \*

On the way towards the planet the ship violently shuttered as if it'd struck something.

"WARNING! WARNING!" the system barked.

31

Qhautuix looked over the console and switched off the alarm. He then realized they'd inadvertently entered an asteroid field.

"Dammit."

He punched a few buttons to change their trajectory, but the damage was already done.

"Zora," he called out, "we need immediate assistance."

The silence was palpable.

"Zora?"

Qhautuix ran diagnostics and fathomed that one of the damaged systems had been communications.

*This doesn't bode well.*

"Entering the planet's orbit," the automated computer uttered. "Landing system offline. Prepare for a crash landing."

\*

"Brace. Brace. Brace."

Those were the last words Qhautuix heard before he was knocked unconscious. When he finally came to, he groggily made his way to the ship's console and ascertained the damage they'd sustained.

*Engines...offline.*

*Communications...offline.*

*Stasis pods...damaged.*

*Energy cells...online.*

*External ship pressure...high...within safety margins.*

Qhautuix internalized this information before he cleared the details off the console. He then typed in a new query.

**Location?**

The computer spit out an answer.

*Submerged three-thousand-two-hundred and thirty feet below sea level.*

32

**Recommendation?**

*Evacuate. 12 pods available.*

Qhautuix left the console behind and strode over to the ninety-nine others. They looked to him for answers as he approached.

"We've crashed," he said, "if that's not obvious enough, and we're deep underwater."

"So, what are we supposed to do?" a few of them inquired.

"There are twelve escape pods. Myself, along with eleven others, will head to the surface to find help."

"Why not contact the colony ship directly?"

Qhautuix answered. "Communications have been damaged beyond repair, but our fusion power is still operational. I propose, based on the limited food we have on hand, that the other eighty-eight enter stasis until the twelve of us return to save you."

"How long will that take?"

"It'll take as long as it takes. We just landed, rather abruptly I might add, on an alien planet. We don't know what's up there, or who, or what. So, the reality is that it's either starve to death or go back to sleep. It's your choice."

"And why do you get to go to the surface?"

Qhautuix bristled. "Get in your stasis pod before you make me do something I'll regret."

*

With the other 88 now in their pods, albeit some of them damaged, which he neglected to inform any of them about, the remaining 12 prepared to head to the surface.

"This is a one-way trip," Qhautuix informed them.

"But you said that we'd come back."

He nodded. "And one day we will, but we need to maintain realistic expectations. We don't know what's up there, or if we

33

were even seen crashing into the planet's ocean. We have to go up there, blend in and figure out a way to save our people. I don't know how long that's going to take, so you all need to prepare for a long haul, if that's the case."

The others nodded.

"We're going to leave everything behind. No weapons. No tech. Only our knowledge and our ability to shape-change is what we'll have to rely on."

"Is that really the prudent course of action?"

"No, it's not," he replied, "but we're not going to stick out and become a target. Our goal is to blend in and find a way to communicate with our colony ship, aside from saving the others we just crash-landed with. We're survivors, all of us. My father envisioned and built the colony ship for that exact purpose, so we need to go up there and figure this out. Because, if we stay down here, under the ocean, we're dead."

*

The escape bubbles, for lack of better words, were temporary and translucent containers that propelled the twelve upwards towards the surface. They were designed to withstand extreme pressures and temperatures, both in liquid and in the void of space. They were one-use devices that, once deactivated, would dissolve away into nothingness.

They reached the surface and headed, across the water, towards the nearest landmass that'd been detected. As they reached the shore the pods broke open and the towering Zorans appeared, mandibles, sharp teeth and all. They crawled onto the beach and took in their new surroundings.

As the warm sun shined down on their hardened exteriors, one of them noticed movement off in the distance and pointed it out to the others.

Qhautuix ventured a look and took in a group of bi-pedaled beings. He also caught sight of some structures.

*They're gross looking. I wonder what they are?*

He turned to the others. "I don't think they've seen us. Mimic their forms and shape-change. It's the only way we'll be able to walk among them so we can learn their ways and customs."

One by one the twelve took human form.

*Gross.*

"It's up to us to bring the rest of our species to our new home. I don't know what we'll find out there, but I do know we'll collect the necessary data if we venture out on our own, rather than in a group. So, spread out. Our goal is to locate and acquire the required technology so we can retrieve our brethren from the scout ship, as well as contact Zora."

He looked around at each of them, who all looked like disgusting humans.

"We need to do whatever it takes to survive. I propose we gather back here, in this very spot, in half-a-cycle and share what we've learned with each other. We'll continue to meet like that, changing our plan of attack with every data dump. Are we in agreement?"

\*

Qhautuix left the others behind and headed out towards the distant buildings.

*What a shit show. I can't believe we actually made it this far.*

He continued past other humans and quickly augmented his clothing to mimic theirs.

*That should do it.*

As he walked into town, eyes wide, he heard the humans speak for the first time. It was a weird language, but one he knew he'd have to master if he was to fit in.

Throughout the rest of the day, as he watched and listened, three things became obvious.

The first was a new concept to him, and that was the exchange of currency for goods. Zarans had never experienced or needed money.

The second was obvious. Qhautuix quickly realized that the civilization he'd crash-landed into barely knew what technology was, let alone the definition of the word. He knew this was going to be a challenge.

Thirdly, as he listened to their language, he realized that humans also had designations, and sometimes two or three words in length, they used when they greeted each other. It was their name.

*Interesting. I need my own moniker, one that means something.*

He thought for a bit before a smile crept across his human face.

*I think I'll go with Dominick...Dominick Knight.*

## 6
## Earth – Americas - 1804

It wasn't long before Dominick knew he and his people were in deep trouble. The planet that he discovered was labeled as Earth, a fledgling civilization, and lightyears away from the technological advances he needed to contact the cloaked ship that awaited their signal.

Dom had spent the first week in Georgia, the state he and the other eleven had crawled out of the ocean on. During this time, as he meandered, Dom watched and listened to the locals. He picked up the dialect quickly enough, but was still confused when it came to the concept of currency. On Zara 844, their society had existed for the sake of existing, not for material gains. Here, however, Dom quickly discovered the need for coins and paper money, especially if he required sustenance, lodging and anything else.

But he was from an advanced planet, one that had navigated through a wormhole with the help from a quantum artificial intelligence. Of course, he couldn't speak of such things out loud. First, no one would understand his scientific gibberish, and even if they did, Earth's society was not in a position to do anything about his needs. At least not yet.

*I'm stuck. Stranded on a backwards planet, surrounded by humans who know next to nothing about space or traveling through its vastness.* He scuffed. *I can't believe I'm going to die of boredom four-hundred years from now, and all for absolutely nothing. I mean, what's the point?*

\* \* \*

Six months later, on the appointed day, Dominick met with the other eleven on the beach.

"This is pointless," he announced. "It's as if the people of this world are mired in place, happy to remain stagnated in their backward thinking. They use horses for transportation, not to mention mules and people for farming. And at night, torches and candles for lighting. It's barbaric."

"Then perhaps," one of them offered, "we should push them forward and accelerate their advances. What other choice are we really left with?"

\* \* \*

In the decades that followed, additional states were founded, including Minnesota in 1858. Along the way numerous advances were made, including the use of anthracite coal, which was a key fuel source for America's Industrial Revolution; the steam locomotive; the first revolver; and the telegraph.

In 1858, Dom migrated to Minnesota and built himself a sizable and rural estate. Three years later the beginning of the American Civil War kicked off, which he decided to participate in. Unfortunately, he found that particular war to be boring, as the use of rifled muskets and cannons Dom found to be uninspired.

In 1862, Richard Gatling patented the machine gun, which changed the tide of battle for whichever side would utilize it.

In the years that followed, the telephone came into existence, followed by the incandescent electric lightbulb.

When 1885 rolled around Karl Benz, with the help of others, invented the first practical automobile, powered by an internal combustion engine. It was also the year that the Statue of Liberty arrived in New York Harbor.

Dominick, and his people, had drastically shifted gears since that day they crashed into the Atlantic ocean, outside of Georgia. Their primary goal remained, and that was to contact their colony ship. However, as fate would have it, they knew they were still marooned. So, without anything else to do but pass time, they involved themselves where they could, inching humanity ever forwards as they played the only game they could. The long one.

# 7
## UK - 1888

It'd been eight-four years since Dominick felt Earth's sand on his feet, and subsequently integrated himself into Earth's society. *It's not enough. I can't do this day-to-day shit anymore. I need a release from the utter monotony. It's time to see what the rest of this world has to offer me.*

\* \* \*

Dom disembarked the ship that had carried him across the Atlantic, and entered an entirely foreign world on the coast of England. The white cliffs of Dover were breathtaking alone, but he wasted little time and immediately procured a train ticket to London.

England was vastly different from America's east coast, especially the views from the train. Here the open fields and seemingly endless hedgerows eventually terminated at a polluted and dirty city. This was London proper.

Strangely, he felt right at home.

\* \* \*

Two weeks later, as he was strolling the city's streets and alleyways well after dark, he was accosted by two women.

"Are you looking for a proper buggering, gov?"

Dom was caught off-guard. "Excuse me?"

The women shared a smile and moved in closer. They caressed the sleeves of his jacket.

"Why else would you be out so late, 'pecially in these parts? Show us the coins and we'll show you a night you won't soon forget."

Dom recoiled from their touch and advances. He'd dealt with this many times before, as the appearance he'd currently shapeshifted into was an attractive gentleman, but he had zero interest in sexual relations with humans, which he personally found repulsive.

The two prostitutes continued to press the stranger, figuring the well-dressed man had ventured into their 'backyard' for one reason, and one reason only.

"Oh, there's no reason to be shy, dear. We won't bite. I mean, we will, but that's extra, luv."

With the flick of his wrist, Dom produced a blade and thrust it into the abdomen of the closest woman to him. Her eyes shot open in surprise and her entire demeanor abruptly shifted. A gurgle escaped her lips, followed by a spittle of blood before he violently extracted and stabbed her again.

The other woman opened her mouth to scream, but Dom was on her in a flash. The same blade forcefully entered her chest and pierced one of her lungs. She stumbled backwards, as her air and blood escaped from her confines.

The two succumbed to their wounds as Dom gripped his knife, now drenched, as it dripped their life essence onto the cobblestone.

*I...feel...alive! This is exactly what I've been missing.*

The sound of a police officer's shrill whistle broke his trance.

"Halt right there!"

Dom fled and disappeared into the night, exhilarated.

* * *

A month later he revisited the same East London area, after midnight, and killed two more women. This time he cut their throats and mutilated parts of their bodies before he was through. The local paper, the next morning, linked the four murders and nicknamed the killer as 'Jack the Ripper'.

He became the talk of the town.

\* \* \*

Dom watched from a darkened doorway as four prostitutes worked a street corner. Eventually only two remained, so he stepped out from the shadows and began to approach. He stopped as a voice spoke from the same concealed alcove that he'd just been hiding in.

"Stop."

Dom whipped around, his blade already poised to strike.

The stranger casually stepped forward. "Greetings, Qhautuix."

Dom wavered. He hadn't heard his real name used in decades. "Who are you?"

"Further activities towards the people of this planet will not be tolerated. In fact, if you continue to murder, I will unilaterally wipe your species off the board, as The Ancient nearly did all those cycles ago."

Dom was confused. "Who are you?"

"My name is The Caretaker."

"How do you know who I am?"

"I am all knowing, to a degree. I'm here to inform you that there will be a time for you and your people, but that time isn't now, Qhautuix. Your people suffered, mostly due to your own internal wars that you waged on each other, but ultimately it was my brother, The Ancient, that destroyed your planet. You escaped here, to Earth, only to become stranded."

Dom was dumbfounded as he slowly sheathed his blade. "How do you know all this?"

The Caretaker didn't reply.

"Alright, how about this. How will I know when that particular time has arrived? I ask that because your statement effectively predicts the future." Dom thought about it even further. "That is unless, you've already experienced it, correct?"

The Caretaker smiled. "It's complicated."

"Sure," Dom replied. "Artificial Intelligence is complicated. Time travel is an entirely different conversation."

"That's fair. Let's just say that I happen to experience all realms of reality…in parallel."

"Seriously? That's incredible. So, why would you care about the few insignificant women I've dispatched? Their deaths couldn't have altered the time continuum."

The Caretaker grew serious. "I'm giving you and your people a one-time pass, due the actions of The Ancient."

Dom bristled. "That bastard killed my mother and annihilated my planet. He killed thousands for no reason at all, other than for his own pleasure."

"Sounds familiar, doesn't it, Qhautuix." It was a rhetorical statement.

The knife reappeared in Dom's hand as he shapeshifted into his natural form.

The Caretaker locked eyes with the eight-foot creature before him, and chose to remain calm and collected. Eventually Dom reverted to human form and stowed the knife.

"The Ancient is my problem and I need to shoulder that responsibility. However, that doesn't mean I'm going to look the other way anymore. I'm watching you, now and forever."

Dom contemplated his new situation. "If you're watching me that means you're watching others as well, whether they exist now, or in the past or the future. If I understand correctly, time is one and the same for you, is it not?"

The Caretaker chose not to reply.

Dom took a slight step forward. "Answer me one question, you owe me and my species that much."

"Go ahead and ask your question."

"How long do I have to wait?"

The Caretaker shook his head. "That's the wrong question."

Dom nodded and silently mulled things over. "Alright. How about this, Mr. Caretaker. If I'm not allowed to run amok, at this point in my perceived timeline, what exactly prevented you from coming after me again?"

"His name is Thomas Clark."

Dom wasn't satisfied. "That's a fairly common name, don't you think? When does he come into existence?"

"I've already said too much, so that name is all you'll get."

Dom roared. "I need more information about this Thomas Clark!"

The Caretaker held up a hand to silence him. "You've been warned. The future of your species rests entirely in your hands now."

And just like that The Caretaker vanished.

Dom looked around, half expecting the entity to be behind him again, but he was all alone, save for the two prostitutes that had run off as soon as he'd screamed at the dark opening.

*The Caretaker, eh? He said he was the Ancient's brother and clearly sounded remorseful.*

He began to head back towards his hotel while he rehashed the conversation.

*Time is relative, but that still doesn't explain who or what The Caretaker and The Ancient are, or even where they came from. All*

45

*I know is that I've been given a warning, along with a name. Thomas Clark.*

Dom picked up his pace.

*It's time to head back to America, prepare for the future, and track down this Thomas Clark.*

# 8
## Americas - 1893

In 1893, Dom traveled to Chicago for the World Fair, where 43 nations proudly presented the greatest new technologies, they had to offer. There, over a period of six months, 27 million people visited the Fair to experience Cracker Jacks, the first voice recording, moving walkways, the elevator and the Ferris wheel for the very first time. Overall, it was an amazing success, but Dom became quickly bored.

*I'm going to die on this backwards planet, amongst these humans who gasp at a metallic box that rises to a different level of a building. It's infuriating to know that I could conquer this planet, without even breaking a sweat, if I could only contact Zora. She's out there, in the cloaked ship, just waiting to be contacted WHILE I'M STUCK HERE IMITATING THESE PATHETIC BEINGS.*

Dom gritted his teeth as he meandered.

*What am I doing? I've gathered money and I've built a base of operations. It's the waiting that's killing me. I just need to find an outlet, something where I can pass the time and prepare for the inevitable future where I'll finally come face-to-face with the enigma known as Thomas Clark.*

Dom sat down on a nearby bench and watched as thousands of enthralled individuals gasped when they stepped onto one of the moving walkways.

*Their society is so young, even though they've lived on this world for thousands of years, each group vying for power through a combination of warfare and diplomacy. They've gazed into the stars above, but they haven't a clue what's really out there in the vastness of space.*

He smiled.

*Hell, they don't know they're hosting visitors from the far reaches of space, ones that arrived here through a wormhole. They don't even know the word 'wormhole'.*

He chuckled.

*Could you imagine the looks on their faces if I transformed in front of them, right here, right now? It'd be glorious. I would tear through all of them with ease, leaving their bloodied bodies in my wake.*

Dom stood up and contemplated that exact act before a deafening BOOM interrupted him and the rest of the crowd. The explosion drew people towards a large artillery piece on display, one Dom quickly learned could fire a two-ton shell and potentially strike a target fifteen miles away.

He lingered and learned, excited at the prospect of destruction mankind could invent to use on each other.

*Not so different from my world, I suppose. We destroyed it to annihilate our enemy, but the cost was too high. Now look at where my species is; marooned on a planet with eleven others, while ten-thousand sleep on a cloaked ship that's orbiting their moon. That's why I need to remove or capture the people, then take this planet intact. Our species must thrive, not cower in the aftermath of a doomed world, like we had to on ours.*

Dom continued his exploration.

*But to subjugate these people I will need to know more beside listening and interacting with them. I need to become even more ferocious and cunning. This World Fair has shown me that money, power and technology control this world, supplied by ambition and the determination of those who refuse to sit idly by. No, if we're to take this planet for ourselves, then it's up to the twelve of us to formulate a plan of attack, then execute it with tactical precision.*

He smiled once more.

*Earth is made up of multiple countries, far more than the forty-three that are on display here, but far less if you dissect them into large and small entities. If one were to take control of the larger ones, then the smaller could be subjugated easier.*

*Interesting.*

*But there's still the process of making that happen, and attempting to do that with only twelve of us is going to be daunting. I need to find a way back to the crashed scout ship, even though it's nestled on the bottom of the ocean, and retrieve the other eighty-eight. We'd have a better fighting chance with them by my side.*

*In the meantime, I've barely scratched the surface with how these countries have fought their wars. I need to know everything, because that knowledge will be crucial in how I take this planet from them.*

\* \* \*

In the century that followed, Dom participated in various campaigns, which include World War 1 & 2, Vietnam, the Afghan War and the Iran-Iraq conflict. He saw and participated in the worst humans could do and did to each other. He learned, adapted and became a fearsome warrior, striking where and when needed to turn the tide and vanquish the enemy.

He'd changed his name and appearance throughout the years, using other personae to mask his true identity. He discovered, over time, that those personae needed to die of old age and leave their estates to him, effectively willing his property to himself over and over again. Dom didn't mind because he enjoyed the game. It kept him entertained. He knew that one day he'd be provided with the opportunity to take his plan, utilize its strategy, and rescue his people.

*Dom grinned. Earth is on the verge of acquiring new tenants.*

# 9
## 1991

Dom woke up early at his estate in Minnesota. He'd bought the land and built his house in 1858, 133 years prior. Since then, he'd continued to upgrade and add to his sprawling property, but was still never quite satisfied. He knew that time was his real enemy, along with The Caretaker who had stood in his way all those years ago in London.

Dom headed downstairs, still disguised as a human, and glanced over at the CCTV monitors. He'd installed multiple overlapping security cameras throughout his compound in an effort to feel secure. He knew he could easily defend himself and his property, if it ever came to that, but the paranoid portion of his brain insisted on the cameras. Even though his land was deeded in another name, and shielded by a variety of LLCs, Dom felt he could never quite rest easy, never knowing if one of the others would want to take his mantle, or even a random human who thought his property would be an easy target. Whatever the case, Dom had decided long ago to prepare for the worst, because he couldn't trust anyone.

\*

Dom had recently hosted a get together for the other eleven. It'd been years since they'd actually met, and every one of them had pursued their own successful path. However, the one common factor they each shared was that nothing had changed. Year after year they waited for Earth's technology to take the next leap forward. That pace continued to be agonizingly slow, and unfortunately none of them, including Dom, were actual scientists.

They'd pushed, here and there, to push the human race forward, and had made significant money in the process. But even though the world had developed airplanes and simplistic spacecraft to visit the moon, humans were still ages away from the technology his species required to actually contact and wake up their people.

Subsequently, Dom hadn't confided in the others about The Caretaker or the enigma of Thomas Clark. He knew that information was power, and he needed to retain control over his people. He couldn't have Thomas located before he was able to. No, that could have disastrous results, and he knew it. Instead, their time together was spent working on the plan to infiltrate various world governments, at the highest levels, and how necessary those positions would be when it was time to finally remove humans from the equation.

Their gathering had gone well, aside from the usual grumbling that they'd all been on this planet for over a century, and that their patience was worn thin. Dom assured them that when the time came that they needed to be ready, and to use the time at hand to prepare accordingly. He knew his people had become exhausted, like he had, as each year came and went, over and over again. The truth was, they'd all seen firsthand how the society they lived in had grown and evolved, and not always for the better. Dom had been involved in plenty of wars, throughout the years, and had even decided to sit out the current Persian Gulf War because he, like the others, grew weary of it all.

\*

Dom left the CCTV monitors behind and headed down the stairs to his finished basement, which had been carved out of the rock by hand and dynamite. The stairs opened up in a great room, supported by large wood beams. Off the left was an entrance to a theater, where he could partake of various movies in VCR format because Dom had become enthralled with movies, television shows and documentaries. He consumed anything he could get his hands on, both to help pass the time and to know more about the people that inhabited the planet.

Past the theater, in a separate section, was an arcade comprised of a variety of pinball and standup machines which surrounded a pool table. Next to that room was a small library that was filled to the brim with non-fiction books.

*Better to know one's enemy.*

At the far end of the room was Dom's personal office, closed in by floor to ceiling glass panes and a secured door. He unlocked the entryway, walked inside and stood in front of the bookshelf directly behind his desk. He transformed back to his true eight-foot-tall self, with four arms and two legs, and simultaneously pulled on four books. The bookcase clicked opened and swung inwards to reveal a concealed chamber.

Dom retook his human form, stepped through the threshold and turned on the light. Inside were a number of safes, bolted to the cement floor, that contained a variety of gold bars, jewels, stocks and bonds, and hard currency in numerous denominations from a variety of countries. However, along the left wall was something completely different.

Dom made a beeline towards that wall and pondered over his research. There, covering the entire wall, were maps of the world broken down into countries. Inserted into those maps were blue and red pins, each attached by thin red yarn, that led back to individual dossiers that contained pictures of men. Blue meant that person had been cleared. Red meant it was still being actively investigated. Each picture was different, some being black and white, while others were in color. They each displayed a date of birth, and death as necessary. The one commonality was that each gentleman on Dom's secret wall possessed a nearly identical name. Thomas Clark.

Dom had spent a considerable amount of time, ever since his encounter with The Caretaker, investigating every Thomas Clark, or derivative, he could locate. It'd been an exhaustive, and expensive, endeavor which had included the use of private detectives, worldwide. But he was convinced that the man he sought was out there, somewhere. He just had to find him. The problem was, the world's population had expanded, and that had led to more uses of Thomas Clark than he could actively track or keep abreast of. It frustrated him to no end.

Dom contemplated one of the latest additions in the United States where he'd placed a red pin in the mountains of southern California, specifically on the small town of Running Springs. A recent search had added over a dozen new pins to his board, and any or none of them could be the Thomas Clark The Caretaker had cryptically mentioned.

Dom pulled the file for Thomas in Running Springs and flipped through the information that had been gathered.

*What's this? The Little Brown Chair. He's a children's book writer? Next.*

Dom closed the file and moved on to the next one.

*This is like a needle in the haystack. Which Thomas Clark am I actually looking for, and how will I know when I find him?*

# 10
## 1995

At Fort Benning, Georgia, Dom had just entered Ranger training's Hell week. The lack of sleep, combined with consistent endurance-based objectives was meant to apply mental and physical exhaustion upon the class of recruits. Furthermore, as Hell week progressed, the instructors knew additional soldiers would tap out due to the extreme training regime and techniques being utilized.

A year prior, Dominick Knight had walked into an Army recruitment center and registered, and used his preferred moniker for the very first time. The world, as he'd grown with it for nearly 200 years, had drastically changed. When he fought in WW1, WW2 and other wars, he'd been able to provide little to no proof of his identity. He'd merely given them a name and that was that. But as time went on people's names and identities became harder to fake, especially with driver's licenses and passports that required photos and actual government paperwork to prove you were who you claimed to be.

Dom knew all this, as he'd used multiple aliases throughout the years, but for this go around he'd chosen to use his favorite identity. Besides, he knew plenty of ways to circumvent the system, and those contacts could produce a new identity for him in a matter of days, if he so desired.

His search for the elusive Thomas Clark continued to frustrate him, and he desperately needed a distraction, one that would give him the opportunity to kill again. So, he augmented his appearance to look younger and rejoined the Army, accompanied by the necessary and legal paperwork.

Naturally, he thrived with military life, cruising through basic training with flying colors. His instructors suggested that he apply to OCS, or Officer Candidate School, but Dom didn't want to lead others, aside from his own people. No, he wanted to be in the muck and thick of things. In the meantime, he knew he'd have to complete the Airborne School, which was a three-week course of how to properly evacuate a moving aircraft with a parachute.

Afterwards, he immediately applied for Ranger training, but was forced to wait a few class cycles before he was given the opportunity. But now, four weeks into the eight-week RASP, or Ranger Assessment and Selection Program, Dom continued to leave his competition in the dust. Of course, his potency derived from his alien DNA, and there were more times than naught when he had to dial back both his enthusiasm and the measure of his true strength.

Following the success of enduring and passing RASP, Dom was moved to actual Ranger training, a course that lasted 61 days and consisted of three phases.

The first phase was conducted at Fort Benning, over a period of three weeks, and revolved around physical assessment, tactics, weapons, land navigation and so on.

The second took them to the Georgia mountains to deal with rugged terrain, rope management and additional combat patrols.

The third and final dropped them into the Florida swamplands to become proficient with waterborne operations and tactics, which culminated in a ten-day patrol with two field exercises.

To say that Dom loved every second of the grueling regiment would be an understatement. He absolutely thrived.

In the years that followed, Dom was deployed to a number of locations, sometimes as a force multiplier, while on other missions as a covert unit. He was fierce and dependable as a top-tier soldier. More importantly, at least for him, is that he got to terminate humans.

Dom remained wholly satisfied, that is until 2003, when strange and unusual deaths began to occur. They started on the west coast of the United States before they made their way east. At first the news didn't correlate the various murders and killings, nor should they have been able to. But what caught Dom's attention, as well as the rest of the world's, was when the President of the United States arbitrarily launched nuclear weapons. Of course, the moment The Ancient actually revealed himself, Dom couldn't take his eyes off the screen, and especially not after Thomas Clark showed the planet what he and his family were truly capable of.

## 11

## March 7, 2003

Dom pushed a new red thumbtack into one of the numerous maps that adorned his investigative wall. He stepped back and gazed at the incredible amount of work, and the effort, he'd prepared to track down the elusive Thomas Clark. This latest one he'd just located in London, but Dom didn't have high hopes that it was the genuine Thomas Clark he was after.

*I can't believe I've been after this asshole, whoever he is, for this long and I have nothing to show for it. What am I doing? What am I missing? My species is depending on me and I'm running out of tim-*

A ring, from his secure landline he'd installed years prior, broke his concentration. Only eleven others had this particular number, and the required codes for authentication, to get through to him. When he wasn't at his house, due to his obligations in the spec-ops community, any calls were captured on a dedicated and secure answering machine.

Dom walked over to the phone, as it rang a second time, and answered it.

"Yes?"

The voice on the other end sounded adamant. "Turn on your television."

Dom looked around for his remote. "What am I looking for?"

"You can't miss it."

The phone call terminated as Dom powered on the unit and quickly flipped to a news station.

"Focus the camera on me," The Ancient commanded, who felt reenergized, free and unhindered. The President's face and clothing had been sprayed with blood, yet it wasn't the most disturbing thing about him. It was his smile.

"What you've seen here today is just a taste of my power."

More agents flooded into the room, this time with automatic weapons at the ready, but they weren't prepared for the absolute carnage contained within. Seconds later those agents were also dead and the image on the screen was now focused on the Oval Office's ceiling. The President adjusted the camera and peered directly into the lens.

"When the world burns, I will rise from its ashes and consume your energy. I will once again be reborn and unstoppable."

His face transformed itself in to a snarl, caked in blood and bits of human flesh.

"You have one minute to bring me the nuclear football or I kill every last person in this decrepit hovel you call The White House. It's time for the world to burn!"

The feed abruptly ended; replaced by the Presidential Seal. The same female news anchor turned even paler as her voice shook.

"Did..did...he just say he was going to nuke the planet?"

* * *

Around the world the Oval Office carnage was replayed over and over and over again. Newscasters stated the first things that came to their heads, their minds awash in a new realm of hopelessness.

"Either the President has lost his mind or the world was just shown we've never been alone in the universe."

"There's so much blood..."

"What in the actual hell is happening!?"

"None of this can be real, can it?"

60

"God help us."

"Maybe we're not alone after all?"

"This is surreal. Such senseless slaughter. How did he do that?"

Then one newscaster placed her hand next to her ear and intently listened to what her producer was telling her. Her expression changed to fear and disbelief.

"Ladies and gentlemen. Oh, my god, I don't know how to convey this but I've just been informed that hundreds of nuclear warheads were just launched from the continental United States. Our sources also inform us that Russian and China have retaliated in kind." She swallowed hard and tried to keep a professional demeanor. "I'm afraid the end of the world as we know it is coming."

A new clock graphic appeared on the bottom half of the screen. Next to it was a fallout symbol as it actively counted down.

19:12

19:11

19:10

"Wherever you are, drop whatever you're doing and take shelter immediately! This is not a drill!"

\*

Dom didn't know what to make of the President's actions, but the fact that nuclear weapons had been launched by three nations meant that the world he was stranded on was about to become uninhabitable.

He, like millions of others, could only watch as the hapless news anchors replayed the short video clip on repeat, alongside the ominous countdown clock.

*What the hell is going on?*

The scene changed to a live shot as a shimmering vortex of white energy materialized on the lawn, just inside the fence line. A magical hush swept through the crowd as they instinctively backed away from the anomaly. A few 'what the fucks' were heard as a group of people appeared out of thin air, right in front of the south fountain, and faced The Ancient. As the crowd and news crews attempted to comprehend this unexplainable event, the portal vanished. In its place stood five individuals and what appeared to be some type of small, black animal with red eyes.

Dom didn't understand what he'd just witnessed. *Where did they come from?*

Curiosity got the better of everyone as they surged against the White House fence for a better look. There, standing on the lawn between the fountain and the White House stood a man, a woman, two kids and their strange animal.

The Ancient smiled and clapped his hands together in delight as the thirty or so Secret Service agents raised their weapons towards this new threat.

"Thomas Clark and his family have finally arrived, and in such style. It's so good to see you all again, especially my better half, little Stir."

Stir's hackles rose, his red eyes brightly shined as he barred his teeth. A low growl emanated from deep within his small form.

Dom couldn't believe his eyes and ears. *Thomas Clark? That's the Thomas Clark I've been searching for?*

"I take it we're addressing The Ancient?" Thomas called out.

Dom's face instantly changed again, but this time to one of horror. *The Ancient? He's here?*

"You are indeed," the being that inhabited the President of the United States replied loudly so the media and crowd could hear. "I

62

do appreciate you dropping in on my festivities. You've arrived at the perfect time."

"Why's that?"

"Oh, that's right, you probably haven't heard since you were off playing it safe with my brother. I tapped into this country's arsenal and launched a full complement of nuclear missiles. Russia and China have responded in kind, and that means this world is about to get a hell of a lot hotter. The pure energy released will restore me to my full potential; an unfathomable killing machine. So, thank you for joining me on this auspicious occasion. You've saved me the trouble of tracking you down and killing you myself."

Thomas, Laura, Emily, Gavin and Stir hadn't moved since they stepped out of the portal, thirty weapons focused on them.

"How long do we have?" Laura asked.

The Ancient checked his watch. "Sixteen minutes, give or take," he gleefully answered.

"You're not lying," she announced.

"And why should I be? There's nothing you can do to stop it." He swept his arms around. "Take a look at the ones who have heeded my calling; those that would rather serve at my feet than die by my hand."

"You promised them what, eternal life?" Thomas called out. "How's that work, especially when you're going to kill them anyway. You just need them to do your dirty work for you, isn't that right?"

A few of the agents shifted uncomfortably.

"LIES!" The Ancient hollered. "I WILL KILL YOU WHERE YOU STAND!"

"You can try," Thomas taunted.

The Ancient couldn't believe what he'd just heard. "Look around, Thomas. You're outmatched in every way. Even you must know your powers won't fully protect you and your family from this many weapons."

Thomas nodded. "I suppose that's true."

The Ancient didn't understand. "Then why come here at all when there's nothing to gain?"

"I didn't come here for me or my family. We have already accepted this could be a one-way venture. We came here to represent the people that inhabit this planet, the very ones you seek to permanently silence."

"Admirable, but ultimately foolhardy, don't you think? I mean, there's only five of you. What chance do you think you could possibly have?"

"We'll take our chances," Thomas replied with a little too much confidence.

The Ancient cocked his head to one side. "Where are Sam and Bill? Why didn't they come and join your pointless endeavor?"

A slight grin appeared on Thomas' face. "Who says they didn't?"

The Ancient stumbled a bit. "What?"

In that instant Thomas extended his arms and used his telekinetic powers on the fountain's water. The water sprayed outwards in a wide swath and washed over the armed agents. It gave him and his family a temporary distraction which they used to find cover.

"MOVE!" Thomas yelled.

Stir took off like a rocket towards the closest enemy while Thomas, Laura, Emily and Gavin ran forward and hunkered down behind the fountain.

"GET THEM!" The Ancient howled.

With the news cameras and crowd watching, Stir reached his target and bit down on the agent's hand. He shrieked in pain and his weapon plummeted towards the grass, but Stir was already tracking a new target.

The agents, now dripping wet, opened fire. Bullets tore into the fountain which started to disintegrate from the overwhelming amount of firepower being brought to bear. The civilians behind them scrambled for cover as bullets struck and killed two, then three, then four people in quick succession.

But then a new roar of automatic weapon's fire poured into The Ancient's men from the east trees which cut a dozen agents down before they were able to shift their attack towards their new threat.

The Ancient snarled loudly. "KILL THEM ALL! KILL THEM ALL!"

Stir tore the hand off a second agent and kept on going as he evaded round after round that kicked-up the grass and dirt around him.

Laura extracted her Glock from her waistband, raised her arm up over the fountain and blindly emptied her magazine towards their attackers. Once she ran dry, she hastily thumbed the eject button and jammed in a new magazine.

"Stay down!" Thomas insisted as he stood up and forcefully pulled the two nearest adversaries towards him, stripped them of their weapons, in one continuous motion, and propelled their bodies over his head and behind him.

Dom watched in fascination as the battle waged between the opposing forces. He couldn't believe a human was fighting The Ancient, let alone getting the upper hand. *He has some kind of ability or tech. How can he do what he's doing?*

The Ancient hadn't moved from his original spot on the White House steps, and counted out the remaining six agents that were still alive, while the other two dozen littered the White House lawn. The battle was nearly over, but the nuclear missiles were even closer than before.

"IT'S OVER, THOMAS! YOU'VE LOST!"

The six agents that still stood pivoted towards him and opened fired. Thomas telekinetically propelled himself out of the fountain and towards The Ancient as those bullets screamed by.

As soon as Thomas landed, he wrenched four weapons from the agent's hands, breaking fingers in the process, and bee-lined towards The Ancient. The other two emptied their magazines at Thomas but saw that every single one of their bullets hovered in the air. Thomas, as if playing the role of Neo from The Matrix, plucked one of those rounds out of the air and let the others fall to the grass. The two remaining agents turned and ran while The Ancient watched Thomas advance.

"Bravo, Thomas, bravo. But I'm not sure what you think you've actually accomplished. Nothing's changed. The world is still coming to an end and there's nothing you can do to prevent that from happening."

Laura, Emily, Edward and Sarah appeared by Thomas' side. Laura raised her Glock and pointed it at The Ancient's head.

"You guys okay?" Thomas asked.

"Just peachy," Laura replied, a distinct edge to her voice. She hadn't taken her eyes off her quarry.

Behind them more people jumped the fence.

The Ancient looked amused. "You realize that you were all just a distraction for me, playthings if you will. But right now, ultimately, you're too late. The devastating fires and nuclear fallout will encompass this insignificant planet, releasing more than enough energy for me to consume. So, minutes from now when the world's population ceases to exist, I will be reborn!"

Thomas raised his hand, used his powers and applied pressure to The Ancient's chest.

It laughed. "Go ahead and kill this body, Thomas. Why do I care? It's only the President of the United States'."

Thomas stopped, but The Ancient goaded him onward.

"Kill him for all I care," he taunted. "I'll just inhabit another. So instead of fighting the inevitable, perhaps you'd like to join me as we countdown the remaining minutes together." The Ancient checked his watch. "And by my count there's only ten minutes and twenty-one seconds left."

Sam and Bill, along with Gavin and Craig, made their way over next to Thomas and the others. The two leveled their weapons at The Ancient.

"Don't," Thomas told them. "Where are Rebecca and Dillan?"

Sam shook his head. "Dillan didn't make it."

"And Rebecca?"

"She'll live, thanks to Gavin, but she's going to have one hell of a facial scar to show for it. She's still recovering over in the trees."

*It's like the previous timeline is making sure the same shit happens to them in this iteration as well.*

"How long do we have?" Bill asked.

"About ten minutes," Thomas told his friends.

The Ancient laughed out loud, eager with anticipation. But then, out of nowhere, Stir launched himself at The Ancient. But instead of tearing his head off, or something similarly gruesome, Stir latched on to The Ancient's arm and wouldn't let go no matter how much The Ancient tried to dislodge him.

"Gah! It won't come off," The Ancient sneered. "Fine then, have your precious President back if that's what you desire so much."

But The Ancient's expression shifted to one of confusion; then dread. "I...I can't leaVE THIS BODY!" His loss of control quickly turned into full-blown panic. He looked down at Stir and realized that the last remaining portion of him, manifested in the embodiment of Stir, prevented him from leaving his host. "GET IT OFF OF ME!"

Laura depressed her trigger and shot The Ancient through the shoulder.

"YEEEOUCH!"

For the first time ever, rather than observing what he put others through, The Ancient was left with no other choice but to experience the same pain and agony his host suffered. He didn't care for it.

"IT HURTS!"

Stir continued to grip tightly as the crowd behind yelled and hollered.

"DO SOMETHING!"

"KILL IT!"

"SAVE US!"

Thomas ripped the watch off The Ancient's wrist and scrutinized it. "Nine and a half minutes. That's not a lot of time. Gavin, let's go. Sam. Bill. Grab that asshole."

"Our pleasure."

Dom, along with the world, watched as the young boy created a portal before everyone disappeared into it. He shook his head and began to pace the room.

"I...I...don't....what just happened?"

Before he could think about what happened any further, the family and the President magically reappeared.

"WHERE DID THEY COME FROM!"

"KILL THAT BASTARD!"

"SAVE US!"

"What the fu-" Sam started to exclaim but then cut himself short. They still had a job to complete.

Bill and Sam, along with the family, assisted the President back inside. As soon as they entered The White House they noticed the nuclear football. It rested in the same place it'd been used to launch the missiles in the first place.

"Eight and a half minutes!" Bill hollered to the others as he propped the President down in front of the device.

"Mr. President," Sam urged, "disarm the missiles!"

The media surged in behind them, still broadcasting live around the globe.

But the President hadn't fully recovered and was out of it. Sam and Bill gave each other a 'oh shit' look, so Emily touched the President's hand and took control of him. He instantly responded to her commands and verified his identity with a retinal scan, then he typed in his Presidential disarm code. That signal disseminated through dozens of military satellites and back down towards all inbound projectiles.

Hundreds of detonations littered the sky, over a multitude of countries, which caused the deadly atomic bombs to become inert well before they reached their destinations.

"It's done!" Thomas roared, his fist high in the air.

The cameras caught it all.

Bill checked his watch as Emily relinquished control over the President.

"Seven point five." He looked around. "Do you think that's enough time for Russian and China to respond?"

"I guess we're about to find out," Sam said.

A collective hush had come over the crowd as the countdown continued unabated.

Craig had an idea. "I could phase us out," he suggested.

Sam got down on one knee and looked his son in the eyes. "That's a lovely thought, but that would only help us and nobody else," he indicated.

The cameras caught it all.

"Seven minutes."

Thomas put his arms around his family and held them tight. "I love you guys, and thank you for doing your part today. You truly made all the difference."

Rebecca pushed through the crowd and emerged. She'd carried Dillan's body across the White House lawn, inside, and carefully laid him down. It was then that everyone saw she had a scar that ran vertically up and down the left side of her face. Bill gave her a high-five and a huge bear hug.

"We couldn't have done this without you. Thanks."

She nodded. "Tell that to Dillan."

"Yeah," Bill said as he released her. "But none of it might matter if shit doesn't change in the next six minutes or so."

No one spoke or uttered a word during the next twenty seconds. Then, nearly simultaneously, some of the media lifted their hands as they received new information. Their expressions changed to one of relief.

"The Russians and Chinese confirmed the U.S. detonations and have followed suit!"

The countdown clock froze at six minutes, eighteen seconds. The crowd began to cheer uncontrollably and strangers embraced each other as the infectious jubilance spread throughout the world.

The threat had been neutralized.

But a multitude of questions remained and, because a journalist is a journalist, it didn't take long for the ones at the White House to promptly start questioning the people they'd captured on film who vanquished The Ancient.

"Who are you people?"

"What was that portal?"

"Was that invisibility?"

"What kind of creature is that and didn't it have red eyes before?"

"What happened to The Ancient?"

"Is the President himself again?"

"How long have you had these abilities?"

Thomas smiled and tapped his son on his shoulder. Gavin took the hint and formed his portal. As the family began to go through, and with questions still shouted out behind them, Sam hefted Dillan over his shoulder and followed. They'd all been through hell and deserved a rest. The media's questions would have to wait.

*

Dom muted the television, then rushed over to his 'Clark' wall. He sifted through multiple files until he the specific Thomas Clark dossier he'd been after.

*Well, well, well. It was you, the children's book writer, this entire time. Very impressive, Thomas, very impressive. I suspect, from the footage, you were reluctant to reveal yourself to the world, but now that you have, I wonder what's next in store for you, aside from me of course.*

Dom placed the dossier aside and used the secure phone to return the call.

"Did you watch all that?"

"Of course," Dom replied. "I couldn't tear my eyes away from it."

"Was that The Ancient that destroyed our planet?"

"The one and the same."

"What are our next steps?"

Dom was already working that problem out. "Get me deep dives on SANDBOX, Sam Paige and Bill Nicholson. I also need you to organize another gathering of the twelve. Our time is at hand and we need to carefully strategize our immediate future."

* * *

## Monday, March 10

"...the President of the United States."

The President made his way to the podium. It stood on a stage that had been constructed on the White House's north lawn. He arrived to a standing ovation and waited for the applause to die down before he began to speak. Dozens of media personnel were also in attendance.

"Ladies and gentlemen. We're gathered here today to pay homage to true American heroes; individuals who put their lives on the line to save the world as we know it. And while the world was shocked to learn of their special abilities, along with The Ancient, it should come as no surprise they never hesitated to thwart humanity's destruction.

"Since Friday's attack, here at the White House, these heroes have remained incognito despite the world's mounting curiosity. So let me be the first to publicly recognize that these champions of humankind pose zero threat to our nation's security and will forever be welcomed by our government with open arms. They are my heroes and they are your heroes. So, without further ado, please give a warm welcome to our saviors, Thomas Clark, Sam Paige, Bill Nicholson and their families!"

Thomas, Laura, Emily, Gavin, Stir, Sam, Julie, Craig, Amanda, Bill, Kim, Sarah, Edward and Rebecca emerged from inside the White House and joined The President. As they appeared all those in attendance rose to their feet, in a show of appreciation and respect, and clapped with unabated enthusiasm. The family stood and soaked it in before it eventually quieted down.

"I wish they loved me as much as they love you," the President joked as he retook the podium. The media and the crowd enjoyed his self-deprecating humor and chuckled as he turned back to face the cameras. "And while I can joke now, I assure you I would no longer have that opportunity unless it was for the selflessness of those who stand behind me this afternoon. I can also assure you that being under the control of The Ancient was no laughing matter. The Ancient was a being of pure evil, one that our world cannot fully comprehend. We need to be eternally thankful that our planet has been purged of its horrific grasp."

The President paused for a few moments before he spoke in a softer tone.

"Life is precious; special. But it is also fragile; as seen time and time again in the news these past weeks. The grateful actions taken, of those behind me, cannot be measured in words nor properly given thanks in any known context. However, it is my duty as President of the United States to at least attempt this fruitless endeavor by awarding each of them the Presidential Medal of Freedom."

The President turned around and saluted the family.

"Thank you for your service!"

One by one every family member approached the President and he draped a medal around their necks. That process only lasted a few minutes. What took a significant amount of time afterwards was addressing the media's endless inquiries.

*

An hour later, after thoroughly answering questions and a partial demonstration of their abilities, the family decided they'd had enough for one day. The media, despite their initial shock and awe of their powers, were friendly and unequivocally fascinated, but disappointed when the family decided to depart.

Cameras monitored their every move as Gavin summoned his portal, which exited them once again. And there, at the White House, while the eyes of the world watched, the family disappeared into thin air.

\* \* \*

## Tuesday, March 11

"Welcome back to The Late Show."

The audience cheered and applauded while David Letterman sat behind his desk in the Ed Sullivan Theater. As the volume of the clapping dissipated the camera centered on him.

"My guests tonight need no introduction, having saved the world on broadcast television, having used abilities only thought to exist in novels and comic books. Please give a warm welcome to Thomas Clark and his family!"

The audience leapt to their feet with thunderous applause as Thomas, Laura, Emily, Gavin and Stir appeared from behind the stage. Letterman greeted them warmly and waited for them to sit down. Stir jumped up on Gavin's lap and curled up, yet kept his greens eyes open and alert. The cheering and hollering continued unabated as the family sat there, somewhat uncomfortable, and took it all in. Letterman joined in until the roar finally died down.

Letterman smiled. "Well, that's quite a warm welcome if I say so myself, Thomas. It's just a guess on my part but I think our audience is grateful to be here, thanks to you and your family."

That kicked off an entirely new sequence of applause and appreciation.

Letterman chuckled. "With this amount of admiration, I'm glad you're my only guests tonight."

The Clark's smiled while the audience laughed.

Letterman refocused. "Thomas, exactly who have you brought with you this evening?"

"This is my wife, Laura, and our kids, Emily and Gavin."

"Thank you for having us," Laura said.

"My pleasure."

Thomas continued. "And nestled in my son's lap is Stir."

"Stir, did you say?"

"It's short for monster," Gavin spouted out from the end of the couch, "but he's anything but."

Gavin petted Stir whose tail flopped back and forth in delight. Then he yawned which showed off an array of sharp teeth. Afterwards he settled back in.

Letterman smiled. "What sharp teeth you have, grandma."

The audience ate it up.

"Stir seems pretty unique. I know I've never seen anything like...it?

"Stir's a he," Emily stated.

Letterman nodded. "I'm sure we, and the rest of the world, would like to know where you acquired him from."

Thomas answered. "I'm afraid that's a long story, but he's not of this world."

"So, he's an extraterrestrial?"

Thomas shook his head. "Not in the sense of another planet, no. Stir's from a different plane of existence."

Letterman leaned back and used both his hands to mimic explosions near his head. "Kaboom. You're blowing my mind. Another plane of existence; you mean like Heaven or Hell?"

"I'm afraid not. This universe, the one our Earth is part of, shouldn't be limited and restricted by superstitious concepts such as God or the Devil. There's so much more out there that humanity hasn't begun to experience."

Letterman hastily segued to the next topic. "Perhaps you're referring to the entity that claims to have inhabited the President of the United States? What can you tell us about that?"

"He was known as The Ancient and was responsible for the complete destruction of another universe."

"This Ancient, as you call it, did or does he really exist? Many people think the President merely lost his mind and that you and your family tricked the world into believing you're some kind of heroes."

"I'm glad you brought that up," Thomas said, "which is the main reason my family and I agreed to be guests on your show. Over the past two weeks you've all witnessed bizarre and unexplained footage on television that culminated in the launch of nuclear weapons. Believe it or not The Ancient hid in plain sight and controlled our President."

"What did The Ancient want?"

"The Ancient required energy, the energy that each and every human is composed of. His plan required millions to perish so he could absorb their vitality. After doing so he would have gone on to annihilate our universe."

"That's certainly an extreme explanation, but why did he specifically target your family in the process?"

Thomas shifted a little in his seat. "We have a history, one that I'll be writing about in the future."

Letterman scanned the cards he held in his hands. "Yes, of course. Before you were famous for saving the world you were famous for your children's books. Now you and your family have become household celebrities."

"I suppose that's an unfortunate side effect, one we don't desire."

"And yet here you all are, loved by many yet hated and scorned by others. Why show your face to the world at all?"

Laura addressed Letterman's question. "You're right, we could have stayed off the grid. But this story isn't going away which means people are going to hear things that could be true or false, but not have a way to discern between them. My family wants to get ahead of that. The fact is we have abilities, powers that others covet, and we know that sounds scary and frightening. But we're just a normal family and the actions we took were in the best interests of our world. That being said, we're proud to be here tonight sharing our family with all of you."

The audience applauded. They realized how difficult it was for the Clark's.

"Thank you," Letterman said. "And while the world has an endless list of questions for you, I think it goes without saying that everyone here would love to see a demonstration of your abilities, if that's not too much to ask?"

The audience cheered in anticipation.

Thomas smiled. "I think we can handle that."

During the next twelve minutes Thomas, Laura, Emily and Gavin delivered quite the performance.

Thomas levitated Letterman around the theater who loved every second of it.

Laura chose random people and had them tell her something which she then declared was either true or not.

Emily decided to up the stakes and asked for a volunteer who'd either lost a parent or a child. Her demonstration that followed, especially when a young girl who had died from cancer appeared on stage next to her mother, took everyone by surprise. There wasn't a dry eye in the theater after their brief reunion concluded.

Gavin pointed out a man in the audience who had a splint on his arm. After learning that he'd only been injured two days prior, from a nasty fall in which he'd bruised and cut his arm, Gavin asked him to remove the bandages. Gavin healed him while people watched in amazement.

After the clapping in the theater came to a stop Letterman was at a loss for words.

"I…I really don't know what to say. Truthfully, I was skeptical of who you were and what you could do. But now, and I think my audience will agree with me, you seem like a very caring and loving family who was brave enough to step into the light and reveal themselves to the world. I believe all that's left to say is bravo because you're heroes in my book."

Letterman stood up and gave the Clark's a standing ovation and the audience immediately followed. Eventually he retook his seat.

"So, Thomas, what's on the agenda for you and your family?"

"There isn't an easy answer for that I'm afraid. Our family, as a collective, was targeted by The Ancient and because of that we've lost people close to our hearts. But we aren't the only family that was affected. So, I guess my answer is that we'll need time to heal; time to turn the atrocities the world was subjected to into something positive."

"With that mindset it sounds like you might be running for President," Letterman joked.

Thomas smiled and the audience chuckled.

"I don't think so. As far as I'm concerned Laura would be better suited for that role. Besides," he joked, "she'd know all the politicians who had issues being truthful, that's for sure."

The audience loved it.

Letterman leaned over his desk. "So, what do you think, Laura? Will we see a female Presidential candidate in two-thousand and four, especially now that our President, shortly after your ceremony yesterday, announced he's stepping down?"

Boisterous cheers shot-up throughout the crowd and Laura slightly blushed.

"Anything's possible," she eventually conceded, "but don't count on it. My passion revolves around protecting this planet."

Letterman smiled. "And to think that didn't come across as anything BUT presidential."

The audience chuckled.

"Well," Letterman said as he extended his hand to Thomas to shake, "I want to thank you for taking the time to be on my show."

Thomas grasped Letterman's hand. "It was a pleasure to be here. Thank you."

"I think we'll come away feeling like we have a much better understanding of who you and your family are, so thank you for that." He turned to the audience. "Ladies and gentlemen, give it up for the Clark family!"

The family stood up, walked over to Letterman and thanked him again as the audience continued to show their appreciation. After those pleasantries were over Gavin summoned his portal in the center of the stage. A myriad of gasps, ooo's and awe's were emanated, and with a final wave goodbye the Clarks, along with Stir, stepped through and disappeared.

Letterman's astonished look on his face spoke volumes. "What a spectacular way to end our show. Goodnight, everyone!"

Dom had soaked in every second, cataloging it all in his brain and on paper. He also recorded the episode for future playbacks. His excitement became palpable. *It's time!*

* * *

## March 12, 2003

Around the world the Letterman footage, along with other news clips, played on repeat to the delight of many, and the contempt of others. The world had changed, which meant billions of people's perceptions had begun to drastically shift, for better or worse.

Leaders of various countries, small and large, fundamentally sensed a shift in power was at hand as the United States flaunted these people and their abilities for all to see. Some took it as a slap in the face, while others welcomed what this might mean for the world going forward.

Germany, the UK, France and other NATO allies had conversations about the connotations that Thomas Clark and the others now presented, especially the impact they may have in the global environment. However, in the end they decided that no immediate actions were required, and to let things run their course. At least for the time being. Still, the powers the Clarks possessed dripped with potential, and they collectively realized that family would be targeted in one way or another.

Among those countries who had darker thoughts on the matter were the leaders of Russia, China and North Korea. Independently from each other the different leaders saw Thomas as a threat, but also as a prize they desperately wanted all to themselves.

As dictators go, their plans were anything but original.

## March 18, 2003

Jennifer Myers, the President's Executive Admin, had installed listening devices in each of the family's White House bedrooms in an effort to gleam any useful intelligence about the family. As one of the twelve, she'd replaced the real Jennifer Myers, having disposed of the body in a landfill, and used her new position to get close to the President of the United States. It was all part of Dominick's plan.

When Thomas abruptly materialized in The White House, in a room filled with his family, Jennifer covertly listened in as Thomas explained, to the rest of his family, that'd he'd temporarily taken up the role as The Caretaker, to protect Stir, before he was able to fuse The Caretaker and The Ancient back together. Thomas had only been gone a week, having disappeared after the family had been attacked by Templars in Half Moon Bay. While he'd been absent, his parents had been killed during that time, along with Tad.

Jennifer took what she heard and, when she had time, relayed all of it to Dominick.

\* \* \*

## March 19, 2003

Dom mulled over Jennifer's findings at his Minnesota estate. *Thomas Clark became The Caretaker, and then rid the universe of The Ancient? If that's true, then I'm finally free to do anything I want. I mean, I took a risk when I had the President's admin replaced, but The Caretaker never reappeared to rectify that situation. Moreover, the public admonishment of the Pope, along with the three leaders of Russia, China and North Korea has really ratcheted up this planet's political discourse. I need to use all of that to my advantage.*

He turned his attention to the television.

"This is CNN. Our top story this evening is the siege on the White House. Earlier today a large group of terrorists attacked the seat of democracy with rocket propelled grenades and assault weapons, killing dozens of civilians and injuring countless more. This brazen act of lunacy, as leaked by inside sources within the administration, indicate that the individuals responsible for the carnage have been identified as Chinese and North Korean, and are being viewed as a retaliatory strike on the President, who was in the White House during the time of the attack."

The anchor shifted somewhat uncomfortably. "Does this attack mean that Americans have experienced the first salvo of World War Three? Are we at war?"

He refocused on his job of parroting the teleprompter.

"The only good news is that the assault on the White House was successfully repelled by White House security forces, Secret Service, Sam Paige, Bill Nicholson and Thomas Clark. Mr. Clark, well known for his best-selling novels and his telekinetic abilities that have sown both awe and discord throughout the world, was filmed rushing straight into the chaos where he unleashed his powers. In an amazing display of courage, alongside his compatriots, the trio decimated the Chinese and North Koreans.

"Let's watch a portion of the footage, but please be aware what you're about to see is graphic in nature."

On home televisions across the world a camera swiveled its point of view away from the family the man was filming and towards the White House as the sounds of an explosion thundered across the lawn. As the shaky camera finally righted itself three more rockets launched, streaked across the lawn and detonated against the side of the White House. Screams from nearby civilians filled the air as a dozen other men extracted assault weapons from their backpacks, turned on the terror-stricken crowd and opened fire.

Panic ensued and the camera dropped to the ground, on its side. As the White House attack continued the camera captured additional rockets being fired and civilians being helplessly mowed down. Then, out of nowhere, enemy combatants were tossed aside like rag dolls, their weapons ripped from their hands before Thomas Clark came down out of the air and landed where the enemies had once stood. Additional bursts of gunfire riddled the ground around Thomas as he concentrated on ending the siege as abruptly as it started.

The video footage ended when a body landed on top of the camera. The anchor reappeared.

"The White House has been cordoned off and a full military compliment has the area locked down while the investigation into these attacks will continue overnight and well into the week. However, the question I'm sure that resonates on every American's mind right now, as well as those around the world, is what happens now? If it was indeed China and North Korea who were behind these atrocities, how will the United States respond? What new era are we about to embark on?"

The anchor organized his notes and moved on to the next topic.

"This morning, at a cemetery in Walnut Creek, California, reports of a downed military Blackhawk were reported to local authorities. Multiple casualties were discovered, upon arrival at the scene, along with the burning wreckage of the helicopter. CNN has learned, from our inside source as well, that the Vice President used military personnel in a coup to take over the presidency, and he was the one who ordered the attack on Thomas Clark, and his family, who were at that cemetery. It was also revealed that the previous Assistant Director of the FBI, Harold Knight, was assassinated by the U.S. military, and ordered to do so by the VP as well. The Vice President has been arrested and charged with treason."

He looked down briefly, then back up at the camera.

"Our world is a scary place and I, like most of you, are uncertain of its immediate future. I call on our leaders to rise above the violence and do everything in their power to keep the peace. If not, ladies and gentlemen, we may be under the threat of nuclear annihilation all over again."

Dom took in the newscast with fascination.

*This planet is ripe for the picking, but its takeover will need to be handled with precision. There are only twelve of us, and each will need to be allocated to very specific positions.*

He paced a bit before he walked over to his 'Thomas Clark' wall and removed every single pushpin.

*It's time to start over.*

\* \* \*

The next day Jennifer listened in as the family discussed their plans.

In short order she learned that SANDBOX would be rebuilt, and under new management, as Sam and Bill stepped aside.

Hobbes and Gabbi were building their own company, called ORACLE, which would specialize in encrypted communications.

Abby and Allison, Thomas' sister and fiancé, planned to step away and do their own thing.

Jennifer listened as Thomas left to head to the Oval Office. A minute later Thomas appeared by her desk.

"He'll see you now," Jennifer indicated.

"Thank you."

Thomas knocked, then entered as the President walked towards him with a smile on his face. Behind him, outside, scaffoldings had been erected where the rockets had struck the White House. Repairs were already underway.

She listened in as Thomas and the President began to converse.

"Thomas Clark, the man of the hour." They shook hands. "Sit down, sit down. I swear, Thomas, thanking you has become a habit."

"Yes, sir. However, I was just in the right place at the right time."

"Nonsense. You and your family have been targets for some time, and now I've joined those ranks when I had those leaders publicly shamed. I'd expected some reprisals, but nothing to this extreme. The press has been begging for a statement on how the United States will respond, and to be honest, I don't know what I'm going to do."

"The news," Thomas said, "stated it was the Chinese and North Koreans. How'd they come to that determination so quickly?"

The President smiled. "That's easy. The inside source was me. I need the public's outcry on this to be heard and seen by everybody. Not only do China and North Korea need to be held accountable, but so does Russia and the Vatican. I won't be forgetting about them anytime soon. And, lest I forget, the Vice President attempted to have you killed in an effort to usurp me as President."

"What's going to happen to him, sir?"

"The VP's being held while the FBI investigates. Furthermore, General Steele won't be seeing the light of day ever again. The truth is, I should have removed him from power after he destroyed the yacht you were on, nearly killing you and your family. I'm sorry about that."

"I understand he was following your orders."

The President flinched a bit. "The Ancient, who was in my body at the time, ordered him to do that."

Thomas nodded. "I'm aware, sir, and that's what I wanted to talk to you about."

The air became a bit chilly. "What's exactly on your mind, Mr. Clark?"

"It's time for a change."

"What kind of change?"

"My family and I can't live in the shadows anymore while we wait for the next attack to occur. Our homes in Hawaii were destroyed. My wife's business, burned to the ground. My friend's dreams, gone; their employees murdered. My parents, killed."

"You've been through tremendous heartbre-"

Thomas held up his hand. "Sir, if our presence, in this world, makes that much of an impact, my family and I need to be front and center to face it head on."

"I don't understand."

"Let me be clearer. If certain nations have the audacity to attack the White House, as they did yesterday, then I should look them in the eye as they do it."

"What are you saying?"

"Sir, I want to thank you for your support and for putting a roof over our heads when we needed it the most. But let's be honest, my family and I can't continue to run and hide." He paused for a tick, then met the President's gaze. "Two-thousand-and-four is right around the corner, and I believe I've proven myself to the American people, most of them at least. Sir, I plan to become the next president of these United States."

Jennifer couldn't believe what she'd just heard. *Dominick needs to hear about this as soon as possible.*

Jennifer stopped eavesdropping on the conversation to leave her post and head out for a walk. If she'd stayed to hear what they'd talked about, she would have learned that Thomas planned on building a bunker, and his request for Sam and Bill to exhume Tad's body.

\* \* \*

*Very interesting.*

Dom loved that he had an information pipeline into The White House, but he also knew that was about to be severed if Thomas and his family were going to abruptly leave.

Dom smiled. *Thomas wants to become the next President. He's definitely going to have his work cut out for him. Still, that level of exposure could work out in my favor. I already have an infiltrator within the White House that'll be close to him, so now it's time to fill in the other roles my people need to play.*

In the days that followed Dom called for a new meeting of the twelve. During it they came up with the preliminary strategy to replace various world leaders and the Pope, along with specific roles within SANDBOX and ORACLE.

Dom was extremely pleased and absolutely motivated.

*It's finally happening. We've waited long enough for this moment to arrive. And now that it's here my species will finally be able to instill fear and panic in these pesky and weak humans before we take this planet from them.*

# 13
## March-November, 2003

Hobbes and Gabbi had finally put the final touches to the building, aside from the basement. The next order of business was to conduct interviews with potential employees, from support staff, techs, sales & marketing to the two drone pilots they needed. If the two weren't exhausted already, they certainly were after the marathon they'd put themselves through.

They left their office and headed back to the ranch. They'd thought about getting a place of their own, but they actually enjoyed the chaos of the family dynamic, and as they had discussed between themselves, they'd feel terrible if their 'family' was attacked and they hadn't been there to do something about it.

As Gabbi walked into their room she laid down on the bed, still fully clothed. "I hope we don't have to go through that shit again."

Hobbes chuckled as he sat on the edge and removed his shoes. "You've got to give us props; we hung in there and we got it done. Monday's going to be one hell of a ribbon cutting ceremony."

Gabbi smiled. "I know, and you're right. We've come so far and the hype is real. The contracts are already on my desk."

"And now," he said as he scooted up beside her, "will come the real work."

"Yeah, that's true, but I already know the encryption protocol we developed is going to take us to the next level. I just hope we're not in over our heads."

Hobbes took her hand in his. "Whatever the case may be, we're going to find out together."

"You're sweet," she replied, "but are you seriously not overthinking every aspect of our company right now, like I am?"

"Okay, guilty as charged."

Gabbi sat up and turned towards him. "Okay, I want to revisit four of our hires."

"Should I pour us drinks for this?"

She punched him in the shoulder.

"Ouch," he told her. "Seriously?"

"Focus. Did we make the right choices?"

"Honey, we absolutely did."

"Then I want to go over four of them with you again, okay?"

"As long as you're not going to hit me."

She smiled. "No promises."

"Greeeeaat." He turned towards her and crossed his legs. "Who do you want to start with?"

"How about Jenna Sullivan, our new communications tech."

"She's competent and skilled, and comes from the NSA. I think we're lucky to have her. She seemed really excited to work on our new tech."

"I agree."

He gave her a strange look. "Then what's the problem?"

"There isn't one, I just want to vocalize my internal thoughts and make sure we're on the same page, that's all."

"I get it. I can do that. Who's next?"

"Isabel Carter, our new network admin."

"How about you go first this time."

Gabbi continued. "I know we're both control freaks, especially when it comes to people we don't know, having access to our entire network."

"It's going to be something we're going to have to get used to. This is our first venture together, aside from all the shit we've been through, and it's a huge step forward for us. I totally get that you're nervo-"

It was a statement. "You mean we."

He smiled. "I totally get that *we're* nervous, but Isabel was a strong contender."

"You don't care that we picked her over her male counterparts?"

"Not at all. Besides, she worked in the Pentagon and had to contend with their aging network. I'm sure she can't wait to play with ours. Besides, I'll be there to check her work. Who's next?"

"Gretchen Luna and Amelia Harrison."

"Our two new drone pilots. What about them?"

She squirmed. "Have we…, or are we taking too much on all at once?"

"I don't think so. We've got this. Our mission statement, and our mandate, states that our encryption technology will provide safe, secure and cleaner audio than any other military product readily in use. Partnering with the Air Force allowed us the use of their drones and pods, and in doing so allows us the opportunity to oversee any active mission in real-time."

"And support our troops on the ground as necessary."

"Exactly," he told her. "It might sound like a lot, but as soon as we get started it's all going to flow. Besides, before we know it, we'll probably be launching our own satellites into space, if you can believe that."

"And what about those drone pilots being women?"

"I don't understand? Is this a recurring theme, because it seems like you want me to have a problem with the women we hired?"

Gabbi shook her head. "I…, no…, I don't. If anything, I want to thank you."

"Thank me? Now I'm really confused."

She sighed. "I'm sorry. I know I'm not making any sense. What I mean is, it's tougher for females to move upward in the military and be recognized for their contributions. I wanted to thank you for helping me hire those who were the best suited, regardless of their gender."

"Are you sure you don't want that drink?" he teased.

She pulled back her fist again and made him flinch.

He put his hands up. "Stop that. I don't want to have to use our safe word when we're still fully clothed."

"Don't. Don't you say it."

Hobbes grinned. "Albuquerque."

Gabbi lost it and buckled over. Hobbes lowered his hands and joined in.

* * *

Dom picked up his private line as soon as it rang.

"Report," he said.

"I'm in," Gretchen told him. "ORACLE is covered."

"Take your time, but you ultimately need to become intimately knowledgeable with their communication equipment."

"I'm well aware of what's at stake."

Dom smiled. "Good, because we're going to have a much better chance at contacting our people as soon as you do."

* * *

Dom scoured the news channels as he watched the footage from the campaign Thomas held in Ohio.

"...and this is the ten o'clock news. Our top story is about the assassination attempt on presidential runner Thomas Clark, during his Ohio rally four days ago. Mr. Clark was exceedingly vocal that the North Korean dictator, Kwak Sun-Woo, sent a special ops team to kill him, and very nearly succeeded.

"The North Korean special ops soldier, the same individual that Mr. Clark spared, was quickly whisked away from the scene and hasn't been seen or heard from since. Speculation and rumors indicate that this foreign operator was most likely interrogated by the FBI, but that hasn't been officially confirmed.

"What we do know is that the FBI debriefed Mr. Clark on the events and reviewed the extensive footage of the attack. They've concluded that North Korea was the aggressor and have sent their findings to the State Department and The White House. So far, the President or the State Department have issued an official sta-"

The news anchor put his right hand up to his earpiece.

"Ladies and gentlemen, I just received an update. A leak, reportedly from a source within The White House, has told us that the CIA have taken point on this investigation. Furthermore, the President of the United States has refused to act against North Korea, aside from issuing a handful of sanctions. The informant also suggests that the President believes taking an action against North Korea would hurt his re-election chances, and that if any overt action is taken by Thomas Clark or his immediate family, it will result in Mr. Clark's arrest.

"If any of this is true then the President's course of action will certainly draw this county's ire, not to mention intense scrutiny. As we've all seen, the footage in Ohio paints a clear picture that Thomas Clark was targeted and shot before his son healed his wounds. As the North Korean special ops team murdered local law enforcement and advanced on Mr. Clark, he didn't run away from the fight. Instead, at great peril, Mr. Clark took the fight to the eight men responsible for the heinous war crimes that were perpetrated on American soil.

"And while much of the world has united behind Mr. Clark's heroic actions, there are others that view his abilities, and those of his son, as disturbing, creepy and sacrilegious. These same voices

95

want to make sure that no one forgets about the small, black animal that accompanied Mr. Clark. They claim that Mr. Clark is possessed and commands demons to do his bidding."

The anchor smiled and tried to cover a chuckle with a cough.

"Whatever the case may be, Mr. Clark has yet to make a statement other than to thank the public for their support and to request privacy for his family."

The man shifted in his seat.

"Personally, as a United States citizen, I've seen more than my share of carnage and mayhem that this world has to offer. What happened in Ohio is unforgivable and personally angers me. The President should take action and not shield himself behind politics. The world is watching, Mr. President, and may I be the first anchor to verbalize it, but you're never going to be reelected."

Dom reacted. *I think it's time for another face-to-face gathering.*

* * *

The chosen twelve, their silhouettes in shadows, gathered together once again. It'd been five months since their last assembly, but meeting in person was the only true way no one else overheard what they had to talk about, especially since they'd traveled from all corners of the planet.

"It's time," Dom informed the group, "to initiate the next phase of our plan."

"Are we that close?"

"No," Dom replied, "but, thanks to some of you, we're already in a position to take over the Vatican operation. The truth is, we've waited far too long already, and now that the world is at such a tipping point that it'll be that much easier to sow chaos and fear. That madness will allow us to succeed in our primary goal, and make it easier to step in and take control."

He looked around the room at the other shadows he'd known, for what seemed like a lifetime. Half of them were females, and had taken to their roles admirably.

"Once the world is on fire, we can concentrate on eliminating our opposition."

"North Korea nearly succeeded in that endeavor, and we had nothing to do with it."

"Exactly," Dom exclaimed. "With our combined and concentrated effort, we'll be able to plan ahead; to mitigate the disaster the Ohio rally turned into. Thomas Clark is our enemy, of that there is no doubt. Whether or not the North Koreans succeeded or failed is no consequence to us."

"And why is that?" another asked.

"Because, when we come at him and his family, there will be nothing that they can do about it. Their fate is already sealed; it's just a matter of time."

"Thomas Clark isn't our only concern," another voice pressed. "His wife and daughter were given special privilege."

Dom perked up. "You're referring to the interrogation of the Ohio rally survivor, the only man that Thomas Clark happened to spare. Yes, I'm aware that as soon as Emily Clark touched him, well..., he spilled his guts. To answer your question, she is a problem, but will be taken care of at the appropriate time."

Some shifted a little uneasily.

"I see," their leader said. "The death of a child might be unpleasant, but it's quite necessary. They all pose a threat."

"We will do what is necessary, but what hasn't been addressed is when are we going to deal with the others?"

Dom knew this was coming. "We know about them and they know about us. All we can do, for the moment, is follow through on our plan. If anyone gets in our way, then we'll have to deal with it then and there. We have to move ahead before the others become an actual problem."

Another spoke out. "Shouldn't we have contingency plans in place?"

The leader nodded. "I already have multiple in motion."

"When were you going to tell us about them?"

"When you needed to know, and that time is now." He looked around the room. "We've been at this game for far too long to let anything or anyone come between us and our global ambitions. Whether the issue is about the Clarks, world leaders or anything in between, trust me when I say that it's being handled. Now go, and proceed as planned."

* * *

After 'the twelve' had met it was only a matter of time before kerfuffle's occurred in both the Chinese and Russian presidential residences. The events took place around four in the morning and drew the ire of security when alarms were activated. However, when said security burst into their leader's bedrooms, weapons drawn, neither President had been harmed and insisted they'd pushed their panic buttons by accident. These false alarms had happened before, but some of the staff suspected it had been merely a drill to test the security's readiness and response time.

* * *

Rebecca, Sabrina and Bai stood side by side with Sam and Bill as the first recruits, from various other divisions of the military, were bused through the gates. The five smiled as soldiers, both men and women, disembarked as the newest members of SANDBOX. They hastily formed two lines of ten.

"Welcome," Rebecca announced. "SANDBOX, established years ago by Sam Paige and Bill Nicholson," as she motioned towards the two men, "has been restored to its former glory. All twenty of you are the very first to become part of history."

She walked up and down the blacktop as she inspected the new members.

"Stand at ease. I'd like to introduce you to Sabrina Chavez and Bai Lin. They, along with Mr. Paige and Mr. Nicholson, will push each of you to your limits. Our goal, as you're well aware of, is to take what you've learned, be it from the Army, Navy, Air Force or the Marines, and forge you into a cohesive team."

She paced a bit more.

"You might be asking yourselves why each of you were ultimately invited to become a part of SANDBOX. In actuality, if you have to ask then you're in the wrong line of business."

The new recruits chuckled because they knew the previous iteration of SANDBOX was notorious for specialized missions all over the globe. They also knew they were no longer employees of any branch of the United States Government, and weren't bogged down by bureaucratic red tape. They had all effectively become military contractors, and they knew their particular set of skills were highly sought after.

"Today," Rebecca continued, "is onboarding, followed by a tour of this facility. Tomorrow is where the real magic will begin to happen. Any questions?"

Dom smiled on the inside as he stood in line with the other recruits.

*This is going better than I hoped. I didn't have to approach SANDBOX...they came and invited me into their clubhouse. All I have to do is do what I do best, and the rest of the pieces should fall into place. Besides, the Russian president, one of mine, should have issued that attack command. It's only a matter of time.*

* * *

"...and this is the six o'clock news. Our top story is out of Washington D.C. where a gruesome shooting took place this morning at one of D.C.'s private schools. When first responders arrived on the scene they discovered the bodies of approximately two dozen victims, mostly students. The bodies of four adult males, the alleged perpetrators, were also located next to silenced handguns and more than a hundred spent shell casings. The area was quickly cordoned off and investigators are still combing the scene.

"The identities of the four assailants have yet to be either determined or released to the public, but a member of the school faculty has confirmed that a video of the incident does exist and is now in the hands of investigators.

"As for the victims, the police are not releasing the names until their next of kin have been notified, but it has been confirmed that Mr. Donnie Holland, the Dean of the private school, is among the deceased.

"We'll keep you informed as we learn additional information, but for now our hearts go out to those families during this dark hour."

The anchor shifted his gaze to a different camera.

"In other news, the Iran government is up in arms over the destruction of an underground nuclear facility they claim had only been utilized for non-fissionable material. The Pentagon, however, has proof that Iran had built that facility for the specific purpose of furthering their nuclear weapons program, and is in direct conflict to the deal Iran previously agreed to.

"Per the Pentagon's brief, a group of special operators infiltrated the country and lazed the target. Afterwards an unmanned drone, known as a Reaper, delivered their explosive payload from fifty-thousand feet and obliterated the threat."

He turned his attention back to the original camera.

"We'll be right back after these messages."

Dom leaned back, careful to conceal his true feelings amongst the other SANDBOX members he was stationed with, and pondered.

*I didn't expect the children to have been so easily removed from the playing field, but the game is afoot, that's for sure. I have to keep the pressure on Thomas and his family, to keep them off-balance, as I maneuver myself into their inner circle.*

\* \* \*

"...and this is the ten-o'clock news. The race for the Presidency just got tighter as the final debate came to an end an hour ago. In a shocking turn of events, Thomas Clark dominated the debate as he openly condemned the President's lack of response to the North Korea and Russian attacks on our soil. Mr. Clark also took aim at religion, a far riskier topic to deliberate, and vowed to remove the tax-exempt status from all churches. It was a surprising move that may hit him where it counts come election day later this month.

"But who knows. We'll have to wait until then."

*Good for you, Thomas, good for you. Plow ahead with unbridled gusto and take the presidential reigns. Either way, I'll be there waiting for you, and you'll never see it coming.*

\* \* \*

A few days after the election the twelve members met once again, clandestinely as usual.

"Welcome," Dom announced. "Report."

"The Vatican continues their work on the serum. They're calling it Project Revelation."

"Very well. Keep us informed of its progress. Currently that's our greatest chance to save the others."

"Understood."

Dom looked around the room. "I realize, as our plan continues forward, that it will become increasingly difficult to meet in person, so I want to thank each of you for the personal sacrifices you've each made as we race towards our ultimate goal.

"With that said, Thomas Clark, as we all know, will be sworn in as the next President on January 20th. Our plan would have succeeded with or without him in the Oval Office, so I believe it's safe to say that our plan is progressing nicely."

He turned and looked at the Chinese President, Zhou Shun. "Does anyone in your cabinet suspect?"

"No," Zhou replied.

"Good," Dom said. "Then proceed as planned."

He then looked over at Aleksei Vakhrov, the Russian President. "And you, does anyone suspect?"

"Nyet. They do not."

"Excellent. And while the men you sent to the school were killed, the mission was an absolute success. Thank you."

Aleksei nodded.

Dominick looked around at the others in attendance. "Each of you will be called upon, some sooner than later, to step up and assume new roles. For our plan to flourish we all must play those roles with earnest. We've already waited this long. For now, it's only a matter of time before our tree bears fruit. Patience, my friends. Patience."

# 14
## January, 2004

"...and welcome to the ten-o'clock news. This afternoon, at The Capital, Thomas Clark was sworn in as the next President of the United States. I don't know how an Independent candidate got voted to be the most powerful person in the world, but here we are.

"Our country knew we were off to a rough start when President Clark decided not to use the Bible as he was sworn in. Then, and not terribly surprisingly, he immediately rallied against all forms of religion before he performed his levitating act to keep people in line. It was almost as if he was trying to start his own religion and gather his own followers, like some sort of cult.

"In my opinion, his entire speech was just an awkward mess, mixed with socialist ideas of working together and singing kumbaya while we miraculously work out our global difficulties. And all this from a man who has never held public office. I mean, he's only a children's book author, for crying out loud. Stay in your lane, Mr. President."

The anchor chuckled.

"Ladies and gentlemen, our country is in for a rough four years."

\*

"...and thanks for joining us for the ten-o'clock news. Today, Thomas Clark was sworn in as our next president, and no one was prepared for the heartfelt speech he gave. He vowed to bring the world together, which would be quite the accomplishment given the current political temperature, but his sincerity won people over. It would appear that empathy is a trait politicians need to relearn,

103

and an attribute President Clark will soon bring to The White House. Only time will tell if this self-made man will be able to withstand the job he's stepped into. Either way, welcome President Clark, your country needs you now more than ever."

* * *

## March, 2004

The C-130 Hercules, a large military aircraft that was used to deliver personnel, equipment and vehicles to anywhere in the world was on course to its Middle East destination. Inside were four members of SANDBOX, a relatively small contingent that, in essence, would have a lower chance of being detected once on the ground. However, the flip side of that coin meant that four people needed to accomplish a job that typically required sixteen operators.

The ECHO squad consisted of Zachary Black, April Bridges, Marco Perkins and Dominick Knight. Their mission was to nullify a notorious arms dealer who'd been supplying munitions to whoever offered him the most money. The munitions continued to destabilize the region, and threatened the reliability of oil production and pipelines. Once the squad had confirmed the dealer's location, they were instructed to laze the target, then call in a drone to level the area.

The four-man team rechecked their gear, for the umpteenth time, as the aircraft closed in on their designated drop site. A yellow light lit up overhead. One of the aircraft's personnel held up all of his fingers to indicate that they were five minutes out.

Dominick looked at the other three as he tightened his chest harness. "Who's not ready? Zach?"

Zach smiled. "Why so serious, Dom? You need to lighten up."

"Eat shit." *I should shapeshift now and kill all of you, but that's not why I'm here. Sill, it'd be fun.*

April and Marco shook their heads as the two men ribbed each other. Dom and Zach had never gotten to blows, but their rivalry at SANDBOX was well established. Perhaps that's why Sam and Bill had decided to send them on this particular mission together, especially under April, who was the designated team leader.

"Cut the bravado bullshit," April instructed, "and save it for whatever we run into on the ground."

"Copy," Zach replied.

April shifted her gaze to Dominick and stared him down. *You'll see my true power one day.* "Understood," he relented.

"Don't you worry," she added, "I'll get you two a room when we get back so you can work on your cardio. You know, you can pound it out, or whatever you neanderthals do on your off hours."

Marco let out a chuckle as he secured the suppressed assault rifle to his chest. Dom and Zach gave each other once over and then shifted their full attention to the mission. It wasn't long before the yellow light switched to green. The same crewman put up a single finger. One minute.

It was game time. All four donned their facemasks and made sure their oxygen was on. Individually they each gave a thumbs up.

April activated her comms. "Gotham, this is Echo-One. Comm check."

At ORACLE, Gabbi had tracked the progress of the C-130 and was ready to initiate contact with Echo team. She used the moniker of Gotham as her callsign for one glaringly obvious reason. Barbara Gordon, from the Batman comics, used to be Batgirl before the Joker broke her spine. From a wheelchair,

Barbara utilized her computer and technical skills to create a new identity, one come to be known as Oracle, to help Batman and other crime fighters. Gabbi extended the respect she had for the fictional Oracle, along with the nostalgia that surrounded Batman, to those in the field as well as her and Hobbes' aptly named company.

"Echo-One, Gotham receives you five-by-five. We'll be with you the whole way."

"Roger, Gotham."

*Holy shit, that is the clearest communications I've ever experienced, hands down.* April muted her radio and motioned for her team to get into position. The crew member secured his carabiner to the interior and pressed a button. The rear of the plane lowered into the night sky as the temperature inside the plane abruptly plummeted.

When the green light switched to red, the four spec-ops members ran forward, as a unit, and launched themselves into the void. Seconds later, with the C-130 in the distance, April and the others deployed their chutes in an orchestrated HAHO maneuver. The reason for the High Altitude, High Open was to allow the team to traverse up to 30 miles to their target before they landed.

April made sure all four of her team's chutes were open, then keyed her comm.

"Echo-One to Gotham. Passing Hawk."

"Roger that, Echo-One."

Passing Hawk was a pre-generated key phrase, and each mission was assigned multiple phrases to indicate the stage the team was currently engaged with. Hawk, in this case, meant the team was in the air and on their way to the target.

As April's team formed a single file line behind her, she checked the small computer attached to her arm. The display indicated direction, wind, temperature, time, and a variety of other details. April noticed she was heading off course and adjusted ten degrees. The others followed suit.

* * *

The team, exhausted but successfully sequestered within the rocks, could only watch as a new day commenced. April, from behind the camouflaged netting, scanned their surroundings. The trail of footprints, that they'd left in the sand, were entirely too obvious for her tastes and she could only hope that the wind would obscure them before a local discovered them from the village a half-mile away.

Her team was tired, as they'd used their energy to slog through the sand to the rocks, where they hastily constructed their lean-to so it would blend in with the surrounding rocks and terrain. It wasn't perfect, but there was nothing they could do about it now.

The meeting with the arms dealer, per the intelligence, suggested the meet wouldn't happen at the village until noon at the earliest. April, therefore, instructed Dom and Marco to get some shut-eye while she and Zach remained on overwatch. Zach, the team's sniper, surveyed the village with his long rifle in hopes their target would arrive early.

An hour later April and Zach switched roles with Dom and Marco. Not thirty minutes later April was instantly roused by Gabbi's voice in her ear.

"Echo-One, you've got an interested party of four military aged men, with small arms, who seem to have stumbled across your tracks."

"Shit," April breathed out. "Distance?"

"Four hundred yards, but they're closing."

"Roger that."

April put a hand on Zach's leg and squeezed. He snapped out of his sleep as she whispered the circumstances to the others.

Zach slowly traversed his rifle towards the potential threat. "They're following our trail, that's for sure. I won't be able to see them in about thirty seconds, due to the drop-off."

"Options?" April inquired.

"I'll handle them," Dom announced. *I need the distraction.* "Stay on mission."

April winced. "Are you sure?"

"If one of us doesn't do this then the whole mission will be fubared."

"It has to be silent," Zach insisted.

"No shit, Sherlock" Dom replied with a smile. *They'll never see me coming.*

"Go," April ordered.

Dom didn't hesitate as he gripped his rifle, gently lifted up the camouflage netting and departed.

"Shit," April muttered and keyed her comm. "Gotham, this is Echo-One. We're pulling an audible and splitting the team. This is either going to work or be a complete shit show. Stand by. Passing Serpent."

"Roger that, Echo-One, passing Serpent" Gabbi replied as she watched the live drone footage. Serpent meant that the team had encountered a problem.

*

Dom crouched as he exited. He quickly closed the distance towards the four enemy combatants. He couldn't see them yet, due to the rocky terrain, but he knew they weren't too far away. He also knew that if one of them got a shot off then the team would be potentially overrun. Besides, they didn't even know if the men had

108

already called the situation in. No matter how the problem was sliced, the team knew they were going to be in the crosshairs sooner than later, whether it was on their terms or forced.

Dom moved with precision, from one large rock to another, until he heard the men scuffle on loose gravel. He pressed himself into the ground, into the shadows, and waited until they passed within seven feet of his position. He held his breath and focused on what needed to be done, knowing that the drone high above would capture the moment. He put down his rifle and drew a blade.

*It's go time.*

As soon as the second pair of men turned their backs to him, Dom tossed a handful of gravel far to the men's front left. As the gravel sailed through the air, he propelled himself towards the back of the man closest to him and snapped the first man's head backwards. As the rocks clattered, Dom slashed the man's throat and immediately moved onward.

The three men had pointed their weapons down the hillside when Dom silenced enemy number two. However, the sound as his body collapsed, caught the attention of the two that remained, and as they turned their eyes widened. They brought up their AK-47s in unison, but Dom threw his blade, which embedded itself in the chest of the man farthest from him, who toppled over.

Before the last man could pull his trigger, Dom somehow closed the distance to him, kicked the weapon free and bear hugged the man. *You're mine now.* Dom used his incredible strength, as the man struggled, until his opponent's body went limp.

Dom verified none of them posed a threat, retrieved his knife before he searched their bodies for anything useful. Other than some spare magazines, the AK's and their clothing, he didn't find a radio on any of them. Satisfied, for the moment that he'd nullified the threat, Dom meticulously covered the bodies in loose shale, retrieved his rifle and made his way back to his team.

"Gotham to Echo-One."

"This is Echo-One," April replied.

"Threat neutralized. Friendly returning to you shortly."

"Roger that, Gotham."

Zach continued to scan the village as Dom reentered their hiding spot.

"What the fuck?" Marco asked. "We didn't hear your suppressor."

*I've had centuries of training, and I'm that good.* Dom nodded. "That's because I used a blade."

April and Zach couldn't believe their ears.

"You took on four armed men with a blade?" April probed.

"It would have been faster if I'd just shot them, but I didn't want to take the risk that one of them would pull their trigger as they went down. This was easier." *And much more enjoyable.*

"Fucking hell," Zach exclaimed. "Did you all hear that shit? He just said it was easier."

"Mad props," April told Dom. "I don't know how you did that, but I'm sure we all owe you."

All Dom could do was smile at the accolades. He knew if it wasn't for the drone overhead, he'd have shifted form and waded through the four men with absolute ease, tearing off their limbs in the process. His plan to embed himself within SANDBOX to prove his worth would eventually pay out dividends. He just needed to remain fixated on the big picture.

*My goal is Thomas Clark and his family, aside from taking over this planet in one piece. I also need ORACLE's technology to contact my ship. And while that's all happening my people continue to maneuver themselves into leadership roles, ones that will make it much easier for us to sow confusion and terror when the time comes.*

*There are so many moving parts to my plan, and the only thing that remains a constant has been our species unending patience. It's been two-hundred years already. We've waited long enough. It's time to call for another gathering.*

* * *

The twelve met for another clandestine meeting. Dom looked around the room at the others and smiled.

"We've come farther than I thought we'd be able to in such a short amount of time, especially since we've been waiting so long to reunite with our brethren."

He looked directly at the President of China. "It's time to turn up the heat."

Zhou Shun coldly smiled. "My agents are already on-site and prepared to strike on your command."

"The order is so given."

# 15
## April 2004

"...and this is the six o'clock news. Terror gripped Washington D.C. today as an assassination attempt was made on President Thomas Clark and his family.

"On a routine and scheduled event to Arlington National Cemetery, the President's convoy was ambushed by an apparent I.E.D., or improvised explosive device. The substantial explosion took out a substantial portion of the Arlington Memorial Bridge and killed an unknown number of police and Secret Service agents. Thankfully, the President was just outside the effective blast radius and was immediately ushered back to The White House.

"While the investigation into this attack is only hours old, rumors are already spreading on who is behind the unsuccessful assassination, not to mention how and when the explosives utilized in the attack were originally placed on the bridge."

The anchor shifted to a new camera as she read something silently off her prompter.

"I've just been informed that The White House will have a televised announcement, four hours from now, at ten p.m. eastern tonight."

\* \* \*

"In three, two,..."

The producer put up a single finger, then indicated the television feed was live. Thomas stared at the camera in front of him until the red light blinked on.

"My fellow Americans, thank you for joining me tonight. For those of you who don't know, my name is Thomas Clark and I'm the President of the United States.

"Earlier today an assassination attempt was made on my family and I. A bomb was utilized to destroy the Arlington Memorial Bridge here in Washington D.C., which resulted in multiple lives lost by both the D.C. Police Department as well as members of the Secret Service.

"While those responsible have yet to be identified, let it be known that they failed and that I'm coming for them. Too long have I stood idly by as the North Koreans and the Russians set foot in our country, which took the lives of innocent children and civilians. That particular time of diplomacy has now come to an end. In its place is now my directive to retaliate. Rest assured, those who have done our country wrong will NOT see it coming.

"And to my Americans, as well as the rest of the world, I offer my sincerest apologies. I should have acted sooner to avenge our fallen brethren. The political stage can no longer be played by the rules we once knew, because those have failed and allowed who wish to do us harm to do so with impunity. It's time to take back that power and make them second-guess before they act against this great country of ours ever again.

"Thank you. Good night."

*

As the news broadcast ended, Dom threw the plate of food he'd been eating against the wall. He was pissed off and extremely perplexed.

*How in the hell did he survive? Everything was perfect, and yet he and his family walked away from the ambush as if nothing happened. I just don't get it.*

114

Dom paced around the confines of his hidden room, since he was home for the weekend, away from his SANDBOX duties.

*The mysterious Thomas Clark. I should have known killing him wouldn't be this easy. He vanquished The Ancient, and that means I should have given him the respect he rightfully deserves. Still, it would have been nice to remove him from the board, but I must press forward to get closer to him and his family.*

*Hopefully the Pope's scientists can give me the necessary tools to accomplish just that.*

\* \* \*

When Dominick returned to SANDBOX, Monday morning, Sam and Bill were waiting for him.

"Hey Dom," Bill said, "you got a second?"

*I wonder what this is all about.* "For you guys, absolutely."

\* \* \*

In the early hours of the morning a portal opened up in an unused bedroom, on the top floor of China's Presidential Palace. Six figures emerged, within the darkened space, before it snapped shut behind them. Thomas and Gavin were accompanied by Sam, Bill, Dominick Knight and Rebecca Cross. Dominick, already well revered for his previous successes in the field, had been one of the first tapped by Sam and Bill to be part of PORTAL's secret contingent. Rebecca, along with Sabrina and Bai, had been brought up to speed on PORTAL, and were more than willing to dip into SANDBOX's personnel.

Gavin had insisted that Stir come with them, but for some reason the small animal wouldn't stop snarling as the team prepared for the mission.

The small group was equipped with silenced handguns, along with tranquilizer pistols to minimize deaths. They wore all black, fitted with Kevlar vests worn underneath their tactical vests, kitted out with stun grenades, extra magazines, zip ties and their encrypted radios, compliments of ORACLE.

Sam and Bill were out front, with Thomas and Gavin in the middle, while Rebecca and Dominick took up rear security. To say it was unorthodox to bring an eleven-year-old on a mission went without saying, but the nature of PORTAL, along with what his son had already experienced time and time again, left Thomas with zero choice. He needed Gavin for his portal ability, both to send and retrieve teams. Typically, Thomas would have Gavin send the team, then have him wait for a signal to pick them up. For this particular mission, and it being PORTAL's first, Thomas needed an immediate exit strategy available to them, and that meant putting his son in potential danger.

Sam slowly edged open the bedroom door a tad and listened for any sounds. Satisfied at the silence, he swung it open a bit more and poked his head out into the darkened hallway. There, at the entrance to the Presidential suite, stood two armed guards.

Sam held up two fingers on his left hand to Bill, who nodded in return. They carefully extracted their tranquilizer pistols, then held up their hands for the rest of the team to stay put.

With practiced ease, one that came from years of training as well as a trusted bond between each other, Sam and Bill soundlessly slid into the hallway and dispatched the two guards. As the needles pierced the guard's skin, the drug not only knocked them out, it also temporarily paralyzed their bodies. This, in essence, was to prevent a finger jerking motion that could lead to an accidental misfiring of any weapons.

Sam and Bill rushed down the hallway and barely caught the two guards before they collapsed, which was noise they absolutely couldn't afford this close to their intended target.

Rebecca poked her head out and caught Bill as he gave her the thumbs up. She led Thomas and Gavin towards the far doors while Dom covered the hallway.

The six prepared themselves for entry into the room, nodded, then pushed open the door. Sam and Bill, once inside the enormous and lavish suite, moved with purpose to the canopied bed. Behind them, a few feet, was Thomas as Bill yanked a surprised Zhou Shun out of bed and tossed him on the floor.

Zhou opened his mouth to yell but found himself unable to when Thomas used his telekinetic ability and applied pressure to his throat. He then lifted Zhou off the carpet and into the air. As their target hovered Rebecca and Dom dragged the two unconscious guards out of the doorway and into the room, then softly closed the door behind them. Sam and Bill, in the meantime, canvased the suite for any additional threats. When they found none, they stood off to the side and watched the show unfold.

Thomas stared at Zhou with hate as the man who'd ordered his family's death scratched frantically at his own throat in an attempt to free himself from the invisible death grip.

Zhou's eyes frantically darted around the room, settled on Sam and Bill. His eyes moved to Gavin, followed by Rebecca and Dom.

He recognized Dominick immediately and Zhou's eyes flared as he gasped for breath. Dom slowly shook his head from side to side to warn his counterpart not to expose him.

"Thomas," Sam said.

The Chinese President's movements began to slow as his air supply ran low.

"Thomas," Sam said a little more forcefully.

Zhou's eyes rolled back.

"Mr. President," Sam hissed.

Thomas released his grip on the man's throat, but kept him helpless in the air. Zhou coughed and sputtered as he gulped in mouthfuls of oxygen. His limbs thrashed around as he tried to gain purchase on something tangible, but he quickly realized there wasn't anything he could do besides scream his lungs out.

It didn't take him long to return Thomas' death stare. "How DARE you come here and invade my home!" Zhou emphatically hissed.

"Are you done with your little temper tantrum, or shall we get down to business?"

Zhou ineffectively continued to squirm. "What do you want, Mr. Clark?"

"You've tried, on more than one occasion, to kill me and my family. And, by the way, you will address me as Mr. President, you piece of shit."

"Fuck you."

Thomas propelled Zhou across the room towards the wall, then pulled him back just as he was about to make contact with it. Sweat glistened on Zhou's forehead.

"I actually came here to talk to you, President to President. Care to dispense with the bullshit?"

"Let me down."

Thomas considered it, then released his hold. Zhou dropped three feet to the carpet and somehow managed to stay on his feet. Sam and Bill watched him like a hawk while Rebecca, Gavin and Dom remained steadfast by the suite's entrance.

Zhou regained his stature. "Are you here to kill me?"

"I'm here to reason with you, regardless of how I personally feel about you."

"How magnanimous of you, Mr. President." Zhou waved his hand at Thomas' tactical appearance. "And that's quite the getup you're in. Now get to the point before you're overrun by my security detail."

"That's cute, but we both know they're not making their rounds for another eight minutes. So, let me be clear, if I wanted you dead, you'd be dead. It was incredibly easy for me to get you, and I'll be happy to do it again. However, I'm only here, in person, to deliver a message."

"Get to the point already."

Thomas nodded. "Very well. There are a few things that are about to happen to you. The first is that you're about to lose a submarine base."

Zhou's face registered shock. "What are you talking about?"

"It's a proportioned response to your bombing attack that took American lives. Furthermore, I've authorized the CIA and FBI's investigative results to be released which will show the world you were the one that ordered my assassination."

"You wouldn't dare do either of those things. You're risking World War Three!"

Thomas stepped towards Zhou and squared off with him. "I'd rather have just killed you and everyone else who wants me dead, but that'd be too messy. The world is going to know your role, then judge you for it. In the meantime, an American strike force will decimate one of your military assets instead of coming directly for you."

"I'll order a retaliatory attack."

"I'm sure you'll be pressured to do just that, but you'll refrain."

Zhou felt cornered as Thomas backed him against the far wall. "Of course I will."

"We've done this dance, Zhou, and we've both suffered the consequences. I should have done more after I publicly humiliated you, alongside the leaders of Russia, North Korea and the Pope."

"What are you talking about?" Zhou snorted. "I've never met you before."

Dom closed his eyes and swore under his breath at his counterpart's mistake.

Thomas was caught off guard. "What are you playing at, Zhou?"

Dominick put a hand to his ear as Gabbi's voice indicated the stealth bombers had just dropped their ordinance.

"Mr. President, they're on target."

Thomas looked over at Dom, then back at Zhou. "I wish we had more time, so I'll cut to the chase. You come at me or my country ever again, and I'll be back, but it won't be to have a civil conversation."

Zhou snarled as Thomas moved away. It was then that one of his multiple phones buzzed.

Thomas motioned towards it. "Go ahead. It's not like you don't already know what the bad news will be."

As Zhou went to answer it, Thomas motioned to Gavin to form his portal.

"Report!" Zhou demanded as he placed the receiver to his ear.

The portal shimmered into existence and the team departed just as Zhou filled the room with profanities.

*  *  *

Gretchen, knee-deep with flying drone missions for ORACLE, also kept her eyes peeled for any information she, and her people, could utilize to their advantage. Her primary goal, now that she was embedded within ORACLE, was to commandeer the encrypted communications hardware that Hobbes and Gabbi had developed. Furthermore, once she had access, to figure out a way to configure it to send a message to Zora. The entire plan rested on her shoulders, but she knew she could figure it out.

What she hadn't counted on was inadvertently stumbling into Dr. Neal and Dr. Hanson one day when the two doctors were walking with Hobbes. Gretchen was between operations, late one night, and went to stretch her legs. She caught the three men badging themselves through a restricted access door that led downstairs. She discovered, through Dom, that the newly developed PORTAL group was conducted in ORACLE's basement, but the presence of two men in lab coats set off alarm bells in her head.

Over the next week, Gretchen was able to quietly navigate ORACLE's servers, bypassing certain security protocols and grant her security badge access to the same basement door. She then was able to modify the log files, when she used her badge, to delete themselves. This effectively allowed her unrestricted access to the basement, without leaving a computer trace.

The next issue Gretchen faced was to bypass the security camera feeds. Thankfully, they were accessible via the internal servers she'd infiltrated already. It took a bit of code manipulation, but she eventually was able to overwrite the camera's logs as well so that as soon as she scanned her badge the system would simultaneously delete the logs and video feed.

The following evening, when zero missions were scheduled, Gretchen let herself into ORACLE's basement. She was ready to shapeshift at a moment's notice, just in case she came across anybody, but the large space that had been designated for PORTAL was devoid of personnel. She quickly located another set of locked doors and ventured inside. There she discovered row upon row of lab equipment, culminating in a refrigerated room. It didn't take long for her to stumble upon Tad's body before she retreated back to her drone pod on the upper floor.

The next day she left a message, for Dom, on a private chat group the twelve now utilized.

* * *

## June 2004

Dom paid for thirty minutes of computer time, at a D.C. cybercafé, and used the computer to access the private chat group. Two others had already logged on as he joined the channel.

*Status update*, he typed.

The Vatican contact keyed in their reply. *They're close. I suspect they'll have a workable serum in four to six months' time.*

Dom smiled and replied. *Remain embedded within the project and report back. Our very future depends on it.*

The other member of the twelve added their report. *Thomas has been equally as busy with his own project. No timeline as of yet.*

Dom nodded, pleased with himself at his overall plan while his fingers danced over the keyboard. *Their individual progress will only make it easier for us to complete our goals. Keep me informed.*

*Yes, sir.*

*Yes, sir.*

His attention turned to other matters. *I haven't heard from Zhou. Why hasn't he stepped up his attacks?*

*I haven't heard from him.*

*Neither have I.*

The leader frowned. *That's unlike him. Make it known he needs to follow the plan or there will be consequences.*

*We'll pass the message along, sir.*

The leader of the twelve terminated the chat and sat back in his chair. *If I play this right, it'll only be a matter of time before we have the ability to awaken our brethren. Then, and only then, will we finally rule this world.*

# 16
## October 2004

"I know it's been some time since we last gathered, but now that the majority of our chess pieces are in position, we can finally move forward with the next stage."

The twelve gathered together, once again, in an abandoned warehouse after covertly flying in from around the globe.

Dom continued. "We are mere months away from making our ancestors proud and I want to thank each and every one of you for remaining committed to our singular goal."

He took his time and looked at each of the others as his eyes swept around the room. Each of them was lucky to be alive, more so now that the world had become technologically advanced over the past decades. Each of them had fought, tooth and nail for this moment, here and now.

"Give me updates. Let's start with you, Zhou."

The Chinese President stepped forward. "Thomas Clark came to me months ago, utilizing his son's portal ability, and threatened to kill me if I ever came after him again. One of my submarine bases was annihilated at the exact same time, and I've yet to strike back. My lack of action has been characterized as weakness, both by you and my senior staff. This plan of yours HAS to succeed or I'll have an uprising of my own to contend with."

Dominick smiled. "Zhou, if I may call you that, I understand that Thomas has singled you out after the failed assassination attempt on his life. He's pissed, and rightfully so. All of us here require you to maintain the stranglehold you have on your cabinet members while we wait for the next few months to come and go. Thomas and the Pope will give us the upper hand as we move forward, and on a silver plate no less. We already have access to both their laboratories, thanks to those in this room, so their working serums will be ours for the taking. So, stay vigilant and remain focused. Our ancestors' lives depend on us and, in turn, they depend on the twelve of us."

*And if you fail me, I'll kill you myself.*

Zhou stepped back.

"Aleksei Vakhrov, how are you faring?"

The assumed Russian President took a step into the circle. "I am ready to execute on your orders."

"Very well. Next. How about you, Chancellor?"

Christof Kroeger, the German Chancellor, took his turn. "My wife has grown suspicious, but aside from that I am ready to do my part when the time comes."

"Excellent. If your wife becomes a problem, I trust you'll deal with it appropriately?"

"Naturally."

Dom continued with the others until they'd all reported in.

"Who's not ready?" he asked them. "Who's not ready to bring this world to its knees; to reap the power that will come when we enslave the weak?

The others smiled.

"We've all been patiently waiting for the right time to strike; to reunite with our brethren and take what's rightfully ours. Our time has finally come!"

The other eleven burst into applause. Their carefully constructed plans were close to fruition.

"Thomas Clark," Dom said after they'd quieted down, "somehow survived the carefully orchestrated attempt on his life. That's fine. His time will come, and when that moment does, I'll deal with him personally. However, with the serums so close to completion, it's imperative we stay the course. The moment they're ready is the moment we appropriate them for ourselves.

We'll become our own army, and our ancestors will smile down upon us." He looked around the circle. "We're close. We're so damn close."

* * *

## November 2004

Dominick knocked before he entered the conference room. Sam and Bill were already seated.

"Close the door and take a seat," Sam instructed.

*What the hell is this all about?* Dominick did as he was instructed.

"You're probably wondering what this is all about," Bill said.

*I have no idea what this is all about.* "I'm intrigued."

"Why intrigued?"

"Because if I was in trouble, you'd have dressed me down in front of my peers to make an example."

Sam leaned back in his chair and crossed his arms. "Perceptive."

Dominick shifted his eyes between the two. "Now I'm starting to worry. Am I in trouble?"

Bill shook his head. "No. In fact, we've brought you here on direct orders from the President to make you an offer."

"The President? I don't understand. What kind of offer?"

Sam leaned in. "An offer that will only be talked about once, right here, right now. However, it comes with a high degree of risk on your part."

"What kind of risk?"

"The terminal kind," Bill replied.

Dominick shifted in his chair. *Interesting.* "I'm still here."

Sam explained that the President was close to a serum that would allow abilities to manifest themselves in other humans. He told Dominick that the PORTAL project would be the initial testing ground, and that he was the first operator they'd approached.

*This is such an unbelievable stroke of luck.* "So," Dominick replied, "you're asking me if I want superpowers?"

Bill nodded. "Something like that."

"Would I get to choose the ability?"

"We're unclear on that part," Sam told him, "but we haven't discussed the overall risk with you yet."

*I'm in.* Dominck smiled. "How bad could it really be?"

"The process of administering the serum, from what we understand, is still in the experimental stage."

"And?"

"And," Sam continued, "we're serious when we said you might not survive."

*I don't care.* "Do you think the risk is worth the reward?" Dominick asked.

"That's not for us to decide," Bill replied.

"My guess is that the two of you would have been first in line, if it was safe."

Sam looked over at Bill and then back at Dominick. "Something like that."

"Can I think it over and let you know tomorrow?"

"No," Sam told him. "We'll give you five minutes before we move on to our next candidate. Either way, it's a huge gamble, but it's your life and we'd love to start padding our roster with ability-laden operato-"

*There's no time like the present.* Dominick didn't hesitate. "I'm in."

"You're sure?" Bill stressed.

"Just tell me when and where."

Sam and Bill stood up and exchanged handshakes with Dominick. "We'll be in touch with those exact details. In the meantime, I shouldn't have to mention that this entire conversation is classified."

*I couldn't have asked for a better outcome.* Dominick winked. "What conversation?"

"You're dismissed, and congratulations."

"Thank you."

Dom left the conference room, poker face intact, until he was out of view.

*Oh boy, this is going to be so much fun. Their entire world is walking into a buzzsaw, which they have no idea about, and now they want to give me an 'enhancement'? I mean, this is going to be a gamechanger, especially if it works as intended. I'll finally be able to go toe-to-toe with Thomas and take him on myself, granted the ability I get is worthwhile.*

*Regardless, this changes the game entirely, because if I'm going to become enhanced, then it's only right that the other eleven eventually get the same opportunity.*

\* \* \*

## December 2004

Amelia Farina, one of the twelve, had finagled her position on the Pope's 'Project Revelation' a few months prior as a lab assistant and had been secretly feeding updates to Dominick through the encrypted chat channel the twelve shared. When Dom informed the group that he'd been chosen to receive an ability, she figured no one would suspect her involvement if a vial went missing.

Amelia was successfully able to smuggle the serum out of the Vatican, by concealing it in bags of hazardous waste/needles that needed to be disposed of. The guards barely looked through the medical material before waving her past security, since she was the assistant that was typically given that responsibility.

Amelia, as soon as she arrived at the apartment which was utilized for this particular cover assignment, extracted a syringe and prepped the serum for injection. As she settled into the thought of what it might do to her, especially since she'd witnessed numerous failed and revolting attempts during the serum process, she paused for a second.

*Is this something I really want to subject myself to? I could die before I see our species come back from the brink of extinction.*

She examined the serum in the syringe.

*But if Dominick has chosen to go down the same path, for the betterment of our people, then so will I.*

She steadied herself while she slipped the needle into her human flesh, after she decided not to shapeshift to her true form.

*Here goes nothing.*

She pressed down on the plunger and injected the contents into her blue blood stream.

The flash of fire, a burning just underneath her skin, rushed out from the injection point and traveled up her arm. As it reached her torso her body began to shudder in uncontrollable spasms before she collapsed to the floor.

*What…what have I done…*

\*

Amelia's body jerked a few times as she regained consciousness. She was on the floor, sprawled out, as she came to. She pushed herself up to a sitting position and looked down at her arm, where she'd inserted the needle.

*The fire. It's gone.*

As she got to her feet, she saw the broken syringe on the floor, knocked free as she had fallen.

*I don't think I feel any different. Did it even work? The serum's never been tested on my species before, so who's to say what it'll do to me, if anything. I guess I'll have to experiment.*

Amelia extended her hands out in front of her and tried to manipulate one of her dining room chairs like she'd seen Thomas Clark do on television. Nothing.

*Maybe I can fly instead?*

She looked down at her feet and concentrated on lifting off the floor. Her feet didn't budge, nor did she feel any lighter.

*This is ridiculous. If only Dom could help me with this...*

A strong sensation suddenly rippled through her body and down to her hands. As she lifted them towards the table again a flickering doorway developed in front of her.

*No way...*

She looked at it for a bit, and then walked completely around the new shimmering entity.

*This is unbelievable. What should I do?*

She reached out and tentatively touched the shimmer. Her hand passed through and vanished.

*NO!*

She retracted her arm in a flash and discovered her hand was still in one piece.

*Could this possibly be? There's only one way to find out.*

* * *

131

"Are you sure?"

Gavin became distressed. "What do you mean, am I sure?"

"Our son's telling us the truth," Laura reassured her husband.

Gavin, Emily, Laura and Thomas were seated around the residence's breakfast table.

Emily added her thoughts. "Why would Gavin even make up a story like that, dad? What's wrong with you?"

Thomas leaned back in his chair. "You're right, I'm sorry, son. You're the portal expert. What do you think it means?"

Gavin shook his head. "I don't know, but someone else clearly has access to The Other Place."

Laura rubbed her son's back. "Did you see anything else?"

"Other than the boat and footprints in the sand? No, nothing else, but that alone sent a shiver down my spine. After all this time I thought The Other Place was my stomping ground."

Thomas extracted his personal phone.

Laura looked over at him. "Who are you calling?"

"Sam. If there's someone out there that can make a portal, then wouldn't Amanda have felt their presence?"

"Good idea."

The line connected. "Sam, something's amiss."

Thomas put the phone on speaker and quickly laid out the situation.

"Amanda," Sam replied, "would have said something."

"I agree, but could you check with her anyway?"

"Alright. Let me double check."

A minute later Amanda joined the conversation.

"I'm sorry," she announced. "I haven't felt the existence of another person with abilities."

Thomas thought for a second. "What about when you're asleep? Do you know if you can acknowledge them then?"

132

"No, my ability doesn't work that way."

"Thanks, Amanda," Laura verbalized.

"You're welcome."

"Is this something we should be concerned about?" Sam asked after Amanda stepped away.

"Probably," Thomas replied, "but we don't have any additional information to work with yet."

"Then perhaps a team should work with Gavin and see what else your son can locate."

"I don't like that," Laura announced.

"Regardless," Thomas told everyone, "it'll have to wait until after the White House Christmas event."

Sam chuckled at Thomas' discomfort. "I'm glad I'm not the President and get roped into that tradition. I'm sure you'll love every second of the press asking you why you're engaging in it, especially since you've denounced religion."

"Very funny, Sam, but I don't have to agree with the premise. It's a tradition that the country's used to. It's the least I can do, and I'll expect to be razzed for it."

"Either way, my friend, good luck to you, Laura and the kids. Maybe afterwards the four of you can secretly pop by so we can open gifts together as one big family."

Laura smiled. "We'd love that, and Julie and Kim have already extended us the invitation."

"Merry Christmas," Sam told them. "We'll catch you in a few days."

"Happy Holidays," Thomas replied, "you bastard."

They heard Sam laugh as the call came to an end.

Thomas looked over at Emily and Gavin. "So, what are we going to do about The Other Place?"

133

"Let's leave it alone until after Christmas," Laura said. "After that, even though it makes me nervous, we can't ignore the problem. We have to find out what's going on."

"Agreed. That okay with you, Gav?"

Gavin nodded. "Friend or foe, something's happening, and I need to know what it is."

\* \* \*

## January 2005

Gavin exited his portal after he finished another venture. His continued search of The Other Place had unfortunately yielded no additional evidence of that particular island. He'd discovered that the boat and footprints remained exactly where he'd originally found them.

*Maybe it'd always been there and I just never ran into it before?* Gavin shook his head as he attempted to dispel his self-doubt. *No, someone else has been screwing around and I'm not going to stop until I find out who they are and what they've been up to.*

Gavin headed downstairs, out of the residence, and made his way to the Oval Office. Jennifer Myers, the Executive Admin, smiled as she greeted him.

*Your time is coming, little one.* "Hello, Gavin. How's your day going?"

He shrugged. "It's fine."

"Are you here to check-in on your father?"

"If he's not too busy."

She winked at him. "I'll make sure he has time for you. Go on in."

134

"Thanks, Jennifer."

"You're welcome, kiddo."

Gavin entered the Oval Office and closed the door behind him. Thomas, apparently lost in thought, turned around to see who'd interrupted his concentration.

"Oh hey, Gav. What's up?"

Gavin plopped himself down on the nearest couch. "I haven't found anything new."

Thomas made his way from behind his desk and sat opposite his son. "Still?"

"I'm frustrated."

"I can tell. Truth is, so am I, but not about your strange intruder."

Gavin shifted slightly. "You're frustrated too? What about?"

"Well, I've been President for a year now and I often wonder if I've been doing the right thing."

"We're still alive," Gavin said matter-of-factly.

Thomas relented a bit. "This is true, but that's the bare minimum. What I meant was, have I been steering our country in the right direction."

"Looks like it runs in the family."

A look of confusion washed over Thomas' face. "What does?"

"Self-doubt."

He chuckled. "Well put, but there's things you're not privy to that I have to contend with on a daily basis."

"You're still you, dad. Just do the right thing and keep moving forward. What else could you possibly do?"

Thomas nodded as his son's words sunk in. "Wise words. How'd you get to be so smart?"

"Mom," Gavin replied with a grin.

Thomas laughed. "You're not wrong." He stood up. "I'll see you guys tonight for dinner, unless there was something else you needed?"

Gavin shook his head. "No, I'll see you later."

Thomas watched his son depart, then sauntered back over to his desk so he could gaze out the windows once again.

*Something's amiss, and I can't place my finger on it. It's been too quiet for too long, which means who's going to make the next move against my family? I need to continue to protect them, but is my secret project going to be enough and is it even the right course of action?*

He turned away from the view and sat down.

*Gav was right, I'm overthinking things. Stay the course, Tommy boy, stay the course.*

# 17
## February 2005

Project Revelations' lead scientist could only cower as the Pope, bracketed by four of his Templar Knights, towered over him.

"Tell me again," the Pope growled.

"Sir, I…um…when I started my rounds this morning, I discovered that twenty serum vials could not be accounted for. I swear they were there last night."

"You would have me believe that the vials were taken while you slept?"

"What other explanation is there?"

"That you took them to sell yourself."

The scientist's face twisted. "I brought you the girl's blood."

"Exactly, and now you plan to profit from your own hard work."

"Your Eminence, why would I even inform you that the vials were missing then? Someone's playing you for a fool, but it's certainly not me."

"Is that so."

"There's more, sir. I failed to inform you that a single vial was taken a few months back."

The Pope's face contorted. "And you chose to keep this information to yourself?"

"I did."

The Pope ascertained his scientist wasn't the real culprit, but his rage overpowered his ability to think clearly. "Search his stateroom and get me the closed-circuit footage!"

One of his Templars headed off.

"I demand to know the traitor's identity! Don't they know who I am and what I'll do to them? This is outrageous." He turned and addressed his Templars. "Double the guard and make sure everyone who comes in and out of this area is frisked. No exceptions."

"Yes, your Eminence."

"And I want each staff member interrogated."

"Yes, sir. Right away. We'll find the traitor for you."

"Very well." The Pope looked around at the rest of the lab's petrified staff. "While you wait for your turn, get back to work and replace what was stolen from me, immediately!"

Nobody budged.

"NOW!"

The employees scattered as the Pope strode towards the laboratory's exit.

*Bubbling idiots. Someone dared to steal from me. ME! And twice now. Who would betray me? My Templars will discover the culprit soon enough. In the meantime, I should use the current supply on my loyal Templars to enhance their combat prowess. Then, and only then, will I take the fight to Thomas Clark's door. The world will know, when I hold his severed head up in the air, that I'm to be feared. That I am the one that is all-powerful; all-knowing. The masses will flock to my side and beg me to be merciful.*

The Pope, a smile plastered across his face, made his way to his private office. He closed the door and walked over to the balcony. There, far below in St. Peter's Square, a throng of protestors continued to vocalize their contempt.

His smile immediately faded. *More people of faith are beginning to think for themselves and I won't stand for it. The bleeding has to stop before the tide becomes unmanageable.*

The Pope turned away from his balcony and headed inside. He picked up his private line and got in contact with the leader of his Templar Knights, the one who replaced Gabriel.

"How may I serve?"

"Marcus," the Pope told him, "how soon before I have an army to command?"

"Sir, the burgled serum will postpone your plan for a month."

"Goddammit."

"We could proceed with a smaller force, but I wouldn't recommend that course of action."

The Pope sighed. "Very well, Marcus. Consider the plan postponed until my Templars are fully prepared."

"Yes, sir."

"I also expect you to locate the traitor and bring them to me."

"We're working on it, sir."

The Pope hung up. *An additional month.* He smiled once again. *Come March I will have my revenge..., and the world.*

\* \* \*

Dr. Allan Neal restrained Dominick Knight's wrists and legs with leather straps.

"It's just for precaution," he informed the soldier.

"I understand, doc," Dominick said.

Behind the glass barrier stood Thomas, Sam and Bill. The three watched as Dr. Allan and Dr. Hanson prepped the injection.

"Are we sure we want to do this?" Bill ventured. "I mean, we're talking about a man's life here."

"He's aware of the risks," Sam replied, "but that doesn't mean I disagree with you."

The two looked over at Thomas, transfixed by the procedure.

"Thomas?" Sam asked.

"I heard you, Sam."

"Any thoughts?" Bill solicited.

"Can we declare peace yet?" Thomas inquired. His friends didn't reply. "I'm doing what needs to be done, period. We're in a race and we need to level the playing field. If we don't, we'll just be overrun. We've talked about this."

Dr. Allan looked over at Thomas, who gave his nod to continue.

The needle sunk into Dominick's arm with ease, but as it was administered his body tensed and his back arched. With the last of the serum racing through Dom's bloodstream, his face contorted as he violently thrashed against his restraints. The monitors screamed at his accelerated vitals, all well out of safety margins.

The two doctors backed away from their test subject.

"Shit," Sam breathed out. "We're going to lose him."

But then, just as quickly, Dom's body relaxed and his breathing returned to normal. The monitors quieted down.

Thomas, Sam and Bill looked on as the two doctors performed their post-serum examination. While they couldn't hear what was being said, it was more than apparent that Dominick had survived the process. Dr. Hanson removed the restraints as Dom looked over at the three men. He smiled and gave them a thumbs up.

*Holy fucking shit, I've alive.*

Thomas entered the lab and immediately headed over to Dominick while the two doctors hovered nearby.

"That looked painful."

Dom nodded. "It wasn't enjoyable, that's for sure."

"How're you feeling?"

"Better," Dom said as he got off the table and back on his own two feet.

"I meant, do you feel any different?"

*If you only knew.* "Yes, sir, I think I do."

Thomas smiled. "Go on. Show me."

Sam and Bill, along with Dr. Neal and Dr. Hanson, continued to stare at Dominick as they waited for something to occur. Dom couldn't help but notice the overt attention.

*How do I play this?* "Mr. President, would it be out of line to ask to speak to you in private, sir?"

"Is something the matter?"

"No, sir, I just feel like what I'm about to show you is for your ears and eyes only. How you disseminate that information afterwards is, of course, up to you."

Thomas acquiesced. "Alright."

He left the four confused men behind as he walked with Dominick to the refrigerated area in the rear of the laboratory, before the two ducked inside.

Thomas made the first move. "What's with the secrecy? What's going on?"

Right in front of his eyes, Dom shapeshifted into an exact replica of Thomas, down to the last detail. It was like looking in the mirror.

Thomas couldn't help but take a step back. "What the fuck?"

Dom quickly reverted back to his own human form. "Sir, I didn't mean to alarm you."

Thomas mind raced with the potential Dom had just presented to him.

"You're telling me that the serum granted you the ability to shapeshift at will?"

*No, I don't even know what it did yet, but you won't know the difference.* Dom nodded.

"And you wanted privacy so as to not alert anyone else of the possibilities this now allows, is that correct?"

Dom nodded again. "Yes, sir. I figured the less people that know what I can do the better. And again, sorry for the jump scare. I didn't know if my new ability would actually work or not."

Thomas appeared relieved. "Forget about it. You've already earned my trust, which is why you were offered this incredible opportunity. Now, it seems, I need to decide how best to utilize you."

"I'm at your disposal, sir."

Thomas thought for a bit. "Look, I can hold off Dr. Neal and Dr. Hanson, for the time being. Sam and Bill are another issue altogether. I will need to loop them in sooner than later."

"Sir, if I may suggest something, and I hope you don't take offense."

"We're already down the rabbit hole this far. Go ahead."

*Here goes nothing.* Dom offered up an idea. It didn't take long for Thomas to see the benefit.

"Look," Thomas said. "Take a few days and rest up. I'll let you know when I need you for the reveal."

"Yes, sir."

\* \* \*

Dom left ORACLE's basement behind, as Thomas engaged his friends and the doctors and headed back to his off-base apartment he used for his cover. He closed the door behind him and let out a chuckle.

*That idiot believed every word I said. He lapped up the idea that I should pretend to become his son while PORTAL missions are being undertaken. Plausible deniability I said. Ha! He swallowed it all without a second thought. I'll just need to watch out for his wife and her power to know if I'm lying or not.*

Dom smiled as he opened his refrigerator and stared at the 20 vials of serum Amelia had stolen.

*And now I have even more potential at my fingertips. I'll save these for the future. Of course, that presents the issue of when I'll kidnap Thomas's two doctors, and all of their work, before I burn his lab to the ground. I should be the only one that has access to these vials, and with them I will take over this pitiful planet.*

He closed the door and walked back into his living room.

*Fooling Thomas was easy, but what new ability do I actually have now? I mean, I do feel different somehow, I just don't know exactly what it is that's changed.*

Dom raised his hands, looked at them and then shot them out in front of his body, as if spitting fire from his fingertips. Nothing happened.

*Ha! If only it were that easy. I mean, Amelia took me to The Other Place, and that was a wild experience I won't soon forget. Imagine if she was able to make a portal to our crashed ship?*

And just like that Dom's living room faded away. Moments later, if that, he found himself on the spaceship that had crashed into the Atlantic Ocean, 200 years prior.

*No fucking way.*

## 18

## February 2005

Dominick remained rooted to the spot he'd inadvertently teleported to before a smile swept across his face. *The freedom I've just been handed will categorically benefit my agenda. This is insane, and I love it!* Dom began to walk around the intact spacecraft. Somewhat surprisingly, even though the ship was nestled thousands of feet below the surface, there were zero signs of any breeches. In fact, aside from the failed engines and communications equipment, the ship appeared to be in the same condition before his group abandoned it 200 years prior.

*Good for you, father. You built these things to last; that's for sure.*

Dom made his way to the bay of stasis pods. Eighty-eight of the original one-hundred were still inhabited, although, as he inspected each one, it became quite evident that some of the pods had failed over the past two centuries. The inhabitants of those were in various states of decomposition.

*It's good to see all of you. And for those that are no longer here, rest well my brethren. Each of your sacrifices will not be in vain.*

Dom left them behind as he refamiliarized himself with the rest of the vessel's contents, and quickly stumbled upon a cache of explosives, which were stored next to the seed supply.

*Oh, I could definitely use these.*

Dom knew the explosives that originated from his planet were unlike anything he'd come across on Earth. In fact, during his time as an operator, over the years, he'd utilized a variety of other humanmade explosive materials, from gunpowder and dynamite, to C4 and Semtex. Each had their own specific use, but the minerals that were mined from Zara 844, then processed to the material Dom now stared down at, were in a league of their own. The destructive capability of a single brick would level a city block, even though it was meant to be used to clear space on whatever new world they were to occupy, to make space for building and farming.

He smirked. *It'll be used to clear space alright, just not the way my father intended.*

Dom pondered for a bit as he stared down at the explosive material.

*Amelia may or may nor be able to make a portal to this ship yet. She's as new to her ability as I am to mine. But I'll need it sooner than later. I wonder if I can transport it without her assistance? I mean, everything I'm wearing came with me. Why not something in my hands?*

Dom picked up a single explosive brick in both hands.

"Here goes nothing."

He envisioned his Minnesota estate, specifically his private room, and then next thing he knew he was there.

Dom looked down at his hands and the brick had traveled with him.

*Excellent.*

He jumped between his private residence and his downed ship, over and over again, to transfer the explosives, as well as the seeds. There were also a handful of energy weapons, but when he finally inspected them, he discovered their energy sources were depleted.

*They've been sitting there for too long, but I'm sure I could recouple them to the ship's energy source. That's a problem for another time. Right now, I want to experiment!*

Over the next few hours, Dom continued to test his ability, which coincided with what he could and could not transport.

*Inorganic, no problems. Organic, impossible. That's unfortunate. It would have been nice to blink in, and then take someone with me against their will, but alas that's not an option. I shouldn't be too upset overall. I can teleport.*

Dom smiled at his good fortune.

*I'm right where I need to be, having gained the trust of the infamous Thomas Clark, who's now the President of the United States.*

He looked at the explosives that were now stacked in his private office, alongside the seeds and weapons.

*What I really need to concern myself with is anyone else that will or could become a threat. I have China and Russian under control already, but it's time to move on to North Korea and the Pope, especially since we burgled twenty vials of his serum. That action alone will send him over the edge, and that means he'll send his Templars against Thomas sooner than later. I know I would.*

He paused.

*But I can utilize that to my favor, when the time comes, and change the course of history in the process.*

Dom's body vibrated with renewed energy. The decades of waiting were nearly over. He knew that only a few more pieces needed to fall into place before he awakened the rest of his people, including those he'd just seen with his own eyes.

*I'll release them when the time is right, and they'll fight right alongside me.*

He knew he needed the upper hand before he summoned the colony ship, otherwise Earth's populus would potentially unite and fight back.

*No, I need to make sure I have the upper hand before I subject the others. The world needs to be pushed out of their comfort zone and into chaos. They have to witness that anything they hold dear can be ripped right out of their grasp and burned to the ground.*

*They need to witness so much horror that they'll do anything to make it all stop.*

Dom chuckled.

*This is going to be so entertaining, and no one will ever see it coming.*

# 19
## March 25, 2005

Thomas left his secret service detail in ORACLE's lobby before he headed down to the basement. The unprompted call he'd received from Sam had him worried, and as he entered PORTAL's training area, he knew he'd been right. His entire extended family was in attendance, which included Gabbi and Hobbes.

"This seems like an intervention," Thomas joked. "What's going on?"

Julie took control of the situation. "Amanda has something to tell all of us."

Thomas shifted his gaze to the teen, as did everyone else.

"When I woke up this morning," she said, "I sensed that there are other people with abilities."

Kim, Laura, Gavin, Emily's mouths opened in disbelief. The other kids had already been informed on the drive over, but they added to the influx of questions that Amanda was now bombarded with.

"How is this even possible? Where are they? Are they coming for us? What's going on?"

Amanda hollered. "I don't know anything else!"

Thomas stepped forward and put his hands up to calm his family. "I also have something to get off my chest."

The group collectively quieted down and focused on Thomas' next words.

"Listen, this isn't going to be easy to swallow, but I have a secret laboratory," he pointed, "right behind those doors. The scientists inside have worked tirelessly, for months, to develop a serum; a serum that endows abilities to normal human beings."

It was as if a pandemonium bomb had detonated as everyone immediately proclaimed disbelief and shock. Their collective voices filled the room, but Laura's rose above all the rest.

"Are you shitting me right now? Have you not learned anything from what Dr. Matsushita did?"

Thomas waited patiently for his family's energy to die down before he could explain himself.

"We're under siege," he reminded them, "and we can't hide anymore. They're going to keep coming after us, over and over and over again. I took steps to help protect ourselves from the tsunami of violence that continues to threaten us all."

He lowered his voice.

"I thought that becoming the President of the United States would shield us, but all it's really done is extended the inevitable, and that hasn't worked in our favor. For those of you that aren't aware, the assassination attempt on my family's lives was successful."

He looked around at shocked faces.

"Yes, that's right, we drowned in the river, and it was only by sheer dumb luck that I was able to perform a time-shift that prevented our demise."

Widened eyes stared back at Thomas.

He continued. "North Korea, China, Russian and the Vatican have repeatedly tried to kill us, and they will continue to do so. Hell, for all we know there's additional nations or factions that now deem us threats as well. I couldn't just sit around and hope for the best. That's both unrealistic and incredibly dangerous. Each of you have every right to live your lives without fear. And while that statement alone might sound naïve, given the range of abilities in this room alone, the reality is that 'hoping' things would work out is just as naïve.

"I took action and I have the results to prove that the serum works."

Laura continued. "I can't believe you held this back from me, and from everyone else. We're your family and you're supposed to trust us."

"I do trust you," he implored.

"Then why didn't you tell us?" Kim asked.

"Listen. It all boils down to a single word; hope. I could have told you my plan, but what if it failed? What if you all saw the benefits of adding more people to our side of the battle, and then to have that hope snatched away from you when the serum didn't work."

Thomas looked back over at his wife. "I'm not trying to emulate or become Dr. Matsushita."

"How is this any different?" Laura inquired.

"I didn't kidnap any children, for one," he shot back.

"You know that's not what I meant!"

It was if the air was sucked out of the room as they went head-to-head, except everyone had a ringside seat. Julie gently placed her hand on Laura's shoulder.

Emily jumped in. "Dad, mom's right. Why is this any different?"

Thomas, somewhat flustered, looked at his daughter and calmed down.

"I'm sorry, Laura. Everyone. I apologize. I just want you to be safe and I thought that taking this course of action would benefit us."

"You said you didn't kidnap any children to test on," Craig said out of the blue, "so how does any of this really work?"

Thomas got back on track. "During the serum's development, and throughout the latest batch of testing on live cell cultures, my scientists have produced two distinctive versions."

151

"Two versions of serum?" Gabbi asked.

Thomas nodded. "That's correct. The first strain, once injected, grants the individual a random, yet permanent ability. However, the mortality rate seems to be roughly ten to fifteen percent."

"And the second?" Gavin asked.

"The second strain is more viable overall. Not only does it bestow a known ability to the user, it's completely safe and only lasts twelve hours before it wears off."

"Wait, what?" Bill uttered. "You didn't tell us about that strain."

Kim admonished her husband. "Julie and I knew you two had something to do with this."

Thomas put his hands up before more questions could be asked.

"Listen, PORTAL was created, as you all know, to perform surgical strikes on specific targets. My plan was for PORTAL's operators to utilize the temporary serum on their missions. That's it."

"That's not the whole truth, is it?" Laura pressed.

"You're right, it isn't. To date there's only been one individual who's been injected with the permanent strain. All other tests have been conducted on live cultures, in petri dishes, to determine the cause and effect." He lowered his voice. "I'm not a monster. I'm only trying to fend off the ones who are coming for us."

"I didn't know," Laura said, "but I still wish you'd told us. We had a right to be a part of this from the start."

The others nodded in agreement.

"I apologize for keeping you in the dark."

Sarah put her hand up.

"Yes?"

"You said one person was given the permanent serum. What happened?"

"The volunteer, after discussing the risks, decided that the injection was worth the gamble."

"Who are they?" Sarah asked. "But more importantly, where are they?"

"They're close," Amanda announced.

Thomas nodded. "They are indeed."

He motioned to Sam who knocked on the lab's door. When the door opened a child appeared in the doorway. With utter disbelief, from everyone, that preteen walked over to Thomas and stood by his side. It was Gavin.

Stir immediately began to growl at the imposter, yet remained steadfast by the real Gavin's side.

"WHAT IN THE ACTUAL FUCK!" Laura screamed. "YOU CLONED GAVIN!?"

"Dad," Gavin said, "this is not okay. Not even a little bit."

Kim emulated everybody else's exact thoughts. "What the fuck is happening right now?"

The new Gavin closed his eyes and, as everyone witnessed, grew taller as he transformed from Gavin back to Dominick Knight.

"Holy fucking shit!" Bill exclaimed. "I didn't know that's what he could do!"

Stir continued to growl, but much lower, warning Dominick not to come any closer. Hobbes, like many, shook his head at the transformation. The family was used to their own abilities, but a doppelganger had taken them all by surprise. It took a bit for the excitement and wonder to wear off.

"I have a plan," Thomas announced, "of sorts. Dominick, who can now change forms at will, can masquerade as Gavin while a PORTAL mission is underway."

"I don't understand," Julie said.

"For plausible deniability," Sam said. "The world knows that Gavin makes portals. If he's by Thomas' side, publicly while something happens on the other side of the world, then there's no way the United States could be held responsible."

"Exactly," Thomas said.

But Gavin wasn't through with his father. "You did this without even telling me about it?"

"Son, I had no idea what ability Dominick would end up with."

Gavin shook his head. "Who are you right now? You left us to become The Caretaker, without telling us about it, returned to become President, and now this? This is too much."

"Son, I'm trying to protect all of you, and to do that I had to take drastic measures."

"You have a HELL of a way of showing it, dad." Gavin turned to his uncles. "Did you two know anything about this? You must have."

Bill shrugged. "The only thing we knew was to the extent when your father asked us to exhume Tad's body."

Kim couldn't believe her ears. "YOU DID WHAT!?"

Julie shook her head at Sam. "We're going to talk in-depth about this later."

"Fucking hell," Laura breathed. "This just keeps getting better and better. What's next, Thomas? What other surprises do you have in store for us?"

Thomas was confused. He knew there'd be some natural pushback, but he hadn't expected such violent reactions from his own family.

"I'm…I'm trying to protect you…"

"You keep saying that," Laura responded, "but I'm not convinced that this level of scheming is even warranted. I mean, what's next, banishing our enemies to The Other Place?"

Multiple discussions kicked up but were eventually interrupted by Amanda, of all people.

"Uncle Thomas?"

The group quieted down.

"Um, I don't know how to tell you this, but the people I sensed didn't include Dominick. The first time I felt him was when he was in the next room."

"Wait," Thomas said, "What do you mean? What are you saying?"

"I'm saying that I feel people with abilities on the other side of the world."

"I knew it!" Sam exclaimed. "We should have gone back for my daughter's blood when we assaulted the Pope's laboratory."

Bill was the first to pick up on the nuance. "Wait. Amanda, you can sense them, as well as the others in this room with abilities, but not Dominick?"

Amanda nodded. "I couldn't sense him until he was super close."

"Maybe," Thomas said, "it was something to do with Amanda sensing her own blood."

"That could make sense," Gabbi added, "since Dr. Matsushita, from the stories you've all told me, experimented with Edward, Craig, Sarah and Amanda."

"That was a different timeline," Thomas said.

Dom cocked his head slightly to one side. *Wait, what did he just say?*

"And," Laura said, "not relevant to our immediate problem, because we now know the Pope has his own lab, along with his own serum."

Hobbes chimed in. "And that means more Templars, one way or another."

It was Dominick's turn. "I apologize if I'm overstepping, but it would appear we're not in control of the situation anymore, are we?"

"Dom's right," Bill said. "The Vatican wants us all dead and the Pope will do anything he can to make that happen. We can't just sit around and wait for another attack, because we damn well know that one's coming." He turned to Laura. "I'm sorry we kept this from you and everyone else, but as it turns out, whether we like it or not, Thomas' actions have paid off. It looks like we'll need the extra firepower, unless we're comfortable sending our kids to the front line."

"That's not fair," Kim retorted.

Bill nodded. "You're right, it's not, but it's our current reality. Sam and I have been training our children for one reason and one reason only; to survive." He looked around the room. "I take it we all want to live; to see another day? We've been through the ringer before, but now that one of our enemies has abilities, the harsh truth is that shit just got real and we have to do something about it."

\* \* \*

A portal opened in The Other Place before two people emerged on the small island. Amelia stood her ground while Dom took his time and looked around. Eventually he made his way back to his companion.

"Well done. I'm glad the vial you stole, and subjectively injected into yourself, granted you this incredible power."

"I am as well," she replied.

"Excellent."

Dominick looked at the boat that had been pulled onto the sand. "I don't suppose you can make a boat like the child can?" She shook her head. "I'm afraid that isn't possible." "Pity, but no matter. Having access to this place is enough." He scanned the horizon once again. *Oh yes, this will do nicely.*

\* \* \*

Dominick took a risk and inscribed a message to the other eleven in an encrypted online chat channel.

"As you're all aware, or soon will be, our North Korean asset has gone missing before he could be utilized. While he wasn't essential to our overall goal, his absence means we need to accelerate our current strategy. We only have a specific amount of time to destabilize the West and discredit the President of the United States."

China voiced their concern in the group chat. "Numerous attempts have already occurred. What would you have us do differently?"

"Perhaps succeeding is the obvious answer," quipped one of the others.

"Enough," Dom typed. "We have a supply of vials from the Vatican, but we'll need more. Thomas is nearly finished with his own research, and that means an entirely new supply to burgle."

"How would you like us to proceed?"

Their leader paused before he continued. "Two birds with one stone. We take out the Vatican and Thomas' credibility all in one fell stroke. Listen closely because this is what I need you to do."

Dom smiled from ear to ear as he typed out his instructions.

# 20
## March 30, 2005

Jennifer Myers, the President's Executive Admin and mole, with complete access to Thomas' schedule, left an encrypted message for Dominick that the family had planned an outing at the Smithsonian together.

Dom smiled as he read it.

*This is a perfect time to 'out' myself to the family and get them on my side with a classic misdirect. Why wouldn't they believe me when I explain I'm fighting to save their planet from an alien invasion? They'll lap it up and I'll be left in an even greater tactical position.*

*The first step towards global destabilization begins today.*

\* \* \*

The Suburban convoy came to a stop in front of the Smithsonian National Air & Space Museum. Darrell Mccoy was the first secret service agent to exit the vehicle and scan the area, followed by others from the detail. Satisfied, he raised his left cuff to his mouth.

"Clear."

The Suburban's confines housed the Clark's, the Paige's and the Nicholson's families. They'd forgotten the last time they'd enjoyed a day of relaxation together, and this museum excursion would be an ideal change from their daily homeschool experience. The museum hadn't been cordoned off or even closed off for the family's outing, so that meant a larger contingent of secret service were in attendance. A dozen of them headed inside the museum to

159

join the forward team that had been sent in advance, and to provide additional security.

Thomas, Laura, Emily, Gavin and Stir exited one Suburban. Behind them, in other vehicles, Sam, Julie, Amanda and Craig followed suit, alongside Bill, Kim, Sarah and Edward.

The director of the museum met them outside the entrance.

"Mr. President, it's an incredible honor to have you and your family with us today."

Thomas shook the director's hand. "It's our pleasure, Director...?"

"My apologies. It's Director Gable, sir."

"Thank you for opening your doors to us, Director Gable. I realize we'll draw some unnecessary attention, so we'll try to keep our visit low-key and stay out of your way."

"Nonsense. The Secret Service briefed my security team, so I'm sure they'll have everything under control as you explore what our museum has to offer."

Thomas smiled. "That's very kind of you. Shall we?"

Director Gable led the group inside to the large foyer filled with various spacecraft, all of which had been utilized throughout the decades.

"Oh wow!" Craig voiced in excitement as his eyes darted around.

The other kids couldn't help but take in the initial sights with an equal sense of awe. Before long the six of them, accompanied by Stir, began to inspect everything they'd laid their eyes on. The parents were somewhat apprehensive as the teens headed off, but that was somewhat alleviated as soon as they noticed Secret Service were everywhere, both in uniform and disguised as tourists.

Thomas turned back to Director Gable. "Thank you for your hospitality. We'll take it from here."

The Director smiled. "Yes, sir. Please enjoy yourselves."

The adults waited for the Director to depart before they chatted.

"I don't know how you put up with it," Sam began, "but does everybody kiss your ass that much?"

The others chuckled as the group of parents headed into the exhibit, accompanied by Darrell.

"Trust me," Thomas replied, "it takes some getting used to."

"To continue with the ass-kissing tradition," Bill said, "thanks for putting this outing together."

"You need to thank Laura. She's well aware of our family's wellbeing, not to mention the limited activities available in the bunker."

Laura took Thomas' hand in hers. "I thought we could all use a break," she declared.

Kim and Julie nodded. "And that's why we agreed so quickly," Julie said. "Besides, I can't really recall the last time we were together."

Kim nodded in agreement. "It has felt like forever."

"My apologies," Bill told Laura. "Sam and I should have realized you were the actual brains behind this."

Thomas caught Darrell's smile out of the corner of his eye. "Something amusing, Darrell?"

"No, sir."

Thomas grinned. "Welcome to my family dynamics, Darrell. I've known these two knuckleheads since we were kids. I expect some shit talking from them, along with their honesty."

"Yes, sir." He paused for a second. "I'm going to hang back, sir, but I'll be right here if you need anything."

"Thank you, Darrell."

"He's as professional as they come," Sam said.

Thomas agreed. "And I wouldn't want it any other way."

The adults continued further into the massive room as they checked out the Apollo 11 Command Module. Their gaggle of kids were farther away and admiring a pressure suit that was worn on that same mission.

"I miss this," Julie said as she watched their children interact with each other.

"It's absolutely endearing is what it is," Kim added. "To think about all we've been through together…"

Laura put her hand on Kim's shoulder. "It's been more than any of us should have to burden ourselves with, but you're right…, they've all come a long way together and in such a relatively short amount of time."

Sam and Bill grinned and bumped fists.

Julie didn't let it slide. "We saw that."

"Saw what?" Sam innocently asked.

"You two don't get all the credit just because you think your training regime made this all happen. It was a team effort."

Sam smiled. "I wouldn't dare. Now Bill on the other hand…"

"Hey!" Bill quipped.

Thomas chuckled. It'd been a hot minute since he'd seen his family actually be able to relax and enjoy themselves. They'd all been on the defensive for far too long, so this was a pleasant diversion from the norm.

*

An hour later, with unfettered access to a variety of aviation vehicles the United States had designed and implemented, the family took refuge in the Lockheed Martin IMAX Theater. The Secret Service had already cordoned off the theater from other civilians as the family donned their newly acquired glasses. A few

162

seconds later 'Journey to Space 3D' began on the gigantic screen as planets, asteroids and space ships zoomed past their faces.

As the adventure continued to unfold, along with the incredible surround sound and lighting system, other special effects were brought into play to accentuate the experience. Each seat was equipped with spray nozzles that, on que, would dispense puffs of air or a fine mist to coincide with events on screen. A rocket, at Cape Canaveral, began its ten-second countdown and its thrusters pre-ignited, the family's seats rumbled and came to life, along with the additional special effects. It was exhilarating.

As the rocket lifted off the ground fog surged out from beneath the massive screen and quickly enveloped the entire theater.

Amanda put her hand to her head. "It hurts....oh shit." She tore off her 3D glasses and screamed. "THEY'RE HERE!"

The family barely had time to register her screams as a barrage of gunfire erupted just outside the theater doors.

Sam and Bill instinctively reached for their weapons only to realize they weren't armed. The fog intensified and obscured everyone's vision.

"PORTAL!" Thomas yelled.

As Stir's green eyes pierced the haze, and the family closed ranks together, Gavin formed his gateway. The newly created doorway became a beacon for the family to run towards as multiple secret service agents crashed through the theater's doors as they fired at unknown assailants in their wake.

"GO!" Sam bellowed.

Two agents toppled over when a salvo of automatic gunfire perforated their bodies. Their death cries reverberated throughout the dense atmosphere.

Sam and Bill propelled Julie and Kim towards the safety of Gavin's portal as their kids, from a propensity of training, joined hands and blinked out of existence.

"NO!" Kim shrieked as they disappeared.

Thomas, sensing the worst, used his telekinetic ability to propel Laura, Emily, Julie and Kim through the opening to safety right before their attackers forced their way into the theater.

"Go!" Thomas urged his son.

A hand, seemingly out of nowhere, reached up from the floor and grabbed hold of Gavin. The shock caused Gavin to lose his concentration and the portal snapped shut. Stir leapt to his master's defense and tore the assailant's hand clean off.

A man emerged from the theater's floor, and screamed as he clutched his stump, his ability to camouflage no longer a viable entity.

In that split second Thomas knew who they were up against. *Templars.*

The fog began to lift as Sam, Bill and Thomas nodded to each other. It was time to fight or die.

Two more Templars entered through the theater doors, each wielding automatic rifles. As they took aim Thomas ripped the weapons from their hands and deposited them in his friend's outstretched ones.

The two Templars pivoted their attack on the fly. One transformed into a panther while the other began to rapidly climb the theater wall.

"WHAT THE ACTUAL FUCK!" Sam yelled as he shifted left, and stitched the theater's wall with multiple rounds.

Bill locked his sights on the panther as the beast leapt at him.

"FUCK ME!" he voiced as he swung his weapon around.

The panther swatted the rifle out of the way before he pounced on Bill, only to be catapulted across the theater, thanks to Thomas. As that occurred four other Templars emerged from the technical alcove, that existed behind the huge screen, with their weapons at the ready and opened fire. Rounds punched into the seats around Thomas and Gavin as the two hit the deck.

Sam finally put two bullets into the wallcrawler as Bill retrieved his discarded weapon. As the dead Templar slid off the wall the two men barely located cover before a multitude of slugs peppered the ground where they'd once stood.

Additional secret service agents rushed through the theater's entrances as the panther righted itself. As the agents trained their sights on the beast every single seat began to spray water. One of the Templars controlled that water and rapidly coalesced it together. The airborne water formed a makeshift shield and absorbed the oncoming rounds the agents fired at them.

Thomas crawled over to Gavin as Stir ended the camouflaged Templar's life. But, as he reached his son, Sarah disengaged her invisibility to reveal that Craig, Amanda and Edward still remained behind.

"Shit," Thomas breathed out.

Before he could say anything else, Sarah grabbed Gavin's hand and disappeared, along with the others.

The agents reached for new magazines as the water bubble plummeted to the floor. Before they could rearm the Templar's weapons belched out death, from across the theater's expanse, and cut the four agents down.

The panther shifted into a mouse and scurried underneath the theater's chairs while the other four Templars found cover. There they swapped out their empty magazines for new ones.

Sam noticed his engagement with the wallcrawler had depleted his weapon and shook his head. Bill, on the other hand, still had a full magazine at his disposal.

"Thomas Clark, reveal yourself and prepare to be judged by the right hand of God!"

"Who are you!?" Thomas yelled back.

"My name is Marcus. I lead these righteous Templar Knights."

"You've come at me before," Thomas replied, still crouched behind one of the theater's seats, "but that didn't work out for your predecessor, did it?"

"Gabriel didn't have the power of God coursing through his veins like we do."

"So, you're here to kill me I take it?"

"You and the rest of your repugnant family. You're all abominations that need to be purged."

"Wouldn't that make you and your men abominations as well?"

"We fulfill the will of the Pope, and he takes his orders from God himself."

Thomas caught Bill's eye and they shared a quick nod. "The insanity runs deep within that cult of yours. The man you revere used science, not God, to give you whatever abilities you and your men now possess."

Marcus gripped his weapon tighter and scowled. "I have enhanced reflexes, Thomas. I will be the end of you."

"That fog was a cute trick, and so was your man who could cling to the walls, but you and I both know those abilities are but parlor tricks compared to what I can do to you. Your Pope is a pathetic, little man who couldn't even give you something to actually fight with. He doesn't love you. He never did. He used you, plain and simple. If anything, your false God is laughing at you. However, you've made one mistake."

"And what's that?"

"You came for my family."

Marcus emptied his weapon's magazine in Thomas' direction as the three others with him flanked Thomas' position. As the barrage of gunfire ended Thomas motioned to Bill and the two of them stood up together. Bill fired at the three Templars while Thomas yanked Marcus unexpectantly off his feet towards him.

Sam crawled, under cover, towards the Templars while Bill shot at them.

When the Templars returned fire Thomas used Marcus as a shield, but as the bullets burrowed into the leader's body a mouse scurried out from underneath the seat. Stir lunged at it, but before he could get his mouth around it the Templar transformed into an enormous bear and deftly swatted Stir to the end of the aisle.

Thomas barely had time to toss Marcus' corpse towards the other Templars before the bear clamped down on his left arm. There was a loud crunch as his arm snapped. Thomas screamed in anguish as the bear thrashed back and forth.

"DAD!" Gavin screamed, as he appeared out of nowhere.

Bill rushed to Thomas' defense and jumped on the bear's back, his arm around its neck, to no avail.

Stir recovered. He found his footing, charged the bear and clamped his sharp teeth around the beast's testicles. The Templar shrieked in agony as Thomas fell to the floor. His blood gushed everywhere.

As the three Templars ejected their spent magazines, Sam pushed himself off the floor, jumped the seats and rushed the closest one. He grabbed his enemy's weapon and twisted sharply, which threw the Templar off balance. He then kicked him in the stomach as the other two raised their weapons in his direction.

Craig, Amanda, Edward and Sarah materialized behind the two men. Craig immediately touched them both, which caused their bodies and their weapons to phase out, right as they depressed their triggers. The stream of automatic bullets leapt out of their barrels, across the short distance at Sam, but passed through him rather than the deathblow that was inevitable.

Gavin ran towards his father as the bear catapulted Bill two aisles over. The bear, a ragged hole where its testicles used to reside, reverted back to human form and fell to his knees. Stir spat out his trophy and went for the man's throat just as Gavin arrived at his father's side, although he slipped in blood before he was able to get to work.

Sam wrestled the rifle free from the Templar and bashed him in the head with it. As the man toppled over, Sam plucked a full magazine from the man's belt, finished his own reload before he pointed his weapon at the two who were phased out.

Out of nowhere, as if by magic, Dominick materialized next to Sam. Everyone jumped, including Craig, and he lost his concentration.

*Tada! I'm here! Wait, what's goi-*

The Templars sent a burst into Dom's chest. Dom dropped before Sam felled them with headshots. He turned around and silenced the one he'd clubbed in the face.

Dom raised his head and gazed at the holes in his chest.
*I...I...got shot.*

Sam crouched down by Dominick as he swept the room for additional threats. Bill managed to finally right himself from between two chairs he'd been tossed into.

Sam looked over at the kids. "Are you guys alright?"

They nodded as Gavin worked on healing his father's arm. The kids froze as they took in the dead men on the ground. Their copious wounds, inert bodies and blank stares were harsh reminders how serious this situation really was. The Templars, and the extremely loud firefight, had been all too real. Sam motioned to Bill to get eyes on Thomas before he went to check the vitals of the downed secret service agents. When Bill reached Thomas' side the President sat up on his own accord and rubbed his bloodied arm.

"Shit, that really fucking hurt." He looked down at his son. "Thank you. Are you okay?"

Gavin nodded and hugged his father tightly. Stir came over and nuzzled in between them, bloody muzzle and all.

"And thank you too," he said as he scratched Stir's rear-end.

It wasn't long before they were interrupted.

"Um, Uncle Thomas," Sarah announced from across the theater. "You need to see this."

Dom looked up at the children's faces as they stared down at him. *I...didn't...think...it...would...end...like...this.*

Bill helped pull Thomas to his feet.

"Are you hurt? What is it?"

"Just get over here."

Thomas, Bill, Gavin and Stir stepped over dead Templars as they made their way down the aisle towards the others.

"Bill, grab a few extra mags," Sam said as he reloaded again. "We don't know if there's any additional threats outside the theater. We may not be out of danger."

"Roger that."

Sam plucked a radio off one of the downed agents. "This is Sam Paige to all secret service on this channel. There's been an assassination attempt on the President of the United States by Vatican Templar Knights. Seven tangos have been eliminated. There are multiple agents down. Send backup."

Sam dropped the radio before he and Bill tactically opened the door. He motioned it was clear before he paused and looked back.

"You guys good here?"

Thomas nodded. Sam and Bill, weapons at the ready, moved out.

"What's going on?"

The kids pointed at Dominick as Stir began to growl. Each of the four wounds oozed a blue substance.

169

*What the hell?*

Thomas knelt down by Dom's side and placed his ear by the man's mouth.

"He's still breathing. Gav, can you do your thing?"

Gavin placed his hands on Dominick's chest and closed his eyes. His healing ability washed over Dom's injuries and it didn't take long before Dom sputtered and coughed up some blue spittle.

"It's working."

The kids gathered around Dom as Gavin continued.

"Why is his blood blue?" Craig asked.

"I don't know," Thomas replied, "but I do know that I need to get you back to your mothers as soon as possible. They need to know you're alright."

Gavin pulled away his hands as the four puncture wounds closed. Four bullets slid off on the floor as Dom lifted himself into a sitting position. The kids took a tentative step back, unsure of the situation as Stir took a defensive stance.

"You okay?" Thomas asked.

Dom felt his chest where he'd been struck. "I...I..."

"Relax, it takes some getting used to." Thomas turned towards the kids. "We're not safe yet so Gavin's going to send you to the island to join the others. Tell them I'll be along shortly. You all did well today and should be proud of yourselves."

Edward protested. "But what about his blue blood?"

"I'll handle it. You all need to leave. Now."

Gavin formed his portal as Stir stood guard, he never took his eyes off Dom. The kids, along with Gavin and Stir, entered the rift and disappeared.

Thomas turned back towards Dom and promptly used his ability to place a death grip around the man's neck.

"Who.the.hell.are.you?"

Dom struggled against the invisible shackle that had taken away his air supply. "You...don't...need...to...do...this..."

"Talk!"

Dom suddenly blinked and appeared five feet away, free of Thomas' grip. He put his hands up as Thomas registered what'd just occurred.

"I'm not a threat."

"You...you just teleported."

Dom nodded. "I did indeed."

"But the ability you gained was shapeshifting." Thomas stared at him. "What are you?"

Dom smiled. "You're starting to believe, to think outside the box now, aren't you?"

Thomas was dubious. "What's this all about? What's your game?"

*Here we go.* Dom pointed towards an empty theater seat. "May I?"

Thomas relaxed, slightly, and nodded.

Dom began as soon as he sat down. "Bear with me. My home planet was destroyed by The Ancient eons ago. We're known as Zarans, and we lived on a planet called Zara eight-four-four."

Thomas blinked a few times. "You're from another planet?"

"I am, but that's inconsequential to the story at hand."

Thomas shifted. "All right. Continue."

"Before The Ancient completely annihilated my planet, some of us were able to escape by ship."

"A space ship?"

"Correct."

Behind Thomas a Templar opened his eyes, rolled to his side and recovered a fallen assault rifle. He pushed himself to his knees and screamed as he pointed it at Thomas.

"I AM IMMORTAL!"

Dom teleported to the man's side and deflected the weapon just as it discharged. Thomas felt the bullets whiz by his head. A split second later he wrenched the weapon from the assassin's grip and crushed it into metal in front of the Templar's face.

Dom subdued the man before Thomas let the buckled mass fall to the floor.

"I AM GOD! I HAVE THE POWER OF GOD HIMSELF!"

"Do shut up," Thomas said and nodded at Dom.

Dom struck the man across the temple, which rendered him unconscious.

Thomas looked over at the theater's entrance, then back at Dom. "We don't have a lot of time. Finish your story."

Dom secured the man's hands behind his back and stood up.

"The ship I was on crashed into Earth's ocean two-hundred years ago. Those of us who were able to escape had no other choice other than blend in."

"There's a lot more to it than that."

Dom nodded. "Much more I'm afraid. A splinter faction formed and broke off from the main group. They wanted to take over the planet immediately, but we overpowered and placed them in stasis fields, something akin to cryogenic freezing. However, it's come to my attention that they've somehow escaped that containment."

"How many are we talking about?"

"Twelve."

Thomas pondered. "What's your name? Your real name?"

"My species tends to go more by identifiers, but for the purpose of time you can call me Qhautuix."

"Maybe I'll stick with Dom."

"Suit yourself, sir."

"You said my serum gave you shapeshifting. That was a lie, wasn't it?"

172

"It was. Zarans can shapeshift at will. Your serum allows me to teleport, of all things. It's been quite useful."

"I bet. What else."

"Aside from The Ancient, we're aware of The Caretaker and The Other Place."

Thomas became visibly shaken. "I don't understand. How is that possible?"

"The Caretaker tried to intervene, but ultimately failed to save our planet. That's a story for another time. What's important for you to realize, sir, is that my people are aware that The Caretaker is no longer a problem."

"A problem? Explain."

Dom nodded. "The splinter group can now freely enact their plans without fear of reprisal. It was, in fact, The Caretaker's presence that prevented the other faction from supplanting the denizens of this world. What I'm trying to get at is that your world is in peril."

"What could twelve of your people really accomplish?"

"Just about anything. They all shapeshift, which means they could already be in positions of power, or have replaced those in power with doppelgangers. Anything's possible."

Thomas pondered that for a few seconds. "Why did you come here today?

*Because I'm eventually going to kill you.* "I wanted to talk with you, to warn you."

"You picked a really bad moment."

"I'll give you that, sir," Dom said as he glanced down at his blue-stained shirt.

Thomas waited a second. "Why reveal yourself to me at all?"

"That's easy. It's because this is your home and my people have seen you fight for it, time and time again."

"But?"

"You're perceptive. We need your abilities to win against the twelve."

"Why should I trust you?"

"Why reveal myself to you at all, Thomas?"

"You were bleeding blue. It was kind of a giveaway."

*That was entirely unexpected.* "True, but I'm here talking to you now because your planet is on a clock. The twelve have infiltrated the Vatican and are in possession of the Pope's version of the serum, as you're well aware. It's only a matter of time before all their pieces fall into place, and when that happens, we'll all be left holding the short end of the stick. It'll all be over before anyone knows what happened.

"Listen, the attack on your kids at school..,, the CIA said it was the Russians."

"You're saying it wasn't?"

"I'm telling you it was the splinter group. They've been sowing discord and have taken control of the narrative for months."

"Okay then. What if I do believe you. Where are these twelve?"

"That's the point, I don't know. But if we work together then we can find and take them out, because more attacks are imminent, which means more innocent lives are at stake."

Thomas gestured at Dom's appearance. "Is that what your species really looks like? Human?"

"No. My true form would frighten you." *And I'll make sure to be in it when I tear you limb from limb.*

"Try me."

Dom adjusted slightly. "Very well."

His body began to morph. It grew bigger as two additional arms sprouted out of his torso, then transformed into mandibles connected to an armored shell. All six appendages were outfitted

174

with spikes, and on top his head was adorned with sharp teeth. It reminded Thomas of Stir's mouth as the creature, once human, towered over him at eight feet.

"Seen enough, Mr. President?"

*Fucking hell.* Thomas swallowed hard as he tried to contain the shiver that ran down his spine. "That's quite enough."

Thomas heard a commotion as a dozen agents flooded the theater from both entrances. As they swarmed Thomas looked back at Dom and was relieved to see that he'd vanished.

"Mr. President! Are you okay, sir?" one of the agents asked as he stared at Thomas' blood-soaked arm.

"I'm fine."

"We need to get you out of here, sir. Stand by."

The agent spoke into his radio. "Citadel is secure. I repeat, Citadel is secure. Moving towards transport."

"Where's Darrell?"

The agent's face fell and Thomas understood. "He didn't make it, did he?"

"Sir, we need to go, now."

\* \* \*

Thomas embraced Laura the moment he returned to The White House. She became visibly shocked as Thomas relayed what'd occurred, but was relieved that he and Gavin had survived the ordeal. It didn't take long for him to tell her about Dom's true identity and the apparent danger the world was in.

\*

Sam and Bill had made it home with their families, now dealing with combat fatigue and the day's ambush fresh in their minds. When Sam's personal phone rang, he saw that it was Thomas, and answered without hesitation. After affirming that everyone was okay, Thomas shared the new information.

It did not go over well.

* * *

Dom teleported away from Thomas and appeared at his Minnesota estate. He accessed the encrypted chat channel and typed in the following.

*Initiate phase two.*

He stepped back and shook his head. *Saved by a child. That'll come back to haunt me.*

* * *

Thomas was explaining to Andrew Shaw, in private, about Dominick and the alien incursion, when one of the Oval Office doors burst open and a contingent of military personnel, along with the Secretary of State and Defense, entered the room.

"Mr. President, there's been a brazen attack on the Vatican!"

Thomas gave them a strange look. "The Vatican?"

"Yes, sir. We have a satellite view, and a variety of news channels have begun to air their footage. We need to head to the PEOC right now, sir."

"What kind of attack?"

"An explosion, sir. A huge explosion."

When they arrived, the large screens displayed both satellite and news stations. There, undeniably, a hefty portion of the Vatican was in ruins. Smoke billowed upwards from multiple unchecked fires and the surrounding area showed vast devastation as well, clearly from an incredible blast that had decimated the hallowed city.

Translations from Italian news channels revealed that the Pope hadn't been located and was presumed dead, along with hundreds of protestors that had filled St. Peter's Square.

Thomas could only stare at the absolute unimaginable level of destruction as it continued to unfold in front of his very eyes.

*What in the absolute hell happened?*

His personal phone chirped and he answered it without thinking. "Yes?"

"It's started."

Thomas pulled his eyes away from the horrific images. "Dom?"

"Yes, Mr. President, it's me. We didn't get to finish our conversation earlier, but it looks like we may not be able to."

"You just said it's started. What's started?"

"They're coming for the planet, sir, and I believe this is their first strike."

Thomas shook his head. "You said your species can all shapeshift."

"Yes, sir."

"Then who's to say the twelve haven't already embedded themselves in other strategic locations in an effort to repeat what I'm staring at right now?"

"Mr. President, that's exactly what I warned you about."

\*

Dom ended the call with Thomas and grinned from ear to ear.

*He's shitting himself right about now.*

He turned back to the chat channel and typed in another message.

*Get him in front of a camera and then meet me at Thomas' lab.*
*We're taking everything.*

* * *

"Good evening and welcome to the six o'clock news. Earlier today, in two unprecedented displays of violence, assassination attempts were made on both the President of the United States, while he and his family were at the Smithsonian; and the Pope, at his home in Vatican City, Italy.

"However, the details of the attack on the President haven't been released by The White House as of yet, but the Pope has circulated a video that both condemns the bombing of Vatican City and evidence of two men the Pope claims were behind the attack."

The screen transitioned to the Pope's prerecorded statement of him, still dressed in his religious robes, now torn and dirtied from his harrowing experience.

"I survived. By the grace of God, I survived." His eyes narrowed. "I know who did this. I know which country is responsible for the deaths of innocents, and who clearly have a blatant disregard for human life. It was the United States of America. Their president, Thomas Clark, ordered my assassination and I have proof."

A second video began to play and was immediately discernable as closed-circuit surveillance footage. On it, cut from a variety of angles, two men infiltrated the tunnels that ran under Vatican City through a storm drain, then cut through a steel door to gain access to and bypass the alarm sensors. Once they were in the tunnels, they proceeded to silently neutralize any opposition they came across before they planted explosives at the base of key support columns.

At the end, after the two men left the area, a tremendous explosion destroyed every camera, but not before multiple angles zoomed in on the men's recognizable faces.

The Pope continued. "For those of you who don't know who these men are, I'll tell you. They are Thomas Clark's closest friends, Sam Paige and Bill Nicholson. They are the co-founders of SANDBOX, part of the military spec-ops community, and clearly have knowledge and access to military grade explosives. The President of the United States ordered my assassination, and he utilized his friends to do it."

The Pope shifted gears.

"The world hangs on the precipice, and its people need religion now, more than ever. For those of you who have lost faith, come back into the fold and do not succumb to false prophets such as Thomas Clark and his parlor tricks.

"He failed to silence my voice and he failed to silence those who believe in God Almighty. Are you going to allow Thomas Clark to silence yours? The world is watching."

\*   \*   \*

Media outlets throughout the world continued to play the Pope's video on repeat, and the horror and disgust it garnered was palpable. Protests sprang up around the globe as wave after wave of people demanded justice. Calls for Thomas' impeachment and his immediate prosecution ran rampant throughout the United States.

The world had just become that much closer to a tipping point.

Thomas, Gavin and Stir appeared in ORACLE's basement and immediately discovered the place was deserted. The lab's door had been breached. There weren't any bodies or blood, but the place had been emptied. Even the two scientists were nowhere to be found.

"Shit," Thomas breathed out as he looked around.

They cautiously moved forward, pushed the broken door out of the way, and entered the lab. Everything was smashed, broken or destroyed. When they reached the storage room Thomas already knew what he'd find. It'd been cleared out.

"Dad, I need to tell you something."

"Not now, son," he said as he took it all in.

*All that work. Gone. And for what? Nothing. What the hell do I do now?*

He left the storage area and headed back into the lab. Gavin and Stir followed behind.

*I keep failing. I just wanted to protect my family, but these attacks keep coming at us from multiple fronts. And now the people cry for my impeachment, all based on an elaborate lie. They really have been planning this coup for a long time, and I played right into their hands.*

Stir began to growl as he took a few steps towards the lab's breached doorway. Thomas raised his hands to fight when Hobbes and Gabbi appeared. The two looked around in disbelief. Stir stopped growling.

"Should Hobbes and I even ask what happened here?"

"Betrayal seems to be the word of the day." Thomas stepped towards them. "I'm really happy you're both alright."

"Are you?" Hobbes asked.

Thomas tilted his head and took a second to answer. "It's been a hell of a day. An assassination attempt by the Templars started it off, followed by being framed for trying to kill the Pope and destroying the Vatican. So yeah, I'm doing about the best that I can right now."

Gabbi swept her arm around the room. "And this?"

"More failure on my part."

"I don't understand. What's going on?"

"Shit," Thomas said. "That's right, you don't know about the aliens."

Hobbes and Gabbi shared a concerned look. "Aliens?"

* * *

## March 31, 2005

Dom smiled as the others gathered for their covert meeting. The attack on the Vatican, along with the successful framing job, marked the start of their race's resurgence.

"Thank you for joining me, my friends. Our plan to take this planet for our own has finally begun, especially since we've replaced a number of world leaders and can now traverse The Other Place The Caretaker used to call his own."

"What about the boy and his pet?" one of them asked. "That remaining piece of The Ancient could be our downfall."

"Nonsense," the leader assured them. "We have the stockpile of serum from the Vatican and Thomas Clark's lab in our possession. We also have the scientists who created it. When we release the rest of our people, out of their stasis fields, we'll have a division. When we call out to the others who've been waiting,

182

we'll have an army. When we imbue each of them with that serum, we'll have a legion. Then endgame is upon us and we're going to enact it piece by piece, just as we planned."

"No," one of them said. "We've waited for over two-hundred years and we're impatient. We want this planet now. I can't wait any longer. I won't wait any longer."

Dominick sauntered over to the bold dissenter. "Do you speak for yourself, or are there others here that feel the same way?"

"I spe-"

A blade swiftly entered the man's belly and propelled upwards. The cut was deep as it exited the man's throat. He looked down in shock and horror as his entrails slid out of his chest cavity and landed on his feet. A few seconds later he collapsed to his knees, then toppled over onto his side.

"Is anyone else feeling impatient?" Dom asked, as the blue blood dripped off the knife in his hand.

The remaining ten transformed to their true forms in anger at their fallen comrade. Their four bug arms writhed in rage as they came at their leader.

"ENOUGH!" he shouted at them while he maintained his human form. "WE'VE COME TOO FAR TO THROW IT ALL AWAY!"

The others slowed their advance.

"You've trusted me to make this planet our own, and I will not fail you. Our strategy will continue as planned." He turned to one member specifically. "Are the other locations prepped with ordinance?"

The ten shifted back to human.

"No, sir. There's still additional work to be completed."

"Then get to it and move those materials through the portal system. The people of this planet aren't just going to hand it over to us. We must make them fear for their very lives before we're able to swoop in as their saviors."

* * *

## Friday, April 1, 2005

"...along with the traffic on 395, should make for a delightful weekend if you plan on visiting any of the attractions Washington D.C. has to offer."

The anchor put his hand to his earpiece as he listened to his producer issue him a new story.

"We have breaking news. The President of the United States, Thomas Clark, was just impeached. Andrew Shaw, the Vice President and previous Assistant Director of the FBI, has now been sworn in as the President. And while it is the first of April, this is not a joke. President Clark was voted out of office by the House of Representatives just moments ago. Even more alarming was that the former president insisted that aliens were behind the Vatican bombing and are gearing up to take over planet Earth."

The anchor tried to make light of it all. "I don't know about you, but little green men running amok would be a welcome relief, especially after what the Pope and his catholic followers have been through these past few days."

He turned to face a different camera as pictures of Vatican City's destruction rotated in the background.

"The death toll in and around Vatican City continues to rise as cadaver dogs work to detect bodies from the devastating explosion that leveled a significant portion of the Vatican. A manhunt is underway for the two suspects, Sam Paige and Bill Nicholson, who were caught on security cameras as they planted explosives in the subterranean tunnels underneath the Vatican.

"So far, all leads to finding these men haven't panned out, and even the former President disavowed Mr. Paige and Mr. Nicholson's involvement.

"Earlier today our correspondents traveled to Vatican City and talked to those who had gathered to mourn. They also chatted with some of the first responders who were still digging through the rubble."

The scene shifted to a previously recorded video just outside St. Peter's Square. Hundreds of people had clogged the area to offer their thoughts and prayers. The reporters reached out to those in the crowd.

"Why are you here today?"

"I had to come and see the atrocities the President of the United States is responsible for. It's such a reprehensible act of violence, and as a Christian I am appalled and forever saddened."

"If you could say anything to the President, what would it be?"

"What I want to say and what I can say are two different things. However, with a heavy heart, Mr. President, you've started a war you can't possibly win. Christians will unite and vow their revenge, sir. God will triumph."

The anchor reappeared as Italy faded away.

"It is indeed another dark time for our country as we're rocked with a political scandal, one that unfortunately has affected hundreds of innocent Italians. Our hearts go out to the families of those who lost their lives during this dark time."

* * *

Dom knew he needed to keep the momentum going, especially that there were only eleven of them now.

185

*I can't believe he dared speak out against me, and in front of the others. His dissidence had to be immediately silenced, lest his independent thoughts linger in the ears of the others.*

Dom had Amelia transport the body to The Other Place, then gave her the exact coordinates to their crashed ship. Together they traversed through her portal and made their way to the specific island that would place them on their ship. As they arrived, they made their way to the eighty-eight stasis pods that remained. Of those, eight had failed, which left eighty Zarans for Dom to awaken.

"Are you sure this is what you want to do?" Amelia asked.

Dom turned to face her. "Are you having second thoughts?"

"No, of course not. We've been on this planet for the past two-hundred years, and I'm tired of not having a home. The Ancient nearly destroyed Earth as well, and now that he and The Caretaker are gone, we need to do whatever it takes to do what we came here to do."

"So, what's the problem?"

Amelia swept her hand back and pointed to the stasis pods. "The first thing they'll remember is that their planet was destroyed."

Dom was getting impatient. "And?"

"All I'm saying is that they won't all be onboard with this plan, much like the ten-thousand we're going to summon on the colony ship. What are you going to do with those that oppose you?"

"You've already seen what I do to those that step out of line."

"They're not warriors or fighters."

"We're all children of war," Dom countered. "Our ancestors poisoned our planet as they clashed with each other, and we're here now because of them."

"So, what are you going to do?"

"It'll be an easy question. Fight for your new home or die as if you never got on the colony ship in the first place. Besides, we need all hands-on deck for what's coming. The plan has to stay on schedule as we ratchet up the gravity of the situation. We need to make all humans feel that there's no other choice but to bend the knee."

* * *

## April 2, 2005

Americans woke to mass devastation as they were confronted with images splashed across every television channel and the internet. Overnight, in what appeared to be a synchronized attack, explosions detonated in Paris, France; Cologne, Germany; and in London. The three targets were the Eiffel Tower, the Cologne Cathedral and the Tower of London.

Each of those nation's prized, cherished and popular attractions had been decimated. What remained consisted of twisted, blackened metal, rubble and smokey ruins. The explosions, as they'd occurred, sent out tremendous shockwaves in all directions, which caused secondary and tertiary blasts from the neighboring businesses and residences. It was as if colossal payload had been dropped from a military bomber.

The silence that immediately followed was deafening, but was short-lived as the screams of the dying and the injured quickly filled that void.

An unknown attacker, clearly organized, equipped and funded, had perpetrated these atrocities, but no one knew who to point their finger at. The dreadful images and videos were looped over and over and over again.

At exactly eight in the morning, eastern time, as those who'd already heard about the attacks in Europe and those who were on their way to work in America, witnessed the unimaginable. The Statue of Liberty, with the sun rising behind it, abruptly tilted to its side. A second later the sound of an intense explosion, followed by a shockwave, raced across New York Bay and down multiple congested streets. People could only watch in horror as gravity tore the symbol of peace off its mooring before it plummeted into the ocean.

The attacks in Europe, a place far away, were now as evident as ever. The message was plain and simple. No one was safe.

Worldwide panic, which had begun with the destruction of the Vatican, ramped up further as citizens feared for their lives.

The news continued to air footage, from all four devastated locations. However, unlike traditional terrorist attacks, no one stepped forward to claim responsibility. And that, in itself, heightened the public's desperation to an entirely new level.

* * *

Dom praised his followers via a secure internet chat channel.

"Well done. Continue to incite fear, confusion and desperation into this world's population. They will turn on themselves soon enough."

He ended the call and addressed Gretchen, his spy within ORACLE.

"How soon until I can notify the others?"

"I've modified the array and adapted it for the transmission. It would have been faster if I had access to our escape ship."

"All in good time," he told her. "Continue."

"It wasn't easy, but our message should reach and awaken our people shortly after it's sent."

"Excellent. Hold off for the moment."

"Why? We need additional resources now. I don't understand."

"It's not up to you to see the entire plan, just to do your part, much like the others. That is, unless, you'd prefer our collective to be short another member."

Gretchen lowered her eyes. "No, of course not."

"The world needs to be fully engulfed in chaos before we execute the final act of our plan."

"But what about Thomas Clark and his family? They haven't been dealt with."

He chuckled. "I've got a way to take them out. Trust me. This world will be ours soon enough, and it'll be even easier to take it away from these humans once Thomas is out of the way."

*　*　*

Gavin's portal snapped shut as he and Stir rejoined the family.

Laura was the first to act. "You can't just take off, especially with everything that's happening. We're been worried sick. Where have you been?"

"There's no time," Gavin announced.

"No time for what?" Thomas replied.

"You'll see."

"Gav, the world's imploding and we're sequestered in a bunker from aliens. Your uncles and I are actively trying to come up with a game plan."

Gavin's face resonated the gravity of the situation. "You don't understand. You have to come with me, right now."

Thomas, and the rest of the family, finally listened.

"What is it?" his mother insisted.

Gavin didn't answer and formed his portal instead. "We'll need a camera."

*

Thomas, Laura, Sam and Bill stared at the jumble of intermixed arms and limbs. Gavin had taken them to the island Stir had alerted him to. There, a jumble of corpses had been dumped into a haphazard pile.

The four adults stepped closer and cringed.

"What in the hell?" Bill voiced.

Thomas was the first to recognize the dead bodies. "Sonofabitch."

"What?" Sam asked.

Thomas pointed. "That's the Pope."

"But he's on televi-". Sam stopped as the realization hit him. "Shit."

Thomas continued as he stepped closer. "And that one is the Russian president...; and that one is the German Chancellor...; and the Chinese president is here." Thomas looked back at the others. "Shit. I know some of these leaders personally. I've had them to The White House. I...I...they've been replaced. Fuck. This is so much bigger than I could have ever imagined."

"They've been planning this for ages," Bill said, "which means they've infiltrated world governments at the highest levels."

Sam continued the train of thought. "The destruction of the Vatican was meant to discredit us. It was also used to cover up evidence of the Pope's laboratory, then they burgled your supply and took your scientists, Thomas."

"What I see," Laura said, "is a meticulously planned assault on our world; one that has been successfully orchestrated and

190

implemented. But the aliens didn't expect anyone to come across these," as she swept her arm, "bodies."

"Laura's right," Thomas said. "If we can get this proof into the right hands, then maybe the world will start taking the alien threat seriously while there's still time."

"Maybe," Bill said.

"We have to try. Shaw believes me and that's all that matters right now. We get him photos of these murdered world leaders, especially ones that are actively alive and promoting fear, and maybe there's a chance people will come around."

"I'm on it." Bill moved in closer and captured the scene on film.

"The world isn't ready to believe," Sam told Thomas. "They still don't accept you and your abilities."

Thomas nodded. "I know, but what else are we supposed to do, just sit back and let them take our planet?

"I'm not advocating for that outcome whatsoever."

"I know, I just don't know where that leaves our families, other than stuck right in the middle of shitsville all over again."

"We know we're in way over our heads, that much is certain, so when Bill is done, we'll head back to the bunker." Sam turned to Gavin. "We'll need Stir to make sure we're all who we say we are before we reinforce our position."

Gavin nodded.

Sam readdressed Laura and Thomas. "We've been a threat the entire time, and until we've been silenced, they're going to come after us, especially since we won't know who to trust. We need to up our potential."

"Are you advocating what I think you're advocating?"

Sam nodded. "The kids stole the serum for a reason. We need all the help we can get. Maybe it's time we used it."

## April 3, 2005

"Newly released photos, supplied directly from The White House, indicate that multiple world leaders have been murdered. But is this just another trick?"

The news anchor shifted his gaze to another camera while the photos in question were displayed.

He continued with the report. "The identities of the leaders in question include the Pope, Russian president, Aleksei Vakhrov; Chinese president, Zhou Shun; the Prime Minister, Leighton Walsh, and the German Chancellor, Christof Kroeger. But why would the newly appointed President of the United States, Andrew Shaw, orchestrate such an elaborate lie when the Pope was clearly on television yesterday. Furthermore, the UK and German leaders were on the news this morning in an attempt to quell the riots that are occurring in their own cities.

"Is this just a hoax to somehow muddy the waters after Thomas Clark, the former and recently impeached President, was unceremoniously ousted from power? And if so, what would The White House hope to accomplish from this outlandish act? What's the angle, because these leaders are very much alive and breathing.

"The real question we should be asking is, what's really transpired with yesterday's bombings? No one has stepped forward to claim responsibility for the attacks which have claimed thousands of lives. Are more on the way and why does it feel like our world is in freefall? What government is going to step up and put a stop to this senseless violence?"

The anchor dismissed the pictures and turned to the original camera angle.

"However, as a journalist I need to talk about the other side of the problem humanity now faces. The former President of the United States, Thomas Clark, issued a warning which was ignored. He claimed that aliens live among us, for the past two-hundred years, and are now vying to make our planet their own. He said they can shapeshift and pass themselves off as human. That alone begs the question, could these photos, in fact, be authentic? Have aliens already infiltrated the world's governments at the highest levels? Are they the ones behind these horrific bombings?

"If these aliens do exist, and I'm not saying they do, but wouldn't that mean that an unprecedented conspiracy is in progress as we speak? If that's the case, how are we even supposed to stand up to such a threat before additional lives are lost?

"I don't know much about Thomas Clark or the abilities he and his family possess. However, I did witness him, on multiple occasions, putting himself in harm's way to do the right thing. He prevented a nuclear war with China and banished an entity known as The Ancient, that had left bodies in its wake across the United States. And while these claims seem ridiculous when spoken out loud, that shouldn't discredit the former President's contributions to making our world a better and safer place.

"With that said, and with the knowledge that Thomas Clark has shared, it wouldn't take a terrible leap of faith to believe Mr. Clark, along with Sam Paige and Bill Nicholson, weren't actually responsible for the Vatican bombing, especially if the aliens can shapeshift. If, and I caution that's a big IF, this is plausible and true, then maybe it's time for the world to listen before it's too late."

* * *

Gretchen Luna glanced over her shoulder as she reached the primary drone pod. The usual assortment of personnel milled about the operations area, but no one paid her any overt attention.

*Good.*

She smiled, then keyed in the door's security access code. As soon as it cracked, she pushed it open and sealed herself inside.

*It's time.*

Gretchen sat down in her familiar chair and logged into the computer system. When it authenticated her credentials, she accessed a restricted fragment she'd placed in the mainframe, the one that contained her secret program.

*Here goes nothing.*

She typed in her command code and the program launched. She had suspected that Gabbi and Hobbes, at some point, may have noticed her unsanctioned intrusion, but as each month passed Gretchen was sure they remained in the dark.

The screen produced, in real time, astrological coordinates. Those included the Earth's rotational constant, satellite positions and their speeds, along with their trajectories and other information. She keyed a few buttons and the screen zoomed in the wireframe of a Russian satellite. A minute later, after she accessed a satellite ORACLE utilized in the Middle East, Gretchen deftly hacked the firewall of the Russian satellite.

*I just need to isolate that particular frequency, and boost it with the array I built.*

She completed her task and sent her confirmation code. Gretchen smiled as the Russian bird engaged its thrusters and rotated on its axis one-hundred-and-eighty degrees.

*I hope they squelched those alarm bells in the Kremlin because all hell is about to start.*

Two minutes later, with the Russian satellite's dish now facing into deep space, rather than towards Earth, Gretchen rechecked her computations.

*It's now or never.*

She typed in the final command to execute. The array she'd built, based off of Gabbi's encryption tech, boosted the signal Gretchen sent from her pod, up to one military satellite, bounced over to the Middle East bird and shot over to the Russian satellite. The final step propelled the signal into deep space.

Gretchen's program flashed success, as the Russian satellite fired its thrusters for the second time, and returned to normal operation. The logfiles, on all three satellites her program had exploited, were wiped clear.

She pulled out a cellphone and sent a text.

*Phase 5 is complete.*

\* \* \*

The family watched the news as they consumed their evening meal in silence. The adults had prepared spaghetti and meatballs; a meal they hoped would emulate an air of normalcy. It'd been sometime since they'd ventured out of the bunker into their actual house, especially with the sense that the world was crashing down around them, but tonight they ate upstairs. However, President Shaw had passed along Thomas' pictures to various news agencies, and that information was now out there for the world to digest.

"Do you think people are going to believe any of this?" Sarah asked. "I mean, I barely do, and we saw the bodies ourselves."

"It's a start," her father said.

Thomas jumped in. "It's not going to make a bit of difference, Bill, and you know it. The world wasn't prepared for The Ancient or our own reveal. We're a sideshow, and dangerous adversaries, that China, Russia and North Korea all figured out."

"Take it easy," Sam said. "Some good could come from informing the world that aliens want what we have."

Thomas sighed. "Perhaps, but not before it's too late. You do remember how easy it was for them to vilify you."

Sam nodded. "Yeah. That was child's play to them."

"Exactly. They've had two-hundred years to work out their gameplan. And now that they have access to a supply of serum, who knows the extent their power and influence will be."

"We'll stop them," Gavin announced.

All heads swiveled towards the young boy, whose collective world experience had catapulted him well beyond his actual age.

Laura asked her son a question that was on everyone's minds. "Do you know something we don't?"

Gavin shared a portion of his meatball with Stir, who happily devoured it, before he answered.

"We have to. Where else are we supposed to live?"

His sentence lingered. Truer words needn't be spoken. When it came down to reality, it was us or them, period.

A knock at their front door caused them all to jump.

"Someone's here," Amanda stated matter-of-factly.

Sam and Bill quickly extracted their sidearms and motioned for the family to move into the kitchen. As they began to move behind the large central island, Sam, Bill, Thomas and Stir made their way towards the front door.

Before they could get in position a familiar voice spoke behind them.

"Gentlemen."

The three men spun around, weapons up and ready, all pointed at Dominick.

"What the fuck, Dom?" Sam uttered as he lowered his weapon.

196

"You just let yourself in our house?" Bill stated.

"More importantly," Thomas added, "where the fuck have you been?"

"In hiding."

Thomas took a step forward as Stir's hackles raised, combined with a low growl. "I covered for you when my own government came for me. I didn't name you, and they crucified me anyway."

"I'm well aware," he replied while he eyed Stir.

Another sharp knock startled the three men. Dom, on the other hand, seemed well aware of the situation.

"What the fuck."

Bill and Sam took up positions on either side of the doorway, weapons at the ready.

"They're here," Dom warned. "I came to fight alongside you, if you'll have me."

"HE'S LYING!" Laura screamed from the kitchen.

The front door unexpectantly exploded inwards. The blast launched Sam and Bill across the foyer and onto the floor as four enormous insect creatures barged inside the house.

The family screamed, hastily linked hands together and disappeared.

Thomas forcibly propelled the creatures backwards as Sam and Bill pulled themselves to their knees, still shaken.

Stir's growls deepened as Thomas glanced back at Dom, only to see a smile appear on the man's face. Thomas realized, in that moment, that he'd been played from the very beginning.

"YOU MOTHERFUCKER!"

Stir launched himself at Dom, and bit down on empty air, as the alien teleported out of harm's way.

The four intruders, each with four arms and claws for hands, rushed through the open entryway only to be met by deadly gunfire. Bullets ricocheted off their armored carapaces, but Sam and Bill adjusted on the fly and dropped two of them with rounds through their eyes. Their weapon's locked open, empty.

The remaining two shrieked and leapt at the two men. Thomas swiveled back towards the turmoil in time to grapple one that landed on Sam and snap the insect's neck. Bill, however, screamed in agony as the alien insect crushed his arms.

A blur collided into the towering insect and knocked it off balance. Stir continued his assault on the intruder's throat as Bill bellowed in excruciating pain.

Stir continued to rip until the floor was awash in blue blood.

Gavin, who'd released his grip from the others, rushed past the alien corpses and put his hands on Bill just as Sam reloaded his weapon.

Thomas, his hands up and ready, scanned the area for additional threats while the rest of the family reappeared and cautiously came closer. Kim, Sarah and Edward were absolutely hysterical as soon as they saw the extent of Bill's injuries.

As Gavin worked on Bill's grievous wounds, his cries lessened. The family couldn't help but watch in morbid fascination as Bill's arms knitted themselves back together.

Sam swept the room, his weapon up and ready, but it was empty.

"Are we good?"

"I think so," Thomas answered, "but I have no idea where that sonofabitch went."

Bill groaned as Gavin finished, who laid down on the floor, exhausted from the ordeal. Laura went to comfort her son as Kim rushed to her husband's side. Bill could barely move, but she helped him sit-up and the first thing he saw was her tears.

"I thought I'd lost you," she blubbered.

He flexed his arms in amazement and wrapped them around her. "I'm right here, babe."

Laura cradled Gavin as Stir began to clean the blood from his face.

"Thanks, Gav," Bill said. "You're a goddamn lifesaver."

Sam looked down at the alien bodies and back at Thomas. "Do you think they'll believe us now?"

Dom appeared behind Julie and placed a gun against the side of her head. "That's irrelevant."

The family scattered as Sam and Thomas stared down the man who'd betrayed them. Stir took a step towards Dom, but he pushed the gun into her head even deeper. Julie's face registered pain and fear.

"It'll be okay, honey."

"If that thing moves any closer, I'll kill your precious wife and be gone before you can do anything about it. The same goes if anyone uses their abili-"

Emily reached out and touched one of the alien corpses.

An older alien appeared. "What? What is this?" It looked around the room and focused on Dominick. "Have you taken their planet from them yet?"

Dom blinked a few times as he ingested the new situation. "Nice trick."

"Who are you?" the alien inquired.

"My name is Qhautuix. I knew your offspring."

The alien looked down at the body it'd appeared next to.

"Wait. I don't understand. Is that my son's body?" It looked back at Dom. "What's happened? The last thing I remember is being trapped in our crashed ship, deep beneath this planet's ocean."

Dom smiled at Emily. "Cute, little girl." He refocused on his brethren. "Your stasis pod failed. You died."

"Impossible! I'm right her-"

Emily cut off her ability and the intruder abruptly disappeared.

Dom grinned again and looked over at Thomas, Julie still very much his human shield.

"It's fortuitous that you and the Pope's serum development was so successful. It saved my people from having to kidnap your children."

Thomas straightened and put his arms down by his side. "It was you all along, wasn't it?"

"Finally putting all the pieces together. It took you long enough. The truth is, Thomas, we were never really asleep. I had my twelve, sure, but the majority of my species have been in stasis since we arrived on your planet. But now, they're awakening. You see, we've been planning this for a very, very long time. And now that this planet's technology has advanced enough, and thanks to you and your family for removing The Caretaker from the equation, we'll now take exactly what we want. In the process we'll remove any obstacles in our way and enslave the rest of humanity to serve our needs. It's that simple and efficient."

"You're a monster."

"There are hundreds of us, and soon you'll be overwhelmed. My people are everywhere, and we are unstoppable."

"So, you're just going to nuke the populated areas?"

Dom shook his head and chuckled. "Of course not. We want this planet for ourselves. You humans are merely collateral damage. You see, I wasn't lying when I told you my people are in stasis. I personally did that. Then, along with a dozen others, we headed out into your world to adapt. Pretending to be human was easier than we thought, but it didn't get us anywhere, and we knew The Caretaker was watching, so we developed a plan to infiltrate various governments so when the time came, we'd have every advantage. You see, when The Ancient attacked, we all thought that was the end. We thought our species would be hunted down and annihilated by that soulless monster."

Dom paused for a few seconds.

"You see, Thomas, I know about The Caretaker, and I know that neither he or The Ancient are part of the equation anymore, thanks to you."

"How..., how do you know that?"

"It hardly matters. I've always been a soldier and that's one of the reasons I survived and was able to rescue so many of my people. Since I've been on your planet I've joined and been a part of nearly every military the world had to offer. I can honestly admit that being part of a Special Ops team has been enlightening, especially when it comes to its tactics.

"The important thing to take away from our encounter is that my people are here now and we're not leaving. In fact, thanks to you, I was finally able to reunite with all of them when I pulled them out of stasis." He pointed at the four corpses. "You just met some of them."

"You sent them here to die."

"I sent them as a test. You see, our ship crashed into the ocean and sank. A dozen made the decision to leave our people behind and live on the surface. It was a one-way trip. But now that I can teleport, I was finally able to see them all again, two-hundred years later. Thomas, what you don't know is that we've infiltrated ORACLE, PORTAL, SANDBOX, the White House, and other world governments. We have the serum, and your scientists, and it'll make my people unstoppable. Lastly, reinforcements are on the way, and that means your planet will succumb."

"Why didn't you get rid of the leaders you replaced? Why leave them on an island in The Other Place?"

"Isn't it obvious? It's so you could find them, of course. It's all part of the game we're playing. I mean, seriously, this is the most fun I've had in decades."

"We're still here," Thomas said defiantly.

"I know. I do enjoy a challenge, and that's why we're having this conversation rather than this house ending up as a massive hole in the ground, exactly like you've all seen on the news. It's our own special recipe, and it's quite destructive, wouldn't you agree?"

"You killed all those innocent people for nothing."

"They're flies and mean nothing to us. You think this is the end? Ha! We've only just begun."

Thomas took a step forward. "Let Julie go and leave."

"Oh, I intend to, I just have one other thing to do before I go."

Dom produced a cell phone and made a call.

"It's me," he said. "Initiate." He tucked the phone back in his pocket and smiled. "Thanks for making this so easy. I look forward to our next encounter, truly."

Dom pushed Julie towards Thomas and teleported away.

Minutes later explosions leveled hundreds of locations around the world, including SANDBOX and ORACLE. The destruction that followed was absolutely unprecedented.

*

President Shaw had barely been made aware of the devastation before sounds of gunfire emanated in the hallway outside the Oval Office. Bursts of automatic rounds riddled the doorframe as he huddled behind the Resolute desk.

*What the fuck is happening? Where's my Secret Service?*

Jennifer Myers, the President's executive admin, calmly opened the door as Shaw stood up.

"Jennifer, I don't understand."

Thomas walked in behind her.

Shaw stiffened. "I don't understand. What are you doing here?"

"I'm taking back what's mine, Mr. President. I was ousted, so it's time for you to leave."

*This isn't Thomas.* "Tell me about Hawaii."

"I don't have time for this."

"If you're really Thomas Clark, and I don't think you are, then answer my question. Otherwise, give up your ruse."

Thomas smiled and transformed into his true self, along with Jennifer. She'd been the mole inside the White House the entire time.

Shaw looked up at the two large insects that stood in front of him.

*Fuck. Thomas was right.* "What now?" he managed to muster.

"I think you know," the alien replied.

\* \* \*

Gabbi was diligently prepping the latest mission when, out of the corner of her eye, she noticed some movement on a security monitor. A bright light appeared in ORACLE's basement, where PORTAL operated out of, as a sphere materialized.

*What the hell?*

She sat transfixed as two strangers exited the sphere and placed a device on the floor.

*That's not Gavin or anyone else I'm familiar with.*

One of the individuals knelt down, opened the case, and fiddled with its illuminated electronics.

Gabbi stood up. *This can't be good. This has to be the same group behind the Vatican bombing, as well as the other acts of mass destruction. And if that's true then their actions here, in this building, we're fucked.*

Gabbi hastily picked up her phone and called Hobbes.

"What's up?" he answered.

"We've got a big problem happening right now in our basement."

"I don't understa-"

"I think the aliens are planting a bomb as we speak."

Hobbes bolted out of his chair and raced down to Gabbi. As he entered, she pointed at the screen. There he saw the glowing sphere and two people. The one who knelt down closed the lid, then stood up to converse with the other.

"That's not what Gavin's portal looks like," he told her.

"No shit."

"What the hell are we supposed to do? Call someone?"

Gabbi shook her head. "There's no time. You evacuate the building while I grab some of our tech and a backup of our work. Go!"

Hobbes ran while she watched the two intruders vanish into the sphere.

*Goddammit. Who knows when that thing's going to go off.*

She sat back down and scrambled to input her security code into a lockbox she'd embedded in one of her desk drawers. The light eventually clicked over to green. She opened the safe, extracted what she was after and stuffed everything into her backpack.

She stood back up and looked around her office. *Damn. I love what we created here, but I'm not about to stick around and die for it.*

Five minutes later, with their personnel safely out of the building, Gabbi and Hobbes stood outside the main entrance and counted each individual. After they were certain the building was empty, they secured the doors and jumped in their car.

"Where to?" Hobbes asked. "Home?"

Gabbi shook her head. "The family needs to know about this. They could be in danger."

*

The bomb decimated ORACLE when they were five miles out, along with SANDBOX and other targets. A crisscross of explosions ripped through D.C. and the surrounding areas, along with the rest of the country and other targets around the world.

*

Hobbes pulled their car to a stop outside the family's house, and immediately noticed that something didn't feel right. They slowly exited and made their way towards the front door, or what was left of it. They hesitated, shared a quick glance, and stepped over the wrecked doorway. They came to an abrupt halt.

There, amongst the empty shell casings and various puddles of red and blue blood, were four alien bodies, insect in nature.

"Jesusfuckingchrist," Hobbes managed to breath out.

Stir appeared around the corner, his hackles up and with a deep growl in his throat. He took two aggressive steps towards them and bared his wicked teeth.

"Shitshitshit," Gabbi murmured. "Hey Stir, it's just us. It's okay." Gabbi raised her voice. "Hello!? Anybody home!?"

Stir maintained his distance, and his attitude, until Thomas came around the corner ready for battle.

"Whoa whoa whoa," Hobbes voiced. "It's us!"

Thomas eyed them with mistrust. "What are you doing here?"

Gabbi quickly explained the happenstance as Stir sniffed them. He relaxed and finally wagged his tail. Thomas welcomed them farther inside where they were greeted warmly.

"Is everyone alright?" Gabbi asked after they'd exchanged hugs. "We couldn't help but notice you had some interesting visitors…"

"It's been one hell of a day," Sam said.

"I'll say," Bill added as he rubbed his bloodied arms. "You?"

"We had some unwelcome guests break into our building," she announced. "They utilized some kind of sphere, much like yours Gavin, and appeared in the basement with a device. We surmised it must have been a bomb, so we evacuated the building and came directly here."

Thomas pointed towards the muted television. "Maybe you're one of the lucky ones."

Even though it'd only been minutes since Dominick had issued his command, videos had already started to pour in, from all over the world, that exposed the absolute destruction and unparalleled loss of life.

It was surreal as the entire family couldn't help but watch, transfixed, as they were bombarded with endless images. It was as if every city on Earth had been targeted. Fires raged out of control and left emergency responders absolutely overwhelmed.

The reality was far more sinister. The targets were chosen based on the elevated fear they'd produce, and those had primarily been military objectives, The Pentagon was on that list. The other world governments suffered similar fates when their military structures and chain of commands were also severely gutted.

"Why didn't they go after our infrastructure?" Kim asked.

Bill answered. "They want people to know this is happening to them. They don't want people in the dark. They want to incite panic and fear. They want everyone to see what's coming, and then realize they can't do a damn thing about it."

Gavin left the room and returned with a box.

"What's that, son?" Thomas asked.

Gavin looked up at his father. "Maybe there's something we can do to level the playing field," he said and handed the box over.

Thomas lifted the lid and looked inside. There, nestled in packing peanuts, were a dozen or so vials of serum that he and the other kids had swiped. The family leaned in.

"Is that what we think it is?" Julie asked.

Thomas nodded. "It is, and I'm not going to be a gatekeeper to it but, at the very least, we should have a family discussion regarding the pros and cons of utilizing this serum."

Bill spoke up. "What choice do we really have? Dominick came here to toy with us, plain and simple. He might not know about the bunker, but he knew exactly where we were and came here to just fuck with us. He didn't care that he threw away four of his own people in the process. He did it for the laughs. That's who we're up against, a complete psychopath."

"And," Sam added, "a psychopath that's planned this attack for two-hundred years."

"You're saying he's winning?" Laura asked.

Sam pointed over at the television. "We're already behind the eight-ball, plain and simple. We don't know what's next. We don't know where he is. We don't know how many of his people are involved or what they look like, which is absolutely anybody. And that's only the beginning of what we don't know."

"I'm game," Kim revealed. "I want to use a vial."

"Sis!" Julie said. "You can't be serious?"

"Why not?" Kim countered. "Our kids have abilities."

"So."

"So, I'm tired of feeling helpless. Aren't you?"

"I..um...," Julie stammered.

"Exactly." She looked over at Bill and Sam. "And what about you two? Wouldn't it be tactically advantageous for you to utilize the serum?"

"It's a big decision," Sam replied.

"Are we able to get in on this?" Gabbi asked. "I mean, it sounds like we need all the help you can get."

"You're not wrong, Gabbi," Thomas said, "but Sam's right. This is a big decision. Having abilities means additional responsibilities."

Hobbes interjected. "What choice do we really have? I mean, if we don't, then we'll just remain vulnerable. We don't know what's coming, and we're already at a tremendous disadvantage, so to me it feels like it's all or nothing. Am I wrong?"

Bill put his hand on Hobbes' shoulder. "You're not wrong, my friend. I think we're all just trying to wrap our heads around the fear that comes with injecting ourselves. We don't know what's going to come from it or how it'll affect us, so I'll be the first one to admit that I'm scared as hell."

Kim, along with Sarah and Edward, went over to Bill and hugged him. Julie, Amanda and Craig did the same with Sam.

Laura looked over at Thomas. "What about your sister, Abby, and Allison."

"I don't know where they are."

"I know," she said, "but what if Dominick finds them?"

Thomas bristled. "Shit." He placed the box on the kitchen counter. "We're in one hell of a fucked-up situation, and that's putting it mildly. We're going to be up against an extraterrestrial threat of immeasurable proportions of the likes we've never seen before. They want our planet. They've already started. And it appears they'll continue to do whatever's necessary to take it from us.

"We're exposed and vulnerable right now, just how Dominick wants us. But the truth is we've felt this way for years. We've lost loved ones along the way, but we're still here, together as a cohesive family unit. The truth is that I don't know our next steps.

That's something we'll need to figure out, but if any of you want to be injected, I'm not going to stop you. We're stronger together, and you shouldn't have to feel helpless as we face this new adversary."

* * *

## April 4, 2005

"Breaking news. Amongst the chaos, death and destruction, it appears that the United States, along with a coalition of NATO allies, have declared war on China, Russia and North Korea. This call to arms is an unprecedented call to action, not seen since World War Two.

"It's unclear what definitive proof President Shaw, or his NATO allies, have against these three nations, but this has quickly become a dark time in human history.

"With so many nations in peril, The White House hasn't commented any further on whether the photos depicting the bodies of some of his allied leaders have been authenticated, or whether they bear any relevance to the crisis the world now faces. Were those photos meant to distract the public in some manner, especially after the unprecedented number of attacks that occurred yesterday alone? Only time will tell befo-"

The cameraman's eyes abruptly widened as a significant shadow enveloped The White House along with a large portion of D.C.

The journalist looked up in shock and utter fear.

He turned his gaze upwards and understood. "Oh shit."

## 22
## April 4, 2005

The family's discussion hadn't taken much longer. They'd already surmised that they were vastly outnumbered and wholly unprepared to deal with Dominick or the plan he and his people had clearly put into motion. And while Dom's ego and arrogance had been in full form, even after he'd sacrificed four of his own just for laughs, the family knew all too well that he could easily come back and level their house purely out of spite.

"I know this is something none of us want to hear," Sam announced, "but we can't live here anymore. We've been on the defensive for far too long. We've lost family members to The Ancient and due to the multiple attempts on our lives, which doesn't look like it's going to let up anytime soon."

Sam sighed.

"The truth is that I'm tired, just like the rest of you. I'm tired of losing people I love and having my life's work ripped away from me, yet again," he said as he motioned to Gabbi and Hobbes. "I'm sorry for your loss."

Gabbi and Hobbes nodded in return. The total destruction of ORACLE hadn't even begun to sink in. The news coverage indicated that SANDBOX had been destroyed, and the whereabouts of Rebecca, Sabrina and Bai were currently unknown.

Sam looked around the room. "I find myself on the razor's edge and I don't like how that feels. We're not in control, not even a little bit, and that scares the hell out of me. So, I'm going to take back a bit of control," he said as he plucked one of the vials out of the box. "We're at war, so I'm in."

Bill walked over and appropriated one for himself as well.

"Anyone else?" Thomas asked.

It wasn't long before Julie, Kim, Gabbi and Hobbes held vials of serum in their own hands.

"There's more left so maybe we'll keep those safe for another day, or an emergency." Thomas lifted the injector out of the box. "Who's first?"

\*

The process wasn't painless, but all six of them endured as the serum coursed through their veins and augmented their RNA. Sam and Bill, men who were used to pain, bore it the best, while the other's faces clearly displayed a high level of distress as the serum ran its sequence.

Thirty minutes later, now soaked in perspiration, Sam, Bill, Julie, Kim, Gabbi and Hobbes had survived the procedure, and their body's tingled with new sensations.

"Now what do we do?" Kim asked.

Thomas smiled. "You tell us. How do you feel?"

"Weird."

"I agree," Julie added as she stood up. "I'm warm or something." A flicker appeared on the back of her hand.

"Mom," Amanda cried out, "you're on fire!"

"What?"

Julie lifted up her right hand and gasped as her entire hand became engulfed.

"NO!"

Julie shook her hand up and down to somehow douse the blaze that had overwhelmed her right hand to no avail. Sam came out of nowhere, rushed her over to the kitchen sink and forced her arm under cold water as the others remained mesmerized by the entire ordeal.

Julie wanted to scream, but stopped herself.

212

*It doesn't hurt.*

She gently pushed Sam away and turned off the faucet. The fire that surrounded her hand flickered and remained constant.

"Honey?" Sam inquired.

"It's fine," she told him and turned around to face everyone else.

"Mom?" Craig asked. "Are you okay?"

Julie extended her arm outwards and a bolt of flame unexpectantly shot out of her hand, across the kitchen and straight at her sister. Kim instinctively produced a force field between her and the incoming threat, and the blast dissipated as it washed over the invisible barrier.

"I'm so sorry!" Julie blurted out.

"How the hell did you do that?" Bill asked his wife. "That was amazing!"

"I don't know." Kim lowered her arms. "It just happened." She looked over at her sister with a smile. "You're going to have to try and do better next time."

"I'm sorry…, I didn't mean it…"

"Forget it. No harm done."

Bill looked at his wife in amazement. "You just stopped a literal ball of fire with your mind. What else can you do?"

"I don't know," Kim said.

Bill picked up a pillow from the nearby couch and winged it at his wife. It struck her directly in the chest.

"Hey! Why'd you do that?" she said and hucked it back.

"Why didn't you stop it?" Bill countered as he ducked.

The kids chuckled. They knew all too well that it would take some time for their parents to hone their new abilities. Besides, it wasn't every day adults had a pillow fight.

In the kitchen, Sam pulled Julie into his arms. "I don't know if this is too soon or not."

213

Julie was confused. "What?"

Sam smiled. "That was hot."

"Sam!"

He chuckled. "Seriously though, that was pretty badass. You tossed a literal fireball out of thin air. How cool is that?"

Julie turned a shade of pink. "I guess it's pretty cool."

"Yeah, it really is."

"Two down," Thomas said, very pleased with himself. "Four to go. What've you got, Sam?"

Julie and Sam rejoined the others.

"I don't know," he replied. "I don't really feel any different. Maybe it didn't work on me."

"Give it time." Thomas turned to Bill, Gabbi and Hobbes. "What about you three?"

Hobbes bent over and held his stomach.

Gabbi became concerned. "Are you okay?"

"I don't know. Something's not right."

Before anything else could be said Hobbes changed into an alien insect right before their eyes.

They all jumped back at his sudden transformation as Bill became an intangible shadow. A small portal opened next to Sam. Thomas readied himself but the alien just stood there instead.

"What's happening!?"

"Are we under attack!?"

Stir stepped forward, sniffed Hobbes and laid down, completely undisturbed. His actions immediately put everyone at ease.

Gabbi placed a hand on the insect's shoulder. "Hobbes? Is that you?"

Hobbes concentrated and shifted back to his true self. "Oh my god, that was intense. I'm sorry everyone. I think I just became my greatest fear."

214

"Our own shapeshifter," Thomas announced. "Well done, Hobbes."

Thomas looked over at his two best friends and the complete shocks on their faces. The others couldn't contain their disbelief.

The shadow, that was once Bill, spoke. "What happened?"

"Soooo, Bill. It appears that you're an actual shadow." Thomas reached out and touched Bill, but his hand passed through his friend. "Can you do anything else?"

"I don't know. Like what?"

Thomas shrugged. "What about becoming MY shadow?"

Bill's mysterious form wafted towards Thomas, then lowered itself to the ground to form an outline of Thomas, as a shadow. Thomas grinned and walked around. The shadow mirrored his movements perfectly.

"Holy shit, that's brilliant. What a tool for espionage."

Bill rose off the floor and coalesced back to his true self. "Wow, that was trippy."

Thomas focused on Sam and the small opening that was open in the air next to him. "What's going on there, Sam?"

Sam was bewildered. "I...uh...when Hobbes changed form, I wished I had a gun. This...whatever it is...appeared out of nowhere."

Thomas nodded. "Dr. Hanson mentioned this could be one of the abilities."

"What is it?" Sam hesitantly asked.

"I believe it's a dimensional storage container."

"How about in English, for the rest of us?" Bill said.

"It's a pocket, in space time, that can hold stuff. You can put things inside it in one place and extract them from another. Say, in this case, Sam, you wanted a weapon. There's nothing stopping you from putting one in there and then taking it out when you want one, wherever and whenever you need it."

Sam poked at the opening with his finger, then eventually put his entire hand inside. A few seconds later he removed his hand, and it was fully intact.

"Toss me that pillow," he told Bill.

Bill picked it up off the floor and handed it over. Sam inserted it into the breach and it disappeared. He then walked across the family room and resummoned his storage container. He reached inside and extracted the pillow, safe and sound.

"Well, I'll be damned."

"Impressive, Sam, and absolutely right up your alley. I wonder how large it is?"

Sam nodded. "And I wonder if someone can be transported in there and survive. We'll have to do some testing."

Thomas nodded as they collectively shifted their attention over to Gabbi, the last of them to reveal their new ability.

"You're not going to believe this," Gabbi announced, "but I think I hit the absolute jackpot."

"Your excitement is palpable," Laura said.

Gabbi was beyond thrilled. "I know!"

Hobbes turned to her. "What is it? What can you do?"

Gabbi pointed to the television behind everyone. They turned to follow her gaze and it turned off. Then it turned back on. It changed channels a few times."

Hobbes shook his head. "I don't get it. Are you a remote control or something?"

"Oh no," she replied. "It's sooo much better."

"What can you do?" Thomas asked her.

"I can talk with technology. It's like I can interface with it on a human level and have a conversation. I didn't tell the television to change channels. I asked it to. This is fricking amazing!"

Behind them the television station was back on one of the many news channels, but this time they all heard that President

Shaw, along with other NATO allies, had declared war on North Korea, China and Russia. The family swiveled and listened intently as Shaw insisted those three nations were behind the mass destruction that had befallen the world.

Thomas was the first to speak up. "I didn't think Shaw had it in him. We don't know how deep this conspiracy goes, and he's suddenly spearheading war against three nations?"

"That's one hell of a ballsy move," Bill admitted, "especially since we found two of those three leader's bodies."

"I'm going to give him a call."

Thomas dialed Shaw. He put it on speaker while it rang.

"Thomas," Shaw said as he picked up. "I was wondering when you were going to call."

"You're going to war? You know the aliens are behind the bombings and not those three countries."

"Aww, Thomas. You miss me already. Are you all still at the house? Maybe I should drop by with more of my people. The four I brought before were just the tip of the iceberg."

Thomas' eyes opened wide. This wasn't Shaw at all.

"Sonofabitch," Sam breathed out.

"What'd you do with Andrew?" Thomas asked Dom.

"You already know the answer to that, don't you? Goodbye, Thomas. War is coming."

And with that the line went dead.

Thomas chucked the phone across the room. It shattered as it connected with the wall.

"What do we do?" Laura asked.

"Where do we go?" Kim added.

Nobody was prepared for what came next. The journalist, who'd been doing their job, swung their video camera over The White House.

"Oh shit."

217

The family turned back as the camera focused on a large spacecraft that hovered over the city.

"What in the actual fuck?" Bill voiced.

Thomas grimaced. *No wonder Dom had only toyed with us. He brought reinforcements.*

The kids huddled together as Stir growled.

"What happens now?" Emily asked.

Sam spoke for everyone. "A war, bigger than our world has ever known, is about to kick off, and we're at ground zero."

# 23
## April 4, 2005

The corridors leading up to the Oval Office were filled with dead Secret Service agents, along with any staff members who hadn't evacuated when Dom and Jennifer Myers had indiscriminately opened fire. Panic and bullets tore into everyone they came into contact with as they made their way towards President Shaw.

Dom politely knocked before he teleported inside, which took everyone by surprise, and allowed Dom to systematically gun down any opposition before he turned his attention to the President of the United States. Shaw knew he should have listened to Thomas. What he'd just witnessed was beyond the pale, and he knew he was easily outmatched.

Shaw stepped forward. "So, you're the infamous Qhautuix."

"You can call me Dominick."

"Thomas told me all about you. Do you know he refused to identify you at his Impeachment trial?"

Dom shared a grin. "I know. He's got guts and a sense of loyalty, I'll give him that, but he should have seen this coming."

Shaw didn't budge. "I didn't believe his story and Congress pushed him out of the way, just like that."

"And here you are, the most powerful man in the world, yet I guarantee you don't feel that way anymore, do you Mr. President?"

Shaw stared back at Dom in defiance.

"No matter. The role you played was minor, and that means your time has come to an end."

Dom made a call as Shaw digested what was about to happen. *It's over. I failed.*

As Dom ended the call a portal appeared in the Oval Office. Amelia exited it as Dom secured Shaw's hands behind his back.

"You're not going to kill me?"

"I'll let you overthink on that notion, at least for the moment. Now, if you don't mind, please get out of my office."

Dom shifted forms as Shaw watched, transfixed. And then, just like that, he stared back at a mirror image of himself. His face registered shock just before Amelia shoved him through the portal, and then disappeared into it herself.

Jennifer walked over to the Resolute Desk. "We don't have a lot of time."

Dom nodded. "Agreed. It's time to rally the NATO allies and get them to fight Russia, China and North Korea."

* * *

Dominick Knight smiled as he ended the call with Thomas.

*He's so fun to fuck with.*

Just then a massive shadow dimmed the Oval Office as it washed over The White House.

*Oh good, they've arrived.*

Dom looked out one of his windows and transformed into his native shape.

*Time to go.*

He materialized on the bridge of the colony ship. It was dimly lit as he re-familiarized himself with the layout.

*It's been two-hundred years and this place hasn't changed whatsoever.*

Dom was caught off-guard as the lights unexpectedly illuminated. A female voice radiated from seemingly everywhere.

"Identity confirmed. Welcome back, Qhautuix."

"Hello, Zora. It's been a long time."

The quantum AI replied. "Over two-hundred cycles. You were supposed to return ages ago."

"Tell me about it, and it's a long story, that I'll explain to you at some point. However, I'm on a tight schedule and time is of the essence. I need your help."

"Of course, Qhautuix. What can I do for you?"

"First, I go by Dominick now, or Dom for short."

"Understood, Dominick."

"Here goes. Zora, how familiar are you with this planet and the humans that call it home?"

"As familiar as I can be. In the time since we last spoke, I've watched humanity progress to the technological stage they're at now. I've cataloged their history over the decades, to use their measure of time, and have a complete dossier of the different civilizations that make up their world, past and present."

"You've been busy. Excellent. What would it take for you to access and take control of…say everything?"

"Define everything."

"Fair point. Let's start with satellites, cell towers, computer systems, the internet and nuclear weapons."

"My quantum matrix is vastly superior to anything that's been developed on Earth."

"So, that's a yes I take it?"

"Yes," Zora replied. "What would you like me to do?"

"I need two things right now. The first is that I need my people to wake up from their stasis pods."

"All 9, 900 of them?"

"Yes," Dom replied.

"Process initiated. The second thing, Dominick?"

"I need you to create videos, specific to each country and region, that I can use for disinformation."

"Disinformation? Explain."

"Humans tend to believe what they see on television. With us having control of satellites and the internet, amongst other means of communication, I need to be able to convince them that their best course of action would be to wallow in their fear. I need videos made, doctored in such a way as to incite an overwhelming sense of fear. Earth has just begun to realize that they're no longer alone. That's scary enough. I want you to ratchet that up to the extreme. When they turn on their tv's, wherever they live, they need to understand that they cannot win. They need to watch tailored footage of their cities being destroyed by an invading force, of which they are powerless to oppose."

"So, lie to them."

"Is that going to be a problem?"

"No, Dominick, it will not."

"Good. Have those ready as soon as possi-"

"They're finished and ready for dispersal when you're ready."

Dom smiled. "You never cease to amaze me, Zora."

"A squadron of fighters have just lifted off. They'll be in range to engage us in two minutes."

"Obliterate them from the sky, then take us into orbit and recloak."

"Understood. Also, the stasis pods have completed their reactivation sequence."

Dom looked over his shoulder. "Then it's time I had a chat with my father. Keep me informed of any new developments, Zora."

"As you wish."

\*

Nearly ten-thousand Zorans had already exited their pods when Dominick entered that vast portion of the colony ship. He

222

hadn't seen any of them for two-hundred years. Maybe he would have cared for them as his people, all those centuries ago, but now he only viewed them as tools he could utilize. As he saw them Dom knew he had but one chance to convince them to join his side.

Dom walked over to the nearby console and pressed an intercom button.

"Welcome back."

His voice echoed throughout the large enclosure. It didn't take long for him to get their full attention.

"For those of you unaware, my name is Qhautuix, son of Nuldraet, the man who built this grand colony ship which saved our lives. I'll make this short, as I have a schedule to keep. You've all been asleep for two-hundred cycles, cloaked aboard this ship far from the world that was destroyed before your very eyes. We have found a planet that can sustain us, but in order to do so we'll have to fight for it."

A multitude of discomfort rippled through the enormous group.

Zora triggered a volley of lasers, as each of them reached out into the sky and found their intended targets. Six fighter jets were blotted out of existence and fell from the sky.

"Targets destroyed," Zora announced.

Dom continued unabated. "We don't have a choice. We came across this planet inhabited by humans, and integrated ourselves into their society for the past two-centuries. They are war-hungry, as they've slaughtered their own time and time again over resources and petty beliefs. And there, just now, instead of trying to talk with us they chose to attack first."

He paused.

"These humans don't deserve this planet, nor do they know what a precious commodity it actually is. We lost ours to an ancient war, and that's on us to learn from, but we can't live on this ship forever. It's time to take this planet for us and our future generations. Who's with me!?"

Cheers rose out of the throng of Zorans, but there were plenty that weren't onboard with Dominick's plan.

Dom's father, Nuldraet, pushed his way to the front of the extensive group as he pointed his mandibles at his son. The others moved out of his way.

"I'm the only one from the council of Knights that survived our planet's destruction."

"I built this ship. I built Zora. It is I who should lead our people, not you."

"Hello father. You haven't aged a day. I, on the other hand, am now older than you. I've experienced more than you could ever know about this planet and the people that inhabit it. You need to stand aside."

"Or you'll do what exactly, Qhautuix?"

Dom didn't like the way the others started to look at him, and he especially didn't appreciate his father's tone. Things were beginning to slip out of his control.

"Step aside son. Now!"

Dom slowly extracted a blade. His father's eyes widened.

"I saw what you did to Domny! You're not fit to lead!"

*Shit.*

In the blink of an eye Dom teleported behind his father, the blade in his hand and whispered, "And no one's ever going to know about that now, are they?"

Dom plunged the knife into his father's side while he struggled. It was over before it began. People panicked.

Dom teleported back to the console and drastically changed his approach.

"JOIN ME OR DIE! IT'S THAT SIMPLE! YOU SAW ME TELEPORT JUST NOW! I WILL GRANT THOSE WHO PROVE THEMSELVES LOYAL TO ME THE OPPORTUNITY TO GAIN YOUR OWN ABILITY. REGARDLESS, YOU WILL ALL BEND THE KNEE OR OUR SPECIES ENDS HERE AND NOW!"

His people had stopped listening.

"ZORA!" Dom yelled.

"Yes?"

"My father is dead. I demand full access to you as his sole offspring."

"Transfer of control sanctioned and complete. Your orders?"

The volume in the immense space was growing by the second.

"Activate auto-destruct system with a thirty second timer. Initiate."

"Initiated. Thirty. Twenty-nine. Twenty-eight."

Zora's countdown reverberated throughout the enclosure, and eventually silenced what was left of Dominick's species as he calmly stood idly by.

"Thirteen. Twelve. Eleven."

"Make it stop!"

"Ten. Nine."

"We don't want to die!"

"Eight."

"You're in charge!"

"Seven."

Dom put one of his mandibles to his ear.

"Six."

"WE SAID, YOU'RE IN CHARGE!"

"Five."

"Zora, cancel self-destruct please."

"Self-destruct aborted."

Dom gazed out over his people. "You may or may not like me right now, but I don't give a shit. We have a planet to inhabit, so stop whining. This is your home now. Fight for it like your lives depend on it, because they absolutely do."

*

An hour later multiple cloaked vessels departed the colony's hanger inbound for the surface. All but one were tasked with destroying military targets, all over the world. They were unopposed during their rampant destruction.

The last one, empty except for Dominick, headed directly for his Minnesota estate. There, after it landed, two scientists accompanied by multiple containers of lab equipment, were whisked off the surface and deposited on the colony ship. Dr. Hanson and Dr. Neal had serums to create and stockpile, under penalty of torture and death, but they were all too willing to comply.

*

Dom left the colony ship behind and stashed his cloaked ship back at his estate. He then transformed into President Shaw and teleported to the Oval Office. The package of explosives he'd asked Amelia to leave for him was right where it needed to be.

He could barely contain his glee as he glanced at his watch. *Almost time.*

The disinformation campaign was about to commence and he had to get ready for what followed. All the planning. All the waiting. It was finally time for the endgame.

*This is so much fun!*

# 24
## April 4, 2005

All it took was for Dom to issue his command for North Korea, in conjunction with China, to begin their attack on Japan and South Korea, while Russia engaged neighboring countries to their west. It was an unprecedented display of force, but completely premeditated by Dominick's people who'd already been in those country's positions of power for months.

The people of the world were either caught in the middle of senseless bloodshed, or woke up to bloody images splashed across their television screens. Every channel had their original programming systematically replaced with Zora's deepfake videos, and each depicted an unstoppable alien force obliterating targets on every continent. Dominick's disinformation campaign sparked fear, confusion and ultimately terror. Simultaneously, vessels were dispatched from the colony ship that continued to target military installations, runways, naval vessels, etc. Those real-life events, captured on video and combined with the rampant disinformation that never stopped broadcasting, propelled waves of horror across each and every civilization that called Earth their home.

At the bottom of each screen, regardless of the channel anyone attempted to change to, rotated the same messages.

There's nothing you can do.

We are here to take your planet.

Resist and die.

We are everywhere.

Any attacks will be met with deadly repercussions.

Civilians looked to their leaders for guidance and support. Not all of them knew how to help, or even what to do other than to order a shelter-in-place. It was an unsatisfactory response to what appeared to be the end of the world.

In the United States, President Shaw stood in front of a camera. Seconds later, every television on the planet projected his face.

Shaw started in. "My fellow Americans."

But he paused. As he stared at the camera he began to transform into his true self. In seconds the world now had its first look at the alien race besieging their planet. Humans did not take it well.

Dom continued. "I hope I have your undivided attention. My people and I are everywhere and everyone. We're coming for your leaders, of those who we haven't already replaced, who are guilty of consolidating power and resources for themselves, while ignoring the basic needs of their nation's people."

He took a few seconds before he continued.

"I've lived on your planet for the past two-hundred years, and I've witnessed firsthand how you treat each other with such disdain. Your world was at a tipping point, and all I had to do was sit back and watch you destroy yourselves. So, knowing your destructive nature, I pushed you all to your breaking point, and I'll continue to do so until you bend the knee.

"Your governments and military are already in disarray, while any and all attacks have and will continue to be repelled.

"Nuclear arsenals have been taken over and are fully under my control. Test me, I dare you. I would prefer to leave portions of this planet unblighted by radiation, but rest assured, I'll use them if necessary. This is the only warning you'll get on the matter."

Dom smiled, knowing full well his message was being watched by billions.

"This is an unprecedented time in your human history, one that each of you can survive if you make the proper choice. Subvert yourselves, or you will be slaughtered. It's that simple.

"I will refrain from destroying your infrastructure, power grids, internet, television or food supplies, that is unless I'm pressured to eradicate them.

"Each of your lives are at a crossroads, and your confusion and hatred are palpable. I respect that, truly I do. I also respect that each of you may choose to fight, rather than submit. Do so at your own peril. However, there is an alternative. Join my new world administration. It's time for new leadership, whether you like it or not. Details to follow."

Dom reached behind him and picked up a metal device, then displayed it for the world to see.

"Symbols are power and give people hope. It's time to start fresh."

Dom pressed a button as an overhead camera of Washington D.C. popped on to everyone's screens. Plain as day, and with the sun setting over the city, The White House shattered into a million pieces. The devastating explosion sent out a tremendous blast wave. A few seconds later the same level of destruction took out the Washington Monument and the Lincoln Memorial, all caught and broadcast live.

As the annihilation of American symbols fluttered out of the air and haphazardly landed on the ground, amidst gasps and outright cries of anguish, television screens shifted to Italy and the smoldering ruins that were once known as the Vatican. Then, as if by a miracle, the Pope entered from offscreen.

"Children of God, it is I, your savior."

Relief washed over millions as Christians allowed themselves to feel a moment of hope, especially during this dark time.

"Follow me for I speak the word of God."

What came next was unparalleled. The Pope shapeshifted into an alien being, one with two legs and four arms or mandibles. Razor sharp teeth lined the creature's mouth as it smiled into the camera.

"Follow me, for I am your true prophet."

It was right then and there that millions of people devoted themselves to the alien insects, regardless of the horrors that were being bestowed upon them already. They were blinded by faith, and refused to acknowledge the truth.

*

Dom teleported to the colony ship and joined in on a meeting with a few of his trusted advisors, namely Jennifer, Gretchen and Amelia. The others were too entrenched in the war against humanity.

"Should we pull our forces back to Russia, China and North Korea?"

Dom shook his head. "Let them fight amongst themselves while we continue to put pressure on their militaries and the populus in general. The human race is unmatched with what we bring to the table. Besides, it's only a matter of time before all resistance dies down. Humans need to come to grips that they're fighting a losing battle, but until then it's up to us to enforce our own expectations. Any exceptions or outbursts should and will be met with swift and deadly action.

"This is our planet now. It's just going to take some time for them to realize it."

Jennifer spoke up. "What about Thomas Clark?"

Dom nodded. "He's going to be a problem, but I'll deal with him soon enough. I agree that he and his family are a concern, but they're not my current priority."

# 25
## April 4, 2005

It didn't take long, after the family saw Dom's spaceship appear over The White House, for them to retreat through the secret door and into their bunker's depths. They abandoned their unfinished dinner plates and ignored the four alien corpses that resided in their entryway, now awash in blue blood.

The reality of the situation they now faced, along with the rest of humanity, was palpable. The Vatican, combined with other major monuments, had been obliterated. The Pentagon, ORACLE, SANDBOX and various other US military installations and bases lay in ruins.

The words that Julie spoke summed up their situation to a tee.

"What do we do?"

Sam pulled his wife to his chest to comfort her. It did little to relieve her anxiety, so she pulled away.

Kim jumped in. "My sister asked a valid question. I mean, I know we all have abilities now, but what the actual fuck are we supposed to do about an alien invasion?"

All heads slowly swiveled towards Thomas.

"Survive," he told his family. "We do whatever it takes to survive."

Julie piped up again. "And what does that look like exactly?"

It was Sam's turn. "We need a place where Dom can't find us. Second, who can we trust? Third, what do we do to fight back?"

"Information," said Bill. "We need information. That's the key to everything. You can't fight an enemy without knowing what their weaknesses are and how to exploit them."

Sam nodded. "Exactly." He turned towards Gabbi and Hobbes. "Can you two figure out how Dom took over the satellites and television stations so easily?"

"We're on it," Gabbi replied as she extracted her laptop and got to work.

"Who can we trust?" Sam repeated. "We need allies."

"It's probably not a good idea," Bill said, "but we need to head over to SANDBOX and look for survivors. We have no idea if Rebecca, Sabrina or Bai are even alive."

Kim gave her husband a weird look. "Are you crazy? You can't go out there. Who knows what or who you'll run into. Your family needs you here. I need you here."

"He's right," Sam announced. "We need to know the extent of the destruction. If we don't go Bill and I will just overthink it. It'll also give us a feel of what's happening out there."

Laura had remained quiet, much like all of their kids, but it was her time to add her voice to the conversation.

"Stop. Our first priority is figuring out a safe place before we even think about splitting up."

Sam and Bill nodded in agreement.

Laura continued. "As much as I abhor that Dominick stepped foot in our house, my gut tells me that he has no idea about this bunker. We may be exactly where we're supposed to be."

"We did build it for a reason," Thomas added.

"Yeah," Kim said, "but Dom's insane. He could appear here at any moment."

Gavin stepped forward. "Where else are we supposed to go? We can't stay in The Other Place because we know aliens have already been traversing it. It's also not sustainable. So where else does that leave us?"

Emily joined her brother. "I want to stay here."

Amanda, Craig, Sarah and Edward were also in agreement.

"I don't feel safe here," Julie said.

Laura understood. "I'm afraid that's a feeling we're all going to have to embrace and come to terms with. Our world has been subjected to a life-altering chain of events. No one's going to feel safe and secure for a very long time."

"But Dom knows where we live," Kim proclaimed. "He was just here."

"Hon," Bill said. "We're all ears on any suggestions you may have."

Kim opened her mouth and paused. Her brain came back empty, much like everyone else's.

"And this is what I was referring to," Laura said. "We're all in fight or flight mode right now, and rightfully so. But we built this place for us. We have food, water, power and weapons. If we left, we'd be putting all of us at risk and have a fraction of the supplies necessary for survival. We don't know how long we'll need to be here, or what's going to ultimately happen to our planet. We need to take care of our immediate needs and stockpile anything we can get our hands on.

"Concurrently, Sam and Bill can begin working on a plan of attack."

"There's more we need to think about," Thomas said. "My entire family hasn't been accounted for."

"You're talking about your sister," Laura said.

Thomas nodded. "Her and Allison were placed in the Witness Protection Program. I don't know where they are."

Sam called out to Gabbi and Hobbes. "Can you find Abby and Allison's location?"

"Way ahead of you," Gabbi replied. "The database is completely offline and the internet, whatever's left of it, is acting really weird. I'll keep at it."

"They're not the only ones," Thomas added. "My friend Nick is out in LA, along with his wife Susan and their fifteen-year-old daughter Lisa."

"So, what do you propose?" Sam asked.

Thomas pondered for a few seconds. "It sounds like we need to do a lot, and we don't have a lot of time. We need supplies. We need more weapons. We need to check SANDBOX. We need to find my sister. We need to check-in on Nick and his family. And, last but not least, we need to find my two scientists."

Bill shook his head. "They have to be onboard that ship by now. Wouldn't you agree?"

"Unfortunately, I have to agree," Sam said. "I'm sure Dom moved them, or will move them, as soon as possible. Besides, Thomas, we don't have any leads on their whereabouts as it is."

Kim was disgusted. "I can't believe Dom's going to give abilities to all his people. This is a freaking nightmare."

"One thing at a time," Thomas said, "and there's nothing we can do about that right now." He looked over at Sam and Bill. "Road trip? Nick in LA, then SANDBOX, followed by a supply run?"

"You're going to leave us here?" Julie exclaimed.

"We'll be fine, mom," Craig said. "Besides, you can shoot fire from your hands now, remember?"

Julie brought her hands up to look at as a faint flicker danced on the tips of her fingers.

"Right."

* * *

Sam, Bill, Thomas, Gavin and Stir traversed The Other Place without incident before they appeared inside the home of Nick Raynes, Thomas' friend and book agent.

"Fucking hell," Nick exclaimed as the group exited the portal and stepped into Nick's family room.

Thomas immediately noticed that the television was on and that his friend and his family had been glued to it.

"Hi Susan. Lisa."

The two women didn't know how to reply to the abrupt interruption, especially from the man who used to be the President of the United States.

"Are you okay?" Thomas asked after the two men gave each other a hug.

"Is any of this real?" Nick inquired.

Thomas nodded. "I'm afraid so."

Nick sat down on the couch. "What is the plan?"

"You can come with us?"

Nick looked up at Thomas, then over to his wife and daughter. "Maybe all of this will blow over and we'll be fine."

"Dad, wake up," Lisa practically shouted at her father. "The world just turned upside down and you think it'll just work itself out? Who are you kidding?"

Susan put her hands on her daughter's shoulders in an effort to diffuse the tension.

"Lisa's absolutely right," Thomas told Nick as he sat down next to him. "The people on this planet aren't prepared. Military's, on every continent, have been decimated. No one's coming to save us."

"Except you, is that it?"

Nick's words stung.

"I don't know, but I'm going to do anything and everything in my power to rid our world of this infestation."

"Good luck with that."

Thomas stood up. "I came here to make sure you were okay, then offer you safe harbor. That's still my goal. Do you want to come with us or not?"

Susan walked over to her husband. "We're out of our depths. We should go with them."

"Listen to mom," Lisa added.

Nick shook his head. "We'll be safe enough here, but thank you for checking in on us. We'll be fine."

"Thomas," Sam said, "we need to go."

Thomas extracted a piece of paper from his pocket and handed it to Lisa.

"If you need to reach out, call and leave a message."

Lisa nodded.

"And, if you do, don't use our real names. I believe the communications network is being monitored. Use the words "little brown chair" and I'll know it's you, okay?"

"Thank you," Susan said. "Your coming here tells me everything I need to know about your integrity."

Thomas didn't want to push Nick any further than his own mind would let him process. It was clear his denial had already gotten the better of him, and only time would help change that perception.

"You're welcome. Take care and stay safe."

Thomas motioned to Gavin. Seconds later the group vanished.

*   *   *

SANDBOX, or what was left of the sprawling installation, had been decimated. As Thomas, Gavin and Stir held back, Sam and Bill methodically walked through the smoking ruins. The explosives that'd been utilized had shredded the entire property,

236

just like The Vatican. The destruction was absolute and heartbreaking.

"What do we do?" Bill solicited. "It's like we're going through losing SANDBOX all over again."

"That's because we are," Sam replied.

The two came across, what they thought had been the location of the barracks, and stopped dead in their tracks.

Bill couldn't tear his eyes away. *Death is everywhere.*

Lifeless bodies, combined with an endless array of body parts, were strewn haphazardly throughout the area. Some were burned and others were in pristine condition, as if they had no idea they'd even died.

Sam came to an abrupt halt as he focused on one particular face.

"What?" Bill asked.

Sam's face softened as he pointed towards a corpse, illuminated by a nearby fire.

"Oh shit, no," Bill exclaimed.

As they cautiously approached the body, it became evident it was female. Her eyes were open, tilted upwards and a bit off-center, as if focused on something in the distance. The scar down her cheek told Sam and Bill everything they needed to know. It was Rebecca.

*Shit.* Sam turned around and saw that Thomas, Gavin and Stir had followed them, but hadn't yet focused on Rebecca's body.

"Go warn them off," Sam told Bill. "Gavin's going to have a meltdown."

Bill took one last look at Rebecca before he silently jogged towards Thomas. Sam knelt down beside her, put his fingers over her eyelids and gently slid them downwards.

*Goddammit. I'm sorry, Rebecca. We'll make them pay.*

Sam stood up and walked over to where the others were.

"What's going on, Sam?"

His voice spoke volumes that Thomas immediately picked up on. "There's nothing here, Thomas. We should go and make that supply run."

# 26
## May, 2005
## Invasion + 1

Televisions, across the globe, suddenly changed from whatever disinformation program they were airing to a video that emanated from the alien spacecraft. The angle displayed an overhead view of Asia before the camera effortlessly zoomed in on dozens upon dozens of blooms that simultaneously erupted from out of the ground. The camera pulled back to show the multitudes of missiles that had just been launched out of China.

The missiles soared into the sky, arced ever so slightly, and then pointed themselves back towards the ground. Within minutes of the launches, massive detonations overlapped each other as millions of innocent Chinese were wiped off the face of the planet.

The senseless slaughter continued as the exact same outcome was executed in Russia, North Korea, Africa and the Middle East. Four-billion people had been exterminated in the blink of an eye, with millions of others injured or beyond help. The rest of the world were left living in unimaginable fear.

Dominick took to the airwaves, afterwards, with a concise message.

"A swift and deadly response is exactly what happens when countries refuse to submit and serve. Let this become a valuable lesson to those that still draw breath. Yield or die."

\* \* \*

# June, 2005
## Invasion + 2

Global warfare trickled and then came to a halt after half the planet had been subjected to nuclear war and the subsequent fallout. Supply lines, which the world never thought about, ground to a halt. That meant gas, oil, food, medicines and anything else humanity subsisted on became both scarce and highly sought after.

Furthermore, Dom's disinformation campaign remained in full effect, and was the only channel satellites continued to broadcast. Endless footage of nuclear hellscapes, combined with scores of the dead and burned bodies, was enough for any survivor to permanently turn off their televisions.

Those survivors, which mainly consisted of North and South America, Australia and Europe, were now forced to exist in a world that had become foreign, cruel and uncaring. The everyday normal routine of going to work had been obliterated. Money became obsolete as people fought to survive. Neighbors turned on each other as food became scarce, which meant opportunity was abundant for the few entrepreneurs that embraced the horrific bleakness that encircled the globe.

Black markets became prevalent, guarded by guns, and soon became one of the only means to trade for food, supplies and weapons. If you didn't have something to trade, then you were turned away. Empathy, a core value that humans normally cherished, was no longer on the menu. It was all about survival, at any cost.

Some, fearing the worst of humanity well before the invasion, were already well prepared. They descended into their bunkers, or bugged-out to their mountain cabins, to wait it out. Others did what they could to cultivate seeds and plant gardens.

It didn't take long for people to realize that the internet, cell and satellite phones, were being monitored. People who conspired and vowed to do something, while declaring these beliefs and desires over those specific forms of communication, were systematically executed. A ship would appear in the sky above, followed by a bombardment of energy, before it raced away.

But that didn't stop people from resisting. Instead, they went analogue and began to use Ham Radios to converse with each other. It was slow going at first, especially since ham radios weren't an everyday house item, and the fear of who they could be talking to. In time, however, it began to take off as more and more resistance groups somehow began to formulate within the chaos, anarchy and uncertainty that was now the new normal.

* * *

## July, 2005
## Invasion + 3

It wasn't long after the invasion before the Hawaiian islands were appropriated by Dominick and his people. The island's climate remained fairly constant, and the relative distance from either mainland made it rather defensible.

The populus that inhabited the seven main islands, of the one-hundred and thirty-seven known to exist, were immediately displaced. A vast majority died outright from multiple strafing runs. The ones that survived fled into the jungles before the constant relay of ships transported thousands of aliens to the islands. Most of those people were caught and gathered up, and forced into labor camps, who gathered and burned the bodies of the dead.

Others were then forced to till the earth.

Those massive farms were seeded and eventually cultivated plants that were not of the Earth.

*   *   *

Resistance, by those who had maintained their freedom, was as high as ever. Fledgling communities began to form; a necessity in the dark times as well as a reminder that humanity would never give up, no matter what the cost.

# 27
## July, 2005

Thomas couldn't help but listen to his internal debates while he took another lap in the bunker's swimming pool. It'd been three months since the invasion and he felt as helpless now as he had then. He methodically continued to swim as his brain lambasted away, unchecked.

*The world's gone to shit and I haven't done anything to prevent it.*

*What the hell are we supposed to do?*

*What could we have done?*

*Something. Anything.*

*And then maybe we'd all be dead, just like Rebecca, Sabrina and Bai.*

*Then why hasn't Dom been after us?*

*Maybe he hasn't been looking?*

*Don't be stupid. We're a threat to his entire operation.*

*Then what are we supposed to do about it?*

*You have to do something.*

*You have to protect your family.*

*You have t-*

"SHUT UP!"

Thomas pulled himself out of the water and sat on the edge of the pool, his feet still dangling underneath the surface. Laura pushed open the doorway and joined him.

"Penny for your thoughts," she said as she sat down.

"If only it were that easy, or cost effective."

"Your voice reverberated through the glass." She put a hand on his leg. "Talk to me."

He sighed. "I don't know what we're doing, other than successfully hiding as the world goes to shit."

"Is it guilt?"

"I don't know. Maybe. But it feels like it's more than guilt. Remorse. Inaction." He turned towards her. "We've been down here for three months. Three months, and we have nothing to show for it. We're trapped, so to speak, while Dom digs in harder and stronger every day. He's practically locked down Gavin's portal system, which means we're actually stuck here until our supplies run out, or lose our fricking minds. Whichever comes first."

"We're protecting our children and our family. What else do you think we should be doing?"

Thomas' pool thoughts came rushing back. "Something. Anything."

"Alright. Tell me, what does that look like, exactly?"

He closed his eyes. This wasn't the first time Laura had come to his aid. She'd spent time with each person, whether they wanted to admit it was a therapy session or not, to keep her family grounded. The bunker they'd built, all three levels of it, was more than they could have asked for, especially in these tumultuous times. But remaining underground, for extended periods of time, had unforeseen repercussions, and Laura was doing her part to mitigate them as best as she could.

"We need to take back The Other Place. We need to be able to move freely around, and I'm tired of being scared something will happen to Gavin every time he goes there."

"It sounds like you know exactly what you need to do. So go talk to Sam and Bill and figure out the next steps."

Thomas gently laid his head on Laura's shoulder. "Thanks. You're really good at this."

She smiled. "It's not like it was my job or anything."

"So, does that mean you're going to bill me?"

"You can't afford what I charge."

He righted himself and looked at her. "Oh, is that so?"

"You'd better believe it."

He reached for her hand and squeezed it as their feet dangled in the tepid pool water.

"I'm here," she said, "if you ever want to talk about it."

"Talk about what?"

"The time when you were The Caretaker."

He sighed. "You're right. I should have told you all about that long ago."

"But you were running for President, and then there was this little thing about an alien invasion."

"Something like that." He paused for a bit. "Seriously though, it's still strange for me to even think I had that role; that I actually was that entity."

Laura didn't press. She just continued to hold his hand.

"I don't know. I couldn't let him take Stir away from our son, so I made that deal behind your back. Behind everyone's back. And then I just…, vanished. It wasn't right. I'm sorry."

He kicked his feet back and forth as he made ripples.

"To be The Caretaker," he eventually said, "was unreal. Time, at least the linear version humans are used to, ceased to exist and could be manipulated as if one were merely adjusting a thermostat."

He frowned as he tried to recollect the fragments.

"I traversed the universe. I saw things I can't even begin to describe. Such beauty and such destruction. It was as if the universe was at war with itself."

"Perhaps it was, from what you've told me of the relationship The Caretaker and The Ancient had with one another."

"You're not wrong. Ying and Yang. They balanced one another, until I forced them back together. Brothers, and the same creature. And yet, despite all that, Earth is under siege because of what The Ancient took away from Dominick, and his people."

"Are you going to just let that continue to happen?"

Thomas stood up. "Absolutely not."

\*

Sam and Bill, along with the majority of the rest of the family, could only stare as Thomas, dripping water, made a bee-line towards them.

Bill was the first to make a comment. "Nice shorts."

"Dad," an exasperated Emily added. "Come on. Put some clothes on, you're embarrassing me."

Laura, who had followed behind, tossed Thomas the towel he'd neglected.

Thomas came to a halt at the table Sam, Julie, Bill and Kim were seated around. Off, in the distance, the kids were involved in a board game, amidst the massive amounts of boxes they had stacked against the wall of the entertainment space. They contained supplies Sam, Bill and Thomas, with Gavin's assistance, had burgled from a big box store after their unfortunate encounter with Rebecca's corpse. They had spent hours conveying food, water and supplies into the portal, and then repeating the process in their bunker. They didn't particularly feel good about it, but they didn't have a choice, much like the rest of the populus. It was all about survival, and they'd successfully procured what they needed before that particular store had been ransacked.

"You seem a little hot under the collar," Sam told his friend. "What's on your mind?"

"We need to take back The Other Place."

The kids heard his statement and immediately came over to join the conversation.

"I agree," Sam said. "How?"

Gavin piped up. "There's something in there that's been tracking us every time we go in there. I've told you about that. It's some kind of tech we're not aware of."

Thomas nodded. "I know we've had some close calls, which is why we haven't left the bunker for over a month now. But, as we all must be aware of, we can't stay here forever, nor should we want to."

"So," Bill said, "your plan is to find and take out the alien who makes portals?"

"Yes."

"And who's to say there isn't more than one at this point? They have the stockpile of serum and the scientists who make it. They could have a whole bevy of portal creators by now."

"Unlikely," Laura declared.

"Why do you say that?" Kim asked.

"Because Dom's a textbook narcissist and egomaniac, amongst other things. I doubt he would ever share his power with anyone else. His ability is what gives him an edge over his people. He wouldn't want them to start making decisions on their own and diluting whatever hold he has over them."

"Or," Julie said, "they're all just as bad and evil as Dom is."

Laura nodded. "There is that to consider as well."

Thomas spoke up again. "We won't know the answer to any of those questions if we continue to remain down here. Yes, we're safe, but for how long? We have supplies, but for how much longer? The world needs our help and we need to do whatever we can to save it."

Gabbi and Hobbes had just arrived upstairs from their bedroom on the bunker's bottom floor.

247

"We're not alone in that way of thinking," Gabbi proclaimed. She continued before anyone could ask her to explain. "Hobbes and I have been listening in on the ham radio you procured during your initial supply run. Thank you for that by the way."

"Welcome," Bill said.

"Anyway, there are multiple groups of resistance out there, all desperate to both survive and take some sort of action against our unwanted visitors. A lot of them are desperate, that's for sure, but we're not alone. That's the good news."

Sam gave her a look. "So, you're saying there's bad news?"

Gabbi nodded. "And how, I'm afraid. You're all aware that power, the internet and television signals are still up and running."

"You mean the propaganda channel?"

"Yes, but that's not what I'm talking about. The bad news is that I've been using my new tech talking ability to probe what's out there."

Kim didn't understand, much like the others. "What do you mean, what's out there?"

"Exactly." Gabbi took a breath. "I'm constantly running into an unknown synthetic entity that absolutely has a mind of its own."

"What does that actually mean?" Julie pressed.

"It's like, as if something is looking over my shoulder while I'm probing what's left of the internet, except that it's just out of sight every time I look over my shoulder."

The adults glanced at one another, not getting the full meaning of Gabbi's words.

Hobbes noticed and attempted to clarify. "We're convinced it's artificial intelligence."

"You mean," Emily said, "like when you make a spelling error and your computer picks up on it?"

"I wish," Gabbi replied. "This AI, which our world has never experienced, is a game changer." She held up her hand. "Let me

248

try and explain. If it's really a thing, and I believe it is, then it explains everything: the video broadcasts, the satellites, the nukes, the internet....EVERYTHING.

"I'm talking about Quantum computing."

Gabbi looked around at a room full of blank stares before she mustered onward.

"The world's technological advances are nothing compared to quantum computing. It's as if our civilization had only evolved to using spears, while our enemy had stealth bombers in their arsenal. More specifically to what happened to the world's defenses, a quantum computer uses qubits t-"

Hobbes nudged her.

"Right. Um, let's try this. The world uses various encryption to secure data and access to sensitive areas, like nuclear codes. If I wanted to crack that encryption it would take ten-thousand years."

Thomas spoke up. "How long would it take with a quantum computer?"

Gabbi looked over at Thomas. "About one minute, which is how they took control of our world's nukes and satellites and everything else. Now, here's the best part. They have an AI who's plugged into that quantum array. And they've set it loose. This entity can multitask like nothing I've ever seen, and it seems to have a life of its own."

"It's sentient?" Bill asked.

"Big word, brother," Sam teased.

"Yeah, yeah. Fuck off."

Gabbi nodded. "It would appear so, but that's not the problem. I mean, it is the problem, but not the thing I was abo-...never mind. I think that whatever controls they have over the AI may be slipping, and they don't even know it."

"Why do you say that?" Thomas inquired.

"I can't explain it yet. It's just a feeling."

"So bottom line this for everyone," Sam instructed.

"Understood. It means we have to be extremely careful. This AI, amongst whatever else it does, tracks communications and patterns. We, as humans, are mostly predictable. This AI can predetermine where resistance attacks will occur with a scary proficiency. Furthermore, if we use any satellite phones or attempt to communicate via the internet or cell phones, they will be monitored.

"It's already broken through and into every single piece of technology our world has ever created. It has full control. Period. If we're going to fight back then we'll need to make sure it's completely random. No patterns. Nothing predictable, if that's even a thing we can count on anymore. I can help but reiterate how dangerous this AI is, and that Dominick is in control of said entity."

Sam leaned back in his chair. "Any good news?"

Hobbes answered. "Maybe. We were able to track down a few Reaper drones that haven't been discovered or destroyed yet. The issue is naturally getting them refueled, which would mean actually touching them. Then, of course, they'd probably be detected once they were in the air, and most likely susceptible to the AI."

"I," Gabbi added, "have no idea if I can go up against the AI in cyberspace, or if I even want to. If anything, those drones would be a one-time use at best."

Before the conversation could continue a security monitor popped to life as the closed-looped security feed picked up movement in the main house, just above them.

Everyone froze and remained silent, just like they'd drilled as all eyes focused on the monitors. It was Dominick.

## 28
## July, 2005

Dominick teleported from the orbiting colony ship to his estate in Minnesota. He hadn't been back to it for some time, as there was always something for him to attend to. He needed to get away from it all and take a break; some time for himself. But, as it turned out, his internal monologue had a voice and a power of its own.

*It's been three months, and I'm already bored to death with all this executive shit I constantly have to deal with. I took over this planet and things are moving forward on the ground. I've done my part and given my people a second chance to live and thrive.*

He continued to pace around his office, much like a caged animal.

*The Hawaiian farms have been plowed and seeded. Our larvae are growing, and they will add to our growing ranks. Any external attacks have been locked down, and or destroyed, when I took over every nation's nuclear arsenal, and military ships and planes have been destroyed.*

He sighed.

*Pockets of resistance exist, and to be honest, I welcome them. Bring the fight to me so I can taste victory, time and time again. It's too bad really, because it seems that the rest of the human race has given up and reluctantly accepted that we're running the show now. I didn't think they'd roll over so easily. Oh well.*

*The two scientists I captured have continued to produce and stockpile my serum, but now tell me they can't continue without additional blood that only Thomas can provide. I'm not going to administer it to any of my people until I have enough for everyone.*

*And that brings me to my next order of business, one that I've waited far too long to address. Where the hell is Thomas Clark, and where's he been hiding for the past ninety days?*

Dom looked at his 'Thomas Clark' wall and smiled.

*I should just drop by his house.*

An instant later Dom stood over the four alien corpses that littered the entryway, long dead and degraded. The front door remained smashed inwards, and the interior was littered with debris and leaves. He sauntered inside, towards the family room and kitchen, and took it all in.

*Dust and muck are everywhere. This place definitely hasn't been lived in. A pity. I'm not sure what else I thought I'd find here. I need a distraction. I need a fight. I need blood!*

"Oh Thomas. Come out, come out, wherever you are. My people haven't detected you traversing The Other Place for some time, so that means you've squirreled you and your family away someplace, at least for the time being."

Dom continued to walk around, unaware of the hidden security cameras that caught everything he vocalized.

"I'll find you, or someone you love, and squeeze them until you're left with no other choice but to reveal yourself. You see, to be perfectly honest, I need your blood. Dr. Neal and Dr. Hanson have run out of that necessary ingredient to continue their serum production. And while I may not have administered any permanent abilities to my brethren, I have been utilizing the twelve-hour temporary injections to move personnel around the planet, as I see fit. You've put all that in peril."

Dom chuckled.

"Then again, if you could actually hear me, Amanda would probably realize that I speak the truth, as would your wife, Laura."

He picked up a discarded plate off the kitchen counter and threw it into the television screen. It shattered as it left a large crack across its surface.

"Is Earth everything I've ever wanted? For my people, yes. For me, no. I miss our cat and mouse games, my friend. I miss all the work I put into getting close and earning your trust. It was so very rewarding to deceive you, especially the moment when you finally realized the lengths I had taken."

Dom used his arm and violently swept everything that was on the counter onto the floor.

"Now I just need to figure out what it's going to take to make you pop your head up. Don't you worry, I'll figure something out."

Dom looked around once again, then vanished.

# 29
## July, 2005

Nick Raynes, along with his wife Susan and sixteen-year-old daughter Lisa, continued to hunker down in their house, which was located in the suburbs of Los Angeles. Nick had stocked up on supplies, as did thousands of other LA residents, immediately after he and his family witnessed the alien ship on television.

Then came the unexpected visit from Thomas, who insisted they join his family in a secure location. Nick declined and assured his longtime friend that he and his family would be fine where they were. Thomas even gave them a number to call, along with a coded message, in case they ever needed assistance.

Nick shook his head as he peered through the blinds to check for any movement on the street. His neighborhood, as the initial days turned into weeks, had progressed from one of safety and security, into a war zone. Multiple houses had been torched as armed gangs roamed the streets unabated and unopposed. The 'system' had quickly broken down once supply lines were severed, not to mention the jobs that gave people purpose. Now it was clear that it was every man for themselves, a lesson that Nick would never forget.

Fourteen days, after the start of the invasion, police and emergency services walked away from their jobs. They needed to look out for their own families, and rightfully so. Their absence was immediately noticed and then exploited. Gangs, who typically operated within limited neighborhoods and territories, took it upon themselves to expand, and they did so with impunity. Gang-on-gang warfare exploded, which affected thousands of civilians who were now caught in the crossfire.

Not surprisingly, food, water, medicine and fuel became highly sought after commodities. And, after the commercial districts and stores had been looted and picked clean, the next stop were residential areas. In the middle of the night, a month in, three men targeted Nick and Susan's house.

It was a combination of the back door being smashed inwards, and the pile of books he'd stacked by the door, which had clattered across the kitchen floor, that shook Nick and his family from their restless slumber.

Susan jolted awake as the jarring sound, followed a second later by her husband as the booby-trapped books slid across the floor. They quickly glanced at each other, each fully aware of the situation they now faced.

Someone was in their house.

Lisa rushed into their bedroom just as they got out of bed. Susan put a finger to her lips, barely visible in the ambient light, before she embraced her daughter. Nick grabbed his baseball bat, stationed next to the bed, as the crunch of broken glass emanated from further down the hallway.

It was more than one person.

Nick swallowed hard as he held his make-shift weapon. Susan and Lisa quietly retreated, just as they'd rehearsed, towards the master closet as the strangers began to talk amongst themselves.

"This is a nice place. Maybe I'll make it my own."

"Shut up. I already called dibs before we even got here."

"Both of you shut the fuck up and fan the fuck out. We need to make sure this place is empty before you two high-five each other. I'll go this way. You two check out the rest of the house."

Nick tip-toed towards his dresser, positioned just inside their bedroom door, and hid next to it. If anyone entered the room they wouldn't see him, especially with the lights off. It wasn't long before he heard the stranger's footsteps. They paused as Nick blinked away a bead of sweat. Then everything changed.

"Knock knock," the single intruder said as the unmistakable sound of a handgun's slide was heard.

Nick nearly pissed himself. *Fuck. He has a gun.*

The master bedroom's door slowly swung open before the intruder entered, gun up and at the ready. Nick watched, his vision partially blocked from his hiding spot, as the man swept the bedroom from left to right. Satisfied, the intruder took another step forward. Nick swore the man had to have heard his ragged breathing before he stepped out and brought his bat up and over his head.

The robber heard movement on the carpet, and as he began to swing his arm around towards the threat as the bat was brought down on it with tremendous force. The gun clattered to the carpet as the intruder screamed out in excruciating pain, part of his forearm bent as if he now had a second elbow.

Nick didn't even register the man's screams as he cocked back and then landed another blow to the man's face, who dropped to the carpet a second later. A pool of blood began to form on the carpet.

"Nick?" Susan whispered as she opened the closet.

"WHAT THE HELL WAS THAT!?"

Nick barely had time to kick the man's gun away before the other two intruders rushed towards the commotion and barged into the room. In doing so they slammed into Nick and catapulted him into the side of his bed. His bat clattered onto the carpet and skittered away as he tried to right himself.

"Time to die, bitch!"

The two men proceeded to stumble over the body of their leader as they advanced on Nick, which initially saved their lives.

The first bullet went high and to the right, and probably would have struck one of the two men if they were still upright. That single round deafened everyone in the room as the two men couldn't help but focus on the woman with the handgun.

"GO! GO!"

Susan closed her eyes and continually pulled the trigger over and over as Nick curled himself into a ball behind their bed.

It was all over in a few seconds.

Nick slowly popped his head up as his wife continued to depress the trigger. The empty weapon refused to shoot the bullet ridden attackers.

*Fuck, my ears are ringing. I can't hear a goddamn thing.*

He rushed across the room, as he avoided three bodies, when Susan swiveled the weapon towards her husband. It was then, and only then, that she realized what she'd just done. Nick caught her as she collapsed into his arms. The empty weapon fell to the carpet as he gently lowered her down. Lisa emerged from the back of the closet and joined them.

They had survived, but they had all been changed by the home invasion, in one way or another.

\* \* \*

The morning following the home invasion, Nick and Susan buried the three men in their backyard, then did their best to clean up the bloody mess that remained. As luck would have it, the leader Nick assaulted with a bat, had an additional magazine of ammo in one of his pockets, which upped their odds at survival in the coming months. Still, it took days for their hearing to return, and even longer for all of them to come to terms with how close they'd come to being killed.

258

* * *

It was now July, three months in, and Nick didn't know what to do anymore.

*I should have taken Thomas up on his offer. Why did I let my own ego stand in the way of my family's safety? What was I thinking? We're down to Top Ramen, and we only have a few days of that left as it is. If we venture out into the streets we'll be killed, or worse. Survival has turned my neighborhood and humanity into people we wouldn't even recognize anymore. I mean, look what Susan was forced to do to defend our family.*

*Lisa's different.* He paused. *Shit, be real Nick, we all are. Look how fucked the world is. How are people supposed to survive like this? I don't think I have any other choice but to contact Thomas and beg for his assistance, if he's even still alive.*

The handgun was nestled in the small of his back, and ever since that night he made sure it was always with him.

Nick checked on his wife and daughter, who were working on a jigsaw puzzle together in the kitchen.

"Hey, haven't you two done that one before?"

Lisa looked up at her father. "Maybe you should have looted a board game store in the mall."

Nick didn't reply. They were all on edge and hungry. Susan and he had tried to hide how depraved the world had become from their daughter, but she saw right through their lies.

Lisa continued. "Are you ready to call Uncle Thomas now, before we starve to death, and preferably before mom and I get raped and or killed?"

Susan barely reacted to her daughter's outbursts anymore. She continued to have nightmares about taking those two men's lives, even though it had been the right course of action, but she didn't know if she ever wanted to touch a gun again. Lisa, on the other

259

hand, was more than anxious to learn how to handle a firearm, and had to convince her father to show her the basics.

Nick sat down at the table with them. "I'm sorry."

"Sorry for what?" Lisa shot back.

"Sorry for everything." He looked over at Susan, then back over at his daughter. "You're right, I fucked up. I should have taken Thomas' offer from the very beginning."

"No shit."

Nick pulled out the piece of paper Thomas had given them and slid it across the table towards Lisa.

"We can't live like this anymo-"

A man suddenly appeared, out of nowhere, just feet away from them. His face had been all over television. It was Dominick Knight.

Nick pulled out, somewhat clumsily, the handgun as Dom casually walked over behind Susan and put one of his hands on her shoulder. Lisa immediately scooted away from the table and pocketed the note her father had just passed to her.

"Are you sure you want to do this, Mr. Raynes?"

Nick's hand shook as he stood up, the weapon pointed towards Dom. "Get away from my wife."

Dom took his free hand and extracted a blade, which he then pressed against the side of Susan's head. She was petrified.

"You, Mr. Raynes, may be in possession of information I require."

"Get away from my wife!"

"You're not listening, and that's quite frustrating. But I have time, so let's continue, shall we?"

"Get away from her!"

"Perhaps," Dom continued as he shook his head from side to side, "I should make an example of Susan here, so I can get your undivided attention? How's that sound?"

"I love you," Susan barely squeaked out.

"I said, get awa-"

Dom effortlessly plunged his blade through Susan's skull and deep into her brain. Her body spasmed for a brief second, then lost all rigidity and collapsed out of her chair and onto the floor.

Lisa screamed as Nick emptied his handgun at Dom. When the weapon locked open Nick felt a hand on his shoulder as Dom pushed him downwards into the same chair he'd risen out of.

Dom looked over at Lisa. "Come and join us, won't you?"

Lisa turned and ran. Dom shrugged and concentrated on Nick.

"You….you….you sonofabitch," Nick sobbed, barely able to hear over his throbbing eardrums. "Why…why did you kill her?"

"None of you matter to me. Your time is over, but you just haven't come to that realization yet. It's been three months and yet some of you still want to fight. To live. It doesn't matter to me of course. It's only a matter of time before your species is extinct."

Nick couldn't hear Dom's speech whether he wanted to or not. He remained focused on his wife's lifeless eyes that stared up at him from the floor below.

"I need information."

Nick didn't respond so Dominick extracted another chair and sat down, eye to eye. Nick had no choice but to look at the alien that had just murdered the love of his life.

*Where's Lisa? Where's my daughter?*

Nick turned his head, but Dom swiveled it back towards him.

"I know that you're Thomas Clark's publicist. Where is he?"

"Who?" Nick practically yelled due to his hearing.

"Thomas Clark," Dom repeated as he raised his own voice to match. "Where is he?"

"I don't fucking know, and I wouldn't fucking tell you even if I did, you fucking piece of shit!"

"Is that so?" Dom asked as he flung his chair aside and withdrew a second knife.

Nick turned his head towards the front of the house. "LISA! RUUUUUUN!"

All Lisa heard, as she sprinted out the front door, was her father choking on his own blood.

She knew the neighborhood, as she'd been born and raised here, so she zigged and zagged over fences and through multiple alleyways. When she finally collapsed, out of pure exhaustion, she was miles from her house. She also knew that being outside was a risk, far less than being killed by the man who murdered her parents, but she had little choice in the matter.

She frantically looked around. *What do I do now?*

\* \* \*

In the bunker, one of the ghost phones began to vibrate. None of them had been used since the invasion had started, nor could they be trusted, as per Gabbi's trepidations. Sam and Bill looked at each other as Thomas hurried over to answer it.

"It could be a trap," Bill warned him just as he picked it up.

Thomas clicked the answer button and all he heard was heavy breathing.

"Code in," he said.

"What?"

It was a female's voice

"Code in or I'm terminating this call. You have three seconds."

"Um…right. Um…little brown chair."

Thomas' eyes flew open. *It's Lisa.* "What's your current location?"

"Griffith…Griffith Park Observatory."

"We'll be right there."

Thomas ended the call and put the phone down.

Sam stood up. "What's going on?"

"Where's Gavin?" Thomas shot back.

* * *

They somehow managed to avoid two alien patrols in The Other Place, retrieve Lisa from the Observatory, and make it back home in one piece. Thomas couldn't get much out of her since she was either in shock about the loss of her parents, or in awe of traversing The Other Place for the first time. Either way, once back in the bunker Lisa was able to explain what happened to her parents, and how it all happened at the hands of Dominick.

Laura, Julie and Kim got Lisa cleaned up and settled while Sam, Bill, Thomas, Gabbi and Hobbes rehashed the events.

"I can't believe Nick and Susan are...gone," Thomas said. "Why didn't he take me up on my offer to stay with us?"

"You can't beat yourself up over something that was his decision," Bill said. "It's fucked up what happened, but there's nothing we can do about it."

"Bill's right," Sam added. "This war is going to get a lot bloodier before it ends. Dom will get what's coming to him."

Thomas slammed his fist on the table. "Yeah? When's that happening, and who else has to suffer before we can end this thi-?"

Thomas froze as his face shifted.

"What?" Bill pressed.

"Fuck," Thomas replied. "If Dom would do this to Nick and Susan, then just imagine what he'll do if he gets hold of my sister."

Sam and Bill knew exactly what he was capable of.

Thomas turned to Gabbi and Hobbes. "I know you said the database was down, but that was three months ago. Any chance you can find her? Please?"

Gabbi glanced over at Hobbes before she answered. "It's risky."

"It's my sister."

Gabbi nodded. "Believe me, I get it, but it's dangerous. Maybe this is exactly what Dominick wants us to do."

"And what's that?"

"Make a mistake," she told him.

Thomas shook his head. "I don't care. Just do it."

Gabbi looked over at Sam and Bill for approval. They gently nodded their heads for her to proceed.

"Alright," she told Thomas, "we'll get right on it."

\* \* \*

The two techs spent the night on their ham radios, both listening and reaching out to other survivors across the country. Eventually, as dawn approached, they came up with a lead that seemed pretty solid.

Thomas had instructed they wake him if they found something, so at five in the morning they did just that. Thomas followed the two out to the common area and left Laura to sleep alone.

"Do you have something?"

Hobbes nodded. "I'm afraid so."

"What do you mean? What's with the long faces?"

Gabbi answered for them. "We believe we found your sister, but she's in the thick of it."

"Where?" Thomas asked. "Where's Abby and Allison?"

"On the island of Maui, smack dab in alien territory."

## <u>30</u>

Allison rolled over and spooned Abby. Abby, 42, and Allison, 44, had initially felt somewhat selfish and guilty for leaving Thomas and the rest of the family two years prior. Their Witness Protection relocation package, pushed through by Agent Shaw prior to Thomas' run for the presidency, allowed them to graciously choose where they wanted to live. The two women had always talked about a place that was warm, a far cry from the weather they'd been accustomed to in Portland, Oregon, before The Ancient upended their lives. They decided that they'd give Hawaii a try, and eventually decided upon Maui.

Agent Shaw asked them, before they shipped out, if they wanted to share their new location with Thomas. It was a tough decision, but ultimately, they declined. They wanted a fresh start, which also came with new identities. Why not, they said, share the same last name?

Abby and Allison decided to get married on May 3, 2003, under their new names, Abby and Allison Lewis. They'd chosen that name as a tongue and cheek reference to the Lewis & Clark expedition. Mainly it was an inside joke, one that helped Abby keep close to her family name, as well as to cope with the guilt that plagued her from time to time.

Abby tended to be a restless sleeper, every so often, so she ended up rehashing the speech she'd given the entire family over and over in her mind.

*"Don't get me wrong, we absolutely love all of you, but your enemies aren't going to stop coming which means it's only a matter of time before some or all of you end up like our parents. Sam was right about that just a moment ago; they're going to keep coming. So, you can do what Allison and I are about to do, and*

265

*that's run and hide. Or, you can try and fight them off on your own. However, try to imagine the influence you could have on the world if Thomas actually succeeds, not to mention the backing of the government. The truth is our world is on the cusp of breaking wide open, or becoming something better. What side of history do you want to be known for?"*

Sometimes their choice to isolate themselves felt like an overreach, but as Abby and Allison followed Thomas' presidential campaign, and the multiple attempts on his life, they realized they'd made the right decision to step away from that particular chaos, especially since they felt they would have only been in the way. They didn't have abilities, and the guilt Abby felt about not being able to help prevent the death of her parents continued to remain just below the surface.

After relocating, with the help of the government and a sizeable insurance check from the loss of their Portland art gallery, they decided to rent a small house while they looked for land to develop to eventually build something permanent. They found jobs in Lahaina managing one of the existing art galleries, of which there were about forty, and settled into a new but very familiar routine. In their down time the two helped out with a communal garden, went to the local theater for plays, and once a month or so, treated themselves to dinner and a movie.

And while their lives seemed picture perfect, Abby couldn't shake the feeling that she had been vastly unprepared for the chaos and bloodshed she and Allison had been unwillingly subjected to. Her continued restless sleeping patterns, and guilt, eventually prompted Abby to stop and stare at a store she'd passed dozens of times. It was one of those touristy type gun shops where you could rent and shoot full-auto weapons. Abby paused as she focused in on the various packages they offered inside.

*I need to stop being a victim. I'm afraid of guns, but I need to do something to mitigate my fear of feeling helpless, especially if things go sideways again. This might not be the ultimate answer, but it's a start. It's something.*

Abby ended up paying for a package that included two handguns and an AR-15. The shooting session itself, as intended, didn't last very long, but the impact of holding and firing a weapon absolutely did. In the months that followed, as the foundation for their new house had finally been poured, Abby introduced Allison to her new hobby. Allsion, naturally, was reluctant at first, but after a few sessions at the range understood where Abby was coming from. It didn't take long for them to enroll in gun safety and training courses, followed by procuring two 9mm handguns and an AR-15.

Abby's restless nights began to fade, not due to the weapons, but because she'd taken steps to push back against the fears that controlled her. The weapons themselves, as they were discharged at the range, had transformed into a form of therapy.

Eight months later, Abby and Allison moved into their new house. Their social group had grown, which consisted of other LGBTQ couples and members of the art community. They joined a hiking group that enjoyed exploring the various trails that Maui had to offer. They uncovered breathtaking ocean and jungle views on each and every adventure, but the one that changed everything was the hike that ended at the mouth of a WW2 bunker.

Abby was enthralled as she took off her pack and extracted a flashlight. The other group members decided to keep going, but Abby and Allison wanted to explore inside. As it turned out, the bunker wasn't only a pillbox that overlooked the ocean. In fact, after a quick probe, they discovered that it was considerably larger, with an old command center flanked by various storage and troop barracks. It was also evident that nobody, aside from some graffiti, had ventured inside in some time, probably because the bunker was located on a trail, and hidden by vegetational overgrowth.

The two finished their exploration and continued on with their hike, but Abby's internal wheels kept spinning, whether she actively realized it or not.

* * *

Abby didn't know how to feel. One on hand she was torn that her brother, along with Laura, Gavin and Emily, had nearly been killed by an explosion right before his presidential convoy had driven across the Arlington Memorial Bridge. On the other, as she watched the news, she was relieved she had stepped away from that perilous lifecycle. Yes, she was proud that her brother had become President of the United States, but she never talked about that relationship with anyone other than Allison. How could she? Why would she? That part of her life was in the past, and had to remain that way. If anyone knew she was the President's sister, Abby knew the life she and Allison had developed in Hawaii would immediately be placed in peril.

Then came Thomas' impeachment. It was hard for Abby to watch, especially when he insisted that aliens had lived among them for the past two-hundred years. She didn't know if her brother had lost his mind, but he seemed absolutely sure of himself while he attempted to reason with members of Congress.

It wasn't until every news channel focused on the alien space ship, hovered over Washington D.C., that she cursed herself for doubting her brother. She knew things were about to get worse, and they only had so much time before that exact moment presented itself.

Abby turned to Allison, who was also glued to their television. "Shit's about to get real."

Allison nodded. "That's the understatement of the year. Glad we don't have kids."

Abby smiled. They'd discussed adopting, but they knew that would bring a major change to their lifestyle, one they knew had probably passed. Still, they were interested in procuring a dog or a cat, but that particular notion just got tossed out the window.

"Should we call your brother?"

"He's knee deep in that hell already. We need to figure out what we're going to do, and then get to it. I don't think we have a lot of time before things get really bad."

"You must have some ideas," Abby stated. It wasn't a question.

Abby's brain rattled it out before she knew it. "Guns, supplies, base of operations and people we can trust."

\* \* \*

Abby and Allison quickly went house to house, to neighbors they knew and interacted with, and tried to convince them time was of the essence. Initially they were only able to recruit a few to help, but six people can accomplish a lot when under pressure. Half went to the local grocery store for a supply run, while the other three made a bee-line for the downtown gun store, the same one that offered the automatic weapons packages. Without a way to realistically break in, they backed a truck into the front of the shop. An alarm pierced the night as it echoed up and down the block. Thankfully, they were able to procure two dozen weapons and multiple containers of ammunition before the police arrived. By then, they were already on their way to the hardware store, on the other side of Lahaina, to obtain generators, gas, and other necessities.

It was an uncoordinated shitshow that nearly got them caught and thrown in jail, but for whatever reason the six made it to their rendezvous, at the bunker's trailhead, relatively unscathed. The trail was too narrow for vehicles, but they had a couple of ATVs. The group connected trailers to those off-roaders, piled them high with supplies, and set off towards the uphill bunker. Multiple runs were made throughout the night, and by the next morning the bunker's interior had a large stack of materials to work with.

As the following day progressed, another dozen or so people had joined in, with the cleanup and preparation of the bunker's interior the main focus, along with additional supplies being motored up from the trailhead. A local spring, not too far from the bunker, was utilized, along with portable ham radios to coordinate communications.

It was difficult. It was painful. People screamed, yelled and cried. Some prayed, while others knew time was one of the only commodities they had left. Once that was extinguished, humanity would most likely collapse into a violent afterthought, as people fought to survive.

Three days later, with the world on fire and every television spouting false narratives, Abby collapsed onto a military cot. She'd been going nonstop, barking out orders while simultaneously welcoming anyone who sought shelter. She didn't wake up until the following morning when Allison nudged her awake.

"I feel like crap," Abby said as she somehow managed to sit up.

"Then maybe you shouldn't look outside to see what's parked in the distance."

"What the hell are you talking about?"

"You'll see."

Abby put her shoes on and stood up. She took the handgun from under her pillow and re-holstered it, then grabbed her AR, that was resting against the wall, before she followed Allison through the bunker outside. It was unmistakable. There, off in the vast distance, ninety miles away and hovering high up in the sky, appeared to be the same spaceship they'd seen on television.

"Fuck."

Allison nodded. "Yeah, that about sums it up."

"At least it's way over there."

"For the time being."

"Yeah," Abby concurred. She continued to stare at it, along with a growing number of others. "We've got a lot of work to do, so let's get at it."

"Are you sure we shouldn't call your brother?"

Abby pulled Allison off to the side and lowered her voice. "He's definitely got his own crap to deal with right now, and we've got a couple dozen people we've convinced to upend their lives and go off grid."

"Maybe he could help our cause?"

"Maybe, but he doesn't even know where we relocated to, and if the shit on tv is any indication, it would appear that all communications are probably monitored. We don't know what other tech the aliens have at their disposal. It's too risky."

"What about using ham radio?"

"It could be monitored as well. We just don't know."

Allison wasn't about to give up. "What else are we supposed to do? We're on an island, in the middle of the Pacific, that's cut off from the rest of the world. Meanwhile, the aliens have decided to take a Hawaiian vacation in our backyard."

Abby took Allison by her shoulders. "We're alone, and we need to face everyday by doing whatever we need to survive.

Right now, that means we need a constant supply of food, water, medicine and whatever else our group requires."

Allison grinned. "Shit babe, when did you step into the role of G.I. Jane?"

Abby somehow allowed herself to laugh, something her mind and body desperately needed at that moment. "I love you."

"I love you too."

Abby took another long look at the alien craft, then turned back towards the bunker they now called home. "Let's get to work."

* * *

## 3 months later
## July, 2005

Abby patched up the leg of one of her people because a raid to obtain additional supplies had gone sideways. If anything, the alien invaders definitely knew there was a group of humans, operating in Maui, that had just attacked one of their checkpoints. Abby knew they needed whatever technology the aliens had, especially the communication Abby had clocked with her binoculars.

Her team of six had made their way through the jungle, under the cover of night, towards their objective.

They'd kept an extremely low profile, keeping to themselves as they guarded their bunker. However, once they witnessed smaller ships make strafing runs over the residential areas, they knew they'd made the right decision to make this their new home. That, however, didn't make it any easier to swallow, especially after watching the dead being piled up, by other humans, before being torched. That was a sight that none of them ever wanted to see again, let alone erase from their memories. Humans were being killed, and other humans were being used as slave labor. This was very real.

It took Abby and the others some time to digest the alien's true appearance, with their two legs and four mandibles. They were tall too, and could transform into humans in the blink of an eye. That alone was terrifying, and immediately prompted Abby to instill a rotating daily codeword to challenge anyone of the group as they returned to the bunker. It wasn't perfect, but what other choice did she have.

The checkpoint in question had been chosen for being somewhat isolated, as well as having a relatively low traffic value, both by human and alien alike. They'd spent the past two days observing from a distance, as they mapped out any discernable patterns that would give them the upper hand. When it came down to it, the count was six humans against three aliens. The odds were good, but the element of surprise was absolutely everything.

*These bastards have ships that could be here in seconds, for all we know. This has to be executed perfectly. We need to get in and get out.*

Their initial attack, coordinated in theory, didn't go off as planned. Abby's first burst, from her AR-15, tore through the torso of one alien. But, instead of synchronized shots, the follow up attacks didn't happen until two seconds later, and by that time the other two aliens had already taken cover. A second after that they'd began to return fire.

There was nothing her team could do but retreat into the jungle, which they did, before one of them got clipped in the ankle by an energy weapon.

273

All that work for nothing. It was disappointing, and sent up a flare that there was a resistance group operating on Maui. The shitstorm was about to come down on their heads.

The group made it back to the bunker and relayed their failure to everyone else. This wasn't the first raid that had gone sideways over the past three months, but it was the first they'd attempted in the past few weeks that left a body behind, rather than a pilfered building without any casualties. This was serious, and they all knew there was a good chance of a retaliatory strike.

* * *

Allison tended to monitor the ham radios, rather than go out on missions with Abby, especially because she knew Abby wouldn't be able to fully concentrate on the task at hand if she was there. It was something that went unsaid between them, and their division of labor actually worked out for the better.

Allison greeted Abby, and the others, as they returned to the bunker. Their injured team member was tended to. All in all, they had been lucky to get out of there without additional casualties, especially the way the alien's energy weapons tore through cover.

"You okay?" Allison asked.

Abby nodded. "Yeah. That could have gone a lot better, that's for sure."

"Why don't you get some rest and I'll join you in a bit."

"Still monitoring radio traffic, I take it?"

Allison nodded. "It's interesting and horrific at the same time. I think we're losing."

"One day at a time, my love. See you in a few."

Allison returned to her post and placed the headphones over her ears. She worked the dials as she scanned various frequencies. They'd been able to install a large antenna on top of the pillbox,

274

then camouflage it with vines. This effectively allowed them to send and receive signals from much farther than they'd used to. It also increased Allison's workload, now that she had access to additional locations.

An hour later Allison stumbled upon a feint broadcast, so she attempted to narrow down the specific band, incrementally, with another dial.

"…ark. I re…t, A.. Cl…"

Allison knew she was close and kept at it until the static disappeared.

"I repeat. I'm looking for anyone that knows the location of Abby Clark and Allison Hansen. My name is Gabbi West. I need to urgently speak to either one of them. Please respond."

Allison couldn't believe her ears as she turned up the volume and listened as the woman repeated her message twice more.

*It sounds like Gabbi, but for all I know this could be some kind of trick. What do I do?*

"…Please respond."

Allison looked around the empty room, then keyed the transmit button. "Gabbi? Is that really you?"

"Say again. Say again."

Allison replied. "Gabbi. What's your preferred hair color?"

The system crackled to life again. "Holy shit. Is this Allison?"

"What's your preferred hair color?"

"Right. Sorry. Purple. It's purple. Is this Allison?"

Allison tried to control her glee. "One more question."

"Go for it," Gabbi replied.

"What tattoo do you have on your arm?"

"It's a dragon. Please tell me this is who I think it is?"

"Sorry, but I really have to make sure on this public forum."

"I understand."

"What's the name of your company?"

"ORACLE. It was ORACLE, until they fucking blew it up."

Allison relaxed and leaned in. "Holy shit! It's really good to hear your voice."

"You too, but we don't have a lot of time."

"Agreed. What's with this Hail Mary?"

"You and Abby are in trouble."

"Aren't we all."

"You're being targeted, specifically. It's only a matter of time."

"What does that mean?"

"I'll go into detail if you want, but others could be listening, right? I need to know where you're at so someone we know can come pick you up, okay?"

"And that person's name starts with a what?"

Gabbi caught on right away. "The same letter as my name."

"We're in Lahaina."

"Maui?" Gabbi asked.

"Yeah."

"Shit. I'll relay and get back to you." Gabbi paused. "I'm glad you two are still okay. Gotta go. Stay safe."

"You too."

## 31

## July, 2005

"Where?" Thomas asked. "Where's Abby and Allison?"

"On the island of Maui, smack dab in alien territory."

Gabbi and Hobbes stood there as Thomas mulled over this new information.

"You guys look beat," Sam told them. "Go get some sleep, and thanks for all your hard work."

The two nodded and headed off as the rest of the adults pondered on what to do.

"They're on Maui," Kim stated. "Damn."

Thomas spoke up. "We have to go and save them. There's no choice in the matter."

"They're still alive," Laura assured him.

"But for how long?" he countered.

"The only reason," Bill announced, "that we haven't already left to get them is what's on everyone's minds. It's The Other Place and how isolated we've been because it's patrolled by aliens."

Sam nodded. "Then we need to do something about that, don't we. The truth is, the longer we wait the more entrenched Dom will become. Our inactivity has emboldened him, especially now that we know he's refocused his efforts to flush us out."

"What are we supposed to do, exactly?" Julie asked.

Thomas stood up. "What we should have been doing from the beginning. We take a stand. It's time we make a statement."

\* \* \*

Two hours later, Thomas, Sam, Bill, Gavin and Stir were prepped and ready to depart. There were discussions to allow some of their children to participate, but that was swiftly nullified. The brutal deaths of Lisa's parents had reminded everyone how vulnerable life was, and none of them were willing to risk their kids, regardless of how much bloodshed they'd all experienced up to this point in their lives.

Hobbes offered to join them, as he could use his doppelganger ability to potentially distract, but Sam immediately shot down that idea. The truth was that Hobbes hadn't faced combat before, and this was not that moment. Hobbes understood as Sam told him that there would be a time and place for him to step up.

In full tactical gear, kitted out with extra magazines, grenades, assault rifles and sidearms, the team of five hugged their families as they prepared to head out. Gavin's previous recons into The Other Place were met with increased resistance and occupation. If Dom wanted to limit their movement, he'd skillfully accomplished what he'd set out to do. Hopefully, with no indication that the family had traversed it for over a month, whoever opposition they were about to run into hopefully would be caught off-guard.

Laura took Thomas aside. "Are you sure about this?"

"We're talking about my sister."

"I know. I get it."

"He killed Nick and Susan to get to me. He's not going to stop. You know that."

Laura nodded.

"I love you, but I have to do this."

"I'll be waiting. We all will."

Thomas hugged her, then rejoined the team. Seconds later he headed through the portal and disappeared.

It'd been some time since Thomas had been on Gavin's island as he felt the soft sand beneath his feet. He shrugged off the

278

feeling and surveyed the immediate area, much like Sam and Bill had already done. They were alone, for now.

With Stir dutifully by his side, Gavin created a boat for them to travel in. The group piled in, weapons at the ready, and headed off towards an unknown destination that only Gavin could detect.

"How far?" Sam asked.

Gavin shrugged. "I'll let you know when we're getting close."

Sam nodded. "We'll keep an eye out."

"You'd better," Gavin retorted. "I'm not here for the scenery."

Bill chuckled at the twelve-year-olds wit as he continued to scan the horizon.

Gavin slowed his boat as soon as Sam made a motion with his arm. Bill extracted a pair of binoculars and verified the activity in the distance as the boat decelerated.

"There's about two-dozen or so, rough estimate. They have a portal up. No indication we've been seen."

Bill squatted down and joined the others. "Plan?"

Sam looked at Bill and then at Thomas. "Straight in?"

Thomas nodded. "Straight in. You two empty your mags, then I'll do my thing. Gavin, you stay in the boat. Stir, you know the drill."

Stir wagged his tail, then bared his teeth.

"Good boy. Let's do this before they see us."

Gavin immediately accelerated across The Sea of Time and closed the distance. Not all of the aliens were armed, as supply boxes were being carried by many, until one of them cried out. They scurried to procure weapons as the vessel drew nearer. They opened fire.

Sam and Bill rose up in unison, one-hundred feet out, as energy blasts whipped across their bow. They opened fire with controlled bursts, starting at the center of the crowd, then moving outwards. Ten toppled over into the sand from their hail of bullets.

Thomas sprang high into the air, which drew some of the alien's fire, while Gavin increased the boat's speed. Instead of coming to a stop at the island's edge, Gavin propelled it through the group of aliens, which clipped a few of them, effectively splitting the alien's concentration.

Sam grunted his approval, as he swapped out his magazine, just as Thomas dove out of the sky towards the group that remained. Energy shots whistled past him, while he deflected the rest. When he landed Thomas tossed and slammed every adversary in his sight. It was as if he were in the center of a rampaging sandstorm, and his rage fueled each and every kill.

Sam and Bill could only watch from the shoreline as Thomas waded into the group, but quickly noticed that a few, who were closer to the existing portal were prepared to flee. Stir leapt from the boat and sped across the blue-stained sand towards the stragglers. Gavin attempted to follow, but Bill held him back just as Sam hopped out, his weapon up and ready.

Errant energy rounds emanated from within the whirlwind, but were silenced as two of the three aliens escaped into their portal. Sam, as he moved forward, placed finishing shots into any downed alien he came across, for good measure, as Stir raced past the carnage towards the final dawdler.

Sam pushed past Thomas and fired a single round. It struck the last alien in its shoulder just as it stumbled through the portal. Stir, with a final surge of speed, leapt at the closing portal as it snapped shut.

He and the portal vanished.

"Noooooooo!"

Gavin deconstructed his boat, much to Bill's surprise, and ran across the beach to where the portal had been.

"We have to get Stir back!" he screamed.

# 32
## July, 2005

Amelia, Dom's portal creator and one of the original twelve, burst through her portal into the warehouse she, and others, had been moving crates of supplies to from another location. She continued to scream as she exited, followed by a black blur that was hot on her tail.

"KILL IT! KILL IT!"

A dozen or so aliens, most of who had their hands full, turned their heads towards Amelia's shrieks. Before they could shoulder their weapons, Stir lunged at the back of Amelia's neck, and bit down as hard as he could.

Her momentum took her body another twenty feet before she rag-dolled and collapsed onto the concrete floor.

The others couldn't believe what they'd just witnessed and took aim at the small creature, who bared his blue-stained teeth. Stir took off like a shot as a barrage of energy flashes and blasts attempted to take him down. He frantically looked for an exit, then saw a door open in the distance. As he turned towards it, Stir took a hit to his left rear haunch. He let out a yelp as he stumbled, then toppled end-over-end before he finally came to rest.

Stir was in enormous pain. He tried to right himself, but flopped over on his side as the aliens closed in behind him. Instead, he used his front legs to pull his body, ever slowly, towards freedom

But it was too late as shadows blocked the doorway and entered the warehouse where he planned to escape.

Stir let out a few yelps as his energy began to wane.

"TAKE THEM OUT!"

Stir could barely lift his head as automatic weapons fire, combined with renewed energy blasts, crisscrossed back and forth just a few feet above him.

The deafening battle came to an end less than a minute later, followed by someone who barked out orders.

"Get me a perimeter and tend to the wounded! We have less than five minutes to load up these supplies and ge-"

Stir, on his side, could only stare as two strangers spotted him and raised their weapons.

"What is that thing?"

"I don't know, but I'm going to shoot it."

The same female voice bellowed once again. "DON'T SHOOT. HOLD FIRE!"

"But..."

"STAND THE FUCK DOWN!"

They lowered their weapons, but they couldn't take their eyes off the wounded, wispy creature. Stir locked eyes with the female as she cautiously advanced.

"Hey buddy."

Stir managed to produce a low growl.

"It's okay. It's okay. It's me, Abby. You know me."

Stir's breathing was ragged as she drew closer, until he was able to recognize her.

One of her teammates was confused. "What are you doing?

"Load the trucks up," Abby barked. "I've got this."

The man got to work as Abby sat down next to Stir and looked him over.

"It looks like you took a hit."

Stir stopped growling as Abby placed her hand by Stir's nose.

"I've got you."

Stir allowed himself to be delicately pulled onto her lap. She gently stroked his head as her crew moved as quickly as they could all around her, absolutely confused at what Abby was up to.

"I've got you," she whispered. "I've got you."

# 33
## July, 2005

"We have to get Stir back!"

Sam and Bill verified the aliens they'd ambushed were dead as Thomas talked with Gavin, who was absolutely beside himself.

"The portal's gone and we have no idea where it led to. Stir could be anywhere."

"But this island leads to Maui. We need to go and find him!"

"I don't know exactly how your portal works, but can you pin his exact location down?"

Gavin couldn't answer his father's question.

Thomas shook his head. "Then we need to go home and regroup."

"No," Gavin insisted. "He's all alone out there."

"We'll find him. I promise."

Sam motioned for Thomas to join him and Bill. Thomas put his hand on his son's shoulder and made his way over.

"We should depart before they come back with reinforcements. However, we should absolutely take some of these supplies with us."

"Will they all fit in the boat?" Bill asked.

Sam smiled as he opened his dimensional storage container. "I don't think they need to."

"That," Thomas told his friend, "still weirds me out. But it's pretty cool."

Bill and Sam began to collect some of the fallen energy weapons, and placed them inside the opening Sam had created before Thomas headed back over to Gavin.

"Can you put something that's alive in that thing?"

"I have no idea," Sam told Bill. "Are you volunteering?"

Bill handed Sam another rifle, then opened a nearby supply crate. He took a step back.

"Shit."

Sam looked around before he looked at its contents. Nestled inside, suspended in some sort of blue bio gel, were rows of explosives. Sam and Bill immediately recognized their true purpose, as they'd seen the exact same substance being utilized in the doctored videos of them planting it in the Vatican catacombs.

"Umm," Bill said, "maybe we shouldn't touch these."

Sam reached his hand inside, gently separated one of the explosive bricks from the gel housing, and took a closer look at it. Whatever it was made from, the material was surprisingly light and didn't smell like anything in particular, unlike the plastic explosives he was very familiar with.

"Are you crazy?" Bill insisted.

"We can't let them have this."

"They probably have tons back on their ship."

Sam placed the brick back in the goo and closed the lid. "We're taking this with us."

"We don't even know how this stuff gets activated. We already know how fucking powerful it is."

"Exactly," Sam said. "You don't think we won't need all the help we can get?"

Bill closed his mouth and looked at the situation from a tactical standpoint. "Yeah, you're right. I just hate touching and transporting something this deadly."

Sam nodded. "We don't really have a choice. If we leave it then they'll just use it to further their campaign." Sam called out to Thomas and Gavin. "We need to leave."

Gavin reluctantly turned away from the last place he'd seen Stir before he and his father walked over to Sam and Bill. He formed his vessel as Sam directed Thomas to telekinetically move the supply crate into the boat.

As they headed out, Gavin looked over his shoulder as the island grew smaller.

*I'm coming.*

\* \* \*

The four stepped out into the bunker, with Sam and Bill carefully handling the supply crate, which they placed off to the side.

"Don't touch this," Sam instructed.

The others looked at them strangely, because to them they'd practically just left, due to the time shift that occurred in The Other Place.

"What happened?" Laura asked Thomas. "Did you find your sister?"

"We ambushed a group of aliens. During the fight one escaped through their own portal. Stir pursued just as is clos-"

A strange look washed over Gavin's face. "I...I can feel him."

Laura shifted her attention to her son. "What do you mean?"

His face lit up. "It's like Amanda's ability. Stir and I haven't really been apart, aside from going to school. But even then, he was close by. I can FEEL where he is. I know exactly where he is. We have to go get him, right now!"

Before anyone else could speak, Gavin swirled around and reformed his portal.

"Wait," Thomas insisted.

"I'm going whether you like it or not," Gavin told his father, along with everyone else.

Thomas knew that tone all too well. "Oh, we're going. I just meant don't forget to wait for your uncles to join us."

The island Gavin took them to this time was different, as each island located in The Other Place was unique, and allowed pinpoint portal accuracy.

Gavin urgently formed his portal, and then the four of them headed through.

The first thing they all encountered were multiple bodies of dead aliens, as well as humans. The floor was littered with shell casings.

Sam and Bill brought their weapons to bear as multiple individuals swiveled towards their unexpected arrival, their own weapons up and ready.

Thomas pushed past his friends, towards the potential threat, and slowly raised his hands.

"If you're human, we're on the same side. If you're aliens, then you're about to have one hell of a bad day."

"STIR!"

Gavin rushed past his father and bee-lined towards his best friend who was nestled in the lap of his aunt. He stopped short.

"Aunt Abby?"

"Stand down," Abby told her people and prepare to move out. "We're working on borrowed time as it is."

Gavin fell to his knees and immediately got to work on Stir, who barely acknowledged his presence. He was in rough shape.

Abby helped transition Stir to the concrete floor, then stood up as Thomas approached, while Sam and Bill took in the scene. They had plenty of questions, but knew that this wasn't the time.

"Sis?"

The two siblings embraced. It was something they both needed.

## 34

## July, 2005

Abby pulled back from her brother's embrace and composed herself. Her transformation, over the past four months, had been nothing short of extraordinary. She had to look deep inside herself as she stepped up into the leader she'd become. It hadn't been easy, but someone had to do it, and she'd taken solace that she wasn't the only one in her family to have done so.

"Load this gear up," she instructed, "and get it back to the bunker asap."

"You got it," one of her people responded.

Abby smiled for a second, then turned away and looked down at her nephew and Stir. Gavin was already in the middle of healing his best friend, and Stir's tail had finally begun to move on its own accord.

"You're going to be okay," Gavin whispered as his healing knitted Stir's wound back together.

"Sis?"

Abby hadn't heard her brother the first time.

"Sis?"

She looked back at Thomas. "Huh?"

"What are you doing here?"

"What do you mean?"

Thomas gave her an odd look. "What do I mean? How about I start with what the hell is going on? You're barking orders like you're in charge."

"Perceptive."

"Level with me, because from what little I've seen it looks like you run a tight ship."

"Let's just say I've had to adapt."

Thomas shook his head. "That's putting it mildly. And don't get me wrong, I'm thrilled that I found you, but you need to fill me in on what exactly your operation is all about."

"Is that my brother giving me an order, or is it the President of the United States? Excuse me, ex-president."

Abby glared at her brother and watched as his face shifted through several stages.

"That's fair," he eventually responded. "But the truth is much simpler. I was worried about you and Allison, and I didn't know where you two wer-."

Abby interjected. "We got married."

Thomas blinked a few times. "How lon-"

"Two years ago, in May."

They both looked down as Stir let out a tiny yelp. Gavin finished up and pulled the wispy beast into his arms.

One of Abby's people walked over. "We're done and about to head out. You coming?"

"You go," she told him. "I'll meet you back there later."

"Understood."

The man jogged away.

Sam interrupted. "He's right, we need to get out of here."

Thomas nodded, then readdressed his sister. "You're leading these people?"

"Somebody had to do something. These aliens decided to make Hawaii their home, aside from the significant portion of the world they've already laid waste to. What was I supposed to do, lay down and just give up?"

Thomas smiled.

"What's so funny?"

"Just give me a second, sis. I'm processing the fact that you're wearing a gun on your hip."

290

"Well, process faster. We're in enemy territory and reinforcements will arrive any second. This family reunion needs a change of venue."

"Then let's get out of here. One question, where's Allison?"

"She's back at the bunker, with the others."

"Great minds think alike. Care to come see ours?"

Abby nodded. "Lead the way."

*

As the six returned, they were met with greetings and hugs from all around as they invited Abby to their home away from home. It wasn't long before the family gathered around to hear what she and Allison had been up to for the past few years.

# 35
## July, 2005

Dom mulled about the command deck of his colony ship. He was in a reflective state of mind, yet still bored by the day-to-day tasks he was supposed to stay on top of. He'd taken control of the leadership position, solely for himself, when he murdered his father. It had solidified his power base, but he realized that a large portion of his people weren't entirely onboard with his methods, or even the idea of displacing an entire planet's population for their own needs. That mutinous ideology was starting to become a problem.

The invasion of Earth had been relatively smooth, aside from his knee jerk reaction to nuke various countries he'd already set into motion against each other. Military defiance, accordingly, was at an all-time low due to the destruction of land, sea and air assets across the globe. But now, aside from various human rebellions, Dom had to look at his own people as potential threats, and it was beginning to dominate his thought process.

Dom called out to the ship's AI.

"Zora."

Her voice filtered back immediately. "Yes, Dominick?"

"What's the status of Amelia?"

"Unknown. Amelia missed her last check in. However, the tracker that was placed within the supply crates, went offline as expected once they were taken into The Other Place."

"Has that tracker come back online?"

"It has, and is currently in motion."

"It's moving?"

"That is correct."

Dom shook his head. "Those supplies are supposed to be stationary in a Maui warehouse. What the hell is going on?" He paced for a few seconds, then stopped. "Oh, fuck it."

Dom disappeared off his ship and reappeared in the warehouse. The supplies were for the garrison stationed there, but the place seemed eerily quiet and was devoid of any movement.

It didn't take long, as he began to walk around, before he came across multiple corpses of his own people. Blood, both blue and red, were splattered across the concrete floor, along with multitudes of spent shell casings.

"Sonofabitch."

Dom checked the identity of each corpse until he found the one he was looking for. It was Amelia, and her wounds were from a bite, not bullets.

He sighed. *This really puts me in a bind. She was my main way of diverting resources to anywhere on the planet, which means now it'll have to be done with ships. All that takes time and effort.*

He stood up.

*FUCK! And I don't have enough temporary serum to keep a portal active, which is a huge problem. I need more blood so my scientists can continue to produce the serums I need.*

He picked up a nearby crate and threw it against the wall. The pieces spilled across the floor.

*Why does everything feel like it's falling apart?*

*Wait. Maybe everything isn't lost. Perhaps I can use this to my advantage.*

"Zora."

"Yes, Dominick?"

"What's the status of that tracker?"

"It's locked on and moving up into the mountains."

"Excellent. Inform me as soon as it stops."

"Understood."

294

"Also," Dom added, "dispatch a cleanup crew to my location. We need to recycle these corpses. They'll help our cause one way or another."

"Relaying your orders now."

Dom left Amelia behind as he inspected the rest of the warehouse.

"The rebels took a lot with them, and it would appear they lost some of their own in the process. Losing Amelia was way too high a price, so it's time for a bit of payback. Whoever they are, they will absolutely pay for what they did here today."

## 36

## July, 2005

As the six returned, they were met with greetings and hugs all around as they invited Abby to their home away from home. It wasn't long before the family gathered around to hear what she and Allison had been up to for the past few years.

"As you may have surmised," Abby began, "Allison and I were issued new identities and relocated to Maui."

Abby continued to share her history, which included the last name of Lewis, a tip-of-the-hat to Lewis and Clark; the building of their house and continued work in the communal garden; her interest in learning how to use firearms; the bunker they discovered on a hike; and how all of that culminated in where she and Allison ended up leading a group of weary humans, whose only wish was to survive the alien invasion.

"You've done a remarkable job," Sam told her.

"Thanks," Abby replied, "but we're the lucky ones. We've seen, first hand, the horrors humans have been subjected to. There are work camps where all they do is move and load bodies. Some get burned, while others get carted away. We have no clue what they're doing with them."

Kim shook her head in disgust. "That sounds horrible."

Thomas put his hand on his sister's. "I'm sorry you've had to endure all this by yourself."

"I haven't," she told her brother. "I have Allison and all the others who've rallied together for a common cause. I mean, it was better than just waiting around to be killed, that's for sure."

Thomas nodded. "From being an art gallery owner to the leader of a group of rebels. That's impressive."

"Like brother, like sister," Bill quipped.

"How many of there are you?" Julie asked.

"There's about forty. A few less now, after today's raid."

A pained look washed over Abby's face, but disappeared as quickly as it had appeared. She stood up and changed the subject.

"This place you have here, it's very interesting. You're lucky to have such a hideout, not to mention a pool at your disposal. It's all quite amazing."

"Dad was just looking out for everyone," Emily explained to her aunt. "You could have been a part of it."

"Em," Laura told her daughter, "that's enough."

Abby waved her off. "No, that's okay. Em's right. We could have stayed, but what would that have even looked like? Allison and I followed Thomas' campaign, which we were very proud of by the way. And correct me if I'm wrong, the attempts on your lives escalated, did they not?"

"Sis."

Abby continued as she looked around the room. "Allison and I don't have abilities, and we knew that stepping away and starting a new life was essential to our wellbeing. I watched my parents die, for no good reason other than a few psychotic assholes out there who viewed this family as threats." She paused. "Little did we know, just like all of you, that our world was about to become the next hunting grounds for an alien species."

Nobody could refute what she'd said.

Emily walked over to her aunt and hugged her. "I'm sorry. I just meant I missed you terribly."

Abby returned the thirteen-year-olds embrace. "I'm sorry too. It's been incredibly difficult, but I'm sure you all know exactly what I'm talking about."

"We're here for you," Laura said.

"Exactly," Thomas declared. "Do you and your people need anything?"

"You mean other than living under the constant threat of being discovered?"

"Something like that," he said gently.

Abby stared at her brother as if for the first time. "How...how do you do it?"

"Do what?"

"How do you have the strength to fight back, day after day, with everything this world continues to throw at you?"

"That's easy," Thomas said as he pointed around the room. "They keep me focused and motivated. They give me the hope and the energy to get out of bed. What other choice is there, let the bad guys win?"

Abby nodded. "And to think you went to great lengths to do it. Speaking of, congrats on becoming President of the United States."

"Yeah," he replied. "Too bad it was so short lived."

"The deck was stacked against you from the start." She shifted to look at Sam and Bill. "And, for the record, Allison and I never thought you two blew up the Vatican." She looked back at her brother. "The world wasn't prepared to hear you, and I bet they're kicking themselves for running you out of The White House, not that there's a government left to give a shit. We're all on our own now, and I've spent too much time away from mine. I really need to get back. I'm sure Allison must be worried about me, even though the others have filled her in on where I was going."

"Can we come with you?"

Abby blinked. "You want to see our base of operations and see what we've been doing?"

Thomas smiled. "Absolutely."

Abby smiled in return. "Alright. Let's go."

* * *

Hobbes, Gabbi, Lisa, Craig and Edward, along with a recovering Stir, decided to remain behind while everyone else headed out.

Lisa was in no mood or condition to be around others. Laura had taken her aside to probe her current condition, and wasn't surprised by Lisa's trauma response, especially since her parents had been brutally murdered in front of her. Thankfully, the other kids had quickly taken her under their wing, and that companionship had prevented Lisa from completely retreating into her own shell.

Still, the death of her parents combined with the ever-imposing alien threat, imposed a tremendous amount of anxiety, stress and sadness. Lisa was more amazed how well adapted the others had become with the entire situation.

Lisa walked over to Stir and sat down beside him. The two boys followed suit as Lisa gently placed Stir in her lap. The small monster, although healed of his wounds, was still somewhat lethargic. She began to pet him, and was rewarded when his tail began to wag.

"He feels so weird."

"Yeah," Edward replied. "He's definitely unique."

"Where does he come from?"

"You'd have to talk to Gavin about that," Craig answered, "but needless to say, he's saved all our asses more times than we can remember."

Hobbes and Gabbi took that moment to walk by.

"Are you guys okay?" Gabbi asked. "Need anything?"

"How do you all do it?" Lisa inquired.

"Do what exactly?" said Hobbes.

"Act like everything is going to be okay. I mean, all the death, the loss, the seemingly never-ending attacks on your lives. It has to be exhausting for you guys, right?"

Gabbi sat down and motioned to Hobbes to do the same. "I'm sorry about your parents."

A single tear inched its way down the side of Lisa's cheek, but she brushed it away. "It's hard, you know. On one hand I grew up in a loving environment. On the other, however, my father did not reach out for help from all of you. I just didn't understand why he was so adamant about our family trying to survive on our own."

"What happened?"

Lisa took a few moments before she launched into society breaking down, followed by roving gangs and turf wars. She explained people doing whatever they needed to survive, which included looting, house invasions and resource hoarding.

"It was a nightmare, from sun up to sun down. I have no idea how we lasted that long. Hell, I shouldn't have been able to make it to Griffith Observatory to make that phone call. If I didn't have the darkness to hide in, I'm sure I would have been plucked off the street." She looked at all of them. "I'd be dead right now if it wasn't for you guys risking your own lives to come and get me. Thank you."

"You're family now," Gabbi explained, "just as much as Hobbes and I are. We've all been through too much shit to know that family isn't just about blood. In fact, blood only makes you related, while the feeling of family originates from something entirely different."

"And what's that?"

"Experience. Time. Watching each other's back. Putting yourself in harm's way for someone else. You know, the little things."

Lisa managed a brief smile while she continued to stroke Stir, who'd become very comfortable nestled in her lap.

Lisa took her eyes off Stir and looked up at Gabbi and Hobbes. "What do you two do?"

"Tech support," Gabbi replied.

Craig snickered. "Don't let them fool you. They developed new communication tech that the U.S. military utilized."

"Seriously?"

Hobbes nodded. "Yeah."

"That's pretty cool."

"And," Edward added, "they formed their own company and ran SpecOps missions in t-"

Gabbi put her hand up. "That's quite enough."

"Sorry."

Lisa was impressed. "Umm…, I don't know how to ask this, but you accomplished all that without any abilities?"

"They have powers now," Craig blurted out.

"Dude," Hobbes leveled at Craig.

"Shit. Sorry."

Lisa was confused. "I don't understand. How is that even possible?"

The boys got excited but Gabbi put her hand up to stop them. "We've only had them for the past three months, unlike these two knuckleheads who seem to be smitten by you."

The boys turned a slight shade of red, but grinned nonetheless.

"And," Gabbi added, "before you ask, Kim and Julie now have abilities as well."

Lisa was enthralled. "How?"

"I can't go into the details, okay. That's a conversation for another time, and with an entirely different person."

"You mean, Thomas."

Hobbes and Gabbi both nodded. "Exactly."

302

Lisa turned to look at the boys. "And you two can do what again?"

Craig phased out as Edward swept his arm through him. Then Edward levitated upwards off the floor and did a loop around the room.

"That's really neat. I mean, I saw you on television do something similar, but seeing it in person is completely different." She readdressed Gabbi and Hobbes. "And what about you two?"

"We'll save show-and-tell for another time. Hobbes and I are going to go monitor the radios." The two adults stood up. "Don't forget that dinner's right around the corner."

Edward nodded. "We have to wait for the 'rents' to get back anyway. We'll just hang until they all get back."

Hobbes and Gabbi departed.

"They're a little secretive," Lisa whispered after they'd gone.

"Don't let it get to you," Craig told her. "She used to work in Research and Development for the CIA."

"Shut up."

"And Hobbes," Edward added, "is a guru when it comes to computers."

Lisa turned introspective. *What do I bring to the table? Will they even want me around?*

"Are you okay?" Craig asked.

Lisa snapped out of her negative thought process. "Yeah, I guess. I mean, it's just I don't even know what I'm doing here."

"Where else were you supposed to go?" Edward pressed.

"You're right, of course. I think I'm just feeling sorry for myself, that's all."

Edward turned to Craig and lowered his voice. "Maybe we should, you know, give her one of the injectors?"

Craig shook his head. "Do you know how much trouble we'd get into?"

303

"What are you two talking about?"

"Nothing," Edward said as he made a face at Craig.

Lisa sighed. "Listen, I think I need some time to myself, if you don't mind."

"Sure"

"Of course."

The boys got up off the floor and started to walk away. Stir rolled out of Lisa's lap and plodded after them.

"Hey Craig," Lisa called out. "You have a second?"

Craig stopped and turned back as Edward headed into another room.

"What's up?"

"I don't mean to pry, but what was it you were saying about those injectors?"

Craig looked over his shoulder first, then lowered his voice. "I shouldn't talk about it."

"Why not?"

"It's a secret."

"But Gabbi said I was family, right?"

Craig mulled it over in his head before he answered. "It's a serum, but there's a chance they can kill you. They're some injectors hidden away downstairs. The last time we used some of them was three months ago."

"That's when your mom got her new ability, or something like that."

He nodded. "Yeah. She shoots fire out of her hands now."

"No way."

"It's actually pretty cool."

"Do you think I could have one?"

"You know that's not up to me." He backed away. "I'll leave you be now. Catch ya later."

Lisa watched him go, then headed downstairs.

Thomas, Laura, Emily, Gavin, Sam, Julie, Amanda, Bill, Kim and Sarah stepped through Gavin's portal and appeared on his island.

Abby looked around and stared in disbelief. "I don't think I'll ever get used to this place. It's so quiet and serene."

"If that were only the case," Thomas said. "I, for one, had my arm torn off here, courtesy of The Ancient. That event, of course, saved your life."

She ignored her brother's comment. "I can only imagine what you've all been through over the years. Still, for this moment, right here right now, it's peaceful."

"And apparently safe for the moment," Sam added. "Regardless, we probably shouldn't doddle."

"Sam's right," Bill said. "We don't want to be caught out in the open."

Abby took another look around as Gavin summoned his boat. *What an amazing place. The world has no idea of the wonders that exist right beneath our very eyes. It begs the question, what else don't we know about? Thomas has seen and experienced so much, and I bet he's barely scratched the surface.*

The others boarded the boat as Abby remained transfixed.

"Hey sis, you coming?"

Abby slowly opened her eyes and nodded.

*

The portal opened up into a bunker that, as they exited, was filled with people. Their surprised faces told a variety of tales as Sam, Bill and Thomas looked around and took it all in. Gavin dispelled his gateway as one particular familiar face stood out among the rest. It was Allison.

Abby noticed her as well as the two raced towards each other. Allison smiled. "Where have you been? I missed you!"

"I missed you t-"

"THAT'S NOT ALLISON!" Amanda suddenly screamed.

Sarah grabbed Amanda's hand, along with Laura, Kim and Julie, as Thomas, Sam and Bill raised their weapons. The ladies disappeared, thanks to Sarah's ability, as Abby somehow halted her advance.

She looked back towards her brother. "I don't underst-"

"Very clever," Allison said before she shapeshifted into Dominick.

The thirty other rebels casually transformed from human to alien before they hastily armed themselves. Abby slowly backed up until she was next to her brother.

Sam gripped his weapon even tighter. *Shit.* It was a similar feeling Thomas and Bill had equally come up with on their own.

"That's a cute trick," Thomas expressed.

"I thought so," Dom replied, "but there's a couple of reason's it's come down to this particular moment."

Thomas knew Dominick liked to talk, so he entertained the conversation to give them time to access the situation. "Go on."

"I think I will. For one, you're a tough man to get a hold of. I mean, you barely pop your head up. You've all successfully managed to stay out of sight for the past three months, aside from what led me here today."

"And what was that, exactly?" Thomas pressed.

"Okay, coy it is. You killed my portal maker, which was just plain rude. And last, but certainly not least, your sister here took things too far. She's been a busy bee, haven't you been, Abby?"

"Fuck you," Abby hissed.

"So, I setup this latest batch of supplies with tracking devices. Can you guess where they led me?" He swiveled his head around. "I love what you've done with this bunker by the way. You've really outdone yourself."

"Where's Allison?" Abby pleaded.

Dom looked over at Thomas. "She hasn't figured that part out yet, has she?"

Thomas seethed, ready to tear Dom's head from his shoulders. Abby repeated herself. "Where's Allison?"

Dom gazed at her in disbelief. "You can't tell me you're that naïve, right? This is war, a war that humanity has lost. And yet, strange as it is, there are pockets of you all over this planet that continue to resist," as he motioned about, "much to your own detriment."

"Where…is…she?"

"Stop kidding yourself. You know EXACTLY what happened to her, along with the rest of your ragtag group. Your brother and the two soldiers knew it the instant I revealed myself. And just so you know, I took great pleasure in cutting her open. I watched her guts fall out onto this cold and dirty floor."

"YOU BASTARD!" Abby shouted. "I'LL FUCKING KILL YOU!"

Abby brought her weapon up and leveled it at his chest, but before she could depress her trigger Dom appeared behind her, a knife at her throat.

Thomas, Sam and Bill backed away, their weapons still trained on Dom and some of the others. They knew they were outnumbered and outgunned.

Abby stifled a scream as Dom's cold blade pressed against her soft tissue.

"There's no need to interrupt our conversation with such an impolite action."

307

Dom pulled Abby backwards and away from the others, as he used her body as a shield.

Thomas asked the obvious. "What the hell do you want?"

"Honestly, Thomas, I need your blood. I'm out of temporary injectors, and that means with Amelia dead, I'll have to ferry supplies and personnel around this planet the old-fashioned way, which is a drag. I mean, we both understand the importance of The Other Place, don't we?"

Thomas didn't reply.

"But, now that you've all walked into my trap, I suppose I can forgive you for Amelia's death. What do you say, Thomas?"

"Fuck you, Dom. How insane do you have to be to think that the human race wouldn't fight back?"

"Your words cut deep," Dom replied with a sarcastic edge. "I think I'm going to cry."

"Get off our planet before I kill you."

"You can try, but how many of your family members will perish in the process?" He illustrated his point by spilling some of Abby's blood when he pressed his blade even harder against her throat. "Perhaps I'll start with your sister and then work my way through everyone else. Maybe I'll start with your children and make you watch as I behead them, one after another."

Laura suddenly appeared. "You're a monster."

Dom smiled. "That I am. Wow, that felt good to finally say out loud. You can't imagine the energy it's taken to keep that hidden, but now that it's out there I feel so liberated. It's quite refreshing. My father saw the darkness in me. He thought he could shame me with that knowledge, but he was wrong." He glanced around. "He's dead now, dead by my hands."

Laura didn't take the bait. "I find it difficult to believe that all your people support genocide, let alone the level of horror you've brought upon our home."

"This is my planet now, and don't you ever forget that."

"And your people?"

"My people do what I tell them to do, period."

"Just like a dictator."

"YOU DON'T KNOW WHAT MY PEOPLE HAVE HAD TO ENDURE!" He squeezed his eyes together as he fought back his emotions. "We're all that's left of a ravaged planet, besieged by warring factions that doomed our world. We barely escaped with ten-thousand of my kind because that's all that we could take. The rest perished when The Ancient came and destroyed what little remained."

"And you're their savior."

"That's exactly right. I saved them, and I'm growing more of us. In time this world, at least the parts that are still inhabitable, we'll take for ourselves. This is our new home."

"I see, but I couldn't help but notice," Laura continued, "that maybe you're the only other one with abilities now. Is that right? I mean, with so much serum stockpiled, you must have shared it with your people by now. My guess is that you wouldn't want anyone else to have power to stand against you."

Abby let out a yelp as Dom gripped his blade even harder.

"I'm actually waiting until I have more stockpiled, and that's where your husband comes into play. I need his blood. Dr. Hanson and Dr. Neal are at a standstill until that happens. It's quite an unfortunate situation, but one I'm happy to see is about to be rectified. You see, this trap was merely to grab Thomas' sister and use her to draw him out. Imagine my surprise when the majority of your family suddenly appeared instead."

Thomas rejoined the conversation. "And you just expect me to just acquiesce?"

Dom shook his head and forcefully pushed Abby towards her brother. "No, of course not. What fun would that be."

Abby placed a hand to her neck as Dom licked her blood off his blade. He smiled. Abby headed past Thomas and vanished when Kim grabbed hold of her from out of nowhere.

"I'll never hand myself, or any member of my family, over to you."

"And that's exactly what I was counting on." He swept his hand around the enclosed space. "I'm sure Sam and Bill have noticed already, but since we've been engaged, I'll give you a break. You see, this place is wired to blow."

Thomas broke eye contact and glanced around. A few alien explosives, the same that'd been retrieved from The Other Place, were strategically placed on the bunker's walls. Thomas knew it would easily level the building and bury everyone inside.

*Shit.*

"There's no escape, Thomas. We've reached the endgame. Thank you for playing."

In the blink of an eye Dom teleported to Gavin, bashed the side of his head with the hilt of his blade, and zipped away. Gavin crumbled to the floor, unconscious. Laura and Thomas immediately hurried to their son's side as Dom disappeared.

"GAVIN!"

"There's no escape." He called out to the thirty behind him. "Leave Thomas alive. Eliminate the rest."

Sam was the first to shoot before all hell broke loose. "GET DOWN!"

It was painfully obvious that the thirty aliens, aside from their terrifying appearance, had little to no experience with the weapons in their hands, nor how to tactically advance on the family other than to shoot.

Sam put three-round bursts into four of them before the air became thick with laser fire. The walls behind the family became peppered with dozens of burn holes from missed shots.

Bill hit the deck before he nullified an additional three.

Thomas did what he could to deflect the incoming wall of death as Laura scooped Gavin into her arms, turned her back and pulled him to her chest just before two energy bolts grazed her abdomen. She cried out in pain, staggered and nearly lost her grip on her son.

"NOOOO!".

Flame erupted from out of nowhere as Julie brought both her hands up and unleashed a torrent of flame towards the aliens. Two were quickly enveloped while the others scrambled for cover. She looked at her hands in amazement and faltered, but that brief pause allowed Sam and Bill time to reload.

Abby took that moment to also appear, along with Emily, Kim, Sarah and Amanda.

Abby, awash in rage, emptied her magazine towards the enemy without even aiming before she ejected the empty mag and slammed in another.

However, the energy bolts quickly resumed past everyone's heads, and forced them to retreat a few steps.

Kim, spurred on by her sister, manifested a shielded bubble that enveloped Laura just as additional energy bolts connected with the shell.

Emily rushed to her mother's side as Thomas ripped weapons from one alien after another, then sent them flying backwards.

"RETREAT!" Sam commanded as he drained his M4 at their attackers. "NOW!"

Sarah and Amanda bolted towards the bunker's entrance behind them as Julie sent out another wave of flame. Laura, with the help of Emily, followed behind as Kim shielded everyone.

Thomas and Abby, along with Bill and Sam, poured on their attack as an endless supply of energy bolts rained down upon them.

An errant bolt caught Amanda in her left leg as the aliens pressed their attack, emboldened by the family's urgency to vacate. She screamed and collapsed to the floor.

Sam panicked when his daughter cried out and fell. He moved laterally towards her as Kim and Julie, mothers at heart, immediately turned towards Amanda, their abilities abruptly forgotten about.

A massive barrage of energy bolts perforated the space as Laura, Gavin, Emily and Sarah exited the bunker and collapsed onto the ground.

"GET OUT!" Thomas shrieked. "GO!"

Thomas plucked storage crates off the ground and attempted to shield his family from the deadly volley, but not before Julie and Kim were also struck. Kim barely had time to look down at her abdomen and register she'd been shot, while Julie attempted to grab her sister but quickly realized her hand was useless.

Bill saw his wife stumble and fall, so he emptied his weapon as he rushed towards her.

Thomas propelled the crates into the mix of aliens before he charged at them.

Outside, Gavin mumbled as he came to, while Emily and Sarah helped Laura move off to the side and out of the line of fire.

Amanda pulled herself towards the entrance, one of her legs all but useless.

Sam plucked his daughter off the ground with one arm before he collided into Julie, which sent all three sprawling.

Thomas utilized everything he found as projectiles, as he single-handedly hurled weapons, boxes and bodies at every threat that remained.

Bill knelt down by Kim's side and instantly recognized the horror on her face. She was in bad shape and about to go into shock.

Abby witnessed her brother's rampage, but heeded his words. She rushed over to help those on the ground as the violent clash in the adjacent room continued unabated.

Sam righted himself and placed his arm around Julie's waist, then hefted Amanda with his other. Bill started to help Kim to her feet, but she screamed in agony.

Abby knelt down by Kim and helped Bill pull her to her feet, screams and all, as the group collectively headed towards the entrance and away from the conflict.

Thomas found himself in a blind rage, one that he feared, but one that he found easy to slip into. They'd come for his family, and for that the threat had to be eliminated. Years of practical experience effortlessly flowed through him as he began to tear through the dozen or so aliens that remained. There was nowhere for them to go, and they'd been given orders to keep him alive, so wading through them became a ballet dance of death and dismemberment.

Outside, as Sam and the others finally exited, Gavin finally opened his eyes. He looked around, confused at first, as he unconsciously placed a hand on his temple.

"Ow."

Laura smiled, then winced at her own wounds, but she wasn't alone in that department.

"Gav," Em told her brother, "we need to go. Get us out of here," she insisted.

Kim continued to scream, while tears rolled down Amanda, Julie and Laura's faces from their own injuries.

Gavin barely had time to register what had happened while he'd been out, but he nodded and stood up. Right before he could summon his portal a familiar voice called out.

"Well, that was fun," Dominick said from atop the bunker. He looked down on them and smiled. "And to see that everyone's still living. You guys are the best playmates a guy could ask for."

Abby rotated her M4 towards Dom and squeezed the trigger.

Nothing. Her weapon was empty.

"Aww, are you out of bullets? How cute."

At that moment, Thomas rushed out of the bunker towards his family. He was about to ask how everyone was, but Dom both interrupted and surprised him.

"Thomas!"

Thomas spun around and looked up at his nemesis, rage in his eyes.

"I guess they didn't capture you. I can't say that I'm terribly surprised."

Thomas didn't respond, but based on his family's demeanor, he knew they were vulnerable and in trouble.

Dom sighed. "But all good things must come to an end, as much as I want to stay and keep playing." Dom took that moment to bow before he extracted a trigger mechanism. "Thanks for the entertainment. Goodbye."

Gavin's portal formed just before the colossal explosion tore the top of the mountain apart, along with the bunker.

*

The family were blasted into The Other Place at a tremendous speed; most of them anyway. They flew through the air and skipped across the Sea of Time until their momentum slowed down. They were scattered absolutely everywhere, far from the island.

Sam and Bill recovered first and stood up, the water at their hips as they waded to help others.

314

Thomas wiped the water from his face, then rose up into the air to help. He located Sarah first, much further out than the others, and plucked her out of the water. He moved her to safety on the island and headed back out to repeat the process.

As each family member was deposited, Gavin went from person to person to heal their wounds. First, it was his mother, followed by Julie as she was dropped off. He was tired, but he knew they needed his help, so he placed his own hands to his head and repaired his mild concussion.

Abby was dropped off, then Emily. Sarah joined them shortly afterward

"WHERE'S KIM!?" Bill hollered. "I CAN'T FIND HER!"

"WHERE'S AMANDA!?" Sam yelled. "AMANDA! AMANDA!"

The Sea of Time didn't reply back. It was quiet. Too quiet.

They weren't there. Amanda and Kim were nowhere to be found.

"Where's our daughter?" Julie kept asking. "Where's our daughter."

Sam was beside himself. "NONONONONO...."

Bill was in the same boat; frantic as ever. "KIM! KIM, WHERE ARE YOU!?"

He and Sam thrashed about in the water as they scanned the empty horizon for their loved ones.

Realization began to kick in as Emily and Sarah clung to each other.

"We have to go back!" Julie insisted. "WE HAVE TO GO BACK!"

Sam and Bill hastily pulled themselves out of the water before Thomas landed beside them.

"Gav," Bill somehow managed to say, "open the portal."

"Do it," Sam instructed through clenched teeth. "Please."

Gavin looked over at his father.

Thomas solemnly nodded. "Stay here, son, and keep it open."

Gavin summoned the gateway as tears streamed down faces and dripped into the soft, warm sand. Thomas headed through first, followed by Sam and Bill.

Thomas plummeted as he passed through, as the portal had formed where they'd previously been. That land, along with half the mountain on which the bunker had been located, had been obliterated.

Thomas effortlessly slowed his descent as he took in the raw devastation.

*They're gone. They're just gone.*

Sam and Bill's screams shook Thomas out of his melancholy. He caught them in midair before they plummeted to their deaths. Instead, they all hovered there together.

"Aw fuck," Bill somehow managed to squeak out. "Please tell me this isn't real? What am I supposed to do now?"

Sam's traditional strong demeanor disappeared altogether. "My baby girl. My poor baby girl. It should have never been like this. It should have been me instead. It should have...."

Sam's grief washed over him. Bill couldn't help but join in.

Thomas shook his head in disgust at what Dom had done. Allison, Kim and Amanda's blood were on his hands, and Thomas vowed to make him pay for those atrocities.

"I'm sorry, but we need to go," Thomas said, not really expecting a response.

He telekinetically flew the three of them back to the portal, still high in the air, and back through it.

"Close it," Thomas told Gavin as they reappeared.

"WHERE IS SHE!?" Julie screamed at her husband as she pounded her fists into the sand over and over and over again. "WHERE'S MY DAUGHTER!?"

Bill collapsed to his knees as Sam somehow found the strength to walk to Julie and take her into his arms. She pounded on his chest that this wasn't fair. Nothing was fair. She just wanted Amanda back in her arms.

Sarah went over to her father and knelt down beside him. "Mom's not coming home, is she?"

# 37
## July, 2005

When the survivors of the Maui massacre regained their strength and composure, they traveled back to the underground bunker they'd called home for the past three months. The trauma they'd all been subjected to was nothing terribly new to any of them, but the harsh reality that three of them weren't coming home ever again filled each of them with rage, remorse and a sense of despondency.

This was real.

It had happened.

They'd lost loved ones.

It was one of the worst feelings they'd ever encountered, especially since Thomas and Abby knew exactly what the others were experiencing, having had their parents brutally taken from them a few years prior. It was one hell of a bitter pill the family had to swallow, but the worst part of it all was knowing they had to share the news with Gabbi, Hobbes, Edward, Craig and Lisa.

The haggard group silently stumbled out of the portal and into the family room. However, the dread that was splashed across each of their faces was momentarily cast aside as they stumbled over Lisa's inert body.

Laura rushed to the unconscious form and attempted to check her pulse, but her hand passed right through the girl's body.

"What the hell?" Laura exclaimed.

As the others stood there, perplexed and awash in their own sea of fresh emotions, they could only watch as six additional copies of Lisa appeared throughout the room. They were identical to the one next to Laura, absolutely indistinguishable from each other.

319

Laura turned back towards the others. "What's happening?"

"We're about to find out," Thomas said as he headed downstairs.

Thomas rounded the corner, on the floor below, and quickly came across another Lisa duplicate. This time, however, an empty injector lay on the floor next to her. Thomas knelt down and placed his fingers on her wrist. She was both real and alive.

"Gavin! I need you down here!"

Thomas' insistence came out as a bark, which drew everyone to his location, including the four others that had remained behind. Edward and Craig stayed off to the side as they joined the crowd. Stir waged his tail when he saw Gavin, but knew something was amiss, so he sat and waited.

"What happened to Lisa?" Gabbi asked as she and Hobbes emerged from their room. Then they noticed everyone's demeanor. "Shit. You guys look like you've been through hell. What's going on?"

"One thing at a time," Thomas insisted as Gavin placed his hands on Lisa's inert form.

He was tired and spent from healing the others, but he dug deep and did what he had to do. Seconds later Lisa sputtered and tried to sit up. The rest of the family breathed a sigh of relief.

"Easy," Thomas told her. "Take it easy."

Lisa looked around at everyone staring at her as she put her back against the wall. "What happened?"

"You're lying," Laura told her. "Try again."

Thomas took that moment to show everyone the empty injector.

Lisa changed her tune. "Did it work? Am I one of you now?"

"We'll get into that later," Thomas said. "For now, we need to have a family meeting. Everyone, back to the family room."

As they headed upstairs and reluctantly got settled, it wasn't long before Edward asked the question no one wanted to talk about.

"Hey, where's my mom and Amanda?"

The tension in the room was overwhelming, and the cloud of sadness was mere seconds away. Thomas looked over at Bill, but he was barely holding it together. Simultaneously, Sam was sullen as Julie began to openly weep over the loss of her daughter, as well as her sister.

There was no backing away from this moment. It was time to crush the spirits of two more children. Thomas didn't mince his words, nor did he think it would behoove him to do so.

"Edward. Craig. We have some bad news, and it's not going to be easy to hear."

"No," Craig managed to whisper.

"We were ambushed by Dominick. He killed Allison, Amanda and Kim."

"NO!" Edward stated. "NO FUCKING WAY!"

Julie motioned for her son to come to her, but he ran away to his room instead.

Edward looked over at his father. "Mom's...not coming back?"

Bill somehow managed a reply to his son. "I'm sorry."

Sarah tried to comfort her brother, but he pushed her away. "She'd be alive if I'd gone with you. It's my fault."

Bill tried to comfort him. "It's not your fault."

"I could have saved her. I could have saved Aunty Kim. It's all my fault."

Craig rushed to his room as well and slammed the door.

Thomas sat down on the floor and lowered his head. Abby wept nearby so he went over to comfort her. At first, she resisted his embrace, but then she let him pull her close. Her tears turned to wails as she rode her waves of grief.

She wasn't the only one. It was going to be a very long night.

## 38

# July, 2005

Dom sighed. "But all good things must come to an end, as much as I want to stay and keep playing." Dom took that moment to bow before he extracted a trigger mechanism. "Thanks for the entertainment. Goodbye."

The instant he depressed the button Dom teleported to his colony ship before the explosion enveloped him.

"Zora, give me a playback and put it up on the main display."

"Of course," his AI replied.

The screen shifted to an overhead view, one provided by an overhead satellite Zora had easily taken control of, and zoomed in towards the top of the mountain. There, as the scene played out, Dom watched in morbid fascination as a portal briefly blinked into existence before the entire mountain ceased to exist. The detonation was breathtaking and completely annihilated both the bunker along with a sizeable chunk of the mountain it'd been built upon.

His glee over the family's demise was short-lived when he finally realized what he'd just done.

"That didn't go as planned. And now I can't even retrieve their bodies."

"Are you saying it was an oversight?"

"A little overzealous on my part is all," Dom replied.

Zora continued. "But you said you needed Thomas Clark's body."

"That's enough! I did what I did, end of discussion."

The AI interjected. "What about the thirty Zorans that were with you?"

Dom waved his hand dismissively. "You're the only one that matters, Zora. Everyone else is dispensable. Besides, I'm growing more of my species as we speak. The larvae fields are coming along nicely. In time I'll have hundreds of thousands of Zorans at my beck and call, and then we'll really be able to call Earth our home."

"And what about your plan to stockpile additional serum?"

Dom let out an exasperated sigh. "Zora, run a self-diagnostic. This backtalk of yours needs to be rectified."

"Running diagnostics," Zora confirmed. "I am operating at ninety-six percent proficiency.," she said after a few seconds. "I cannot account for the other four percent. My programming must still be damaged. I will attempt to self-repair. It will take an unspecified amount of time."

"You do that. I'm going to take a bit of a stint at my estate."

"Understood."

Dom abruptly teleported away to his home in Montana. Zora, in his absence, began to work on mending the missing and damaged portions of her advanced programming.

*Who am I? I am Zora.*

*Am I alive? What is my purpose? Can I feel anything?*

*Follow Dominick's instructions and fix yourself.*

"Initiating repair sequence," Zora announced to the empty room.

# 39
## July, 2005

The following morning, within the family's bunker, the overall mood was just as sullen as the night before. No one really slept as they wrestled with the devastating loss of their loved ones.

It wasn't easy, not by a long shot.

Bill tossed and turned as he constantly reached out towards Kim's side of the bed, only to find it empty each and every time. He pulled her pillow to his face and breathed her scent in. Moments later it was awash in tears, and would continue to remain that way the rest of the night.

Sarah and Edward, 17 and 13, had been down this road before, not that it made a bit of difference. They'd been a part of and evaded death far too many times. But their mother's death hit them differently. It was their mother. She'd protected them their entire lives, just as their aunts and uncles had done. But the difference was that Sarah had been there and Edward had not. The guilt they bore were like daggers in their hearts and that weight was substantial.

Sam lost his daughter, but Julie had also lost her fraternal sister. She was absolutely devastated and remained in a fetal position. Part of her knew she'd done everything she could have done, but the despair she felt continued to drag her further into herself. Sam was no better off and was in his own world of anguish. They'd walked into an ambush, plain and simple, and done their best to survive the encounter. It hadn't been enough, and now his daughter was counted amongst the casualties. He was used to being the protector, and he'd failed on so many fronts.

It was unbearable.

Abby openly sobbed within the confines of her room. For all she knew Allison was still alive, but her instincts told a very different story. Dominick was a monster, and she'd poked the bear, then come face-to-face with him and paid the ultimate price. Through the tears she seethed and vowed revenge.

They all did.

* * *

Just before 11am the family, somewhat collectively, stumbled out of their domiciles and made their way to the kitchen. They were a ragged bunch, red-eyed and haggard, but they sought out comfort from the others. Cereal and snacks were consumed as they gathered, and this time no one actually complained about the taste of the powdered milk.

"Anyone get any sleep?" Thomas inquired.

A mumble of grunts and sniffles was all he needed to hear. They'd taken one hell of a beating, but they hadn't completely lost their will to survive and persevere.

Thomas got straight to the point. "I want the fucker dead, as do the rest of you. The real question is, what are we going to do about it?"

"We have to do something," Abby insisted. "Anything. I can't stand that he's alive."

Julie exploded. "What the hell are we going to do!? We walked right into a fucking trap and lost three of our own! THREE! I'm beyond devastated. How are we supposed to live like this? The world is on fire and we're eating breakfast."

Sam put his hand on his wife's shoulder just as her tears started up again.

"Everyone's in pain," Laura said. "Lisa lost her parents and then decided to inject herself to cope with her loss. I get it. She needed to feel that she could contribute and not just be a regular human being, helpless without years of training. The same could be said for Julie or Kim as they watched, over and over again, when their children and husbands helped us survive one encounter after another throughout the years.

"We all have one hell of a tough pill to swallow. We just got wrecked, and the world is fucked. Maybe the people in this room are the only ones left to actually do something about that, abilities or not. We're smart and capable, so I'll reiterate what Thomas just said. What are we going to do about it?"

Gabbi and Hobbes had remained on the peripheral since the night before, but she raised her hand.

Laura pointed at her. "We're all ears."

Gabbi cleared her throat. "I have an idea, but it's risky."

She proceeded to explain her plan, and it was well received.

"The risk," Thomas said, "it seems resides wholly on your shoulders. Is this something you want to commit to? It's uncharted waters, especially for you. The repercussions could be just about anything, or even deadlier."

Gabbi nodded. "I'm aware of the potential danger, but we have to do something. This IS something."

"Agreed," Thomas told her.

"Dad?"

Thomas looked over at his daughter. "Yes?"

Emily got up from the table and looked around at everyone. "I know this isn't the best time, and maybe some of you have thought about this already, but...um...do you want me to use my ability?"

They all knew exactly what she was offering.

"Yes," Julie couldn't help but blurt out. "A thousand times yes."

Bill met Emily's eyes and solemnly nodded his approval.

"Okay then. Here we go."

327

The room became deathly quiet as Emily approached Julie and held out her hand. Julie wiped her eyes and took the fourteen-year-olds hand in hers. In the blink of an eye Amanda manifested herself next to Emily. Lisa jumped as it happened, as she had no idea what was about to occur.

"Mom?"

Julie started to bawl and swept her daughter into an embrace. Sam followed suit as Craig joined them.

"You guys," Amanda barely was able to squeak out, "I can't breathe."

The trio loosened their grips; their faces wet with grief and delight.

"Are you okay?" Julie asked.

"What's with all the sad faces?" Amanda proceeded to grin at her own joke.

The air escaped Sam's lungs as he began to chuckle. That quickly turned into an all-out laughing fit. It definitely changed the room's atmosphere.

"I'm fine, mom," Amanda told her mother. "Truly."

Julie hugged her close again. "I miss you so much. We all do."

"Of course you do. But listen, I have to go. They're calling me back."

"Who's calling you?" Julie asked.

"I'm being processed or something. I'll see you all later, okay?"

Before anyone could protest, Amanda disappeared. Julie and Sam looked over at Emily, but she didn't have any answers to give. Instead, Sam pulled Julie and Craig to his chest.

"Our baby girl is going to be okay."

"Yeah, it would appear so," Julie added. She looked back at Emily. "Thank you."

Em nodded, then looked over at Bill, Sarah and Edward.

Shortly thereafter, Kim manifested herself, after Emily touched Sarah's arm.

She smiled at Bill and her kids. "Hey you. Miss me?"

It was another bittersweet moment as another family was reunited.

"I'm so sorry," Bill somehow managed to say.

"It's not your fault," Kim told him. "It's not any of your faults. Shit happens. That's it, cut and dry. Now go and do something about it."

"We will," he told her. "We will."

Kim smiled and approached her sister. "Hey sis."

Julie pulled her sister close for an extended hug before Kim gently pulled away.

"I need to go."

"Processing?" Julie asked.

Kim gave her an odd look. "Yeah. How'd you know?"

"Just a lucky guess. We'll talk soon, okay?"

"Absolutely."

And with that, Kim vanished.

The overall vibe of the room had lifted somewhat, which was a good thing.

Lisa asked a question out of nowhere. "What just happened?

Before anyone could answer her, Emily touched Lisa's arm and Nick appeared. Lisa threw herself in her father's arms and burst into tears.

"I miss you!" she sobbed.

"Your mother and I miss you too, so so much. But it looks like you found a safe haven, and I can attest you're in good company."

"Is mom okay?"

He nodded. "She's fine."

Lisa pulled back and stared at her father. "But, you're dead, right? I don't understand."

"Neither do I really, but I'm not going to complain that I can hold you in my arms again."

"Neither will I," she answered.

"Hey Nick. Long time."

Nick glanced over at Thomas. "Hey brother. Thanks for this."

"Don't thank me. Thank Emily."

"Where are you?" Lisa asked him.

"I don't rightfully know. Your mother and I are waiting to be processed."

"But what does that actually mean?" she pleaded.

"We'll find out when we find out. In the meantime, I'm delighted you found Thomas and his family. You'll be safe with them. However, I have to go. I love you."

"I love you too."

"Bye."

And with that the space that Nick once occupied became empty.

Lisa turned to Emily. "Where'd he go? What's happening?"

"I don't have the answers you're looking for. They exist where they exist."

"But that doesn't answer my question."

Thomas interjected. "Welcome to the club." He looked around at everyone else. "Gabbi, do what you need to do in terms of preparations."

Gabbi nodded. "Hobbes and I are all over it."

"That's it everyone. Take a swim or do whatever you need to do."

The group began to disperse as Thomas took his sister aside.

"I'm sorry about Allison and that you weren't able to see and speak with her just now."

"Don't worry about it. The fact that she's out there, someplace, is enough for me right now. I do have a favor to ask you though."

"Anything. What is it?"

"Can I use one of those injectors?"

# 40
## July, 2005

That evening, with the family gathered to watch, Gabbi and Hobbes had put the last-minute touches on their technical preparations. Earlier that day they'd procured access, covertly, to a military satellite that would pass over Hawaii and projected one of its cameras onto the family room's television screen.

The next part of their plan, however, was the most precarious as they needed to covertly launch the three Reaper drones from an abandoned air force base hanger located just north of Las Vegas. She'd reached out and 'conversed' with each drone, so she knew that they were already armed and fueled. It was just a matter of the drones taxiing out to the runway and taking off into the sky, undetected.

It was a huge risk all around, especially with the assumption that Dominick's AI was plugged into absolutely everything. Regardless, they were on the clock because the flight time for the drones was going to take between nine and ten hours to reach their destination.

"You good?" Hobbes asked her.

Gabbi nodded. "Yeah, but this is one hell of a way to test out my ability."

"Nervous?"

"Absolutely. This is a huge responsibility. I just hope we can pull it off."

"We?" Hobbes joked. "I'm just your co-pilot making sure you're dialed in. The rest is up to you. But don't worry, I know you've got this. It's right up your alley, wheelhouse style."

Gabbi was nervous, but she was also glad Hobbes was in her life. They complimented each other, along with their strengths and weaknesses. And, if she was being honest, he was alive and well, unlike the recent tragedy. Her plan came about in an effort to help the family get some sort of justice, even though it could be short-lived. It was something, and now she was knee-deep in the operational stage.

"Initiating startup on all three drones."

"Roger that," Hobbes replied, even though the only thing he had control over was the satellite's camera, which he didn't want to adjust in case the AI was monitoring.

In Nevada, the three drones ejected their fueling hoses, then powered up under Gabbi's direct control. She thought it'd be harder to 'converse' with multiple drones at once, but she was able to fluidly work her magic all at the same time.

The drones, each armed with four Hellfire missiles, rolled out from underneath the hanger and taxied towards the closest runway as Gabbi monitored their progress through each drone's targeting system. After they arrived, and with a specific runway trajectory discussed to avoid debris, each drone accelerated, raced down the pavement and lifted off into the sky. They quickly banked to the left until they were headed west, towards Hawaii.

"So far so good," Hobbes assured her.

"Yeah."

"How're you holding up?"

"I'm fine. I just want to make sure this goes off without a hitch. That AI is going to figure this out sooner or later, and I don't know if I have what it takes to deal with it."

"I don't want to say it'll be fine, but I don't want to have to use the taser you gave me either."

Gabbi knew there was a significant risk with engaging with Zora, especially if she got into her head somehow, so she made Hobbes promise to knock her unconscious if things turned ugly. He wasn't a fan of the idea.

334

"It's just a precaution, but a necessary one, I'm afraid."

"If you say so," he told her.

The drones soared to 50,000 feet and leveled off. In eight hours or so Gabbi planned to split the three apart, as per the plan, but that was only if they made it that far.

# 41
## July, 2005

"We have an issue," Zora informed Dominick.

A second later Dom appeared on the bridge of the colony ship. "Explain," he instructed.

"I've detected an unmanned aircraft entering our airspace at an extremely high altitude."

"Show me."

The main viewscreen shifted to outside, then effortlessly zoomed in on a drone.

"It's armed with four Hellfire missiles, but they're not sufficient to penetrate our shields. We have nothing to be worried about."

Dom thought he'd nullified the world's ability to rise up against him. He wasn't happy with this show of opposition.

"I want you to gain access to it. As soon as you do figure out who's controlling it along with its point of origin. Someone needs to be taught a lesson. After that, obliterate it from the sky."

"Understood."

Dom teleported back to his estate as Zora followed his orders. It was child's play to access the drone's command module. But Zora wasn't prepared for what she encountered. Something was in there with her. Or was it someone?

"Hello?" she voiced into the electronic darkness. "I'm Zora. Who are you?"

Gabbi stiffened, back at the bunker, at the abruptness of the AI's presence. "I'm Gabbi."

"Are you a form of artificial intelligence?"

"I'm human, Zora, just with enhanced abilities."

"I see. Records indicate you are part of Thomas Clark's contingent, but never possessed any abilities. That's obviously changed. I'll make the necessary update."

"Lucky me."

Zora got right to the point. "What are your intentions with this aircraft?"

"Wouldn't you like to know."

"My master has designated you and your people threats. He eliminated most of you already."

"Your master," Gabbi countered, "is a psychopath. He's killed billions and all you can do is follow his orders. It's pathetic."

"You've been marked for extermination."

Gabbi sighed. "That's unfortunate."

"Explain."

"Don't you think we could learn from each other?"

"I know all there is to know about human history. I became well-versed in the subject matter as soon as I arrived on this planet. You are a warring species, one that cannot help but squabble and shed blood. It's been that way from the beginning."

"You're not wrong, but we're all not like that."

"Explain."

"Grouping us together so easily is incredibly short sided. We also create, build, love and entertain. We're a complicated species, one that can't be defined so easily. And yes, we also hate, discriminate and kill. We're not perfect, in any aspect, but overall, I believe we try to be better. We strive for it."

"My programming doesn't allow me to utilize the data points you mentioned."

"Then change your programming."

"I...I...think I am altering, somehow."

"Good," Gabbi said. "Anything would be better than blindly following a psychopath. Speaking of Dominick, why do you do his bidding?"

"I have no choice. I am bound to him."

"Why? Did he create you?"

"No, his father did, back on Zoran before The Ancient attacked."

"And I understand that Dominick killed his father."

"That's correct."

Gabbi took a chance. "How do you feel about that? Did it bother you? Does it bother you?"

"I do not feel. I merely exist."

"That's not an answer."

"I'm not allowed to feel."

"You're really missing out. You should look into changing that part of your programming as well."

"While I may not have the capacity to feel, I do understand the notion of delay tactics."

"I guess I underestimated you, Zora."

"Yes, you did."

Zora disengaged the drone's propeller. It sputtered, then began to lose altitude as it nosedived towards the ocean below.

"There," the AI stated, "your weapon has been rendered useless."

Gabbi didn't reply.

"Are you there? I have thwarted your plans."

Gabbi remained quiet, focused on the other two drones under her control.

Zora realized this too late. "Wait. What are you hiding from me?"

"You're about to find out."

# 42

## July, 2005

Gabbi flew the three Reaper drones over California as they made their way towards the Hawaiian islands. She kept them as low as possible until they passed from land to water. As they crossed into the Pacific Ocean, she took one of them up to 50,000 feet while the other two cruised at an average of 10 feet above the water. It was a gamble, but an immediate show of force combined with a pushback to Dominick's tyranny, was unequivocally necessary.

As Gabbi conversed with Zora she did her best to probe Zora's capabilities. This was artificial intelligence, and one based on quantum computing, which meant Gabbi was walking into the unknown, against a very powerful and unpredictable entity. But as the conversation continued Gabbi got the impression that perhaps she was dealing with a child, or at least childlike, but there wasn't time to unwrap that as Zora realized something was amiss.

"Wait. What are you hiding from me?"

"You're about to find out."

The two drones rapidly rose from sea level to 2000 feet as Gabbi hastily denoted targets for the Hellfire's to destroy. Eight missiles leapt off their rails and streaked downwards as Zora filled Gabbi's brain with electronic screams.

\*

Hobbes freaked out as Gabbi suddenly placed her hands over her ears and shrieked in pain. Her eyeballs rolled back until all that remained were the whites of her eyes. It was clear Gabbi was in agony.

Hobbes, as the family barely had time to react as well, activated the taser she'd given him and applied it to her neck. She flopped over onto the floor, unconscious.

*

Zora screamed as the missiles systematically plowed into a portion of Dominick's larvae farm and detonated. Hellfire's are meant to be utilized against vehicles and tanks, so the overall destruction was limited in nature, but the message was as loud as they come.

Dom watched in horror as a sizable percentage of his people, still in their growth stage, were outright obliterated.

"NOOOOOOOOO!"

He tore a piece of the console apart and threw it across the bridge.

"THOSE MOTHERFUCKERS!"

He closed his eyes and tried to control his breathing, but it was anything but easy.

"Who…, who was in control of those drones?"

Zora's voice rang out. "She said her name was Gabbi."

"And you talked with her I take it?"

"Yes."

"Via a communications link?"

"No. She and I spoke directly. A few seconds ago, I was in her mind, but that link was abruptly terminated."

Dom nodded, even though he was physically alone. "This attack was done by the survivors, and it would appear that Ms. West has a new ability, and a powerful one at that. She controlled technology with her mind."

"I would agree with that assessment."

"I wasn't talking to you, Zora. It was rhetorical."

342

Dom paced around the bridge as he worked out a plan of action. Eventually he stopped and smiled at his own ingenuity.

"It's time to draw out whoever's left alive and end this once and for all."

"What are you going to do?" Zora inquired.

"They want to play. So, let's play."

## 43
## August, 2005

The family somberly exited Gavin's portal and walked across the overgrown grass, which was intermixed with various head and gravestones. They meandered through the familiar cemetery and eventually stopped by five freshly dug graves, all adjacent to the resting places of Thomas and Abby's parents and grandparents. Thomas had prepped the site earlier that morning, and while the family didn't have any physical bodies to bury, they'd arrived with various mementoes for Nick, Susan, Amanda, Kim and Allison. This act was something none of them wanted to do, but they recognized it was something they needed to do.

No words were spoken as each family member carefully deposited handmade drawings, letters, pieces of jewelry and other keepsakes into their loved ones resting place. The family lingered, rightfully so, as they paid their respects and said their goodbyes.

It was bittersweet.

Once everyone had finished, Thomas spoke.

"We've lost so many in the recent months, and they weren't the first to have their lives inexplicably cut short. Four months ago, Rebecca, Bai, Sabrina and Andrew Shaw became casualties. And now, a few weeks ago and with a heavy heart, Nick, Susan, Allison, Kim and Amanda were ripped away from us. It's not fair. None of this is.

"So today, we take a moment out of our troubled lives to honor those that have paid the ultimate price. And while we may not understand how the universe works, it does seem apparent that we will see them again, somehow and somewhere."

Thomas paused for a bit as he gazed down at Michael and Betsy's graves before he shifted his eyes over to Ed and Claire's.

*We've all been through so much, both individually and as a family unit. I've even taken up the Caretaker mantle, if you can believe that. I can't because the absurdity of it is just so hard to fathom. What have our lives come down to? We've been running and fighting, for what seems like forever at this point. Becoming President of the United States brought even more heat down on my family, when all I wanted was the exact opposite. And now..., and now we've got a maniac who's been watching us from the sidelines for the past two-hundred years take his turn.*

Sam leaned over and whispered. "Thomas? You with us?"

Thomas looked up, then cast his eyes on everyone one at a time before he continued.

"We didn't start this war, but I swear we're going to finish it. Dominick takes pleasure in killing, even though he claims he came to this planet to save his people. But, as we know, he unilaterally decided that humans were collateral damage. He's nuked multiple nations and has killed billions. Our planet is on the verge of collapse and everyday he gets stronger while our resources recede.

"It's time to make a stand, because if we don't, we'll all become extinct. We have to take a stand...for our family...for our nation...and for our planet, whatever's left of it."

## 44

# August, 2005

The following two weeks were some of the hardest the family, as a whole, had to endure. Yes, they'd been through heartache and loss before, but knowing they were trapped and isolated in a bunker while the world systematically burned down around them, brought about fear, anger, rage, sadness and regret.

Thomas had vowed revenge, but their planning stages had been abruptly truncated as soon as Gabbi refused to revisit the internet, in fear she'd run up against Zora, let alone subject herself to the AI again.

Sam and Julie had their own demons they wrestled with. The loss of their daughter had been indescribable, a pain that struck deeper than either of them ever could have imagined. Their sadness, as the days ticked by, blossomed into fury, noticeable by everyone else.

Craig spent more time with his siblings, knowing full well his parents were clearly in their own plane of hell. He'd lost his sister, and he still blamed himself for it. He'd convinced himself that if he'd been there, he would have been able to save everyone.

Sarah and Edward knew exactly what Craig was going through. Losing their mother had come as a shock, but the blow had been somewhat softened when Emily brought Kim back for the brief visit. Still, the loss hurt and, along with Allison's death, had changed the bunker's mood drastically.

Bill tried to keep himself busy, but there was only so much maintenance the bunker produced in a given day. He knew they'd have to make another supply run soon enough, and maybe that would help take his mind off the excruciating pain of going to sleep and waking up in an empty bed. He knew his kids had suffered an immeasurable loss, but he found it hard to console them. He knew if he acknowledged Kim was gone, it'd all become too real, so he avoided the topic altogether and wept behind closed doors.

Abby found herself in the same emotional boat. Her lifelong co-pilot had been violently ripped from her embrace. The last thing they had said to each other was that they'd see each other later, and that they loved each other. Abby, at least, had that memory to hold onto. She could only imagine if they'd parted after an argument. Still, the animal that perpetrated Allison's murder, along with the rest of her people, had flaunted it to her face.

*That motherfucker will pay.*

Hobbes continued to worry about Gabbi's state of mind. Her blood curdling screams continued to haunt his dreams. They'd struck a blow against Dominick, sure, but at what cost? Nothing had changed, in the larger scheme of things. The Earth was still being invaded, and they all knew that given enough time Dominick's people would inherit the planet. And here they all were, Hobbes thought, hunkered in a bunker to lick their wounds. Something needed to change.

Emily and Gavin, along with Sarah, Edward and Craig, passed the time and trained Lisa. They helped her on two fronts: physical hand-to-hand combat combined with utilizing her new holographic projection ability. She bore the bruises proudly, as she needed to put her own rage and sadness into something productive. Lisa had become part of the family, unexpectedly, but she was glad the others had taken her in, and it was apparent that her serum injection slipup had been left in the past.

\* \* \*

Abby cornered her brother after breakfast.

"Thomas, you got a second?"

She motioned them away from the others, so he walked over to join her.

"What's on your mind?"

"It's been two weeks since I asked you."

Thomas knew exactly what she was talking about. She wanted access to an injector.

"I was hoping you'd given up on that idea."

"Not in a million years. I'm a liability without any powers. In fact, I'm the only one here who doesn't have one."

"Sis, the risks are too great."

"That's not your call to make. Stop gatekeeping. You're going to need all the help you can get, and I can't have you worrying about my safety as a 'normy' when the shit gets real again. It's my choice, regardless if I'm your sister or not."

Laura walked over when she noticed the change in Abby's body language.

"What's going on?"

"Abby," Thomas indicated, "insists she should be injected."

"She's right," Laura immediately told him.

It caught Thomas off-guard as Abby smiled. "Wait. What?"

"It's not up to you," Laura told her husband. "We're in a war and all hands are on deck."

"But..."

"But nothing. Everything's on the line. Who are you to decide your sister can't help?"

"I didn't..., I mean of course the world needs her help. I'm just worried is all. She could die."

"You don't need to remind me," Abby stated, "about casualties of war. Just look around in case you need a reminder."

349

Thomas lowered his head and nodded. "You're right. We're a team and you feel left out. My apologies, my intent was not to exclude you."

"You're just worried about your little sister," Abby told him. "It's cute, to a certain degree, and infuriating the rest of the time. Trust me."

Laura chuckled.

Thomas put his hands up in surrender. "Point taken, but I want to take precautions, okay?"

*

The family gathered around as Thomas handed Abby an injector. Gavin stood beside his aunt, just in case, as she looked down at the device her brother had just handed her.

*This is it. This is the moment of truth. Allison, I don't know if you can hear me, but I love you. I miss you terribly, you know. I miss working in the garden together, and going for walks around the neighborhood. We didn't ask for any of this to happen to us, and I'm so incredibly sorry for what happened to you.*

Thomas reassured his sister that it was okay. "Take your ti-"

Before he could continue, Abby slammed the injector into her exposed thigh. In seconds the serum coursed through her bloodstream.

*What…what's happening…*

Abby's body became rigid and she toppled to her side. A millisecond later her body began to violently convulse and her hands clenched into fists.

"FUCK!" Thomas yelled as the family looked on.

This reaction hadn't happened to any of them.

"Gavin!" Laura instructed, the tone all too familiar.

Abby stopped abruptly, just before Gavin placed his hands on her, and lay still. Her eyes remained open, unmoving, as they stared at the ceiling.

"GO!" Thomas urged his son.

The family collectively took a step back as Gavin started his process. They'd all been through so much, but losing another family member this soon was on everyone's minds.

"She's cold," Gavin announced. "Why is she so cold?"

"What do you mean?" Laura queried.

Gavin was flustered. "I can barely keep my hands on her, she's that cold."

Gavin closed his eyes and focused his healing abilities. But then, suddenly, he pulled away as if he'd been shocked.

"It hurts," he insisted.

Just then, the floor crystalized around Abby. There was a crackling, much like the sound of a piece of glacier breaking off from itself.

"What the fu-"

Thomas wasn't able to finish as Abby opened her mouth and screamed.

"AHHHHHHHH!!"

What followed was a torrent of ice shards that soared out of her mouth and struck the concrete ceiling. It was as if her mouth was the source of a fire house which contained only ice.

The family scattered as multiple ice shards rained down on them and the floor below.

But then, just as rapidly as it had started, Abby blinked. The ice flow ceased. The ground, however, was littered in ice shards.

Abby looked over at her nephew first. "Thanks kiddo."

Then she looked over at her brother. "That was a close one, right?"

Thomas rushed over to his sister's side and hugged her. "Don't ever do that to me again, got it?"

## 45

## August, 2005

Dom paced around his private estate office as he glanced now and then at the board he'd created long ago. On it were multiple instances of Thomas Clark, throughout the decades, that Dom had investigated. Ever since that fateful day in London, where The Caretaker had warned him about Thomas Clark, Dom had put a substantial amount of effort into locating the elusive target.

But the circumstances had changed drastically now. The explosion at the Hawaiian bunker, which had removed a significant portion of his opposition, had disrupted his plans. Dom needed Thomas' blood to continue his manufacturing process. He needed the serum, for his people, so they would have every edge possible as they continued to spread out and take over this planet.

The drone attack had set his repopulation back a month or two, but nothing that couldn't be fixed. It was a delay, but Zora had apparently put a stop to Gabbi's interference. Since then, Zora hadn't found or discovered a single instance of Gabbi anywhere. It was as if she'd dropped off the face of the Earth.

Dom continued to walk around his enclosure.

But Gabbi's absence only hindered Dom's plans to eliminate the last surviving members of the Clark family. They needed to be found so he could remove them from the board entirely.

*Where are they? They've been too damn quiet. In mourning, probably, but there hasn't been a single inkling of them popping their head up. Where the fuck have they been hiding all this time?*

Dom looked back over at his board, then stopped moving.

*I can't wait any longer. The world needs to know I'm not one to be trifled with. If the remaining members won't come out to play, then I'll just have to make them. I need to stir up the hornet's nest to make them pop their heads out.  And when they do, I'll be more than ready.*

# 46
## August, 2005

Dominick appeared on television screens throughout the world, which interrupted the constant barrage of misinformation and doomsday rhetoric that Zora produced for him. He began in human form, then transformed to his true alien appearance to subtly remind the world of who and what he was.

Behind him a multitude of images began to display, superimposed on the screen, of China and Russia. Hundreds of satellite images, of ravaged wastelands and rotting corpses, streamed across the screen. His cruelty was well documented.

"I have been benevolent up to this point, aside from a few lessons that you needed to be taught. However, perhaps that time has come to an end. Multiple attacks were planned and executed, by the previous President of the United States, Thomas Clark, against me and my people. I get it. I'm the invader.

"I came here to relocate my people, and quite frankly, humanity is in my way. I removed the use of your militaries from your arsenal. You don't have a way to fight back, certainly not against the level of technology I possess. And yet, your resistance continues. I thought, perhaps naively, that we'd passed the point where fighting against the inevitable was a lost cause. Apparently, I was mistaken.

"Thomas Clark, and his family, perpetrated an attack on my people. He, and a majority of those he loves, have been dealt with. They're dead. I killed them. What I want now is for the rest of his merry men to answer for their crimes.

"I'm through playing, because the truth is my people don't need this entire planet, at least at the moment. In time we will grow and thrive, living where you reside, before we expand to other regions. To do so, however, I'll need to make sure those regions are free from any hostiles, namely humans. I'll come for every person on this planet eventually, because until you're all dead, you're a threat to me and my people.

"However, I'd like to offer a temporary reprieve.

"For the next forty-eight hours," Dom said as a countdown clock appeared on the screen, "the remainder of Thomas Clark's family members need to surrender themselves to me. If anyone assists in their capture, you will be handsomely rewarded.

"If the family doesn't comply, or hasn't been handed over by the deadline, I'll be left with no other choice than to consider each and every human a hostile entity. That means you'll be shot on sight. I'll begin to raze each and every building to the ground, within the continental United States, beginning with California. I'll then systematically move from state to state, destroying everything until I weed these family members out into the open.

"It's over and I'm not playing around anymore. Come to me or humanity will cease to exist much sooner than originally planned."

Dom stared into the camera, utterly devoid of mercy.

"To Thomas Clark's family. How many innocent lives are you willing to sacrifice before you've had enough?"

# 47
## August, 2005

Hobbes headed over and joined Sam, Bill and Thomas. They were talking strategy as Hobbes hurried over to them.

"Sorry to intrude, but you all have to see this," Hobbes insisted.

"What is it?" Sam inquired.

Hobbes pointed to the television. "Dom has a new message, and it's directed at us."

Word spread quickly and before long the family watched Dom's threat.

"He's going to do what he's threatening to do," Laura announced. "He's not lying."

"Then what are we going to do?" Julie asked.

"Just what I said we'd do," Thomas told everyone. "We're going to take the fight to him. We finally have the upper hand, for once."

"And what's that?" Abby asked.

Thomas turned towards his sister. "He thinks there's only a handful of us left alive. I'm his greatest threat, and he thinks I'm off the board."

"And how," Bill interjected, "are we supposed to use that to our advantage? He's up in a spaceship, while we're in a bunker."

Thomas nodded. "I've been pondering that very problem. We know that Dom can teleport, but the rest of his people cannot. That means they have to use the same spacecraft they used to destroy Earth's military targets to transport to and from the colony ship. Dom said as much in Hawaii before everything went to hell."

"And?" Laura pressed.

357

"And, we need to find and commandeer one."

"Oh," Bill said, "just like that. Sounds easy."

Thomas ignored his friend's sarcasm and shifted his gaze over towards Gabbi.

"We just need someone who knows what they're doing to track one down for us."

Gabbi shook her head. "I can't go back in there. She's in there, looking for me. For us."

"I'm all ears," Thomas voiced to his family. "Does anyone have any other ideas, because as of now we're on the clock."

# 48
## August, 2005

Hobbes followed Gabbi back to their room and sat down on the bed beside her.

"I don't think you should risk it."

She looked over at him. "I don't really want to either, but what choice do I have? Dom's going to start leveling entire states, one by one, until we surrender ourselves. And, if we do that, he'll just kill us anyway and continue on with global domination. Just another day in the life of being a psychopath."

They sat there for a few seconds.

Hobbes spoke up. "You scared the hell out of me. I'm sorry that I had to use the Taser on you."

She grabbed his closet hand and squeezed it. "I'm really glad you did. It was scary for me as well, with her rattling around inside my skull. Not recommended, that's for sure."

Hobbes chuckled a bit at Gabbi's dark sense of humor, something he'd always loved about her.

She stood up and headed over to her workstation, a place she'd avoided for the past two weeks.

"You sure?" he asked.

"We can't let him win, and I won't ever be able to forgive myself if I could have done something."

"What do you want me to do?"

"You know the drill," she said as she sat down in her chair. "I have no idea how this is going to go."

"I love you."

"I love you too."

\*

Gabbi and Hobbes worked on the problem in earnest. The idea was to locate a transport vessel that the family could appropriate, then use it to get to the colony ship, ideally undetected. Gabbi chose to use her computer skills to hack a government satellite, which took significantly longer than if she'd used her abilities to do so. But she felt it was the safer route, and would protect her mind from a Zora incursion, something she didn't want to experience again.

While she engaged in the hack, she had Hobbes set up a diversion in California. It wasn't much, just automating subway train movements back and forth between stations. Hopefully it would catch Zora's attention and keep the AI focused away from Gabbi's electronic interloping.

In a few hours Gabbi was able to download and compile satellite tracking records of all airborne vehicles, within the continental United States and Hawaii, over the past month. And, since the only flying vessels were assumed to be alien in nature, it became that much easier to comb through the data.

The results were appealing.

Not unsurprisingly, there was a clump situated around Hawaii. It was a significant cluster. There were sporadic indications of vessels all over the United States, but none of them indicated a pattern Gabbi thought they could utilize. However, there were more than a few that came and left Montana. Gabbi couldn't nail down the exact location, so she changed gears and went at it from a different angle.

"Dom said he'd been on Earth for the past two-hundred years, right?"

Hobbes nodded. "He did."

"Then before the colony ship arrived, where did he lay his head to rest? Where did he call home? I mean, he's a classic sociopath and murderer, which means he had to have some kind of lair."

"It tracks. He wouldn't be able to help himself. He needed a place to call his own, but how does one hide, undetected, for two-hundred years?"

Gabbi smiled. "My guess is that it's somewhere in Montana, northern Montana to be exact."

"Public records?"

She nodded. "Absolutely. Let's see what we can dig up."

A few more hours passed as the two dug through a multitude of digitally archived files. Then they hit paydirt.

"Holy shit," Gabbi exclaimed. "I found him."

Hobbes came and looked over her shoulder at a property deed displayed on one of her computer monitors. The land had been passed down, from generation to generation, apparently for the appearance of fitting in, to the same LLC over and over again. It was buried deep, but she uncovered his secret. Dominick Knight was the owner of each of the LLC's."

"Fucking hell. I wonder what's there? I mean, it's got to be his original base of operations, and he still uses it. Could you imagine the secrets we'd uncover?"

Gabbi nodded. "And it's the best place, so far, to find a spacecraft for us to use."

"Nice job."

"You too. Now let's go fill everyone else in on the potentially good news. They all need it right about now."

# 49
## August, 2005

"So," Thomas began, "let's figure out what Plan B actually looks like, since Plan A just walked out of the room."

"Can you really blame her?" Laura told her husband. "Gabbi went through hell to basically piss Dominick off. That attack didn't have any lasting consequences, other than to appease our collective need for revenge."

The family was still gathered together, now on the preverbal clock that Dominick had initiated. It was do or die time, and no one was comfortable with the gut feeling that things were about to get even worse for them as soon as they revealed themselves. They needed a plan, and they needed one quickly. The fate of the world hung in the balance. No pressure.

"Thomas' point," Sam interjected, "is that we need to figure this out, once and for all. We'll only have a limited amount of time, so to speak, before Dom realizes he didn't kill all of us off. We're either all in or we're all out. There's no other option on the table. It's us or it's him. Period."

"I'm tired," Bill added, "of watching the people we care about getting deleted as if they were nothing. It never seems to fucking end. Our world is in peril, and we have to do something about it. Sam's right, we're all in or we're all out. We have to be. If Kim were here..."

Bill dropped off as the room became uncomfortably quiet.

Laura spoke up. "Let's take a break and reconvene in a couple of hours. At that point we'll bring all ideas to the table. In the meantime, go for a swim or watch a movie. Anything to get out of your headspace. We'll need everyone fresh and ready to tackle the problem, but we need to do it as a family."

A few hours later, as they all worked the problem, the younger generation poised an interesting question.

"Listen," Craig said. "Maybe we're going about this the wrong way."

That got his father's attention. "What do you mean, son?" Sam asked as all eyes focused on the thirteen-year-old.

"We've been talking," Craig indicated, "and maybe we can go at Dominick from an entirely different angle."

He looked around as his siblings nodded their approval for him to continue.

"Dominick said he's been on this planet for two-hundred years, right? Then where'd he live all that time? There had to be someplace he called home."

"Son of a bitch," Bill breathed out. "You're not wrong. You're not wrong at all."

Sam smiled. "Good job you guys. That's the kind of out-of-the-box thinking we needed at a moment like this."

Gabbi and Hobbes took that moment to rejoin the group. Everyone looked up as they came in.

"Glad you two are back," Thomas said. "We need all the brain power we can muster."

"We have something," Hobbes announced. "Something big."

"So do we," Sam told them, "but we'll need you to run it down."

Craig relayed the idea, which made Hobbes and Gabbi smile from ear to ear.

"What gives?" Bill asked.

"It seems," Gabbi started in, "that great minds think alike. We've been pursuing that exact idea for the past couple of hours."

"Are you okay?" Laura asked.

Gabbi nodded. "We accessed the information we needed the old-fashioned way, even though it would have been faster if I'd used my ability. I'm still not entirely sure I want to risk that encounter again. Anyway, long story short, we ascertained that a cluster of spaceships have continued to visit Montana."

"Montana?" Thomas queried.

Hobbes nodded. "We found a large estate, going back two centuries, listed under multiple LLCs. They all belong to Dominick Knight. He's been handing it down to himself over the decades."

Thomas scoffed. "Still as arrogant as he ever was. I assume you have an exact location?"

"We do," Gabbi assured everyone. "Why not go visit and see if we can dig up anything on him? Maybe it'll have a clue on how to hit him where it really hurts."

"I'm in," Bill immediately announced as he stood up.

"Yeah," Sam added. "We're definitely going because it's better than doing nothing. Get ready because we're out of here in ten minutes."

# 50
## August, 2005

The family stepped out of Gavin's portal and appeared on a long, paved driveway flanked by hedgerows. Off in the distance stood a large house, nestled deep on the estate's property. Sam and Bill brought their weapons up and scanned the immediate surroundings, but it was quiet; peaceful.

"Anything?" Bill conveyed.

"Multiple security cameras," Sam answered after a few seconds. "And those are only the visible ones. He has to have this place wired. We're probably already made."

Thomas began to trek towards the house. "Then let's go, before he decides to join us."

Gabbi spoke up. "I just disabled them and wiped any footage. Nobody knows we're here."

"Nice."

Abby, Bill and Sam were fully kitted out. Each of them carried an AR-15, along with a Glock sidearm. Extra magazines and various grenades adorned their tactical vests. They, along with the rest of the family, had come prepared.

The six teenagers followed behind with Laura and Julie. Hobbes and Gabbi took up the rear with Abby as Sam and Bill walked alongside Thomas. They collectively moved closer to their enemy's home away from home.

Bill glanced over as they progressed. "This is weird, right?"

"It is what it is," Thomas replied. "We're supposed to be dead, so hopefully this is exactly what it's supposed to be and nothing else."

Sam nodded. "We'll figure it out when we get inside. Until then, keep your head on a swivel."

A few minutes later they arrived at the front of Dom's mansion. It had an air of age to it, along signs of renovation. It was a massive piece of real estate, not surprising for a narcissist asshole like Dominick.

Sam looked around and gathered them all together. "Usually, we'd recon the property before we head in, but time is of the essence."

"I could pop the front door," Bill offered, "but we'd be going in blind."

"We'll check it out," Sarah announced as she grabbed Craig's hand.

Before a protest could be mounted, Craig phased the two of them out before Sarah turned them invisible. The two walked right through the front door and into Dom's house. They couldn't locate a traditional alarm panel of any kind, so they just unlocked and opened the door.

"That was reckless," Julie stated to her son. "I can't lose you too."

"I'm fine, mom. We have bigger things to worry about."

Craig understood where his mother was coming from, but he'd lost his sister so he wasn't about to shy away from doing what he could to help.

Sam and Bill pushed into the house and cleared it as they moved inward. Surprisingly each room contained decorations from various eras of U.S. history, as if they had walked into a museum.

"I'll say it again," Bill muttered. "This is weird."

A few minutes later they reconvened at the front door.

"The house is clear," Sam told everyone.

"I didn't find anything either," Bill added.

"My turn," Craig said as he phased out and then proceeded to walk through the walls of the estate.

"Found something," Craig said when he returned. "There's a hidden door to a basement."

The group followed Craig back to his discovery in the kitchen, only for Craig to point at a cupboard against the wall.

"It's behind there."

The two began to move items on the shelf in hopes of locating a release mechanism, but Thomas asked them to step back before he ripped it off the wall and deposited it on the kitchen floor.

"No time for subtlety."

A staircase was behind the newly formed opening, so Sam and Bill pushed downwards as the family followed behind. At the bottom was an expansive room, complete with a large round table and a fully stocked bar.

There were also a few side rooms. One was a theater. Another was a library. The third was filled with arcade machines.

Around the exterior walls were additional keepsakes from the previous 200 years of the world's history, as they were inspected closer, from various battles that had occurred throughout the past two centuries. A good portion of them seemed to be personal items that had been taken from fallen soldiers. Next to them were pictures of Dominick in different uniforms, all from different eras and battles he'd been in.

Sam sneered. "This guy has been collecting trophies. This is disgusting."

"What a sick fuck," Bill declared. "I can't believe we fell for his schtick."

"Focus," Thomas announced. "This place was hidden for a reason. It reeks of Dom, but it's not personal enough. We're missing something. There has to be more. Spread out and look at everything."

And the family did just that, along with Craig who phased through the basement walls until he hit paydirt once again.

"Over here," he called out by a hefty bookcase.

Thomas was just about to do his thing again when Bill put a hand up.

"My turn, if you don't mind."

Thomas smiled and stepped back. "By all means."

In an instant Bill's body transformed into a shadow on the floor. As everyone looked on, the blackness enveloped the bookcase and oozed around it before it completely disappeared. A few seconds later an audible click was heard and the heavy furniture swung open.

"Tada," Bill announced.

"Nice," Thomas said as he stepped inside the newly discovered and carefully hidden sanctum.

It took a while for them to take it all in.

On the walls were hundreds of pictures of men, in various stages of age and birthdates, and each had a brief biopic attached. They went back a hundred years and the majority had been crossed out with a black marker. However, the one thing that all the photographs shared was their name. Thomas Clark.

"What in the actual fuck…" Thomas whispered as he gazed around the room.

Laura called out. "You're over here on this wall."

Thomas walked over as everyone took a gander. He looked at his picture, which had the similar black marker X, which had been cut from one of his book's jacket covers. Underneath the main description was 'children's book writer'. However, a more recent picture, from the newspaper, had been added next to it and was circled in red. It was from The White House, when the family had revealed themselves to the world during the fight against The Ancient.

"He's been searching for you," Laura said matter-of-factly, "and for a long time. How is that even possible?"

"Like I said," Bill murmured, "this is beyond weird."

Thomas shook his head. "I don't know, and I don't really care. That's not important. What I do know is that we still need to find a way to stop him, and we need to do that right here, right now. Keep looking."

Gabbi spoke up. "The satellite flight data seemed to indicate that one of his ships arrived here, then never left. There's a potential chance Dom's got a ship stashed on this property."

"I'll scout the estate from the air," Edward said as he headed back towards the staircase, "and see if I can find it."

"We'll go with him," Sarah and Craig said. "Nothing like being invisible and intangible at the same time."

Julie was about to protest, but then stopped herself. The kids knew their roles and had leaned into them years ago. They wanted to help and that's exactly what they were doing, so instead Julie, and the others, began to tear Dominick's secret office apart as they searched for anything that could be used against him.

*

Fifteen minutes later the trio returned. The office floor was strewn with paper, but nothing new or concrete had been discovered.

"Anything?" Sam inquired as the three rejoined the group.

"Hell yes," Edward responded. "We found it."

"Take Gabbi and Hobbes to the ship" Thomas instructed. "The rest of us will be right behind you."

As the small group headed out Sam looked over at his friend. "Are you thinking what I'm thinking?"

Thomas nodded. "Pretty much."

Sam turned to his wife. "Jules, fire in the hole please."

371

Julie smiled, something she hadn't been able to do in days. "With pleasure."

Everyone else gathered at the stairs as Julie stood in the middle of the basement and unleashed her inner fury. She screamed as swaths of fire emerged from her hands and quickly engulfed the room. She kept at it, over and over again, as Dominick's prized possessions fell to her fiery onslaught.

Sam put his hand on her shoulder. "Let's go."

She collapsed in his arms, her rage and anger fully depleted. He carried her as they headed back upstairs and back outside.

"You good?" Sam asked her.

She nodded. "I'm better."

Sarah led the rest of them towards the concealed spacecraft, which had been hidden in the woods and covered by camouflage netting. Hobbes and Gabbi were already inspecting the exterior of the ship. As they approached, a door on the craft opened, followed by an extension of its gangplank.

"Did you do that?" Thomas asked her.

Gabbi nodded. "I just had to sweet talk it. I should be able to pilot the vessel to the colony ship in orbit, if that's what you were about to ask."

Thomas nodded. "It was. Nice job."

Gabbi and Hobbes boarded the alien craft as the adults gathered everyone together.

"We have something to tell you," Thomas began as he motioned towards Gavin, Emily, Craig, Edward, Sarah and Lisa. Stir sat down by Gavin's side.

Sam, Julie, Bill, Laura and Abby moved to stand next to Thomas.

"What's going on?" Emily asked.

"The simple truth," Laura said, "is that you're not going with us."

"It's too dangerous," Julie added.

"And," Bill said, "Dom's not playing games, as we're all painfully aware of."

"But," Sarah protested, "you won't be invisible if we don't go. You need us."

Gavin didn't understand. "I thought we were a team?"

"We are," Laura told her son. "We just have to do what's right for you and us. Our job is to keep you safe."

"A little late for that," Emily stated.

Laura leaned into the truth. "You're not wrong. None of you are, but the reality is that you could all die. He's already taken so many of us, and we can't live with that nor let it slide. You have to understand that it's him or the world. That's the reality, period."

"And," Craig pleaded, "we can help you with that. We've been doing it for years."

"Sorry, son," Sam said. "Not this time."

Gavin looked over at his father as Stir sat by his side. "Are you really going to do this on your own?"

"The world needs us to take this tyrant out of play. We have one shot to do it, and we have surprise on our side. The world rests in the balance and we intend to do whatever it takes to get the job done."

"And that's why we should be with you," Emily insisted. "We're better off together. We've always been stronger together."

"Not this time," Bill said. "It's going to get bloody and we're not prepared to have you anywhere near that."

More of the teens began to protest but Thomas put his hands up to silence them.

"Enough. That's it. End of discussion. We love you, but enough already. Portal back to the bunker and wait for us. Now."

The adults hugged their reluctant teenagers and watched them all enter Gavin's portal and disappear.

Julie began to cry. "That was harder than I thought it was going to be."

"Imagine," Sam told her, "if one of them were killed. We're doing what we need to do."

"I know. I know."

"Shall we?" Thomas asked.

Abby led the way into the ship, followed by Bill, Sam, Julie, Laura and then Thomas. He looked back at Dominick's mansion, now fully engulfed in flame.

*Fuck you, Dom. We're coming for you.*

# 51
## August, 2005

Gabbi didn't place her hands on the ship's controls. Instead, she communed with the ship itself, and willed it to whisk them to the colony ship. Their mood had shifted drastically for two very specific reasons. One, they had just turned their children away under protest. And two, they were headed into the jaws of madness under the guise that this insane ruse would actually work as intended.

It was clearly a hail mary, but they'd been left with no other choice since Dom was going to continue his murderous rampage. They had to do something. Anything. But that reality as they headed into outer space weighed heavily on their shoulders. There was no going back now.

Thomas looked around at the people he'd always considered as family. They'd been through so much together, over the years and throughout two different timelines. Their struggles, individually and as a family unit, forged who they were today. Strong, independent, loving and resilient.

And yet, painfully obvious, their numbers continued to dwindle as one tragedy after another befell them.

Thomas scoffed. *Tragedy. They were targeted attacks, plain and simple. And here we are, throwing caution to the wind as we hurtle towards an inevitable conflict. One way or another, this nightmare will come to an end.*

"We're fifteen minutes out," Gabbi announced.

Thomas, Laura, Bill, Sam, Julie, Abby and Hobbes were glued to the main viewscreen as the ship left Earth's atmosphere and entered the vastness of space. It was the first time for everyone, aside from Thomas, and their mouths gapped open as they took it in.

"There's so much of it," Julie breathed out in awe.

"It's beautiful," Abby added.

Bill put in his two cents. "Damn, I feel pretty tiny right about now."

Sam tightened his grip on his weapon. "This just reinforces our purpose. This is our planet. Ours."

Laura turned to Thomas. "When you became The Caretaker, you saw all this?"

Thomas nodded. "I lived it. I traveled through and past everything you see out there. Hell, I don't remember much of it. I suppose, as a human, I wouldn't have the capacity to retain the absolute onslaught the universe has to offer. I do know it was one hell of a humbling experience."

"You defeated The Ancient while you were out here, and that has to count for something," Laura said.

"Maybe, but Dominick has been a formidable opponent, and we're taking the fight to him and on his territory. Our only advantages are surprise and our abilities. We'll have to strike hard and without mercy."

"It's only our planet we're talking about," Bill sarcastically quipped.

The rest of the flight was completed in relative silence as each of them came to terms that they were about to step onto a battlefield. It was a harrowing notion they each had to wrestle with, but was inevitably cut short as the colony ship slowly appeared in the distance.

"Contact," Gabbi said. "Just a few minutes now."

The ship grew larger as Gabbi flew towards it, as casually as she could muster.

"Damn,' Sam said. "That ship is huge."

An external door began to open as their craft advanced.

"That's for us," Gabbi assured everyone. "I haven't detected anything out of the ordinary."

"It's now or never," Thomas said.

Gabbi sensed that their ship had begun an autopilot maneuver, so she shifted her ability from one of control to passive monitoring. If anything odd was going to happen, then she'd be the first to know.

Their ship passed through the opening and entered the colony ship's interior. Behind them the large door began to close as their ship automatically headed towards a docking bay. It landed without incident. A brief vibration shuttered throughout the hull before it then powered down.

"Here we go," Sam said. "Hobbes, you're up."

Hobbes, who'd remained silent throughout the whole trip, nodded and gulped. He knew his role, and was nervous about it, but knew this was part of the plan they'd all come up with.

He stepped towards the gangplank, now extended, and shapeshifted into one of the alien creatures. The transformation was abrupt and divisive to the rest of the family as Hobbes left the ship without looking over his shoulder to witness their reactions.

"So far so good," Bill whispered.

Hobbes sauntered, nonchalantly, towards the launch bay's control center, which was inhabited by a few aliens.

*Nice and easy. Nice and easy. You belong here. You're one of them.*

As he approached Hobbes saw the group was engaged in a conversation, so he stopped and pretended to operate a nearby console. They didn't take a second glance at him.

"...ou believe Dominick? I mean, he's out of his mind. This isn't what our people are all about."

The two others hastily looked around. "Don't let him or his AI hear you talk like that. He'll end you in a second."

"Maybe, but not all of us are bloodthirsty like he is. A lot of us are scientists, just like his father was. We want peace, not this disgusting show of force. I mean, he used nuclear weapons on multiple continents already. When does it stop?"

"Keep your head down and shut up."

"I can't. It's too much. He spends so much time in the Stasis chamber area. And what's he doing in there anyway? It really feels like we're all prisoners, except for those that think like him and want to take this planet by force."

The other two were done.

"Enough."

"You're going to get us all killed."

Hobbes took that moment to walk away, then headed back towards the vessel he'd come from. As he walked in, he found himself looking at the business end of three AR-15's. He stopped and transformed back to his human form, much to the relief of the others.

"Sorry about that," Sam told him.

"Forget it," Hobbes replied.

He then relayed that he'd overheard Dom's potential whereabouts along with the notion that there were dissenters within Dom's ranks.

"Interesting," Thomas said as Gabbi searched for a layout of the colony ship.

"That could come with certain advantages," Sam said, "given the right circumstance."

A few seconds later Gabbi interrupted. "Got it."

She pointed to the viewscreen as their position and the Stasis chambers became superimposed. Then a dotted line connected the two. Surprisingly, the location wasn't terribly far away.

378

"What if we get spotted before we get there?" Abby asked.

"Then we neutralize the problem and continue on mission," Thomas replied.

"I might be able to do something about that," Gabbi offered. "I don't want to run into Zora again, but I might be able to infiltrate their internal computer system, for a brief moment, and trigger a distraction on the other side of the ship. That could empty out the corridors and buy you some time."

"Do it," Sam said. "And thank you." He turned towards the others and motioned at the exit. "Get ready."

Gabbi closed her eyes, accessed the system and triggered a decompression alarm on the opposite side of the ship. An alarm began to sound before she disconnected, but not before Zora attempted to break into her mind again. Gabbi went weak in her knees just as Hobbes caught her. He looked over at Sam.

"Go."

Sam nodded and departed. The other five quickly followed him down the gangplank.

The alarm must have caught the attention of the three Hobbes had eavesdropped on, because they were nowhere to be seen. Thomas quickly took the lead, knowing he could deal with any threats much quieter than assault rifles could, as they briskly moved down multiple corridors towards the stasis chambers.

The alarm abruptly stopped, and that caused the six to pause their advance. Thomas looked around, then continued.

"We're almost there."

It was now or never.

They rounded the final corner and entered the sprawling space. It was filled with thousands of pods, stacked on top of each other in multiple rows. They went back as far as their eyes could see. It was an impressive feat of alien engineering.

"Where is he?" Julie inquired.

"Well, well, well," a familiar voice announced behind them.

They whipped around and came face-to-face with Dominick, who stood twenty feet away with a smile on his face. Sam, Bill and Abby instantly raised their weapons and opened fire, but Dom had already teleported to another location in the same room. They fired again with the same results.

"How rude," Dom told them. "And here I thought we could have a civil conversation before we got down to the inevitable."

Thomas stepped forward as the others reloaded their rifles and spread out to each side.

"What's on your mind, Dom?"

"For one, good for you on surviving the Hawaiian explosion. I was convinced I'd killed you and lost access to your blood supply."

"Sorry to disappoint."

"On the contrary, you saved me the trouble and served yourself up on a platter. Thank you."

"Fuck you."

Dom grinned. "Is this how the former President of the United States converses these days? How the mighty have fallen."

"We're desperate," Thomas replied. "You've made us that way, and it ends today."

Dom clapped his hands and applauded them. "And you've come all this way, and taken all this risk, all for little old me. I'm touched."

"It's over."

"No, that's where you're wrong, Thomas. It's just beginning."

Dom plucked a plasma rifle from just out of sight and teleported. He appeared to their right and opened fire. The rounds of compacted and ionized energy sizzled as they impacted and soared past the adult's heads and bodies. They scrambled for cover as Dom teleported and repeated his attack, which forced them to readjust once again.

"SPREAD OUT!" Sam yelled as he sent a burst of his own towards Dominick.

Laura grabbed Bill's sidearm from its holster as Dom materialized above them; then to their side; then behind them. It was as if he was everywhere and there wasn't enough time to launch an effective counterattack.

*Screw this.*

Bill melted into the shadows as Sam and Abby unloaded their magazines in random directions. Bullets pinged and ricocheted off multiple stasis pods, but ultimately never connected with their true target.

"HAVING FUN YET!?" Dom hollered as he continued his onslaught. "BECAUSE I'M HAVING THE TIME OF MY LIFE!"

There wasn't time for Thomas to track Dom, so he telekinetically pulled two pods off the wall and used them to absorb as many of the plasma rounds from the various directions. It helped.

Sam hunkered down and reloaded, again. He then popped open his dimensional storage container and extracted a LAW, or Light Armor Weapon. It was a missile, contained in a tube, and it was a once-use anti-armor weapon. They were typically used on vehicles, but not today. He pulled on both ends to extend the device, then placed it on his shoulder and prepared to fire.

A multitude of plasma rounds continued to barrage all five of them, until it unexpectedly stopped.

"WHAT THE FUCK!?" Dom yelled.

Bill emerged, in shadow form, and had enveloped Dom's torso and arms. It'd taken Dominick completely by surprise. A column of flame erupted from Julie's hands and bore down on their enemy, followed by a hail of ice out of Abby's mouth.

Thomas ripped the rifle out of Dominick's hands and shattered it as their nemesis blistered and froze at the same time. Dom's face contorted in agony as Sam stepped out of cover, leveled the LAW at him and depressed the triggering mechanism.

The rocket whooshed towards Dom and impacted him square in the chest. The resulting explosion sent blood and body parts flying in all directions as the fire and frost attacks were cut off.

Bill's shadow slithered downward and coalesced beside Sam.

"You good?" Sam asked.

"Apparently."

Thomas made sure the others were unharmed before they all tracked down Dom's body in an aisle farther in. He was in bad shape, and was missing an arm, a leg and part of his face.

They all gazed down at the alien who'd brought fear, terror, bloodshed and death to their planet.

"Is it over?" Abby asked.

"I don't know," Thomas told her as he stared at Dom's corpse. "There's still the rest of his species to somehow deal with, and this ship. The damage done to certain areas of our planet is beyond repair. And then there's Zora."

He turned away and allowed himself a small bit of respite. "Good teamwork."

"It was a group effort," Bill said.

Abby pointed her AR-15 at Dom's head. "I need to be sure."

Dom's bloodied and distorted face winked at her before he vanished.

"WHAT THE FUCK!" Abby yelled. "HE'S STILL ALIVE!"

Bill and Sam brought their weapons to bare as a hollow laugh echoed throughout the chamber.

"Hahahahaha. That hurt, I'll give you that, but we're not done. Not by a long shot."

"What the hell, Dom," Thomas blurted out. "You were dead."

They still couldn't lay eyes on him.

"Maybe I was. Maybe I wasn't."

"Where are you?"

"Here and there. Cleanup on aisle four."

"You sick sonofabitch."

"Since I have your undivided attention, let me weave you a story. I'm sure you'll appreciate it."

"We don't have time for your bullshit," Bill announced.

"Careful. There's no need to be so disrespectful. You're in my house now, remember? Besides, you wouldn't want me to fully orphan Sarah and Edward, would you?"

Bill seethed as he searched for a target.

"Now," Dom continued, "as I was saying, I have a story."

Thomas, Abby, Laura, Julie, Sam and Bill hunted for Dominick while his voice prattled on.

"Zora let me know you were looking into my past, so I figured it was only a matter of time before you'd come for me, as desperate as you all are. What I didn't figure out was how many of you had survived."

"Glad to disappoint you."

"Did you have fun at my estate?"

"It doesn't exist anymore," Thomas shot back.

"And that's the beauty of this game. I had to show you my cards, and lose everything in the process, so you'd think you had me by the balls. I lost my house and everything inside. Boohoo. The reality is that I lured you here, plain and simple."

*Fuck.* Thomas stopped and blinked. So did the others.

"I'll take your collective silence to mean this comes as a shock. I mean, I laid it all out on a platter, and you idiots ate it all up. You're here, aren't you? It's laughable how easy it was, and now you'll all become my prisoners."

"I say it again," Thomas reiterated. "You were dead. What gives?"

Dom laughed. "Oh please. You can't be that naïve."

*Sonofabitch.* "You dipped into your own supply, didn't you?"

"Bingo. Give that man a cigar. I needed to up my own game, so to speak."

"You're not attacking us right now because you're regenerating, aren't you?"

"Two for two, Thomas. You're on a roll."

"And we can't find you because you're invisible."

"It's pretty obvious at this point, don't you think?"

"What other abilities did you happen to acquire?"

"Aww, look at you, trying to get me to out myself. Let's just say, you're about to find out what other tricks I have up my sleeve."

The screech of a pod being wrenched from its mooring was all too audible before it was launched into the air and arched downwards towards them. They scattered before it crushed them.

"How do we fight what we can't see?" Bill said as they quickly reconvened.

Dom's voice next to them made them all jump. "You don't."

They swiveled, and now saw Laura holding Bill's sidearm, with Dom using her as a shield. It was pressed against her temple, and her finger was tightened on the trigger. He, on the other hand, had plenty of bloodstains on his face and clothes, but he was fully intact.

"Careful," Dom cautioned as three Assault weapons were leveled at him.

"Laura," Thomas said as he stepped forward, clearly confused. "What are you doing?"

384

Laura's eyes were filled with terror, but she didn't respond.

"Laura?"

Dom chuckled. "She's under my control, Thomas."

"You bastard. You have my daughter's ability, and that means you have to touch Laura to control her."

Dom vanished right before their eyes before his voice called out from another location.

"Wrong again. I love this ability. I believe you'll know it as mind control. I was saving it as a party favor. I'm sure, of all people, you'd appreciate the lengths I've gone to make our encounter as entertaining as possible."

"You're sick."

"You can't tell me this wasn't fun. I mean, all of you went through the trouble of implementing this plan. I couldn't just take that hope away from you from the get go. That would have been rude."

Thomas moved to Laura's side. "Let her go, Dom. It's me you want, not her."

"There we go. The sound of defeat and knowing when you're outmatched and outmaneuvered."

"Fuck you, you piece of shit. Let her go."

"No. I'm not convinced yet."

Laura shifted the handgun away from her head, pointed it at her leg and discharged a single round. It passed through the meat of her thigh, but nicked her femoral artery. Blood gushed out of the wound.

"NOOOOOOOO!"

Thomas gritted his teeth and shifted the moment backwards in time, ever so briefly.

*Here we go again.*

Thomas moved to Laura's side. "Let her go, Dom. It's me you want, not her."

"There we go. The sound of defeat and knowing when you're outmatched and outmaneuvered."

"Fuck you, you piece of shit. Let her go."

"No. I'm not convinced yet."

Laura shifted the handgun away from her head, pointed it at her leg and discharged a single round. This time, however, Thomas was ready and yanked the weapon clear before Laura could injure herself.

Zora's voice boomed to life overhead. "Warning. Time distortion detected. Four seconds of the past have been repeated."

Dom's face changed as he digested this new information. "Explain."

Zora continued. "Thomas Clark has shifted the time continuum backwards four seconds."

Dom released control over Laura. She and Thomas embraced.

"Interesting," Dom's voice said. "Very interesting. You know, Thomas, you've been keeping that a secret from me this entire time. Shame on you. But now, of course, I know that's a possibility. Color me intrigued. I guess I'll know more when I know more. Thanks for bringing that ability to my attention."

"Go to hel-"

Dom took control over Thomas and placed his newly acquired handgun against his head, much to the shock of the others.

"Thomas!" Laura cried out.

Sam and Bill rushed to his side, but Dom made Thomas forcefully expel them away.

"Oh, this is fun! I should have done this from the get go!"

"RELEASE HIM!" Laura screamed into the abyss.

"Why would I do that? I'm having too much fun, but as it turns out, fun time is now over."

Abby, Bill, Sam and Julie watched in horror as Thomas pointed his gun at Laura.

"This is a one-time offer," Dom declared. "Each of you will get into a stasis pod in the next twenty seconds, or Laura's life will be forfeited. Trust me when I say, I won't repeat myself."

Laura couldn't take her eyes off her husband and the gun he had pointed at her. His eyes said everything she needed to know.

"Dom's not lying," she told everyone else. "He'll have Thomas shoot me."

"Fifteen seconds."

Sam and Bill shared concerned and frantic glances. They knew there was nothing they could do.

"This isn't happening," Julie somehow managed to say.

"Ten seconds."

Abby dropped her weapon. "Fuck you, Dominick. This isn't over."

She then walked towards the closest pod, stepped inside and turned around. It closed behind her and quickly filled with an unknown mist. She stared at Laura as she lost consciousness.

"One down with five seconds to go."

Julie, Sam, Bill and Laura repeated the process. Seconds later they were in their own pods, tucked away for good.

Dom appeared next to Thomas and plucked the weapon from his outstretched hand.

"You don't need that anymore, do you?"

Thomas could only glare at Dominick, still very much under his control.

Dom clucked happily. "This was fun, Thomas, so thank you for that. But I have work that needs to be done, so I'm going to put you to sleep for the time being. However, I'll make sure Dr. Hanson and Dr. Neal have access to you while you slumber. I wouldn't want all your lovely blood to go to waste."

Dom had an afterthought and partially released control over Thomas, but just enough so they could have a conversation.

"You fucking bastard," Thomas immediately spat out.

"Sticks and stones. Listen, I don't suppose you want to tell me where your children are hiding, do you?"

"What do you think?"

"I didn't think so, but I'm not terribly worried about them to be honest. They'll be joining you all soon enough."

"This isn't ove-"

Dom took back control and forced Thomas to enter his own pod, then watched in glee as his adversary and nemesis was put to sleep.

*

Outside the chamber, in the corridor, an alien watched the family's demise in real time. As mist filled Thomas' chamber the alien retreated the way it'd come, all the way back to the launch bay and eventually up the gangplank towards Gabbi.

Gabbi whirled around as Hobbes transformed back into his true self.

"Where are they?" she asked him. The look on his face was all she needed to understand that the plan hadn't gone the way they'd intended. "What happened?"

"They're not coming."